It is a chilling saga of shocking political conspiracies, of human perseverance, of human faith and survival instinct in the face of terror and death. It is also a story of mean political games, vested interest and dangerous motives to keep the Indian sub-continent politically unstable.

ON THE BRINK OF DEATH

A novel by

SANJAY SONAWANI

PUSHPA PRAKASHAN LTD

First Published in March 2001
Second Edition July 2001

Published by **Pushpa Prakashan Ltd.,**
302, B, Narayan Chambers,
555, Narayan Peth, Pune - 411 030.
E-mail: service@pplbooks.com
Web site: www.pplbooks.com

Printed in India by
V. Rajendra Art Press, Pune.

Publisher's Note – This is a work of fiction. Characters, events,
incidents, organizations used in this novel are either the product of
the author's imagination or, if real, used fictitiously without any intent
to describe their actual conduct.

ISBN - 81 - 7448 – 085-4

O pleasant dreams,
Come with me as I go
To the world beyond,
To the realms of truth...
To grace every heart that craves for you.

Don't get bewildered
But bear with me the life's ups and downs,
for my path is littered with obstacles
and my feet are sore.

But come with me as I go
... the world needs you !

Without mentioning their names - as requested by them - the author thanks all those who patiently helped him collate background information for this novel from various sources. He thanks Mr. Anil Roy who has assisted him with his impeccable editing and his invaluable suggestions.

ON THE BRINK OF DEATH

One

The name on the brass plaque on the large iron gate reflecting the light from my motorbike's headlamp matched that on the visiting card I held in my hand. I had finally located the residence of Mr. S. Varadrajan. I tried to attract the attention of the dozing chowkidar, who after several loud calls opened his eyes and peered at me myopically through the small window of his security cabin.

"What's it?" He asked, visibly irritated.

"I'm here to meet Varadrajan *Saab* for some urgent work."

"At this hour!" He asked incredulously. It was almost midnight. Hence, I did not grudge his strange behavior.

"Yes. He has asked me to see him immediately…that's what the message said."

"I am sorry, but *Saab* is sleeping now. Come tomorrow."

"But the message, you see, said it was very urgent... that I see Varadrajan *Saab* immediately. So, why not open the gate and let me in?"

"No, *Saab*," he said, resolute in performing his duty to the `T', "I cannot let you in. I don't think Varadrajan *Saab* has called you or else he would have left instructions for me."

"Look, the message was left for me by Thyagarajan *Saab*. You know him, don't you? He can't lie. Neither am I a fool to knock on other people's doors at this time of the night," I said trying not to lose my cool. "Thyagarajan *Saab* told my wife that even if I come home at midnight, I should see your *Saab* at once regarding some urgent work."

I do not know whether he heard me completely, but Thyagarajan's name seemed to bring him to his senses.

"It's strange," he grumbled under his breath as he got up from the comfort of his chair to come up to the gate.

"Do you have anything written with you?" He asked, wanting to make doubly sure before letting me in.

"No," I said, patiently.

"Then, you tell me, how I can wake up my boss, huh? He will simply kick my arse and throw me out of the job."

"That is not my problem, *Tambi*," I said with a shrug, trying to keep a check on my rising irritation. I was tired and badly in need of a good night's sleep. Many days of sailing in rough waters had taken its toll on me. "Okay, I will come tomorrow, during the day…and I'll tell your *Saab* how insolent you were tonight."

I turned towards my Yezdi, angry with Thyagarajan. If he weren't my strong support, I wouldn't have paid any heed to any message, urgent or not, at such time of the night, weary as I was.

"Wait a minute...let me check." The chowkidar called out as he shuffled back to the cabin, leaving me to contemplate on the other side of the massive iron gates studded with sharp spikes.

I did not know who Mr. S. Varadrajan was. Lately, I had met very few gentry. Since the death of my father a couple of years back, I had adopted a fisherman's vocation. Before that I had been employed as assistant manager at Tarapore Fishing Corporation in Chennai. Though, frankly speaking, the designation did not reflect the work I had to perform. I was, for all practical purposes, just an ordinary clerk, preparing bills, sending memos, kowtowing to my umpteen number of bosses, voicing a respectful 'Yes, sir', 'No, sir', depending on what I felt at that moment their inflated egos needed to hear. God! What a dull, monotonous life was I leading! Then the death of my father at the hands of the Coast Guard changed my world completely. Many truths emerged forth that shook the very foundation of my sedate world. How could I ever have known that my tight-lipped, frail-bodied father with all his dumb, ignorant ways was involved with the LTTE! But I had to digest the bitter reality, howsoever shocking it might seem. Isn't life like that, after all?

The chowkidar was speaking in a very humble tone to

someone over the telephone. After few moments he put the receiver down and rushed to the gate. A visibly servile behavior and the scowl on his face told a different story altogether - that he had been chastised by the voice on the other side of the phone.

Opening the gate, he asked me to enter.

"Go right in. Just knock on the door," he said deferentially, muttering in the same breath, "These bosses…hell! Why can they not inform me who is coming?"

Leaving my motorcycle under the watchful eye of the scowling chowkidar, I walked briskly up the gravel driveway lined on either side with neatly trimmed bushes silhouetted by dim lamps that lit the way right up to the house, my mind too preoccupied to appreciate the well manicured lawns sporting a large pond with goldfish and water lilies in it. I was wondering why on earth would some unknown person send urgent summons for me, that too at an odd hour like this.

My hand was poised to ring the bell when the door was opened by an old maid.

"Come in, Mr. Venugopal… *Saab* is waiting for you upstairs."

I climbed slowly up the wide staircase trailing my hand on the ornately carved balustrade as my awestruck eyes took in the exquisite beauty of the main hall done up in deep leather-covered couches, exquisite antiques placed on low, intrinsically carved rosewood tables, the walls lined with paintings by masters, a plush Persian carpet that covered every inch of the floor, and a huge aquarium in which beautiful fish swam, as though keeping a silent never ending vigil.

Upstairs, at the far end of a wide gallery that lead to a huge French window overlooking the lawns, I was confronted with the sight of an old man dressed in a white linen shirt and a white *lungi* reclining in an easychair.

"Good evening, Sir. I am Venugopal. Mr. Thyagarajan told me to…"

"Sit down," he said, cutting me short, nodding towards the straight-backed chair placed in front of him.

A shiver coursed through my body as I lowered myself into the chair. This always happens to me whenever I have any strange encounter - like this one - with unknown persons.

Minutes slowly ticked by as I waited expectantly for the old man who sat seemingly lost in some deep thought to say something. Even given my wild imagination, I could not fathom what sort of urgent work could this old man have with a person like me. The silence was disconcerting.

"So, you are Venugopal?" He said, at last.

"Yes, sir."

"I heard that you own a trawler and that you are a very hardworking and honest man. Is it so?"

Did he not know of modesty? How could I boast of my abilities?

I said nothing, trying to gauge as to what he was getting at.

"I am sorry I cannot offer you anything at this moment. I hope you will not mind."

"It's alright," I said most amiably, not that I could not have done with a large whisky to relax my tired bones.

"Do you know for whom your father worked?"

The question struck me like a bolt of lightning. Never since the death of my father had I been reminded by anyone as to which organization had he worked for and why.

Immediately my guard went up. I said nothing, preferring to maintain a cautious silence.

"I knew him well… a great soul indeed! A man of great determination, faith and valor. Yes, that he certainly was. I respected him deeply...intensely. Do you know he lost his life for the cause of the Tamils? For the land of Dravids? His sacrifice has come to mean a great ideal to us. You do not know of what a great soul you are an offspring. He was a quiet, secretive and determined person who would go to any length for the cause he believed in. Never would he disclose anything to anybody, even to his own self. A great man, indeed!"

What he was saying was nauseating. I had never been able to get myself to forgive my father for what he had been - an undercover agent of the militant group, the Tamil Tigers.

It then dawned upon me that this old man too was a member of the same Tamil Tigers for whom I had a deep-seated hatred. Weren't these the very people who had very recently caused the horrifying death of the great, charismatic, Indian leader Rajiv Gandhi? Ironically, that too in Tamil Nadu, the state belonging to the Tamils! They were the brutal murderers of a young, dynamic man who was determined to uplift a nation, to give it a global identity.

I remained silent, knowing it would be pointless to debate this fanatic, trying hard as he was in the middle of the night to impress upon me as to how deeply he respected my father. Hah!

"Sorry," he said, in a voice that could warm the coldest of the hearts. "Destiny has been written. The day is not far when the Tamils will win back their lost pride. They will have their own homeland…. This is the truth and truth is bound to prevail.

"You know how the Tamils are being tortured mercilessly in Sri Lanka. How can we sit tight and watch the genocide of the people in whose veins our own blood flows? Your father too was much concerned about it… I mourn his death. But it's only after many patriots like him sacrifice their lives will the goal be achieved."

Controlling a desperate rage that was growing within me to hammer some sense into the old man, I sat still saying nothing.

"...And a great responsibility is awaiting you too," he continued, looking me straight in my eyes, a pleading in his gaze.

I shifted uneasily in the chair, fearful of what lay ahead. This old man was trying to pull me in the same bloody game they were a part of!

"I am sorry, sir, but I cannot be involved in anything like this. I have my own life to lead. I know who my father was, and I do not forgive him for what he did. I know the Tamils are facing problems in Sri Lanka, but I do not have any sympathy for them, since they, for whatsoever reason, have with conscious deliberation elected to go against the law of the very land they rushed to settle in centuries ago. Ethnic problems are meaningless in the light of the technologically advanced boundary-less world we live in today. Bloodshed and conflicts will yield nothing but hatred. And I'm against that," I said in a heady rush, not hearing my own voice over the loud thumping of my heart.

Sanjay Sonawani

The old man heard me without batting an eyelid.

"I understand," he said with a wan smile as I finished.

"You are young and youngsters have the right to entertain wild thoughts, at times. They lack in logic and an understanding of the threads that form the fabric of society of which they are but an intrinsic part. My son, true understanding is reached only after suffering many pains and disgusting experiences. Refrain yourself from the thoughts that possess you. I am not asking you to carry guns and shoot people aimlessly. No. Trust me, I simply want the little help you can render me without disturbing your life."

"I'm sorry, I cannot be of any help to you," I said, resolute in my belief that militancy would never get any support from me and began to rise from my chair.

"Sit down." His voice was changed now. There was no sign of the earlier gentleness of an old man indulging a young child; it cut through the dark night with the keenness of a finely honed razor. "First, listen what I wish to say, you young fool. Then reject it, if you must; you know not of the consequences of such action of yours."

Logic is useless before such diehard fanatics. I had no choice but to listen to the obnoxious old man.

"Your father was greatly respected by the Tamil Tigers' high command. He shipped weapons and men for our cause. He never disobeyed our orders because he knew very well what fatal outcome its disobedience could bring upon him! Now, you too, listen to me."

Blood rushed to my head, the pent-up angst against my father and the old man's derisive manner was ready to explode in violence at any moment now. For the first time in my life, was I being subjected to such impropriety, and that too from such a senior citizen. Exercising restraint, I sat down once again.

His tone changed again. Words began rolling off his lips with the same gentleness with which he had first addressed me.

"We need you, young man. For once, at least! May be, when you have completed the assignment, you can be on your own; no one from our side will ever bother you."

I said nothing sitting still, my mind was a whirlwind of wild thoughts.

"Listen, son," he leaned forward and whispered at last, "Let's not beat around the bush. We need you. At present, there is no one that I can think of who can do the job for us. This job can fetch you a fortune. You can even buy a new trawler and live happily ever after."

So, this was it, I thought to myself. They must be in some sort of a jam and at the eleventh hour can't get any assistance from their own numerous trusted people. But what on earth did they want of me?

"I am sorry, Mr. Varadrajan, I am not interested in any of your assignments. I have already told you that. I can't be used against my will. Not even for money."

The old man leaned back in the chair with a sigh, his legs outstretched, staring out of the window at the pond below in the centre of the lawn.

He must be gathering his thoughts and working out how I could be made to do his biding against my wishes, I thought.

"We can get people. There are thousands who would consume cyanide without a question, if ordered so. But the situation at hand is tricky.

"I truly lack in bargaining skills. But threats, I hate them. But what else can I do at such times when an obstinate young man shuts his eyes to the stark realities of life? Let me cut it short. First, let me tell you what kind of a job we want you to do for us."

He leaned forward and looking me straight in the eyes for a few moments and continued, "We have a package that we want to ship immediately to the north coast of Sri Lanka. Once you deliver the package, we will never contact you again. This is a promise of a gentleman. But the package should reach the coast safely at any cost. Once the job is done you can come back, collect your reward, and be a happy man.

"...Of course, as you have rightly said, you have every right to refuse my offer. We cannot force a person against his will. We believe in freedom of speech and freedom of action. And that is the very cause we are fighting for. But you are also aware that people do change depending on the situations they are faced with. Well, at least during such crucial times when one is desperate to reach one's chosen goal. One has to neglect certain violations of ethics in the larger interest of the cause."

His voice was growing fervid and his eyes blazed with the passion of a man possessed, as he continued.

"And such violations mean a lot of things, my dear obstinate child! For instance, we can arrange that no one buys your catch. No sailor or fisherman works for you. That you get no harbor facilities. Your fishing licence too can be revoked. Oh, and if you do somehow manage to overcome these obstacles, we will see to it that you are delivered a pair of the finest crutches to help you go about your daily chores. Yes, yes, you know we would most certainly do that for you, even if you are not willing to follow my instructions. After all, you are the son of one of our most respected men!"

A chill ran down my spine. I knew very well that they could easily do this to me given the state government's clandestine support and the organization's large network of informers and supporters within the public. But even then, it was not so simple a matter to accept the job and sail the open seas ferrying contraband to the Sri Lankan coast. The Indian Coast Guard had so greatly intensified patrolling the waters separating the two nations that even a fish would find it difficult to enter the coastal waters without being detected.

Uneasily, I changed my position and stared at the floor, trying to think of a way out of this predicament. I cursed myself for having decided to come here on the behest of that bloody chap Thyagarajan. Now, here I was in a Catch 22 situation, caught in finely laid trap. I had little doubt of the subtle threats just given by this old man. I knew very well how deeply the LTTE had spread its tentacles in Tamil Nadu. Everyday since the bloody assassination of Rajiv Gandhi, shocking stories of the militant group's deeds were being reported by the media. And rumors were never ending. The entire state was in turmoil.

Just then it occurred to me, why not say yes to this treacherous old man and go directly to the police from here and inform them about this bastard and his plans? They surely would protect me. They would arrest this bastard and put him through the wringer.... The thought pleased me.

"Okay, I accept," I said in a defeated voice. "You have

left me no choice. But I sincerely beg you, can you not find someone else who can be of better assistance to you?"

"No. To our knowledge, you are the best. We know we can trust you. After all, you too are a Tamil. We know you will not let us down."

"No," I said quietly. "This is a little difficult to explain. I do not as yet know of the risks involved in this undertaking. I am putting my trust in what destiny has in store for me when I accept your assignment. Not that I am afraid of threats. When I set sail on the vast waters of the sea, I am never sure that I will return safe and sound. But I am a sailor, and I love the sea, and the challenges it throws up. I only hope that I will come back and begin a new life with no trouble from you people.

"Also, let me make clear one more thing. If the Coast Guard suspect me and search the trawler and if your package is dangerous enough to indict me, naturally, you too will not be spared the heat."

"Son," the old man chuckled, "Don't worry yourself too much about the package. It is safe. The Coast Guard will not suspect you if you keep your mouth shut and act smart. The chances of you being caught are one in a hundred. So, why worry?"

There was a strong note of assurance in his voice which surprised me.

"It is my wish to remain a sailor as long as I live," I said averting his gaze. "I dream of the day when I will own a large fleet of trawlers. I will need all the money I can make... So may I ask, how much will you pay me?"

"Good, good," said the slimy bastard without any trace of

emotion on his face. "Money is not a problem. As I have told you, you will deliver this package at the given destination and you will get fifty lakhs of rupees, in cash."

Never in my life had I made a deal of such sorts. I did not know whether I put it rightly as I said, "Half before I sail, if it suits you."

"You really are a shrewd businessman," he laughed in self-contentment. "Okay. This can be arranged. Half before, half on completion of the assignment. We never cheat, you know. Your father never ran after money. After all, he was a man of the cause. But you belong to the young generation. So far, you have no values that you respect. But it's alright, you'll get your money."

"What about the package? Are there arms involved?"

He gave me a bemused smile.

"It may be anything, Son. Why worry?"

"But there is tight security on the shore. The Coast Guard checks all trawlers before they set sail. How can I be sure that I won't be caught red-handed with some contraband?"

"The package you are to ferry across is very small. No one will ever suspect you of anything. Believe me, unless we were absolutely sure of it, we wouldn't have relied on the services of an amateur like you. Satisfied? "

"When am I supposed to sail?"

"Tomorrow. Be at home. As soon as we are ready, someone will contact you over the phone."

"I am not feeling safe. Suppose I get arrested?"

"In the first place, this won't ever happen. But even if by any unforeseen chance such a calamity does befall you, we will see to it that you are released with no charge."

I nodded reluctantly. My mind was already rushing elsewhere. Whom I should confide in? Which police station? Which officer? I had so little knowledge about the law enforcement body.

"Thanks for accepting our little job. I will remember this forever. Now you may leave."

I stood up and without any further exchange of pleasantries headed for the stairs.

"Just a moment, Son," he called out from behind.

I froze on the spot.

"Don't even let the thought of double-crossing us come to your mind. From this very moment, you are being watched. So, don't fool around, just go home and have a good night's sleep."

Stunned, I looked back. His lips were twisted in a mirthless smile. A knot tightened in my belly, and my legs became wooden stumps. It seemed as though the bastard had read my mind. I wanted to say something...I wanted to shout at the motherfucker who knew he had me by my balls. But my throat turned dry, I could not utter a single word.

Run... run away from this stupid dream, someone yelled from within the realms of my mind.

At the gate, as I kick-started my battered Yezdi to life, I saw what he said was true. Two cars were parked on the opposite side of the road, and as I took the road home, both the vehicles started following me at a respectable distance.

Unwittingly, in answering that bloody Thyagarajan's urgent message what a royal mess I had landed myself in. I had no courage left now to turn my bike towards the police station. I knew very well that they must be armed. And if I did try anything stupid, I would end up with the word 'Late' before my name.

I drove fast towards home.

On the Brink of Death ❖ 23

no courage left now to turn my bike towards the police station. I
know very well that they must be armed. And if I did my anything stupid, I would end up with the word 'Late' before my
name.

I drove fast towards home.

❖❖❖

Two

Janaki was waiting for me at the door. "What happened?" She asked in a worried tone.

"Nothing. I am hungry. Serve dinner."

"What happened?" She repeated. She must have noted
how ashen I looked.

"Nothing to worry about, my dear," I said with as much
control as I could muster in my voice. I didn't want to upset my
wife with my terrible experience. She was a simple woman and
I loved her very much.

"Mr. Thyagarajan had come. He was inquiring about you.
I told him you got the message and went to see that.... What's
his name? I forget...."

"Never mind." I tried to assure her. "Please serve the food, okay?"

She knew me well enough to gather that something was bothering me deeply, and it was this quality of hers that further added to my irritation.

Unused to such strange behavior of mine, she followed my instructions mutely.

A storm raged within me. I wanted to kill that bastard Thyagarajan for having pushed me up shit creek. I wanted to shoot that son of a bitch, Varadrajan, who had manipulated me- a straight man, leading a simple life and earning his livelihood through honest means- to obey his orders. But how futile was my rage. I did not know what I should do in such extraordinary and dangerous circumstances. After what Thyagarajan had done to me, I had no one in whom I could confide. I was frightened. I was worried.

It occurred to me that I could telephone the police station. Would they come here and release me from the clutches of these dangerous people? I gave a careful thought to this ray of hope. Then I remembered the recent newspaper reports about the involvement of local government officials in LTTE affairs. What if the police informed them instead? And the initial hope ebbed away as fast as it had occurred. I finally thought, 'I have no choice but to act on the instructions of those bastards. If I am lucky, I will be safe. If not, I will tell the police the real story. That is, if at all they do not shoot me at sight. I have to trust my luck and let my reputation of being a clean and honest person stand by me.'

Janaki served me rice and fish curry. She was an excellent cook, but today, I had lost all taste for food.

After dinner we retired to the bedroom, but sleep was furthermost away from me. I lay wide-awake the whole night, my restless mind trying to think of a way out of the mess I found myself in.

Janaki lay fast asleep beside me.

I touched her swollen belly and for a moment, I lost myself in pleasant thoughts. I wondered what the destiny would present me with? Son or daughter?

At least, my wife and child should not suffer the agonies of life as I do, I thought. I was a law-abiding person, never had I done anything in my life that could invite the wrath of the law. But, now, I could not escape from it.

I did not want to die. I had a loving wife, Janaki, a warm and welcoming home, a flourishing business, and I was a Tamil - a cursed debt with which I was born and which I now had to repay by performing an illegal act, whether willingly or otherwise; that too without even knowing what its outcome could be.

How cursed could a man be, I thought pitifully of myself.

◆ ◆ ◆

The clock on the wall slowly ticked its way to noon. The weather was warm and sticky. The noise of vehicles passing by on the road added to my uneasiness. I paced the room, anxiously waiting for the ominous ring of the telephone to announce the commencement of my journey into the vortex of the world of crime. I wondered what the package I was to deliver to the Lankan Tigers would possibly contain. My mind raced wildly imagining all sorts of dangerous situations that could possibly befall me in my endeavor. I was rattled.

Janaki looked at me questioningly, trying hard to comprehend what it was that had changed me overnight, as she went about her routine household work. But she said nothing.

Each time the phone rang, I rushed to grab it before Janaki could attend to it, but it was not the expected call. For lunch, I reluctantly swallowed some rice with *rassam*, impatiently waiting for the call that would end the suspense.

It came at 4.30. "*Tambi*," said a deep voice from the other end, "The package will be delivered to you at 8.30 sharp. Top up the fuel tank of your trawler and keep enough spare on board to ensure an uninterrupted to and fro journey. Also, ask your boat hands not to come today. You will be undertaking the journey alone. Understood?"

"But how can I manage alone?"

"That is your problem. Just follow the instructions. Check the engine and whatever else. You have enough time."

"Okay," I said in a weak voice.

"Good. Now tell me, can you use firearms?"

"No."

"No problem," said the unknown voice. "You will learn it, once you are in deep waters."

The very thought of carrying firearms sent shivers through my body. Far from firing a gun, I had never even held one in my hands.

"Now get going with the instructions."

"Okay. But... the money?"

"It will be delivered, as promised."

"There is no phone on the port"

"We know that."

"Then?"

"The money will reach you before you leave. We know you will not play any funny games with us," said the voice and hung up. So that was it. Varadrajan was trying to ensure that I would not let them down.

Just then the doorbell rang.

A man in his late thirties stood there holding a large leather case.

"Mr. Venugopal?"

"Yes," I answered, weakly.

"This comes with compliments from your friends," he said, as he placed the bag on the floor. " Just as promised."

I nodded. I knew what the bag contained.

"Would you like to count?" He asked with a smile.

"No. No, thanks."

Just then Janaki entered the hall from the bedroom.

"Who's it?" She inquired.

"Nobody," I said and asked the man, who had not introduced himself, to leave.

Janaki looked at me suspiciously. "What's this? What's in the bag?"

"It's none of your business," I said curtly, as I lifted the bag and took it into the bedroom, where in a corner stood a large cupboard. I carefully placed the bag on top of it and sat down on the edge of the bed.

'What should I do with all this money? Where do I hide it?' My mind raced, caught in a whirlwind of thoughts. I could sense all sorts of dangers awaiting me outside, at sea, on my way to the Lankan coast. I was not sure I would ever return safely and see my beloved again. Desperation welled up in my heart.

Janaki came in and stood watching me silently.

"You are in some sort of trouble, Venu?" She asked softly. "Tell me, I have never seen you so worried."

I was never good at making up stories. But I had to tell Janaki something without raising any undue alarm. Already, she had sensed something strange in my behavior, since my return from Varadrajan's place last night. Now I would be out for at least two weeks and I had to explain to her why I would be absent for such a long time.

"It's nothing, Janaki. Please sit down. I want to talk to you."

"Well...what's going on?"

"Nothing to be worried about, my dear." I was thinking hard. The story was not yet shaping up. "You know how things are nowadays. I have been assigned a job by the Coast Guard. They want to use my trawler to keep a watch at sea. The rumor is that some LTTE militants are trying to get to Sri Lanka. They are well equipped and can very easily evade the Coast Guard patrol boats. But the Coast Guard hopes that if they hide themselves in a fisherman's boat, the militants could then easily be trapped. That's all."

"But... it is so dangerous!"

"Yes, I know it is. The militants may open fire...they never surrender easily, you know. But don't worry, the Coast Guard is not even sure whether the rumor is true. Possibly nothing will happen and I can come back safely."

Sanjay Sonawani

"Then why are you so worried?" She looked at me search-ingly.

Avoiding her sharp gaze, I turned to look at the bedspread.

"Well, you know I have never involved myself in anything like this before. They have paid me handsomely, but.... Well, you can understand, this is an unusual incident in my life and that's what is making me nervous. Janaki, trust me. I am helping the law - unlike my father."

I could myself not believe what I was saying. Memories of my father flashed through my mind and made me uneasy. I could see the same reflect in Janaki's eyes. We had never ever discussed my father's past or his activities. We had tried all the time to lead a normal life.

"Forget everything, Venu," said Janaki in a soft voice. "Helping the law is good, but are you sure there is no danger involved?"

I avoided looking her in the eyes. How could I! I knew whatever I was telling her was a figment of my imagination, the very opposite of the truth. "Look Janaki, these days danger is a common phenomenon even in ordinary life. Even Rajiv Gandhi, our former prime minister, was assassinated just a week ago, don't you know? Anyway, I am not that important and then, you see, there's the Coast Guard, heavily armed, to protect me and themselves."

"Okay, Venu. I'll wait for you. Do not involve yourself in any mess and come back safely. Promise?"

"Okay, I promise," I replied.

"One more thing, Janaki...."

"What?"

"You will not tell anyone about this, not a single word. In fact, why not go and stay with your parents till I return?"

"No. I'll stay here."

"Okay," I said, not wanting to get into any argument with her.

"And this bag, does it contain money?"

"Yes."

"Since when the government has started paying cash rewards, in advance?" She said sternly, seemingly unconvinced by my story.

"You think too much," I said casually, trying hard to hide my discomfiture. "I have to leave now. It's already late. Take care. I'll be back soon."

Janaki said nothing. She just planted a kiss on my forehead - "I love you, Venu."

"I love you too, Janaki. Be careful. Say nothing to anyone. And this money, will you please hide it somewhere? Actually, don't bother, I'll take care of it." But I didn't know anyone in whom I could entrust such a huge amount. I snatched the bag from the cupboard and readied to leave.

Janaki watched me silently as I hurried out of the door towards the sound of the ebbing tide. My otherwise rationale mind had come to a standstill, but destiny, I suppose, was leading my feet on. If I could keep myself away from the Coast Guard patrol, I could foresee a good future. Or, else, the consequences of this act of mine could take my life.

Well, nothing matters when one is dead.

Sanjay Sonawani

Three

The quay was crowded as ever. Everyone was busy. The trawlers were ready to set sail. The familiar sight of the trawlers and the smell of the sea gave me a sense of belonging. I felt slightly relaxed. This was my realm. I had grown up here. To me, the sea was a trusted friend. Its sight alone was enough to soothe my troubled mind.

I climbed aboard my trawler, anchored beside a bunch of dinghies bobbing up and down in the ebbing waters that came in and after kissing the shore, scampered back like a shy damsel. Mine was a fifteen-year-old trawler that had weathered many storms, but its engine still held the deep, trusting throb of power that could take on the roughest of seas without any trouble. Since it was only yesterday that we had returned from sea after five days of trawling for tuna, my boat hands were not expected to report for work today. All alone, I got busy getting things ready for the journey ahead of me. I checked the stock of diesel on board as a matter of routine; the first thing on our return yesterday, I had got the spare tank filled up. I checked the radio; no trouble there - all frequencies unaltered. I had nothing to worry about at that moment, but I was not sure whether I could sail such a distance alone. I had never before done such a long trip on my own. I didn't even know what the package would contain! 'Whatever it is, why worry when there is nothing left that's going to change?' I said to myself philosophically.

"Venu. Oh Venu" - someone shouted from the wharf. I came out of the cabin. It was the fisherman, Raju, from Raghavan's trawler. Raju had an uncanny knack of guessing where one could find the best catch.

"What's it, Raju?"

"You were not expected today. Are you sailing?"

"Yes."

"But I see no one around?"

"Today I am taking my wife to sea, to celebrate her birthday."

"Oh, ho!" He grinned cheekily. "Enjoy...but be careful. The Coast Guard's on high alert. Do you know, Govindraj's trawler has been seized?"

"What! But Why?"

"They unearthed a whole load of firearms on it," he said. "Imagine. I'd never have suspected Govindraj of being involved in such dirty work."

Sanjay Sonawani

I felt as though somebody had punched me hard in my solar plexus. My throbbing heart was caught in a tight bind. The nightmare had begun.

"What happened?" Raju asked.

"Nothing." I tried to sound casual. "It's shocking!"

"You look unwell, Venu!"

"Forget it, *Tambi*." I said irritably, angry with myself for not being able to control my fears.

He looked at me askance for a while, then threw his hand in resignation - "Don't go too far. The weather is likely to change suddenly for the worse."

"Yeah," I answered.

"Good luck and have a good time, and wish Janaki on my behalf," he said, as he turned to leave.

My legs seemed to turn to jelly and I sat down heavily on the wooden deck. How helpless was I at that moment. I cursed my father for his association with these bastards. In the past, they had ruthlessly killed hundreds and thousands of people and now, would not hesitate, even for a moment, to kill me.

The sun hurriedly went to hide behind the distant houses and trees and cast a warm orange glow of a pleasant evening everywhere. Yet, the ever-soothing sound of the gently splashing waves made me uneasy.

Okay, I thought, if that's what I have to do, I shall do it once and I shall do it well. Then I'll say good-bye to this business and this city; I can always find shelter in this vast world.

As dark shadows came out to play in the dying light of the day, I got up and entered the cabin and, lighting a lamp, went

Sanjay Sonawani

through with the usual last minute checkup once again.

Sharp at 8.30 p.m., a young man dressed in jeans and T-shirt approached my trawler.

"Venugopal?"

"Yes," I said nervously. My heart was pounding like a drum.

"The package will be here at any moment from now," he said in a low conspiratorial tone. "You won't have to wait for long."

I remained silent. I had no choice; I could do nothing but wait.

The light on the seashore was rapidly getting dimmer and by now the wharf was desolate, with just a few small boats and trawlers dancing on the waves.

A little while later, I heard the clatter of a ramshackle tempo in the distance that grew louder as it struggled closer before screeching to a halt on the pier.

Then the sound of hurried footsteps.

Silhouetted figures approached my trawler.

They were two, one holding a bag in his hands.

I could make out neither of the faces, not that I wanted to.

"Tambi, come down," said a voice. "Help this man up."

Without a word the man with the bag ascended the trawler.

"This man will sail with you, " continued the voice. "In the bag there are weapons, maps and some other important stuff, so hide it somewhere safe."

The man handed me the bag without a word.

"Take utmost care, *Tambi.* Avoid all Coast Guard and

Navy patrol boats. This man is very important to us. If you fail in your task, we won't forgive you. Understood?"

I nodded mutely. There was no courage left in me to resist or to ask him the many questions that had been racing through my mind.

The man then turned and hurried silently back into the darkness. I too turned slowly towards the cabin into which the unwelcome cargo had disappeared.

"Go into the hold downstairs and stay there till we are out in the open sea. The Coast Guard is on high alert. They are watching everything," I told the man tersely, who without a word turned about and descended the narrow stairs into the hold, littered with smelly bundles of nets, hooks, and a lot of other junk.

I was so preoccupied with my concern to get going that I forgot my fears and hurriedly started the engine and wove my way through the other boats towards the deep sea.

The voyage had begun.

♦   ♦   ♦

The vast ocean was rhythmically moving up and down, reflecting the crescent moon and the millions of stars that adorned the sky. In the distance, I could make out the lights of the port of Madras. From Madras to Sri Lanka was a long journey. I never had travelled that far alone. The Indian and Lankan coast guard boats were keeping a sharp vigil for any suspicious movement at sea. Since the assassination of Rajiv Gandhi, many Tamil militants were on the run and were trying to seek safe haven. Many had escaped to Karnataka, Coimbatore and Trichi before trying to get back to Sri Lanka. Everyday the Special Investigation Team (SIT) was unearthing one or two of their secret hideouts.

Sanjay Sonawani

Militants barely in their teens were swallowing cyanide pills and embracing death willingly, rather than be caught.

The militants had the sympathy not only of the common people but that of many high ranking government officials too. The fight that the LTTE had put up against the powerful army sent in by the Indian Government to Sri Lanka was being admired even today by everyone. The small bunch of militants had forced the peacekeeping force to retreat to India! The locals took great pride in the LTTE's victory. Someone else was doing things that they could never possibly do. Alternatively, they were lending support to the militants, not only sympathetically but also with safe havens and funds. That was the reason why the LTTE had been able to spread its network in Tamil Nadu.

I, personally, never had any sympathy for them. I always thought that those who had migrated hundreds of years ago would have adapted to the culture and ways of that land by now. But ethnic problems I could never understand. Imagine trying to maintain an identity separate from the natives for thousands of years and, yet, expecting a share in the power. It was all too ridiculous for me. In Sri Lanka, hadn't the Sinhalese avenged all that had happened in the past? They, after gaining freedom, had never allowed the Tamils to get ahead in any field of life, using every possible means to oppress them. In government jobs, education, business, everywhere, the Tamils were treated like lepers. And it was this very oppression that had inflamed the discontent within them and had led to the formation of the Liberation Tigers of Tamil Elam (LTTE). Since then, bloodshed had spread from Colombo to the luscious fields of hinterland Sri Lanka, with hundreds of thousands of lives being targeted to drive home the message.

The Indian government in its naivete, bolstered, perhaps, by its earlier success in Bangladesh, had added fuel to the already raging inferno by sending in the peacekeeping force. The hatred grew. The Tamils openly supported the LTTE and vehemently abused Rajiv Gandhi for his anti-Tamil policies. Now, even after his bloody assassination, this civil war was not showing any signs of abating.

And, today, I too had, perforce, become a part of the ethnic war. I feared the outcome.

Half an hour later, I sighted a couple of trawlers cruising slowly towards the coast. I speeded up my trawler and changed direction a little. The last thing I wanted at this moment was to confront any acquaintance. It was as though I was trying to escape existence itself. I then turned to the bag that had been handed to me for safe keeping till reaching the Lankan coast and opened the zippered flap. Inside lay an AK-56 carbine, rows of neatly arranged magazines of ammunition and some papers. Among the latter was a map which I thought was of importance. I unfolded it and studied it carefully in the dim glow of the cabin light. A 'Z' shaped line was drawn on the map in red, extending from the Madras port to the Lankan coast, suggesting our direction of travel. I folded the map back and laid it on the table. I was on the right course.

"You can come up now," I called out to that unknown 'package' from near the hold.

He came up, coughed a little and muttered, "I would have

died of that obnoxious smell down there, had I stayed there for another few hours."

"This is a fisherman's trawler, mister, not a luxury liner," I retorted curtly. "If you want, you can sleep in the cabin."

"No, thanks. I feel better here in this fresh air."

"As you wish." I was exhausted and in no mood to converse with him. A strong urge to sleep was almost overpowering me. I locked the rudder in place to ensure that we maintained proper direction during the night and then fixing my bed, put the cabin lights off.

The first rays of the rising sun greeted me back into the world of weary realities. I immediately checked our direction; the waves might have altered our course during the night. It had. I set our direction right once again and then turned to look at the deck.

He stood there watching the soft rays of the sun dancing on the crest of the waves. The wind was gentle and the sky a spotless, azure canopy.

I looked at him as he stood with his back towards me, his slender body resting against the brass rail.

"Haven't you slept?" I asked.

He gave a start and then turned around with a quizzical look.

It felt as if I had been slapped hard in the face. I stood motionless, frozen on the spot.

"Krishnan! Is that you?" I exclaimed, not trusting my eyes. Time had not made any alterations to his face over the years.

"O my God, I can't believe this. You too..." my voice choked with emotion.

He too, for a moment looked overjoyed, and then, in the next instant, seemed detached.

"You, Venu!" He rushed towards me. "My friend, Venu! I could never dream of this... imagine meeting you again. Does this trawler belong to you?"

I was speechless, as though confronted by an unbelievable dream.

"How are you? How have you been?" He asked, holding my one hand tightly in his.

"Fine...just fine," I mumbled, unable to make out my own words through the flood of emotions that swept through me.

"I heard you got married? I always wanted to see you, you know? How is she?"

"She is fine, indeed," I muttered.

"Oh how I wish to see that lucky woman! It is godsend that you are accompanying me on this voyage. I would have got bored if some illiterate fishermen were designated to sail with me! Now we can enjoy the journey!"

But none of his eager enthusiasm was touching the strings of my heart.

"Krishnan, how...how did you get yourself involved in this mess?"

"What do you mean?" He asked, releasing my hand.

"You were not like this. You were a different man!" I said, peering deep into his eyes, trying to fathom the changes the passage of time might have brought about him.

"And you? Aren't you also in this?"

"It's my misfortune that I am in this, Krishnan. Your people forced me."

He watched me silently for a few moments, then, throwing up his hands in a gesture of helplessness, turned to sit on a drum on the deck. His eyes were red and a little swollen, as though he hadn't slept all night.

"So... you are not with us?"

His question angered me.

"How can I be with these demons? You all are criminals...third grade criminals, I should say!" I said in a shrill voice. Anguish gripped me. I looked all around helplessly. I wanted to hit him. I wanted to cry. I wanted to abuse him. I wanted to curse the people he now worked for. But I was at a loss for words. "You, Krishnan, of all people! I could never have imagined that a person like you could get involved with such heinous people."

So, this was the package I was to deliver to Sri Lanka. The man the militants would risk everything for. The man whom I had once looked up to - most intelligent, a genius, perhaps!

"Calm down, Venu," he said softly.

"How... how can I when your people have put my life to risk for a criminal like you?"

"I am not a criminal. Nor are any of my friends. It is fate that has brought us here together. Calm down, my friend. Anger will not change things now."

Unfortunately, what he said was true. I had to get a grip on my emotions.

"Right," I said and slumped down on the deck in defeat.

Krishnan watched me thoughtfully for a long time, not saying a word.

"The night was beautiful. To sleep on the open deck under the stars gave me immense joy."

I said nothing, my heart saddened by the bitter reality that stood exposed in front of me.

I got up and splashed some water on my weary eyes from the sweet water tank on the deck and went to the cabin to prepare coffee.

Krishnan followed me to the cabin.

"I'll prepare the coffee...you know I make good coffee."

I handed over charge and sat back.

Krishnan was an expert in many things. And coffee was one of the things he made exceptionally well. In the days past, we had shared many a cup prepared by him discussing everything that caught our fancy, right from the creation of the universe to the life-style of the hermit crab that was burrowing a hole in the soft sand by our feet, under the coconut trees, where we sat in front of his house.

Silently, I watched him make coffee.

"You should have taken along a few assistants," he muttered after a while.

"How could I? When back at Madras, I don't want to get caught."

He nodded sadly. "Yes, that's true. One cannot trust anyone these days. But...again, the fact is that Tamils do not defect that easily. They have compassion for us."

"That might be the reason why the police is informed where the militants are hiding. The informers must not be Tamils!" I said sarcastically.

He put down his mug.

"What you are saying is but half the truth. The police is trying hard to capture militants, but what of it? All they have been able to lay their hands on are a few inconsequential people. We are taking good enough care of our important people," he said, with a mischievous smile on his face.

The pent-up rage in me burst forth.

"Then that bastard, Sivrasan, must be enjoying his life somewhere!" I retorted harshly.

For a moment, he looked at me in astonishment and then roared with laughter. "So you too are one of the so-called nationalists?" Then controlling himself, asked, "Are you one of those men who have nothing to do with the pride of the Tamil people? Why are you so agonized over Gandhi's death? Wasn't he the man responsible for the turmoil in Jaffna? Was he not the one who sent in the Indian army to fight us? Look, *Tambi*, no person with any self-pride will accept any attack on his freedom. Rajiv Gandhi tried to crush our movement and was punished for it. Just forget him. Now no one will ever think of using the army against us."

I was shocked. Was this man the same Krishnan I once admired? He who used to be a friend and philosopher to me. But today, I felt completely alienated from him.

"What do you people think of yourself?" I asked angrily. "Do you think you are doing the right thing? How can you kill somebody so ruthlessly…only because you've got arms? Aren't you people following a wrong path?"

"You are but a child, Venu. You have shut your eyes to

stark reality. You are not yet ready to confront the truth," he sighed, as he rose from the stool, his face full of compassion, as though I was a child getting angry on futile matters.

"Truth? What truth? Don't tell me about it," I fumed. "Truth is a slave of the powers that be. Whatsoever they say is truth. I am weak, a commoner, but don't tell me about truth, Krishnan. There exists no such thing. Tainted images are presented before us as truth. It has always happened in the past. Don't try to feed me with your warped philosophy. You are racial, you are cruel, and you are a fanatic - and that is the truth, nothing else. Look beyond these fractured images only then shall you find the truth."

I was trembling in the storm of emotions raging within my heart. Fate had played a cruel game with me. It had united me with a long lost friend, but under such bizarre circumstances. Look how radically he had changed!

"Krishnan, I should not discuss anything with you. You are not the same man I once knew, the Krishnan whom I admired. You people have forced me to tread this bloody path. I swear Krishnan, I swear, you will repent for this one day."

"Never!" He muttered, turning his back at me. "Never, Venu. I shall never repent."

I wanted to laugh at him.

"You are a fool, Krishnan. You know from the pages of history that no one can achieve their goals through bloodshed."

"Then should we accept injustice?" Krishnan roared, loosing control of his emotions. "Should we allow them to crush us under their feet? Should we accept the life of dogs? No, my friend. No. They think they are the masters of our destiny and want to mould us in anywhich way they please. They have large armies armed with the most sophisticated weapons and can easily crush any rebellion. They can use the media to tell the rest of the world how wrong, how cruel, we are. But do they speak about their own brutalities? The media is their slave. We are poor. We live in the jungles without any amenities, always on the run, not knowing when a bullet will get us in the back. But what we have is our self-respect and an ambition, which gives us the determination to fight for our freedom. We know, one day will come when we will return the lost pride to our people.

"...We have lost our relations, *Tambi*. There is no family that has not lost somebody to the cause. We have no family life left. You want to know why we lead a dog's life? We do it in order to save the lives of the families of our fellow brethren, to secure them an honorable future. And you? You don't have any respect for it?" His face twisted and his eyes blazed as he trembled in his emotional outburst.

"You too are an ordinary person, a commoner!" He shrieked pointing at me. "You too have fallen prey to their poisonous propaganda. You have respect neither for your race nor for the language. Do you know how in Sri Lanka every day the spirit of the Tamils is being crushed? All this can come to an end, *Tambi*, but who wishes it? All those bloody politicians go about preaching humanity and social equality, but do you know what they actually practice?"

The wind had risen in tandem with our voices. The hum of the trawler's engine had become deeper as it surged ahead with more power to counter the strong currents of the sea. The sails, though lowered, were flapping as though they were trying to avoid taking sides in our angry conversation, which continued over the sound of the waves.

I slumped down exhausted, as if the lifeforce within me was draining away.

"No, *Tambi*, I don't have answer to your questions," I said weakly. "But you tell me, why have the Tamils in Sri Lanka become so important to you now? Should not one be a part of the social fabric in which he lives?"

"It is an illusion, Venu," he said, still furious. "The majority always wants to enslave the minority. They hate the minority because they fear their unity. They want to use them for their own vested interests, but never want to hand over any rights to them. They fear what if this minority begins to rule the majority? And, it is due to this unfounded fear that they go on oppressing the minority class in their attempt to ensure that it is always kept separated from the majority."

"Why tell me this irrational philosophy, my friend? The world we live in is not a place any more where all this falsehood will be accepted at face value. No country can these days rest secure on the pillars of language, race, religion, or caste. The clash between them never yields peace. It always brings about disaster."

He nodded sagaciously to my point of view.

"It is so easy to preach, Venu…till you are yourself confronted with injustice. When your very own existence comes under the shadow of danger, who thinks of tomorrow then? We are not fighting for tomorrow. Our rebellion is for today.

"Injustice?" I asked incredulously. "What injustice have you suffered, Krishnan? You grew up in Madras, just like I did.

You even went abroad for higher education. And you speak of injustice!"

Krishnan laughed.

"True, Venu, true. But how ignorant you are. You don't know, my dear friend, the hell I had to undergo. You cannot even imagine the pain I have suffered. And, Venu, when it happened you were far away from me," he said in a voice filled with anguish. His eyes held a pain I had never before seen in him, a reflection, perhaps, of whatsoever he had experienced years ago.

Krishnan's image as I had known him in the days long gone by appeared before me. "You were not like this, Krishnan. You were so gentle, so lively. So curious about life were you, always optimistic. How poetic was your mind then!"

Krishnan and I were friends since childhood, since the time we had attended school together. He was always jolly and, I, in contrast, was always too serious about everything. I was the only son of an ordinary fisherman, whereas he belonged to a wealthy family. But the bond of our friendship was strong.

After matriculation we both joined Vaishnav College. He, to my surprise, chose the arts stream, while I opted for commerce. Our classes were different, but even then most of the time we could be seen together.

In those days, a girl fell in love with Krishnan. She was a pretty girl. Her eyes reflected her dreamy, romantic nature. But Krishnan never reciprocated Vani's weak efforts to gain his heart.

One day, Vani caught me while I was going home. After chatting nineteen-to-a-dozen about fellow colleagues, she directly

Sanjay Sonawani

looked into my eyes and confessed - "I am interested in your friend, Krishnan."

I was not at all taken aback. I knew all along why she had approached me.

"I am aware, Vani. But you know how Krishnan is. Nevertheless, I will try and help you."

Next day, I indirectly started praising Vani, her beauty, and exaggerated stories of her intelligence. I told Krishnan how she could bring a hearty romance into his dull existence. One day, I even dared to get the two of them to meet at the lovely Marina beach and then left them alone to learn the first lessons of love. But their affair did not last long. Vani failed to understand this jolly philosopher friend of mine. Her perception of life was that of a romantic. She wanted to live in the dream world of fairy queens with heart full of romance. And Krishnan, how indifferent he was towards such things! Vani soon left him for one of our professors, a so-called literary genius.

Krishnan, not at all unhappy with the outcome, told me philosophically - "Such girls never succeed in life, Venu. She is trying to seek a lotus in the barren sands of Rajasthan."

I too laughed with him.

Happy times don't last forever. Our college days too came to an end. We spent an evening on Marina beach and watched the sun set in the ebbing waters, reflecting the many dreams we had seen about the life that lay ahead of us. We thought of building together a business empire. We wanted to become powerful. We wanted to be virtuous. We wanted to change the world. We discussed vehemently what could bring true peace to this troubled earth; no one won that debate. Later, after darkness enveloped the vast beach, we entered a bar and tanked up on umpteen bottles of beer. We discussed, we joked, we laughed, we made promises, we fought, we swore, we embraced, and later staggered out on to the road shouting pleasantries, trying to hide the deep agony of parting.

Life was different that evening onwards. We had experienced the first lessons of life and the agonies that are associated with it. No matter how beautiful they might be, not always do dreams come true. We had to abandon all those dreams we had shared and adopt separate paths. I joined college for a diploma in fisheries. As for Krishnan, he wanted to go abroad for higher studies in sociology.

One day Krishnan got the chance he so much desired. He got a scholarship to go to England, to take the course he wanted to at Cambridge University. We spent the last evening together again at our favorite Marina beach. But how different was this meeting! The waves were rushing in to crash headlong onto the beach with a roar of a wild beast in rage then retreating in defeat, only to gather strength for yet another assault.

It was almost midnight. We sat in silence on the now deserted stretch of sand. The dim lamps of Annadurai Memoriam in the distance were trying to reassure our hearts that were filled with an unknown emotion. The wind blew as if trying hard to overcome some invisible barriers. The sea, like a dark blanket, was spread before us, reaching out to the horizon, and the crescent moon was trying to prove her brilliant supremacy amongst the countless stars. We did not know what to speak and how to react; yet another lovely dream was soon to disappear.

Sanjay Sonawani

Krishnan broke the silence. He held my hand in deep thought for a while and said, "Venu, have you seen how treacherous life is? Most dreams never come true. I wish life were simpler. Its complexity perplexes me... I'll soon be far away, without you to share what we had dreamt about. No castles shall we be building, but are going to trudge the same old beaten path of life. All the vigor that existed in us is meaningless now. I have to go. I say it is for higher education, but I am ignorant. Why would I want to be someone I do not know? I don't know who has filled ambitions in our little hearts, Venu." His voice was choked with emotion as he spoke. I had no words to express myself; I've always been at loss for words when emotional. I just glanced at the reflection of the moon in his watery eyes and then at the vast expanse of the sea. Who has understood life anyway? We just go on nibbling at the life form like a worm. That's all.

Past life, lovely as it had been, could not accompany me forever. The next day, I bid Krishnan farewell at the airport. A few years passed by. In the beginning, we were in regular correspondence with each other. But gradually, the letters became few and long spaced. I had to face a new life. The problems were new and the answers, though not often pleasant, too, were new. There was not much affection left between my father and me. There was a rumor going around the town that he was associated with the LTTE.

And now, I was meeting Krishnan once again, under such strange circumstances - the system I hated most, he represented it with all his might and vigor.

◆◆◆

Four

Almost two hundred leagues were behind us. We could not sight any trawler or Coast Guard patrol boat in the vicinity. Our direction seemed to have been well chosen by those unknown conspirators. We stood on the deck amongst the fishing nets looking out at the sea glistening in the morning sun, reflecting the many hues of the sky above. Occasionally, the fish leapt above the water, paused for a moment in mid air before crashing back and disappearing into the deep sea like a dream.

Krishnan did not speak much after our initial bout of unpleasant discussions. But I was curious to know why a brilliant young man like him had chosen to follow this dangerous path of life. Who could have influenced him so strongly that he, instead of preaching love and peace, was now supporting violence? What injustice could he have suffered? Was he on the run? Or, was he on some dangerous mission to assassinate someone? Was he in any way related to the death of Rajiv Gandhi? Many questions filled my befuddled mind, but I could think of no suitable answer.

After leaving him on the Sri Lankan shores, any future communication between us would be virtually impossible. I glanced at him through the corners of my eyes. He stood still like a statue carved in wood. What was he thinking? What was he planning? What was he scheming? Every possibility seemed to me a real life situation. Thousands of alarms sounded in my mind and their echoes deafened me.

I thought, 'I must forget that he is my friend. He is alien to me now. The past ties of our friendship have drowned in the vast sea of bygone times. This person here in front of me is a new man, dangerous and treacherous. I have no affection left for him. I should not be compassionate. I must deport him at the earliest.'

I thought of Varadrajan. His personality could so easily deceive the people who upheld the law of this country. He seemed to be a rich man; must be having good connections. And that bastard, Thyagarajan? Who could ever have suspected him of being connected with the LTTE? That organization definitely had deeply penetrated into all sections of society. I could feel Krishnan's eyes on my back like a sharp dagger. I looked at the shimmering sea in distress and then, without a glance at my friend, turned towards the control room.

We were speeding at almost thirty knots. I glanced at the map provided by Krishnan's colleague. Our proposed way was drawn in red. This was a longer route than what a person would otherwise take, but a necessary precaution to avoid the Coast Guard and Naval patrol boats. I consulted the compass. We had drifted a little off course. I carefully corrected our direction and fixed the wheel.

The sound of the roaring engine could not console my heart. Janaki's image came before my eyes. She was beckoning me, drifting over the mist. She had a sad face, her eyes full of tears. I wanted to reach out and embrace her, to take her in my arms and console her, to reassure her that this nightmare would soon be over and those happy tunes of life, we had shared in the past, we would sing all once again. But as I tried to reach out for her with outstretched hands, she distanced herself from me. I stood up. I wanted to run to her. But the mist drifted taking her along with it into the distant realms of the dark sea.

I sat down cursing myself. Why am I doing this? Why could I not have rejected this assignment? Why did I succumb to their threats? Hadn't I the balls to fight them?

I was a man of simple means. A middle-class man with hardly any knowledge of the masks worn over faces in a world of double standards, in a world where newspaper coverage was mere gossip, nothing that affected my routine life. I never had any idea how the devils in society work unobstructed. I didn't have that imaginative and scheming a mind. I had great love for my country and a certain ideology about life and its ultimate goal, which was all so easy to preach, to discuss and easy to adapt. But this was different, a strange facet of life that I had never before encountered. Was this really a part of the same world I lived in?

"Venu, quick, bring the binoculars."

Krishnan's hasty call pulled me back from the desperate drawing of the sea of madness. I stood up and rushed to the deck with the glasses. Krishnan was leaning over the rails, peering into the horizon.

"What's it, Krishnan?" I asked, anxiously trying to focus the glasses in the direction he was pointing.

"I think it's a Naval boat," he said, calmly.

Just then as I spotted a large boat in the western horizon. It was a Naval boat.

"Go back and reduce the speed," he said in a low voice.

I ran to the control room, my heart thumping loudly against my ribs. I pulled back the throttles and the speed dropped.

I rushed back to the deck.

Krishnan had, in the mean time, cast a net in the sea and was carefully handling the levers of the system. I was not sure that this ploy would save us from the approaching danger. Those people must have been watching us minutely, I thought... they could sense and understand our frantic actions. I was like a rabbit confronted by a hound. My heart was beating so rapidly I thought it would burst.

The approaching boat seemed to engulf the horizon in its path. I could now read the letters '*I.N.S. Bishvas*' painted in white on its prow. It was an Indian Naval boat.

"Control yourself and stop trembling like a leaf, Venu. Don't be afraid. You need not worry." Krishnan tried to reassure me.

I was sweating, my legs suddenly getting weak, as if life was leaking out of my body, moment by moment. I wanted to abuse him but my throat was suddenly parched with the fear of the impending danger that approached us. I looked at him in disgust; I could have killed him for his poise. What will I answer these armed men? I thought. That this is a fishing trawler? Then, where are the sailors? I had on board a man most wanted by governments of both, India and Sri Lanka. I did not have any answers. All I had was a gun....

By now armed men could be made out standing on the deck of the patrol boat. 'They know who we are! Somebody has leaked the information to them. They were searching for us and have found us. There's no escape now.'

"Don't be afraid, Venu," Krishnan repeated softly. "And don't behave stupidly...try to be at ease. Let them not suspect us; I am sure they know nothing about me."

Krishnan's confidence was unbelievable. He was as calm as a monk. So indifferent to the danger in front of us that it annoyed me. He was the real culprit, a wanted man. And I was an accomplice. What punishment would I get for this crime? What if I told them the truth?

The approaching Naval boat did nothing to attract our attention. It moved swiftly along without any change in speed or direction. The armed men waved to us as they passed us by. Krishnan acknowledged their enthusiasm with an equally eager wave of his hand. I too gave a limp wave.

It speeded past towards the northeast.

Sanjay Sonawani

Exhausted by the tension, I leaned on the warm rails.

Krishnan patted me on my shoulders. "You are looking pale, Venu. I'll fetch some water for you."

I said nothing as he went and brought water in a pail for me.

I drank from it as though thirsty for ages. I was still trembling with fear. I still thought it was a trap...*they will come back...they will shoot us...we will die...my trawler will be sunk.*

Krishnan embraced me tightly.

"Venu, I am sorry," he said. "I didn't know it would be you. Otherwise, I would never have accepted you as my sailor; they would have listened to me. They would have let you go. My poor Venu. Please, calm down."

The pent-up rage and frustration within me exploded. I hit him on his face. "You bastard, it is you who has brought this mess upon me."

Without a word Krishnan wiped blood from his split lips with the back of his hand.

"Hit me back if you want to, you son of a bitch. Look what you people have done to me. I hope you rot in the hell!" I sobbed in rage and self-pity.

I sat down on the deck. Gentle waves were rocking the boat. I had to steady myself by placing my hands on the planks. My throat was choked. I was furious and, at the same time, desperate to listen to Krishnan's soft consoling words. I wanted to cry. I looked up at him. His face was as beautiful as a child's.

"What you are afraid of, my friend?" He whispered. "I have gone through the same a thousand times. Life is not as pleasant as it seems to be. It plays cruel games with us. Please, calm down, Venu."

I tried to control my wrenching heart and clear the gathering mist of sorrows.

"Krishnan, all is over. My life is wasted. This is all cruel. Why me? After all, couldn't you people get your own men for this mission?" I sobbed.

"I am sorry, Venu. But how was I to know that it would be you? What can we do now? Curse me. Hit me, if you so desire. Do anything you want to me, my friend. Unfortunately, destiny has brought us together under such odd circumstances. I don't want to believe in this, but I know this is the truth.

"Venu, just leave me ashore and return. I will speak to the authorities and then no one will ever bother you again. I understand we now stand on different shores of a void. Neither you can understand me, nor I can understand you. You are a happy, middle-class man. You know very little about life. You do not even want to know why some people invite deadly dangers upon themselves when they too can live the contented life of ordinary people. What inspires them to become rebels you know not. You want to live in a dream world of ideals and so-called comforts. I too have ideals...though they have changed drastically with the passage of time. But wasn't it your own beloved society that forced me to take this bloody path? Did I ever want to become a militant?

"... Forget it, Venu. Don't bother to try and understand me. Be as you wish to be. Just think of this as a nightmare, which will soon be over and the life known to you will warmly embrace you once again. And, Venu, don't worry. No danger will befall you as long as I am by your side... I am Krishnan, your friend, not your enemy!"

The sincerity of his words filled my heart with compassion for this criminal friend of mine. I took his hands in mine and sat down with tears in my eyes amidst the turmoil of emotions that welled inside me.

"Do you remember Vani?" He asked. "How desperately you tried to get us together."

I said nothing.

"How pleasant were those days. An idyllic dream. I can't believe we ever lived them."

"True!" I muttered. "But you were a different man then, Krishnan."

"Yes, I was. I believed in humanity. I believed in all humans being equal. I believed in non-violence. I always praised Mahatma Gandhi. I had a secret dream; I wished to become a preacher of a sacred philosophy; I wanted to unite all the peoples of the world and mould them into one nation. No capitalists, no communists, no socialists, no fascists. Just one, single, united nation…the entire human race engaged in the upliftment of the society, with no armies left on the earth, no nuclear weapons, no missiles to destroy each other. I wanted to become the leader of this sacred philosophy.

"But my friend, I am ethnic now. I am fighting for the well being of the Tamils, forgetting all others who too have a heart and have the same blood flowing in their veins. Yes, I am a drastically changed person. And, yet, I exist….though, my dreams keep tormenting me as I sleep. I want to share my love with all living beings on this planet. I, a terrorist, believe in ethnicity.

Sanjay Sonawani

Do you know why? Because the existing social and political system has generated leaders who have wicked minds. Leaders who have nurtured hatred amongst the people for their own vested interests. They do not want peace on earth. Please, Venu, try to understand this. This is a world where individual ideologies are trampled upon by the masses. The masses have no head…it doesn't think. It just rumbles along. It thinks it is powerful because it is large in numbers. It does not respect an individual's freedom. And it's the representatives of this majority, who know nothing, that form governments. And what does the minority get? Just a few crumbs, for the sake of so-called democracy.

"I represent the minority," he said with deep conviction. "I have a head, which can think, which can act! I have feelings. The same feelings which, once upon a time, Valmiki would have had, the same feelings which Gautam Buddha would have had! I am not an alien but I am forced to be one. They have deliberately outcast a man who had pure intentions towards his society, similar to Buddha and Valmiki. So, my friend, do not blame me for I am not responsible for what I am today, I hope you understand what I am trying to tell you. I pity your condition. I blame those who forced you to participate in this course of life. Had I known, I would never have allowed it to happen."

As he spoke his soft voice gave away the torment that was eating his innards. But nothing could soothe me. I was only thinking of my own self. I was thinking of Janaki carrying my child. I was thinking of all the disasters that I had been forced upon me.

He tussled my hair.

I gripped his hand tightly - "I am scared, Krishnan."

Sanjay Sonawani

"Of what?"

"Of life."

He laughed gently.

"You silly fool. Stop thinking like some petty, middle-class man. Just make yourself powerful and there'll be nothing to fear on this bloody earth."

"But if everybody was to do the same, the whole planet would be bathed in blood."

"Then, so be it," he roared. "Those who deserve death, let them die. Those who cower before weapons, they must be kept frightened all the time. They deserve to be crushed under foot."

The trawler fell quiet on the dancing waves. I said nothing; there's no use debating fanatics.

♦   ♦   ♦

It was night. We were now much closer to our destination. The wind blew in gusts and our trawler was tossing about like a bucking mare, under the gaze of millions of stars gathered in the sky to witness some secret game.

Sitting beside a net, I rested my head against the brass rail and looked at the sky. I felt oddly relaxed from the strained emotions I had been experiencing since I had met Varadrajan. Softly, I began to hum...

"The dreams are spread
before me
let me collect them all,
my dear dreams
They belong to me

Sanjay Sonawani

let me gather them,
my dreams
weak and frightened they may be
but my dreams...my dreams."

I stopped abruptly. I realized Krishnan was watching me.

"Go on, Venu, sing loudly. Your passionate voice is a delight to hear."

But the urge to sing had suddenly abandoned me.

"You are angry with me. Aren't you?" He asked.

"No."

"Don't lie," he said softly, "You have every right to be angry with me."

I looked at him askance. Was he really the same Krishnan who used to be my friend once upon a time?

"Krishnan, tell me, why did you become like this? As for me, I was forced into it. But you?" I asked trying to fathom the depth of his heart and mind through his impassioned voice.

Krishnan, under the dim light of the billions of stars shining overhead, desperately tried to pour his heart out through words.

"You don't know anything, my dear friend, nothing at all. Do you really think I ever wanted to become like this? Didn't I want to be a preacher, as I told you earlier? Even today, somewhere in the depths of my heart, I am the same Krishnan you once knew. But what an injustice they committed on me, you know not, my friend. You simply know not. Do you think I wanted to do all this? Do you know what I used to think of the LTTE? India is my motherland! How could she be my enemy? After all, can a son ever become an alien to his own mother?

No, Venu, my friend. Everyone seeks life in the security and comfort of a warm blanket. Which fool would ever throw away that cozy blanket and rush blindly into the jungles of death? No, I never thought my life would become like this."

"Why, *Tambi?* Why then?" I wailed.

"My friend, secretly we have always desired that India assist us in our noble cause. But we failed in that. Instead, she sent a powerful army to destroy us."

"Why do you say 'us'?"

"Because I am one of them now, that's why. Though we are small in number, our unity is most powerful. But, mind you, not at all are we India's enemies, even though she sent an army to finish us instead of protecting our goals."

"All this what you say is confusing me, Krishnan. It is absurd. It is not becoming of you. Many join this stream per force; my father and myself are perfect examples. But we are all insignificant beings. You, however, are considered dangerous. Why?"

"Yes, I am dangerous," said Krishnan in a deep, soft voice. "I am a wanted man because I have masterminded horrible plans that have shaken the world. I implemented them meticulously. I am responsible for the assassination of two Sri Lankan ministers. I took active part in the rebellion against the IPKF, the peacekeeping force sent to Sri Lanka by India. I am the one who set up *Yesu-FTFSFGXY*, the high frequency wireless network in India - we are most powerful now in communications due to this system."

He looked elsewhere as he took a deep breath. Then, with a sigh, he whispered: "I know where Sivrasan is. I am the only man who knows where this man, who masterminded the assassination of Rajiv Gandhi, is hiding. I am the last and final link that will complete the story of Rajiv Gandhi's assassination."

"You!" I gasped in shock. Were all my nightmares coming true? "You know Sivrasan!"

Sivrasan, the most wanted man by the Indian government, who was being searched for everywhere by the Special Investigation Team and the entire police machinery. The man who could throw light on the conspiracy behind the assassination of the former prime minister of India. Newspapers were carrying his pictures almost everyday. There was a huge bounty on his head, the biggest reward ever declared by the Indian government. He was a monster, a cold-blooded murderer… And here was Krishnan telling me that he was involved in all this, that he knew Sivrasan. Who knows, he might have even trained that human bomb who took Rajiv Gandhi's life!

'My God, he is a dangerous man,' I thought.

Krishnan's voice was razor sharp and icy as he continued. "We could not succeed in our goal unless we took a drastic action that would sent shivers throughout the world…and we have taken it. This may lead hundreds of our comrades to their deaths. But unless we shed blood, we can never achieve victory. Rajiv Gandhi sent the IPKF against us. He wanted to portray himself as the messiah of the new era. He boasted of becoming a world leader. He had to be punished for his impudence."

I was benumbed by his words. My mind churned in a whirlpool of agonies. How cold-blooded could a man become? I thought. Krishnan, my friend, was the limit. What could I say to him? Nothing seemed to make sense to me anymore.

Sanjay Sonawani

"You people are cruel and stupid. You don't know how history shapes itself. The deeds of a bunch of evil-minded people like you are just scratches on the vast canvas of history. They cannot change its course. You fool, you people will soon be forgotten for you have no significance on this earth. No one is going to pen praises about you and your deeds, except, perhaps, your fanatic successors. You will be abused, cursed. The coming generations will spit on you."

He stepped forward, towering over me as I sat on the deck. "This is not true, Venu!" He shouted. "All this was inevitable. Injustice demands injustice. I agree that I am no saint, but I could never forgive what they had done to me. You asked me why I joined this path. Want to listen?"

His pursed his lips as if gathering his thoughts. I do not know what went on in his mind. I looked up at the sky, almost resigned to hearing some cock and bull story, for every sinner has an explanation for his misdeeds. The sky was in the silent embrace of countless stars. The vast ocean was vehemently moving up and down.

He began in the same, soft voice-

◆◆◆

Five

It was raining when the Air India flight landed at Heathrow airport. Krishnan was on his way to Cambridge for higher studies in social science. His heart was full of anxiety. First time ever in his life was he visiting a foreign country. That to England, the country which had ruled India for over two centuries. The huge airport impressed him. Its escalators, the massive passenger lounge lined with easy chairs, the rows of duty free shops and the beautiful girls fearlessly serving customers was a sight which he had seen only in the movies. It was incomparable to the shabby the Anna Durai airport, at Madras.

The formalities of immigration and customs were completed very smoothly and Krishnan took the tube from

Heathrow to London; Cambridge University was his destination. When he got down at King's Cross station, the cold breeze made him shiver, as did the excitement of having arrived in a new country. But soon, the charm of being in a foreign country left Krishnan. Many Indians were studying at Cambridge, but very few got well acquainted with Krishnan. He was not worried about it; after all, he had come there for studies. He realized that the Indians living there have some sort of an inferiority complex.

It was a bright sunny September morning when Murlimanoharan, a Tamil student, knocked at Krishnan's door. Krishnan had seen Murli, a senior student who wore thick glasses, many times around the campus. There were a few rumors floating around about him, but none that could be believed in. It was said that he was a strong supporter of the LTTE and that his main motive in attending Cambridge University was to garner support for the cause of the Tamil Tigers. It was also rumored that he was in some way connected with the Khalistani militants in Punjab. There was definitely an aura of mystery about this young man who had come to meet Krishnan.

Murli looked gay and flamboyant in his faded jeans, leather jacket and Nike sneakers. He spoke to Krishnan about his village near Coimbatore and his experiences at Cambridge as if they were long lost pals. Krishnan listened to his enthusiastic chatter with not much encouragement. Then, all of a sudden, Murli asked, "What do you think India will do about sending its peacekeeping force to Sri Lanka? It's all wrong what's going on out there, Krishnan. The Sinhalese oppression has to be denounced and condemned forcefully. It's an international issue now."

Sanjay Sonawani

The sudden change in topic startled Krishnan. He looked at Murli in disbelief and asked warily, "Do you support the LTTE?"

"Yes, I do. They are freedom fighters. The days of oppression are over, but the Lankan government does not think so. It thinks that with the help of the army it can suppress the voice of mutiny. But they are fools. It is the duty of every Tamil to raise his voice against this brutal injustice."

Krishnan wanted to laugh at this young activist but instead, he said, "I read all about it in the newspapers. This country has provided refuge to the enemies of India. They frequently broadcast interviews of the Khalistani leaders on the radio and on TV. They provide them with money, arms and other logistical support. They don't want to see peace established in the Indian subcontinent. I see an international conspiracy behind all this. And it is youth like you who fall prey to their vicious intentions."

Murli fell silent for a moment.

"Tell me, Krishnan, do you support Rajiv Gandhi's move to send the Indian Peace Keeping Force to Sri Lanka? Do you think India should intervene in the Tamils' battle for freedom by supporting their oppressors? Isn't it injustice? Our own army fights our own men. Is this logical, tell me?"

"Murli, all this is politics, and I am the least bit interested in it. Let both the governments decide between themselves what they should do. Let us not forget that we are here to study. So let's concentrate on that."

But Murlimanoharan was no easy customer to convince. He went on vehemently with his sermon about the crisis taking place in Sri Lanka and about the human rights violations there.

Sanjay Sonawani

Finally, Krishnan, tired of all this, refused to hear any more of Murli's pleas and showed him the way out.

The arguments with Murlimanoharan that day disturbed Krishnan but he wiped clean all unpleasant thoughts from his mind and tried to concentrate on his studies.

A few days after Murli's visit, Krishnan received a package by post, containing several booklets and a hand-printed bulletin that highlighted the heroic deeds of the LTTE leader Prabhakaran and spoke of the 'true' conditions in the jungles of Jaffna. Murli also started calling on Krishnan often and would request him in all earnest to join one of their secret meetings that were held in one of London's suburbs. The self-declared general of the LTTE, Naikan, who was stationed at London, would often address these meetings. He would also deliver public statements through the BBC. To Krishnan, all this was disgusting. What was the Indian secret service doing, he wondered? How could they let these people spoil India's image? But these thoughts were temporary. After all, he was just a student and was looking forward to a bright future.

A year had passed since Krishnan arrived at Cambridge, one of the most reputed universities in the world. He was most happy when writing. He found the pen to be the best outlet to express one's thoughts and to develop vision. During the vacations with little else to do, he started contributing articles to a local daily, the first being 'Social Impurities in Indian Social System' followed by another on the 'Impact of South Indian Culture over Indian Social System'. His writings were well received by the readers. And in this way, he started earning a little extra money and the reputation of being a fierce writer.

One evening, Murli, accompanied by another young man, visited Krishnan at his room. Murli introduced his colleague, a frail, dark complexioned young man with sparkling white teeth and big eyes, as Shankar.

"Your this article... it is a fantastic piece of writing, Krishnan. Shankar liked it so much that he wanted to meet the brilliant and ingenuous author right away. I told him, we are pals." He smiled warmly. "Aren't we?"

Shankar shook hands with Krishnan.

"Your article said that South Indian culture developed separately and independently, and denies the influence of Aryan culture. How true! I personally subscribe to this theory and believe that the Aryans were invaders. They were nothing but marauders. They destroyed the original social fabric that India had put together so painstakingly over the centuries. They wanted to destroy the Dravidians too, but our forefathers stood strong against their onslaught. And that's why the Dravidian is the only true ancient civilization still surviving on earth today. They successfully maintained their purity in which the Aryans failed. But now look at the present situation. These impure Aryans want to rule the sacred Dravid race. They never spare a chance to humiliate us. There is not much scope left for our leaders since the new system of democracy has been introduced. Our leaders have to bow before the north to have our genuine demands sanctioned. We have to depend on their mercy to survive.

Sanjay Sonawani

"And look how scheming they are. That Hindi, a most hybrid language, is being forced upon us against our own rich, ancient language! They...."

"Stop it." Krishnan shouted. He was trembling with anger. Both the visitors looked at him dumbstruck.

"Why are you trying to misinterpret my writing? You bloody fuckers are fanatics. You are speaking the same language Hitler spoke decades ago. You are drawing wrong meaning from the pages of history. You say Aryans are ruling over Dravids. How stupid of you people! Have you ever studied anthropology? Many tribal people in north India also belong to the Dravid race. What answer do you have for that? From where they came? Did they migrate to the north from the south? No. You talk about the Aryan race. But did that race really ever exist? Or was it a separate culture? You say Aryans oppress the Dravid race. You are fools. Actually, you people want to separate from India. You want to establish your power centre. You want to destroy the harmony that exists today. You want to plant seeds of hatred in the hearts of the people. The struggle in Sri Lanka is a test of your power. Do not ever again try to mix the issues and get some benefit out of it. I am not that big a fool as not to understand all this. Now look, it's enough. You both get lost from here and never try to meet me again."

Krishnan's direct attack startled both of them. They looked at each other in confusion.

"You are strange," muttered Murli and rose from his seat. "Good-bye. But one thing, Krishnan, before we leave, let me tell you one thing. People like you are rotting in a world of illusions. And the day will come when you will realize..."

"Get out –"

Krishnan was trembling with anger even hours after both had left.

Krishnan's days at Cambridge were soon over. He was now a changed man, with many dreams in his heart. Confident. Ready to accept life's challenges that lay ahead of him as he bade good-bye to his campus life at Cambridge with an Air India flight back to Anna Durai airport.

Krishnan stood near the conveyor belt waiting for his luggage. The journey had been uneventful. Though tired due to jetlag, he looked forward to meeting his parents and friends, for whom he had brought many presents, he knew they would be waiting outside to receive him.

Suddenly, a hand tapped Krishnan's shoulder.

He looked back.

An officer in white uniform stood looking at him gravely.

"Mr. Krishnan?"

"Yes?"

"Your passport, please."

Krishnan was startled. He uneasily handed over his passport to the officer.

"Please follow me, Sir."

"What's wrong?" Krishnan was baffled.

"Just a formality." The officer muttered curtly.

Krishnan could not understand this undue formality. But as he had nothing to hide, he followed the man to a cabin where a bulky officer was seated behind a table.

Krishnan was irritated.

"Why have you brought me here?" He asked.

The man sitting behind the table glanced at him in a most unfriendly manner.

"Sit down. The authorities want you, young man," he said.

Krishnan was unable to understand all this. "But will you tell me what..."

At that moment a high-ranking police officer entered the room. He exchanged greetings with the two airport officials and then turned to look at Krishnan.

"So you are Krishnan. Do you deny this?"

"Why should I? I am Krishnan."

"Good!" He nodded pleasantly.

"Young man, we have to detain you until further instructions," said the police officer. Krishnan's heart gave a leap. He did not know what was going on.

"You mean to say that you are arresting me? On what charge? I have nothing to declare...."

"You have nothing to declare, that we know," he said in a soft voice. "You are involved in a crime much more serious than that. I am sorry for you, young man. You shouldn't have done such a foolish thing."

Krishnan was furious. He could not spell out his anger.

"You were involved in anti-national activities. You were in close contact with the LTTE militant Naikan, the so-called General Naikan. His right hand, Shankar, frequented your residence in London often. You people conspired against the Government of India."

"But... I never did anything! I knew Shankar. But...but, I hated him. I never knew him..."

"Sorry, young man, but you are under arrest. We have enough evidence to prove your active involvement in anti-national activities." He signalled to his subordinates and in a moment Krishnan was handcuffed. He protested, resisted, argued, to no avail. His luggage was seized. He was forced into a van and moved to a jail where he was locked up in a separate cell with swarms of mosquitoes for company. The dimly lit cell was intimidating. His repeated requests to let him make at least one phone call to his parents were ignored. Everyday people from various government departments would visit him and question him endlessly about his activities during his stay in London. He was tired of giving them the same answers over and over again. They did not believe him. They tortured him physically and mentally. His was insulted, his ego trampled upon, in an effort to break him. He was tired, weak and battered. His protests were ignored. He was now a pitiable criminal, suffering injustice at the hands of the very people he once respected.

"Why don't you people produce me before the court?" Krishnan pleaded with the jail superintendent in defeat.

"Unless you tell them the truth, they will not produce you before the court," the jail superintendent advised Krishnan.

"But this is violation of law. I have the privilege to speak to my lawyer. There is also the law that I am produced before court within 24 hours of my arrest. It is also my privilege to make one phone call to my family. I am willing to face trial and prove that I am innocent."

"Forget it. We know when to bend the rules. Unless we do so, people like you become a pain in our arse. Tell them the truth and you'll be set free."

Sanjay Sonawani

Weeks dragged by without a ray of hope in sight. Krishnan's life had turned into a living nightmare. For the first time in his life, he began to despair. He started to hate the system. It was treacherous - It wanted a scapegoat, not the truth. Here was a young man who nourished dreams of serving society and look what he was being served in return.

Krishnan was getting desperate. He would weep, but no tears would flow from his eyes. Gradually, the visits from the authorities began to lessen. Finally, they stopped altogether, as though they had forgotten that there was a man named Krishnan in their custody. But his luck did not change. His unlawful imprisonment continued. Velakkam jail housed thousands of inmates. Who was there to bother about one R.S. Krishnan?

Months passed by. Krishnan lost all hope. He got used to the horrible food served to him and all the pains that could have killed any other weak-willed person. His cell became his haven and the mosquitoes didn't seem to trouble him any longer. He began to forget that he was a well-educated man; the days at Cambridge seemed but a dream.

Then, one rainy night, a member of the Tamil Nadu assembly, Mr. R. Venkateshwaran, was kidnapped from his residence. The news shocked the state government. Newspapers printed the news in bold headlines. The kidnapping of the MLA was not taken lightly by the authorities. A massive manhunt was set in place. After a few days, the kidnappers established contact with the authorities and set forth their demands. One of which was the release of six of their fellow militants, among whom was one R.S. Krishnan.

The State government discussed the issue with the Central government for a few days and at last accepted the kidnapper's demand to release the six militants.

It was the night of August 18, 1988. Krishnan was in deep sleep, dreaming about a reunion with his old life, when the screeching noise of the cell door awoke him. The jail superintendent was standing before him.

"Get up. You are to be released."

"W.... What?" Krishnan exclaimed in disbelief.

"Yes. You are free now. A van will take you out of Coimbatore. You are to be dropped off on the Coimbatore-Bangalore highway."

"But.... Why? Have they finally found that I am innocent?"

"Your friends have made this arrangement," said the jailer bitterly.

"But I don't have any friends," Krishnan said in disbelief.

But then, those who had secured his release from this humiliation must certainly be friends. Those, he once respected had declared him traitor. What feelings, except hatred, could he have for them?

He did not know what this release meant - whether he could return home unobstructed or not. Neither did he express any curiosity to know either - 'Let me suffer whatever is awaiting me.'

Krishnan was dropped off on the Coimbatore-Bangalore highway. The Nilgiri mountains could be seen in the flashes of lightning that light up the dark rainy night. The van, which had transported him here, sped away quickly into the darkness, leaving him standing there in disbelief.

He stood soaking in the pouring rain for a long time, undecided on what to do next. He did not know who had rescued him or what was expected of him. He started walking along the highway.

"Stop!" A voice suddenly called out in the darkness.

Krishnan froze mid-step on the tar road, frightened and uncertain. He then heard the sound of feet splashing through water over the sound of the rain.

"Just walk along with us," someone said.

He tried to look at them. But in the dark and rain, he could only make out two figures. He did not know who they were but reposed his trust in them. They were, after all, his rescuers, his saviors. He hurried along with them through a muddy pathway, under dripping branches, through the woods towards an unknown destination.

After some time, they crossed over to a secluded farmhouse. They knocked at the door. It was opened instantly. In the warm interior of the house, a young man sat carelessly on a sack of food grains. The duo that had brought him to this house were young and ruthless in appearance.

The young man sitting on the sack stood up with a broad smile.

"*Tambi*, how much you have suffered," he said deeply concerned.

Krishnan was overwhelmed by his emotions. He embraced the man.

"We normally restrict ourselves from such forced releases. It gives us bad publicity. But when a comrade is in danger, we neglect the outcome."

"Thanks," muttered Krishnan in gratitude.

He would soon rise to become a pillar of support for the LTTE.

◆◆◆

Sanjay Sonawani

Six

It was long gone into the night by the time Krishnan finished the amazing story of his painful transition from an ordinary, law-abiding citizen to a militant. After a period of tormenting silence, he said -

"Tell me, Venu, if every Tamil is being suspected and treated like this, then what should we do? We shall hate that government. We shall make every effort to undermine their foundations. I never committed any crime in my life before this happened to me. You see what they did to me!"

His voice was now calm, without the slightest reflection of the pain he had undergone. It was just a flat, matter-of-fact statement.

"There must be some mistake... Something must have gone wrong...the government must have been misinformed, misled," I tried to reason out.

"Yes. There was a mistake. But why on earth did they deny me a fair trial? Why did they not produce me before an appropriate court of law? Have you any answer?"

I kept quiet. His argument was irrefutable. I could not rationalize the incidents that took place in his life. There certainly had been a big mistake. I had grown up in Tamil Nadu. My father, too, had been a militant and had been killed by the Coast Guards in an encounter, but I had never felt any discrimination amongst us. I didn't become an avenging terrorist, unlike Krishnan. Tamils decorate a large number of important posts in the Central government, don't you know? The President of India, too, was a Tamil. We had no right to say that the Government was treating us with hostility. But this embittered soul of Krishnan had undergone torture and injustice. It was only fair for him to consider the whole system his enemy.

"Now I am living a contended life. The path I have chosen, I am carefully and faithfully treading it," he said after a long pause, without the slightest tremor in his voice.

"Aren't you afraid of being caught? Or being shot dead?" I asked.

"There is a chance, of course, but I am not worried. I will face that too when it comes."

"What you are going to do when you reach your destination?"

"I don't know," he said honestly. "They have got me out of India. I will go and report to my superiors. Then... Okay, why should I be telling you all this? You too are in danger. Your prolonged absence may stir up suspicion among your neighbors. About the police, I don't know for sure, but you are in danger. I have not liked the way our men have forced you into accepting this assignment. I will talk to my bosses about it."

He had pointed out at the dangers I was likely to face. It troubled me. I remembered Janaki.

"I don't know whether I can reach back or not," I said gloomily. "I will be all alone, and luck may not favor me."

Krishnan held my hand tightly and said apologetically - "I am responsible for this. Due to me…"

"You need not be sorry for this," I said in all earnestness. "It is just my bad luck, that's all. But what I cannot understand is that when you people have such a vast network of your own, why use me?"

He released my hand and looked out at the dancing waves.

"SIT has been keeping a strong vigil on all possible suspects. My life could not be risked in their hands."

"Are you so important to the organization?" I asked.

He stood lost in his own thoughts for a while.

"This is my promise…when you return home, I will see to it that no one ever bothers you again."

Krishnan's statement did not stir any hope in me. I simply nodded, acknowledging his concern.

"No soldier can bring victory if he is forced to fight without motivation. You are not motivated. You are aloof from all this and will be kept so in the future too."

"You will lose your battle," I said. "You can never win. Your ways are treacherous. You are a band of vicious murderers.

You did not kill a man, but the future of this country, Krishnan."

He gave a scornful laugh. "Those who betray us have to be punished. And we have punished him."

His cool, matter-of-fact voice sent a shiver down my spine. I could not stand by his side. He was ruthless. Uneasily, I returned to the control room and checked our direction. The fuel tank needed refilling. But it could wait until morning. I sat down on the chair, lost in thought.

***

"There is a storm approaching," I called out to Krishnan. It was afternoon but the sun was hidden behind huge patches of dark clouds. The horizon was getting darker. The wind was rising. High waves were jolting the trawler. I tried hard to control its balance and direction. Krishnan joined in to give me a hand. Against all our efforts, the raging wind was gaining control over the trawler. Huge waves were crashing onto the deck. My trawler and I had weathered many storms in the past but today, the ageing trawler hardly seemed able to sustain the heavy blows of the waves.

Krishnan's face darkened. This part of the strait was dangerous. We were near the Lankan coast and the storm had created a hurdle in our path. Clutching the rails we tried hard to maintain our balance as the trawler was tossed up and down with tremendous force. The darkness, the howling wind, and the crashing waves were terrifying. All I could do was say my prayers, like all sailors do when caught in a storm.

Hours later, the wind changed direction. "It should recede soon," I shouted out over the sound of the lashing wind to Krishnan standing by the door of the cabin, wet and tired. He gave a weak smile of reassurance.

"We can just pray and wait. We are so helpless before the might of nature," I said.

"Shall I tell you the truth?"

"What?"

"I have no faith in God," he said in a sad voice. "My life's been ruined. I was deprived of my family. I wanted to live the life of gentry. But look at me, Venu, see what they have done to my life."

Never before had I seen him so depressed. I rose from the chair and, carefully balancing myself on the tossing deck, walked across to him.

"You're not happy working with the militants, are you, Krishnan?" I asked hopefully.

His eyes flashed for a moment, then became flat as before.

"Mind the wheel, we are moving towards the shores."

I turned back. The sky thundered and the wind howled, as if outraged. I held the wheel firm in my damp hands and began to say my prayers once again.

The storm receded after a while. The dark clouds sped away on northeasterly winds and the appearance of a weak evening glow of the setting sun in the western horizon brought a sense of relief to us. I pumped out the water the trawler had taken in and corrected our direction after examining the map and the compass. We were nearing the Sri Lanka coastline.

"We will set for coast in the night," suggested Krishnan, his face reflecting an unknown turbulence within him.

I nodded in agreement. Our brief reunion was about to be over in a few hours.

Sanjay Sonawani

"Just few more hours now, and we shall see each other off," muttered Krishnan.

I looked at him sharply.

"It would have been better if we had met under different circumstances. But destiny has it this way. It defeats our dreams and desires," I said morosely.

"I am hungry," he said. "We haven't eaten anything since morning." It reminded me of my own hunger. We went down to the hold where I had stocked eatables and arranged bread and dry fish for both of us. We ate quietly avoiding each other's gaze. The journey had exhausted us.

"Krishnan," I said, when I had finished eating, "You need a lot of rest. You are not cut out for such hard work. Yet, you chose the life of a militant. Think about it, and one day, try to leave the present life... Will you?"

Krishnan looked at me pitifully.

"Venu, I chose this path not by my own wish. They threw me out of the society like an unwanted creature. The same society, to which I had wanted to render my services," he said and added vehemently, "I am an unlucky man, right? But I have not chosen this life by my own wish. I do not wish to waste my life like dead fish. I am a man and I behaved like a man. Trust me, I could not let them devour my soul."

There was not a slightest tinge of remorse in his voice.

"But you cannot accept the present life as it is... You should not!"

"True, Venu. But what choice do I have? I console myself with the thought that maybe God needs me to do the things I am doing. I am not a fatalist, but the more you think, the more you

Sanjay Sonawani

get entangled in the web of life's futile tragedy. I have experienced it many a time since I have become, what you call, an outlaw."

"Krishnan, are you hiding something from me? Why, when you know we will never meet again in future?" I asked in a pained voice.

"What else I can do, Venu?" He asked in a sudden outburst. "I was never a fatalist. I never believed in destiny and its unalterable course. I know that there must have been a fatal mistake committed by those bastards. I am not that big a fool not to understand it - not that I do not occasionally accept things as they appear to be. No, I am not a fool. But even knowing that there must have been some mistake, what else could I do? You cannot challenge all that which tries to obstruct your path all the time. Life is too short for it, Venu. Do you think I really love bloodshed? No, I abhor it. But I have been made a scapegoat. I do not have any personal ambition left to live for. Here or there, what sort of life I have got now? I wish I could kill those bastards who believed in the story that I was mixed up with the LTTE. I wish I could clear that story of my mysterious release. They released me from one hell and put me in another, but where I feel I have more freedom than the previous jail! That's it, my friend, the true, sad story of my life. What can a man do under the circumstances? You have to bend, just the way you too, like many others, have bowed before the circumstances. You fear death, Venu. But death, believe me, is the greatest trade on this planet.

"I too loved my country, as everybody ought to. I too had aspirations of becoming someone special in society. But again, forgive me for being a pessimist, it's destiny after all. Whether you believe in it or not, it rules your soul."

He paused for a while, contemplating the skeletal remains of the fish in his hands and then continued. "I am taught to be secretive. But my life has become the strangest secret of all. I am living a dual life. Someone in my mind and someone else in my heart. Such is the cursed life that I lead. So much for God and his bloody world we are living in! If you want to live, you have to either choose the life of a humble suffering man or you take the side of the people who wield power. You have to adopt some philosophy or the other, without it you cannot live. Moreover, even if you think in depth and try to push forward your own thoughts, you are thrown out of the community. And one cannot break ties with the society he is living in. Today, I am part of a different society and I have accepted its ideology. Yet, being part of this society bothers me a lot, but I too cannot break the laws of the society I have chosen to live in."

Krishnan looked agitated. He was trying not to raise his voice, but failed. His agony was wrapped up in the words he spoke. I pitied him. He was spewing forth the years of hatred and cruelty he had been fed on as he bared his soul to me. In this honest outburst was the true Krishnan I had known earlier.

I wanted to say something but I felt I was standing on a faraway shore from him. His deep agonies and his confusion made me shiver. His outburst was futile, I knew. He had to live in the society he had been forced to choose. He had to scheme and plan brutal executions. Towards what end anyway, I wondered. The rising fog around us seemed to say that one day he too would have to swallow cyanide pills or stop bullets in his heart. I wanted to cry for him. I wanted to stop him. But I knew it was useless. Retreat was not possible now.

I stood up and hugged him closely.

Insane Krishnan...

And who was I? A fool!

***

We sailed towards the East. The coast was covered with coconut plantations and thick woods that looked ominous in the dark, misty night. I had put the lights off, as I did not want to attract the attention of any passing boat. Krishnan had turned the radio on in time for the evening news bulletin. Krishnan liked to listen to the news - according to him, information was power and being well informed was being powerful. The opening lines of the news bulletin were being read at a steady pace.

"The most wanted man accused in the assassination of late Mr. Rajiv Gandhi, the one-eyed man identified as Sivrasan and his female accomplice, Shuba, have been exposed by the Special Investigation Team at Bangalore. Armed police have surrounded their place of hiding and it is expected that at any moment now the police will enter the premises..."

Krishnan recoiled with a gasp. His face distorted strangely.

"What happened, Krishnan?" I asked, deeply concerned.

"This is preposterous, utterly impossible..."

"What? What is impossible...?"

"How could this happen? It was a top secret. No, something is wrong, Venu, terribly wrong." Krishnan was shaking furiously, his face ashen as the newsreader continued with the latest news development in the Rajiv Gandhi assassination case.

I too was curious to know how SIT had exposed Sivrasan.

Krishnan sat down and put his head on his knees.

Why he was so shocked? I wondered. SIT had been trying to hunt down the culprits using all its might. Their arrests were inevitable. Then why had the news of their being uncovered flustered Krishnan so much? Was there any other reason to it? I was sure Krishnan was lying to me. He was hiding something from me. There was something odd about his behavior.

I looked expectantly at him.

"Why are you shocked, Krishnan? This bastard deserved to be caught. He's insane. He killed a man of vision. Good that he has been located and soon will be arrested."

Krishnan lifted his head and looked at me with pity. He tried to say something, which was beyond my comprehension. I kept on watching him in astonishment. Why was he so shocked? Just because his fellow militant was going to be arrested? Had he not himself acknowledged all the time that arrests and death meant nothing to him? Then why did he look so depressed?

"Why are you so shaken?" I asked again. "Krishnan, the traitors must pay their debts. He was bound to be caught one day. It's good for everyone. It will expose all those who were actually behind the killing. At least the people will now come to know the true story."

"Only I knew where Sivrasan was hiding. I had made these arrangements with no help from anyone. No one could possibly know that Sivrasan was hiding at Bangalore I personally took all the necessary precautions. I made sure no one, not a single person, not even in our ranks, knew where he was hiding. It's impossible that SIT could have uncovered them. Impossible."

I was shocked. The truth then dawned upon me and I realized what could have happened. I shivered in fear and the whole universe trembled within me. A cloud of danger had cast its shadow over the trawler. Krishnan was in terrible danger. And so was I. At that instant, I knew what was about to befall us.

The hum of the engine and the rippling sound of waves sounded ominous. I was terribly worried about our safety. "Do you think they will suspect you for this leak? I think many times neighbors get suspicious. They are always watching strangers living around them curiously. Someone might have noticed something suspicious. They might have reported them to the police and by this unexpected piece of luck the police could lay their hands on them. Or, it may be that some one from your own organization leaked the information to SIT?"

"No," he said firmly, "That's not possible."

He rumbled on, "I am in grave danger, Venu."

"But why?"

"You won't understand."

"I must know," I pressed.

"I was looking after communications in this whole sordid business. I transported Sivrasan and Shuba from Tamil Nadu to Karnataka. I selected the refuge for them. I was to take care of their safety till they were ready to be shipped to some foreign country. I was directly reporting to Prabhakaran, no one else. Then tell me, how could SIT possibly have got wind of them? Prabhakaran himself cannot have leaked the news. Neither did I. Then who did? Venu, they will suspect me. They will... they will doubt me and will pronounce my death sentence, they are very strict."

"Stop it, Krishnan. You are frightening me."

We were near the coast, ready to cast anchor any moment now. I was worried for Krishnan.

The newsreader's voice had become inaudible. I was bitter and impatient about the queer happenings in my life. At any moment, Sivrasan and Shuba would be in the hands of the police and their arrest would have horrible repercussions in Krishnan's life.

How did it happen? Who could have leaked this secret information?

All of a sudden, Krishnan sprang to his feet -

"Turn back the trawler. I cannot go there now. They will torture me. I have seen many suffer horribly when suspected of treachery. Someone has defected...who, that I don't know, but, in this case, I will be the prime suspect. I cannot suffer any more."

I stood up.

"Think, Krishnan, think," I shouted, "I cannot turn the trawler back. I have a family. They will destroy me if I don't deport you," I screamed at him in fear.

Krishnan stood still for a few moment staring at me, as if he did not trust his ears with what I had just said. Slowly, he realized what I meant. He nodded sadly.

"Yes... you have a family. Why should I ask you to endanger your life? I am sorry for being selfish. You deport me. Who knows, they may not even suspect me!"

There was no hope in his troubled, guilt-laden voice. I too understood that he had walked into a carefully laid trap.

Sanjay Sonawani

He was my friend, the only friend whom I loved and trusted. The end of our reunion was not happening the way I had anticipated. But I had a wife...she was pregnant and she needed me most. I could not even think of Janaki living alone. I already had been stupid enough to accept this assignment. Whatever would happen to Krishnan, it was his destiny. He had asked for it; I was not in any way responsible. He was unlucky. Fate had played a cruel game with him, what could I do for him?

I knew compassion would not change anything. I was an ordinary man. And the intensity of my feelings was limited to the boundaries laid down by my commonness. I felt ashamed of my selfishness. But there was nothing I could do about it.

"I will deport you, Krishnan," I said in a low, inaudible voice to myself.

Krishnan went to the deck and watched the clear sky dimly lit by the Gods in heaven, while I sat motionless and drowned myself in a filthy viscid sea of unexplainable emotions that surged within me. It was only the hum of the trawler reminded me that I belonged to the world of the living.

I gloomily checked the map. We were somewhere near e spot where I was told to deport Krishnan.

Krishnan silently collected his belongings. He took out a light machine gun from his bag, as if readying himself for battle. He then turned to me, his face pale, and embraced me mutely. A flood of emotions choked me and a strong urge to turn the trawler around hammered on the ramparts of my senses.

"How strange is life, isn't it, Venu?" He muttered. His grip tightened. Tears welled up in my eyes.

"My friend, I never lived a good life, you know. Everything

went wrong for me. If there is such a thing as rebirth, I will ask the Almighty not to make me another human being. You won't forget me, Venu, will you? He asked, almost on the verge of tears.

"No. Never. I will not..."

"Don't cry, Venu. Not for this stupid creature. It was all inevitable. There is a limit to how much one can sacrifice, even for a friend. I do not blame you, nor do you blame yourself. The path I chose had to have a sad end. It was inevitable."

I knew I was pushing my friend into the arms of death by deporting him. I knew something was terribly wrong as I carefully steered the trawler through shallow, calm waters to the landing point. I turned on the headlights and could now make out a few dark images silhouetted by flashing torches beneath a steep rock. I slowed the trawler to a halt and attached a rope ladder for Krishnan to use.

"The water is shallow here. You can wade through. You get down first. Then I will hand over your baggage."

He nodded.

"Good-bye, my friend."

"Good-bye, Krishnan." I responded, choked with emotions, as Krishnan caught hold of the rope ladder and started getting down.

Through the corner of my eyes, I could see the hosts who had come to receive the 'package'. They wore military outfits and all of them carried guns in their hands. Coconut plantations and other vegetation surrounded the area and the only sound to be heard was that of the rushing waves, the rustling of coconut fronds and the occasional chirp of some birds and the hooting of owls. The sky above sparkled with billions of stars.

I was holding his luggage in one hand, the gun in the other, as I watched him descend into the water.

"Get me my luggage," Krishnan yelled. He was standing in chest-deep water.

"Yes, Krishnan," I muttered. He could not hear my feeble voice over the sound of the waves.

"Venu?" He yelled, again.

A sudden movement on the beach startled me.

Suddenly, I was alive.

"Krishnan, get down," I yelled and threw my body down on the deck as a spray of bullets hit the side of the trawler shattering the silence of the night, its thunder echoing into the woods.

Krishnan's gun was still in my hand. I had no choice, but to fight back. I had never learnt how to fire a gun but had watched many movies. I took unsteady aim and pressed the trigger. The bullets sprayed in an uncertain direction. But the effect was soothing. They ran for shelter and continued firing from there.

"Quick, Venu, start the engine. I have caught the rope...turn the boat...speed up." Krishnan yelled.

As I ran to start the engine, my leg got entangled in a coil of rope and I fell down. Somehow I managed to extricate myself and darted into the dark cabin. I fumbled with the control panel and pressed the buttons hard. The engine roared to life. I accelerated the boat towards the sea and setting the rudder in the northern direction ran back to the deck.

Sanjay Sonawani

The firing had not stopped. I could hear the chattering of the guns and the crashing of bullets as they hit wood and metal.

"Krishnan," I yelled.

There was no response.

"Krishnan," I shouted again as I bent over the railing and tugged at the rope. Yes, he was there hanging on it.

"Pull me up, Venu," I heard him call out weakly.

I took a tight grip on the rope and with all my strength started to pull him up. The wet rope chaffed my skin. But my numb hands could feel no pain. Inch by inch, I pulled him up. It was pitch dark and I could not see anything, but I was sure that Krishnan was hurt.

"Are you hurt, Krishnan?"

He made a few feeble gestures, which made no sense to me. I pushed him into the lighted cabin. He was wet and bleeding profusely from his left shoulder.

I looked at the wound. It felt as if it was inflicted on my own body.

"Does it hurt?"

"Yes. It pains..." He mumbled and closed his eyes. His face was pale. I lay him down on the bed gently. It did hurt him and he moaned in pain.

I was confused. I didn't know how to stop the bleeding. Had the bullet hit any bone? Was it still lodged inside him? Or, had it passed through? For a few moments I stood as though in a trance. Nothing came to my senseless head. Then I bent down and tore off his wet shirt. The movement caused him to jerk wildly in pain.

Sanjay Sonawani

I made him sit up, taking every care that he should not fall. The back of his shoulder had a wound bigger than in the front; the bullet had passed through. I was relieved; I had no means to remove the bullet from his body. He was lucky that the bullet had not hit him in the chest.

Suddenly, I remembered the first aid box I had in the hold and the bottle of brandy that I used occasionally to ward off the cold during wet weather. I collected the stocks and hurried back to Krishnan. He was unconscious. The salt water must have tortured him. I gently washed the wounds with the antiseptic lotion and bandaged it across the shoulder. His heartbeat was slow and breathing shallow. I then removed the rest of his clothes and after wiping his body with a wet towel, covered him with a thick blanket.

The sound of the engine resonated in the background, which provided some comfort to me. I uncapped the bottle of brandy and opening his mouth with my hands poured a little of it in.

Krishnan coughed as the raw alcohol hit his throat. I stopped. I then took a swig from the bottle. It burned as it went down my throat and spread like a warm glow in my stomach. I shut my eyes trying to erase the dreadful moments I had just gone through.

How true was Krishnan's guess. What had happened in the outskirts of Bangalore had been learnt by the militants in Sri Lanka in such a short span of time. And they had deduced that Krishnan was the only man who could or must have leaked the information! The suspicion created such a storm within the militants' high command that they had immediately decided to kill Krishnan for his treachery. They had tried to get Krishnan on the beach but failed. Unexpectedly, I had somehow foiled their vicious intentions.

They would be infuriated - with Krishnan, with me, I thought. Was there any ray of hope that could lead me to safety? 'Only death can save you from the oncoming storm. All that will happen before your eyes which you will not dare to witness! They will not forgive you. They will not let you escape this time,' was all that came to my mind.

Fear made me curse my fate. I prayed to God, 'Pull me out of this dirty marsh of nightmares. Let me wake up in my bed at home to the pleasant caress of my dear Janaki. Or let me die...Oh God! Save me...save Janaki...save Krishnan...'

The trawler was moving at a steady pace. The crescent moon's soft light caressed the deck. The sea beyond seemed to sparkle like the eyes of my loving mother. The sky was bereft of clouds and the stars twinkled, as if unattached to worldly things; for billions of years they must have been witness to much more horrifying scenes than what had happened today, but have maintained their serenity, just like an ancient sage.

A vision of a sea of blood danced before my eyes. The LTTE had the most powerful communications system. They were equipped with the most modern armaments and navigation systems. They would not let us escape. The thought bothered me deeply.

I rose to my feet and taking the binoculars went to the deck. I searched in all the directions. The sea was relatively calm. The soft, silvery rays of the moon played on the rising waves. The scene at any other time could have brought out the poet in me, but at this moment, no poetry sprouted in my heart. There was no sign of any fishing boats or freighting activity. Satisfied, I turned back.

Krishnan lay in a corner, unconscious. I clutched the bottle of brandy tightly. It was the only medicine to sooth my troubled heart. I wanted to escape the fear that had gripped me. I wanted to embrace a deep sleep that would make me forget the dreadful events.

I shut my eyes. From all sides, a sticky shower of blood seemed to fall on me. Behind the curtain of blood, someone waited. Beside him stood my dear Janaki. She was bleeding! Someone had stabbed her. But there was a smile on her lips! I could not fathom it. I wanted to call out to her and tell her all that had happened to me, but no sound came from my lips. I wanted to cry but the tears would not come. The man standing beside her looked evil. Was it Sivrasan? Who was that bloody bastard? Was he the one who had stabbed my Janaki? I wanted to rush through the downpour of blood, hold her hand and run.

The night gradually bowed to the coming dawn. I sat, dazed and frightened. I blinked my eyes several times and looked at Krishnan. I got up and felt his forehead. He felt feverish but his breathing was deep and steady.

Thousands of new questions danced a vulgar dance in my head. I had to wade through them. The moment I had left the coast of India, I had surrendered myself in the hands of destiny. Now I had to face the unavoidable. I could not go back to Madras. By now Thyagarajan and Varadrajan would be aware of my deeds. They would kill me on the spot. And I had Krishnan with me, a so-called traitor to the LTTE cause. No. I could not sail to Madras. I had to try some other place. But which?

Another question bothered me even more. All my family members lived in Madras. They would be under close surveillance. How could I reach Janaki? And what about Krishnan? What was I to do with him? He was my friend and badly injured. How could I get him to a doctor who would help without asking too many questions or without reporting us to the police? When shall I bid him good-bye? After all, I could not hide him for the rest of his life. The militants would never stop hunting him down. Even for the time being, where could I take him? I had the money, lots of money, in fact. But could it save us from the disasters? The questions danced and mocked at me like vulgar whores do to a penniless customer.

Krishnan's groans snapped me back into the world of reality. I looked at him. His eyelids were twitching and lips quivering.

"Krishnan..." I called softly.

He opened his eyes. Clouds of unknown feelings swept over his pale face.

"I am alive?" He muttered feebly with a weak smile.

"How do you feel?" I asked.

"Lucky, I suppose," he said and closed his eyes again as a wave of pain swept through his body.

"Why did you save me, Venu?" He asked without opening his eyes.

I looked at him intensely as many unknown feelings welled

up in me. I held his hand tightly.

"You are my friend!" I said trying my best to sound casual, but my choked voice gave me away.

"You too look hurt. Are you okay?"

"No.... not really. I fell down, that's all. I am alright." I assured him.

Krishnan gave a faint smile.

"Life is so strange."

"Yes, it is."

I knew what he meant.

"Now you take rest. You need it."

The faint light of the approaching dawn made things visible in the vicinity. Krishnan was sleeping. I did not know what to do. My mind was perplexed from the sudden incidents that had taken place on the Lankan coast. The horrifying scene still swam in front of my eyes. It was by God's grace that we both had survived the ordeal.

Krishnan opened his eyes. They looked like lifeless ponds. Then as moments passed, a glitter of life came to them.

"Venu..."

"Yes, Krishnan."

"Are you alright?"

"Yes."

"Why did you save a wretched man like me? You shouldn't have done it. Death would have welcomed me; it is the ultimate escape, isn't it?"

"I am not cruel, Krishnan. Had I deserted you, I could never have forgiven myself."

Sanjay Sonawani

"Yes, I know. I have always known that," he said and tears started to stream down his cheeks.

"Do not speak, Krishnan. It will pain you."

"No, Venu, nothing pains me anymore. As I shut my eyes, a peaceful serenity embraces me and on opening them, a torturing present tears me apart. Am I in a dream, Venu?"

"No, Krishnan. Now take rest."

"Alas!" He murmured.

Seven

Gusts of wind slammed my body as I stood on the deck. The shimmering sea and the birds soaring high above us was no more fascinating me with their beauty. I was desperately looking everywhere for any sign of approaching danger.

I thought of the frightening future that lay ahead of me. I had two enemies now; the Government of India and , the LTTE, the most organized gang of mercenaries. At any moment the LTTE wolves could get us. We had defeated them in their ulterior motives on their home grounds. How could they ever let us go? I did not need to know their *modus operandi*, but was aware that a commoner like me could never fight these determined men armed with the most sophisticated weapons. Look how easily they had killed Rajiv Gandhi. These people were fanatics. Insane! They did not care a shit for human life. No values, no morals, only vicious motives resided in their hearts. I had heard many stories of the militants in my life. People whispered of their heinous acts and their commitment to their cause. A shiver ran through me as I thought of how they swallowed cyanide pills if they faced arrest - so committed they were to their cause. And now, I too was their enemy. I was the man who'd foiled their plan to execute a traitor, the man they believed had caused great harm to their impregnable system by leaking information about Sivrasan.

I was crippled by the heavy weight of the feelings that weighed down upon me. I desperately wanted to get out of this mess. But I did not know how. I didn't even know where to take my trawler. How to contact my dear Janaki and ask her to escape with me.

Through the binoculars I watched the fish leaping out of the water in a fine display of their skills. In the sunlight, they looked like silvery streaks trying to bewitch my agonized mind.

I heard a buzzing sound then, unlike any wasp or insect. I turned my gaze towards the sky. It was clear. Then, in the western horizon, I noticed a dark spot. I focused the binoculars on it and froze in shock. It was a helicopter! Who were they, LTTE or the Navy?

I rushed down to check on Krishnan. He was in deep sleep, a most useless creature in the present crisis. I thought of speeding up the trawler, and then realized the futility of such an act. My trawler could never surpass the speed of the helicopter.

I adjusted the glasses once again and watched closely. It had black and yellow strips painted on it.

No, it could not be the Navy.

Nor *LTTE!*

It was nearing us at great speed. My hands turned icy cold. 'Had we been spotted? They will bomb us, maybe even shoot missiles, who knows? They would sink us for sure.'

For a few moments I stood rooted to the deck like a wooden stump. But the instinct to survive was alive in me. I could not accept death so easily. But how could I save my life?

I ran my gaze across the boat. The LMG I had used last night lay in a corner. Crazed with the thought of impending death I grabbed it and ran towards the control cabin. I increased the speed and set the trawler moving in a zigzag manner like a mouse trying to escape a fearsome cat.

I peered at the helicopter from the door of the cabin. It was flying just a few metres above the sea and I could see a gun barrel protruding out of its window taking aim at the trawler. Then a thunderous burst of bullets slammed into the trawler as the chopper flew past us. It turned around for another attack.

I sprang to my feet and took position on the wooden deck. I tried to aim the gun as accurately as possible on the helicopter and pressed the trigger.

Not one bullet hit the target. Instead they were firing at us once again.

I dived back into the cabin. My heart was thumping and sweat was pouring from my body.

A few bullets hit the top of the cabin. Then I heard bombs explode in the water.

I rushed out again.

The trawler was moving left and right like an uncontrolled beast, just as I had set it to. The helicopter was hovering in the air just above me, its rotors making an awesome noise. I saw a man in it looking at me and taking aim. I dived across the deck, trying hard not to loose my grip on the LMG. Bullets struck the wooden deck, puncturing large holes into it where I had been just a moment before. I hurriedly pulled the trigger of my gun. A whipping sound pierced my ears as a burst of bullets from my gun rushed towards the huge metal beast.

> '*God...please help me.*'

I prayed in that brief moment.

The bullets hit the tail and rotor blades. It started to make a screeching noise like a wounded animal. They still tried to shoot me but since there was no coordination between their aim and my trawler's movement, most of the bullets were swallowed up by the ocean.

I took careful aim this time, more confident by my earlier attempt at shooting the chopper down, and fired.

The helicopter exploded in a ball of flames. I ran into the cabin, leaving the gun on the spot, covering my head with my hands. Blazing metal parts showered down from the sky like an inferno. Few burning parts also fell on the trawler. I was scared once again. It could set my trawler ablaze.

I ran and splashed buckets of water on the burning parts.

The fire was extinguished.

I could not believe myself. An inherent instinct to survive had driven me to perform this amazing feat.

But what if the explosion had been witnessed by someone? They might come to check it out. This was a major offence I had committed against the LTTE. I had written the prologue to my own death. I guess, not everyone is so lucky!

I tried to wipe out all thoughts from my mind and gathering my strength, got up and walked like a drunkard towards the cabin, my body drenched in sweat.

Krishnan was wide awake. His look betrayed a deep anxiety mixed with an odd curiosity.

"What happened, Venu?"

"Nothing." I uttered wearily.

"I heard firing then a big explosion?"

"You sleep. You need to rest," I replied.

He kept looking at me with an understanding gaze. There was a hint of gratefulness in it. Then he tried to shut his eyes and his face contorted in agony. He was suffering. He knew everything, but he was so helpless.

I sat on a chair and closed my eyes, my body drained of all strength. I badly needed sleep. A sleep of *Muchkunda* that would last for years.

Eight

The next day, I woke up to a fine morning. The previous night's sleep had eased me of my imaginary tensions to a large extent. I now had to hide this trawler somewhere and reach a safe region as soon as possible. I knew I could not consult with Krishnan. He was still asleep. He had eaten a little in the night. And even though he had been in acute pain, he was very much back to his usual self. I knew he felt guilty. But what was the use of it now? It was all over. We were in mortal danger. I did not broach this topic with him, as I could understand he was yet to recover from the mental shock.

Mahabalipuram is located near Madras. The coast around

it is dotted with sharp rocks and is largely uninhabitated. I knew how dangerous the area was. No one ever dared to sail or moor, even an ordinary dinghy, in these deadly waters. But I had been left with no choice. And so I decided to sail to this coast.

As we neared the coast, I slowed down our speed and looked at the map conforming to the area we were in. I then took control of the wheel and moved the trawler carefully through the treacherous waters.

Krishnan was awake and sitting on the floor.

"Where are we?"

"Close to the coast."

He seemed relieved to hear my reply.

The rocks, hidden in the waters, worried me the most. I did not want any catastrophe to befall us now. The tide was high and the trawler was heaving on the waves. I concentrated on the speed and mood of the waves. The rushing waves were crashing against the rocks making a deadly noise. The towering waves could send shivers in hearts of the bravest of men. My knowledge as a sailor was at test.

Krishnan, too now on his feet, was watching anxiously.

At our left, was a huge cliff. In front, a rampart of huge rocks. To our right, it seemed calm, but the rocks protruding through the rushing tidal water would not let us sail through.

"Where can we moor? Asked Krishnan in a worried voice. "This seems to be a dangerous area."

I did not answer. To reach the coast safely was the only concern on my mind. The crashing waves were menacing. I was tense. The trawler was bobbing up and down like a cork on the waves and every wave seemed an invitation to death. The row of huge rocks was just a few yards away from us.

I then sighted a narrow gully between two massive rocks. It was dangerous. But if I had to avoid the deadly rocks, I had to sail through it. I did not know what waited beyond, but I had little time to think and act. Consulting with the incoming waves and the distance and direction, I revived up the engine and turned the helm to plunge the trawler headlong into the narrow strait.

"Yes!" I shouted aloud.

Krishnan too joined me.

In front of us lay a vast body of tranquil water, which in no way resembled the outrage we had just left behind. Beyond the calm water lay a sandy beach, relieving our strained minds. The pleasant scene welcomed us with its serenity.

The bright rays of the sun touched the sandy bottom through the clear water where a shoal of fish glided gently. I moored the trawler on the beach.

Our journey through the treacherous waters to this spot was unbelievable.

I stood on the deck mesmerized, my mind completely blank.

Krishnan too was in the same state.

"Let's get down."

Krishnan snatched me back from my reverie.

He had started collecting his belongings, which lay scattered on the deck.

"Leave the trawler here itself. I do not think anyone visits this region."

I did not reply.

Krishnan's face was now showing signs of stress. He gave me a worried look. He wanted to speak but restrained himself.

We both were in a confused state of mind.

Soon we were to step on a land of uncertainty and unknown dangers, crowded by enemies.

How rightly Krishnan had said, "No rebirth in this human society..."

Early in life we are taught the profound importance of truth, justice and other virtues plus an unending list of moral values. And later, we go on discovering how futile were the lessons and faiths that were taught. Life is not full of virtues and truth. It is an illusion. And if at all no truth exists…why life?

I spit on it.

"Let's go, Venu," said Krishnan.

What was happening to me? Why was I getting drowned in the marsh of feelings? I cursed myself.

"Krishnan... I have a lot of money with me," I said hesitatingly.

"What do you mean you have a lot of money," Krishnan asked in a confused tone.

"I have almost twenty five lakhs of rupees with me."

"What!"

"Yes...the price for deporting you."

"Oh!" He sighed. "And you brought it with you...on this trawler?"

"Yes, I never wanted that money. I never believed I would come back. I would never let my wife use that bloodstained money, you know? Had we sunk, the money too would have rested at the bottom of the sea."

He gave an understanding smile.

"But we may need it now."

"We cannot carry all the money."

"Yes. Let us take only what we can carry and bury the rest somewhere on the shore."

"And guns?"

"No guns. It will do us no good. People will get suspicious. We want to go to a safe area not to jail. I have a revolver and that should suffice."

I started collecting the necessary articles-some food, clothes and the heavy bag, which contained the money, twenty-five lakhs of rupees.

"We may not be far away from some village, but let us avoid it for a while."

I nodded in agreement.

Krishnan had started thinking and that relieved me; I am a dumb man in such situations.

"Now we have money, guns. Indeed, a good start, except my wounded shoulder and an inexperienced colleague," he said in a jolly mood.

I too laughed.

"I downed that bloody helicopter, don't forget that."

"Oh! Yes, you are a brave heart!"

"By the way, Krishnan, I have another piece of news for you I heard on the radio last night while you slept."

.

"What? Are they caught?"

"No. There was some firing, but they swallowed cyanide pills. The authorities got only a heap of corpses."

"I knew that," he said, nonplussed. "That's the standard procedure we follow in such situations. I knew Sivrasan wouldn't surrender."

"But this does not alter the situation. They will be after us like a pack of wolves. So far we are secure, but how long can we run away from them? Tell me, how do you propose to check them?"

"I don't know. As of now, nothing is comeing to my mind," he said, honestly. "They believe no one. I was a hard core militant. I had planned to smuggle them out of the country. That's why I transported them to Bangalore. SIT on its own could never have found them. But why are they suspecting me? I haven't leaked the news. Something is amiss and I am curious to know what exactly went wrong."

"You didn't do it. Then who could it be?"

"I don't know. I am not as yet sure what is going on. Sivrasan was so important to us. He had successfully executed all the dangerous missions assigned to him. He was our most trusted and reliable man."

I kept quiet.

"Let us get down first. I need some time to think," said Krishnan.

I accepted his decision and got down into the shallow water.

Then slowly I helped him down; the bullet wound had numbed his left hand.

"You were amazing last night," he said, as we waded through the water. "You blasted their chopper to smithereens. That too with their own gun! They could never have imagined that such a thing would happen!"

"Often, even the biggest coward acts courageously in times of crisis. It is the animal instinct of survival that fuels the mind when faced with danger," I said with a straight face.

He laughed.

"Where to bury this bloody money?"

"Look there...the tree with the huge trunk, dig a hole beneath it and bury it there. No one is going to find it there."

I believed in his judgement.

The ground was sandy and easy to dig a hole in. I first removed some money from the suitcase, as much as I could fit in the haversack that held our clothes and food. I then shoved the suitcase in the ditch and filled the hole.

"By chance, if someone uncovers this place, he will be the luckiest bastard on this earth," said Krishnan with a sardonic laugh.

"Who knows! Money not necessarily brings happiness all the time!"

"True. But people struggle and crave for it all their life. How many of them know the futility of it? That's the reason our country, this land of an ancient civilization, of the most profound philosophy, has today turned so mean and treacherous!"

In disgust, I spat on the buried money and adjusted the haversack on my back and muttered-

"Let us move now."

Sanjay Sonawani

He shrugged and started walking towards the deep woods that lay ahead. I followed him.

"Tell me, Krishnan, how did you get entangled in all this. And, please, don't hide anything from me, I deserve that privilege now, I think."

We were walking silently through the dense woods and my sudden question caught Krishnan by surprise. He looked at me in bewilderment.

"You have witnessed how they welcomed us as soon as they got news of Sivrasan's exposure by SIT. I cannot believe that they decided to kill you the moment they heard the news. It is not an easy decision to kill one's most trusted man simply on some unfounded suspicion. And that too so fast. What is the real reason?"

He slowed his pace, as if to digest my statement.

"That's what worries me most," he said. "It's true that they couldn't act so fast. There are ranks and commands to pass on information and orders. As it is, I was walking into their camp unsuspecting. They could have questioned me and even punished me later if they didn't believe in me. No, this has not gone the way they would like things to happen. Something has definitely gone terribly wrong. What must be that, I don't know."

"Is there any other reason, Krishnan?"

"I do not think so.... One moment, Venu, are you by any chance suspecting me?"

"I am not. The chain of incidents is not at all logical. We heard the news at seven in the evening. And at eleven thirty, you were welcomed with a spray of bullets. Why?"

"I don't know."

"Tell me the truth, Krishnan, at least you owe me that."

"I owe my life to you, Venu. How can I tell you how grateful I am to you? Sivrasan was a very important man. Like me, he too was a trusted lieutenant. Only Prabhakaran, Sivrasan and I knew the real things about this whole operation. I personally handled the assignment to ship him to safety immediately after the assassination. I was extremely discreet and met no one, not even from my section. I was totally on my own. I did not report to anybody my actions in this connection. So there is no chance of the interception of transmissions. Sivrasan too was incommunicado soon after he was deported to India. Only I was in touch with him since then. The truth is that there has been some grave mistake. Sivrasan could never be traced unless Prabhakaran, I, or Sivrasan himself tipped off the police. Prabhakaran wouldn't do that, nor did Sivrasan, and why would I invite my own death. Then who is the traitor? And why these fools don't understand that if I were the culprit, I wouldn't have walked back into the lion's den.

"And another point, Venu, I too know that it is impossible to take the decision to kill me in such a hurry. I know the system. Hell! There's too much confusion. Since the day I joined the LTTE, I have been honest to their cause. I hated India. Its so-called stance of being neutral. Its peace loving policy, its secularism and its dirty politicians that has turned a country in to a bastard's paradise. I had devoted myself to the cause of the Tamils. I believed it to be the only ancient, pure and sacred civilization, which needed its past revived in India and in Sri Lanka. I hated Hindi and everything Indian. I preferred Tamil and English to the language of the rulers. I hated Rajiv Gandhi for his decision to send the peacekeeping force to fight us. We made the schemes and plans...and though we lost many lives...we did it. We defeated the powerful Indian Army in the jungles of Jaffna.

"Moreover, we hated the Sri Lankan government. The Buddhists all the time ridiculed us. They kept us away from the important jobs, trampled our egos and our desire for social security, as if we were aliens to the country we had settled in centuries ago. The Indian government too fooled us. Prabhakaran met Rajiv Gandhi in order to find console. He said the fight shall stop and in return the Lankan government will negotiate the burning issues up front. And look what happened! They sent an army against us. Prabhakaran and all the leading commanders had to find safe haven. Our brave militants fought with vigor and valor. We used all possible means to send a chill in their hearts.... Yes, I was so devoted that I too dreamt of the resurrection of the Tamil nation. But the fact remains that they deceived us.

"And look...what they did to me too! First, this bloody government of India and then, the LTTE. In whom should I trust now, my friend?"

I tried to digest what he had just said. His outburst seemed genuine. At least, I felt so.

"Whoever has tipped the authorities has done the right thing. Both deserved the death of a mad dog. Their souls will never rest in peace. Cursed are those who kill a future. You know not, my friend, visionaries are very few. Rare, in fact. And you people, only for the sake of your own revenge, put an end to a fine dream." I roared back in anguish. "Do you know that you have opened the doors to chaos and anarchy? You have generated instability. You have tried to weaken a nation. Let me tell you, Krishnan, this dream of Tamil nationalism will never come true. One day, your people will become an extinct species, just like the dinosaurs. But this nation will somehow survive. What is all this talk of racial pride? Do you, in the real sense of the term, know what race is? It's nature that has defined our body structure and the ways of life. Whites are white because they have been in entirely different circumstances. What is race, after all? What is culture? If we are ready to kill our fellow beings, what meaning is there in boasting of culture? I spit on such culture. Why not stop the bloody violence and look at tomorrow with eyes wide open? See for yourself, today you are repenting because your own people abandoned you and tried to kill you. Now tell me what culture, which race and what philosophy are you going to profess? What feelings are there in your heart right now? You are confused. Your soul is fighting with itself. You don't know what to do, how to react, how to confront the new situation, how to prevent oncoming dangers, how to respond to the moments that are rushing in one after another. You speak of injustice and politics. Do you know what justice and politics is? No, my friend, you are a sucker. You have lost the fight. A defeated soul, that's what you are.

"I don't know, my friend, what goes on behind the iron curtains of the politician's chambers. I simply cannot state how wrong they are. If they are wrong, the aspirations of the community are wrong. Then the people get what they deserve. Why you wanted jobs only because you were in the minority? Why did our brothers in Lanka not try to rise based on intellect and hard work? Why did our people not get mingled in the society they chose centuries ago as a haven? Tell me, why they remained distanced from the people they were supposed to be part of?

"And see, now we both are conspirators - both running away from our own community and law. You are in danger and so am I. You are innocent and so am I; I never wanted to do what I have been forced to do by the culprits; you were on a mission of your own people and yet, your life is wanted by your mentors," I completed my sentence in almost a cry.

Krishnan held me in an embrace.

"I acknowledge your feelings, but my dear friend, you are just a commoner who doesn't have a strong hand to play in the dirty political games that take place behind the curtain. You know the things via newspapers. And most of them are controlled by a bunch of people who let you know only the glimpses of the truth that they feel best in their interest. You live in an era of propaganda. Truth is far away from everybody. You tend to believe the things they want you to believe. We too have a bunch of the so-called thinkers who profess our philosophy in this or that language. It is just like the RSS, another resurrection of the SS of the past. No difference. All rulers are alike. Your government never understood the aspirations of the Tamil youth. Why? Why sent the army to defeat us? Weren't we freedom fighters to gain life in the lands where our people are living for centuries? Why did the Sinhalese try to trample our rights? Wasn't it an unjust act on their part? Who did ever try to tell them what they did was not right? Only because we are in minority? Hell with it! We must win back the lost honor. And you believe in their propaganda?"

I gave a deep sigh. "No, friend, you failed to understand."

But the revelation startled me. How true it was. Didn't I believe in the newspapers? Didn't I always form my opinions based on the information I received through it? In reality, what did I know of the clandestine affairs that took place behind the closed doors?

I sighed again. Krishnan kept looking at me with sympathy. He held my hand in an effort to soothe me.

"Nobody on earth knows the truth," he said. "Truth is a sacred word, but somehow it has lost its meaning. No truth prevails. Only the victorious boast of truth prevails, howsoever false it might be. Venu, my friend, let these revelations not bother you. I've seen it all, I have experienced it, and my heart rejected it, but the brain wouldn't listen to the heart. I obeyed the commands of my brain.... I had to. If I did not, where else would I go?"

The cruel face of the world shocked me. My head drooped and tears started to roll down my cheeks. "Why...why then do we want to live on this earth at all? Death could be a blessing," I mumbled.

"But why should we die? No, Venu, my friend, please don't weep. Only the brave can breathe on this earth. We are not going to die. We will fight it out. We will expose these bastards who did such horrible things to our lives.

"Get up," he said, but then he too sat down on the grass and looked into my eyes. He patted my head, but it could not soothe my agony.

It was a solitary place. The wind rustled the leaves of the tall trees. A silence, which could rake up one's deeply buried emotions, ruled over me.

Sanjay Sonawani

"Venu, please calm down."

I looked at him. His face was morose.

I too held his hand and said, "Alright. If this is the truth, that we are to be sacrificed at the altar of unholy circumstances, then so be it, for now I can't change the course of events. Your own people have now turned our enemies and they won't rest till they kill us. On the other hand, the Government of India too is our enemy. Now how do you propose to deflate their vindictive approach?"

" Good that you've realized the stark reality."

I got up and looked at the shimmering sky through the dense cover of the trees above.

"Someone has ditched you, Krishnan. Think. There must be some mistake on your part. Someone else too knew what you were up to. Who could it be?"

Krishnan waited to gather his thoughts.

"I don't know, honestly. But it appears the way you say it is. I must have committed some mistake, but nothing comes to my mind. Someone else must have defected and the blame is on my head."

"How often did you meet Prabhakaran?" I asked.

"Very rarely, unless, of course, there was some urgent matter to discuss. Otherwise, we would communicate through our wireless system - Prabhakaran is a discreet man, you know."

"You say that only Prabhakaran and you knew where Sivrasan was hiding?"

"Exactly—"

"Any possibility of a breach in the communication system?"

"No. I told you there was no communication since I

personally met Prabhakaran and discussed the final plan. I was prohibited from any communication, as we knew the Government of India would try to intercept all our communications and try to decode them under any circumstances. We couldn't afford to take the risk."

"Were you to transport Sivrasan and Shuba to Sri Lanka?"

"No. We had decided to ship them to the US. Sivrasan had to be operated on - he was blind in one eye, you know?"

"Yes, what then?"

"Sivrasan was invaluable to us. His safe passage was important. He could be brought back to Sri Lanka once the danger had passed."

"But how did you people manage that?"

"Manage what?"

"The assassination of Rajiv Gandhi, what else?"

He looked elsewhere.

"Tell me."

"Well, frankly speaking, Venu, I too know very little about it."

"I can't believe that, Krishnan."

"Yes, I know. Assassinating the leader of a country like India is not something that can be done by amateurs. Indeed, there was meticulous planning. They had the means. They knew how Rajiv Gandhi would greet the people who came to join his campaign. They counted on that. They had human bombs ready to explode themselves at every places he went. Finally, they got the chance in Tamil Nadu. They thought it was the right answer. His destiny was marked. Everything worked out as they had planned. They had a bunch of human bombs ready to receive this honor. I had nothing to do with who did what. My assignment was well defined. I had to take Sivrasan to a safe haven. And I did so. This was my part in the whole operation."

"Then, how on earth was Sivrasan located by SIT?"

There was a wretched smile on Krishnan's lips.

"That's what I do not know."

I kept silent for a while. I had regained my composure.

"There are hints in the newspapers that the assassination was masterminded by foreigners, is it true?" I asked.

"I suspect so."

"Who?"

"I do not know for sure, *Tambi*."

"But you can make an educated guess, I am sure."

"Yes. I can."

"Then who?"

"The CIA."

"The CIA! Why on earth the CIA?"

"It's just a doubt based on some incidents that I witnessed."

"Okay."

"Do you know what happened in Russia?" He asked.

"I know. Communism breathed its last there."

"*They* did it! They infiltrated their men into that country at every level. The process had been going on for years. A few of them even became members of the Polit Bureau. And do you know another story that seems so incredible?"

"Tell me."

"Perestroika is said to be the brainchild of other $uperpowers. Those people initiated drastic changes throughout the globe to make their supremacy absolute. They wanted to end the Cold War. But see, it really has ended. And if this is the case, then India is a far easier target for them where one can buy even Premiers of the nation with money. And yet India had strong potential to become a superpower under the powerful rule of the Gandhi family. Now, with the death of Rajiv Gandhi, future politics is going to shape in an entirely different manner. Actually, this is a newly invented imperialism. Do you read newspapers?"

"Yes, of course, I do."

"Have you read the articles professing that India should abandon its policy of being neutral? They vehemently argue that after the fall of the Soviet Union, India has no powerful allies left on the globe. They say, India should grow under the shadow of America. She should sign the CTBT and the NPT unconditionally. And further, they state that if India follows the tracks laid by America, it can become a strong and developed nation.

"If not, India will lose its importance and would have a miserable status in the global scenario. And, above all, they dare to say that if India befriends the US, terrorism in India will come to an end. Isn't it?"

"Yes, it's true. I must admit."

"India is well equipped to explode and test nuclear weapons. The tests are long awaited. Yet, they cannot do this. Why?"

"You tell me."

"Because, Pakistan too has nuclear weapons. India is not exploding its weapons only because Pakistan too will explode its weapons in retaliation.

"Now, let me tell you a bare fact. The US has infiltrated its men everywhere and with the help of money they are causing havoc in other countries. Of course, we too performed that miracle with the money that flowed in from the countries which had so-called sympathy in our fight. Not only money, weapons too. What was the ultimate gain to those who supplied us money and weapons? I always have thought about this. And where money failed, with our best efforts to infuriate the feelings of the downtrodden people, we succeeded in impossible tasks. It was our power. But what have those downtrodden people got in return till date? Tell me. But that's the very reason why they could do all these things in India, unobtrusively. It's all a big game I too know very little of. Just guesses and doubts...who has concrete proof?"

After a while, he continued. "*Tambi*, India was the first to assist us. The Tamils in Tamil Nadu too helped us with a passion. They too wanted to form Mahanadu. That's the dream they are seeing from the day of India's freedom. But India never had a firm policy and that led the LTTE to form another alliance. There are many countries that want instability in different zones. The US is the topper, *Tambi*. It has the power, the money and the determination to rule the world. Rajiv Gandhi planned India's future in a different way. He wished to bring in a new economy that would overthrow the yoke of the past and take India into the new millennium with confidence and power. His assassination was not a plot conceived by the LTTE. The LTTE knew what great danger they are walking into with the assassination of Rajiv. But they had plausible reasons to kill him. And they had friends who wanted this man, the danger of tomorrow to them, to be eliminated. Again guesses, but the logic holds water, *Tambi*. Tell me, only the US had a logical reason to eliminate this man to safeguard their interests in Asia." He gave a sigh. "Oh! It's tiring even to think about it."

Krishnan's revelation shocked me. I realized what big fools we are - we go on living life blindly. The things that appear so simple are like icebergs with only their tips showing above the water's surface.

"It's all so very horrible," I mumbled.

"I know," said Krishnan in deep voice. "But what can one do? No value to the moralities anymore. Those who are felicitated are the ones who preach the philosophy of the rulers. Only those are in the limelight who devote their lives performing to the tune of the rulers. Then what prevails, after all, is no truth."

"Even then you became a militant," I said flatly.

"I had to survive. I joined them because I did not want to rot in jail. I had to preach the philosophy of my life savers. I had to act as per their desires. I had no choice. Many a time I would think deeply whether I really liked the life I was leading? No. I was frustrated and yet never a slightest hint of it appeared on my face. And I still do not know why on earth I was arrested? Why they detained me illegally? What else you do expect me to do under such circumstances? Worship the establishment! No, Venu, I am grateful to those who rescued me from that hell. It was better to join the surge of violence than serve the society that put a slur on me."

Sanjay Sonawani

"You participated in ethnic violence, Krishnan."

"Yes, if you say so."

"Why?"

"No choice."

By now we had approached a stream with a heavy flow. The water ran deep and the noise was deafening. We looked at each other. Krishnan cried, "Let's hold hands and try the depths."

I laughed.

We held each other's hand and fighting the vicious force of water somehow crossed the stream.

On the other side, the woods were scanty and the chirping of the birds overpowered the silence of the jungle.

It was almost 4 p.m.

The sun rays were slanting.

We kept on walking silently. As yet there had been no sign of any human settlement.

"Tell me, Krishnan, what are we up to now? We cannot enter Madras; they'll be waiting for us. Nor can we run away elsewhere, for my wife is in danger. I am scared, Krishnan."

Krishnan held my hand tightly and looked in my eyes. There was guilt in his eyes.

"No, I won't let it happen."

I laughed ruefully.

"You are wounded, Krishnan, and I am a fugitive with no skills whatsoever. How do you propose to rescue Janaki from the clutches of death? See I have saved you for the sake of olden days. I pity the tragedy that has befallen you. But I am a simple man who wishes to lead a simple and normal life. Janaki is in terrible danger and unless you see to it that she is safe and sound, my heart shall not rest. How should we do that?"

Krishnan did not answer.

"Our little bravado has worsened the situation, Krishnan," I said mournfully.

"You had a choice," he said.

"What do you think, Krishnan, I could have left you in the jaws of death? No. I had no choice. I couldn't have let you die like that, you bastard. All I am worried about now is Janaki. I am deeply worried about her. She is alone. They must be counting on the fact that I will somehow try to contact her. They are present everywhere, you know it. Now, tell me, what are we to do?"

"We both are in danger. I have no one to mourn my death. Even if I die fighting those bastards it wouldn't matter. But you are not alone, Venu, you have a wife."

"Janaki is pregnant," I wailed.

He looked at me awkwardly.

"I can't even congratulate you," he whispered in a desperate voice.

"Doesn't matter," I said, "Tell me how can we get out of this danger? We can't live in this forest forever, we must go to Madras, but I don't know how, Krishnan. I am simply baffled."

Krishnan said nothing. He was in a sort of trance. I stood immobile, confused and exasperated.

After a long silence, Krishnan spoke.

"I've a choice. I can surrender to the Indian police. I may propose a deal with RAW. I may become the government's witness. They may pardon me, for I never actively involved myself in any physical violence. I may provide them with vital information they will simply jump at."

He paused. I kept on looking at him intensely, as if he was the sole survivor on earth.

"But then what about you?" He asked matter-of-factly. "They may provide you protection, at least for a while. But I know them well. They are just like the mafia. They will wait patiently till the security eases. Moreover, no amount of security deters them. For when they can easily assassin a former prime minister, you are easy prey. But I owe my life to you. I just can't let it happen," he said thoughtfully.

Krishnan was confusing me.

"Cut it short, Krishnan, just tell me what has to be done?"

"That's what I am thinking, Venu. I know we are in danger and also Janaki. We have no friends at present. As you did not abandon me, I too will never desert you... mark my words.

"The LTTE is very powerful and resourceful. The government of India is also dangerous for us. We cannot trust either of them. If we can somehow move Janaki to a safer place and once we escape out of Tamil Nadu and find refuge elsewhere, we might be safe. We have enough money to make things easier. Janaki has to be moved... and the sooner, the better."

"But how?" The question rushed out of my mouth.

Krishnan's face lit up with a new found hope.

"I know them. I know their ugly traits. I can penetrate into their system. I know their well-established network in Tamil Nadu. The communications system was developed and installed by me. If luck favors us, I can confuse them. At least for a while."

I looked at him incredulously.

His eyes sparkled and he laughed.

"This is a sort of war and we are the weaker side. The only hope we have is not to give them any chance to counter attack. We may then win. Venu, henceforth, life will be full of dangers. We have challenged this danger and now let us teach them a lesson and with all our might."

"You are talking dangerous things, Krishnan."

He laughed. "Do you really think so?"

"They will simply blow us to pieces. They might even bomb my house. What do you mean be brave and fight, you son of a bitch? Have you gone mad?"

"Then tell me what do you have in your goddamn head. I cannot think of anything else."

"I have no idea ... at least for the moment."

"Then trust me. I can do that."

"You are wounded. You are hallucinating, Krishnan. Think of some practical solution, please."

"Your only problem is how to safeguard Janaki. Isn't it?"

"Yes..."

"Going to the police station to lodge a complaint will be a funny idea," he said. "They will first lock you up and by the time you reach a competent authority, your Janaki will be no more."

"Shut up, you bastard, one more word and you will have bullets up your arse..."

"I am only introducing you to the possibilities."

"They are worse."

"Then just go to Madras, enter your house as if nothing

has happened and take your wife in your warm embrace."

"For heaven's sake, Krishnan, will you stop joking. We are in a dangerous situation. Why don't you think something seriously."

"So, at least, you acknowledge the dangers."

"I have my reasons."

"Good, it is good to be reasonable. You know that you simply cannot walk into your house, don't you?"

"Yes..."

"You cannot trust the police or you can enter your own house, for you know very well that the LTTE is waiting there to welcome you with all eagerness."

"I should have let you die," I said flatly.

"You should have!" Said Krishnan. "But now you can not reverse the course of events. You have blown their chopper to pieces," he said with regret.

"I had no choice. If I hadn't blown up that chopper, both of us would have been at the bottom of the sea."

"So you know you had no choice. You couldn't prefer me getting killed at the hands of my old friends. You know I have been declared a traitor by the LTTE and the Indian Government would first shoot millions of bullets on my body and then would question me, Venu."

"I know that."

"Then why not trust me and assist me so that we can rescue Janaki?"

"I guess, I have no other choice," I said with some regret.

"Look, once we safely rescue Janaki, we can move to the north. The LTTE has no influence in the north, I know that for sure. We could settle there and start a new life."

The idea consoled me temporarily. Is it really possible, I wondered. The danger lying ahead did not seem formidable anymore.

"Of course, it will not be easy," Krishnan warned. "We have to be alert. They must be chasing us, and the worst thing is that your wife knows nothing about us and yet she is in utter danger. They will use her as bait to hook us. First of all, we must liberate her from their clutches."

"How will we reach there?" I asked, perplexed.

"Do you have a telephone at home?"

"Yes," I said enthusiastically. It was a possibility that had completely slipped my mind.

"Good," he murmured. "But I am a little apprehensive as to how safe it would be to contact her on phone. They will tape our conversation. They are very systematic; I know that for sure. And many powerful people in the government are on their side."

"If intelligent men like you assist them, why on earth won't they be systematic?" I said, sarcastically.

He shrugged off my comment. I was irritated and uneasy over the changed course of the conversation. I was feeling great when I was interrogating Krishnan, but now I was facing grave reality.

Nine

The sun sank in the western horizon. The gloomy twilight gave way to maniacal feelings. They grew in my mind with a demonic force, crushing all hopes. The forest started to come alive with shadows of a wild primitive world. In the wake of such moments, you curse yourself for being a thinking and repenting soul. You wish to be a reckless animal dashing down everything crossing your way. Slaughter all those bastards who obstruct your way. Roar with all your strength and frighten the treacherous world.

The world around me, all of sudden, became unfriendly and unknown. As if it was in my dreams that I had stepped into this forest. The chirping of birds seemed as if the earth was weeping. The branches rustled sounding like the deep sigh of a melancholy soul. With the setting sun, I felt as though my soul too had sunk into the weary world of pain.

The tiresome walk made me uneasy. The evening shadows extended their hands and clawed scratches on my existence. As the shadows grew darker, the surrounding became almost invisible.

Krishnan broke the silence. "We must halt now."

"Yes, I think so," I muttered. I was tired. My legs were reluctant to take even another step forward.

I gazed around.

We were standing on a slope. On the left, there was a spring flowing in the opposite direction.

"I could sleep like a log right here," I said with eagerness.

"No problem," said Krishnan.

The very next moment, Krishnan sat down on the grass. He moaned as he rested his back against the trunk of a tree.

I collected some dry leaves and twigs with great difficulty; every bone in my body ached. I arranged it in a heap and set a match to it. A bronze glow soothed us as it caught fire. The fire reaged up with a cracking sound, encouraging and assuring us: 'You are alive, just like me,' it said.

Now as I looked at Krishnan, he seemed pale and dazed.

"Krishnan," I called out to him.

He opened his eyes. The light of the fire reflected in his eyes like the eyes of a wounded lion.

"Huh?" He muttered.

"Are you alright?"

"Yes."

Sanjay Sonawani

"Are you hungry?"

"Yes, like an animal from a drought affected region."

"Come here, you will feel better near the fire."

Krishnan looked at me for a while. Then, suddenly, he pulled out his revolver. I was dumbstruck as he aimed and fired. A thunderous sound echoed into the night's stillness. A wild fowl gave a shriek and fell out of the bushes fluttering. Krishnan smiled.

"Still my aim is accurate," he mumbled and closed his eyes.

I ran to the fowl and held it in my hands as it breathed its last. Its warm touch infuriated my hunger. I brought it back to the fire and after removing its feathers and washing it clean in the stream; I roasted it on the fire.

If anybody had predicted that I would feast on a roasted fowl in the forest, I would have laughed at him. But how miraculous life is! It makes you want to dance on its tunes. Your ambitions, your dreams, your ideologies, just lick the feet of destiny, like a humble dog.

I smelled the fowl to check if it was properly roasted, then satisfied, I served half of it to Krishnan. I could see he too enjoyed it.

"Do you remember Vani?"

"Yes, I do."

"Why didn't you make her your life partner?"

"Do you know what she thought of me?"

"Krishnan, she loved you so much."

"Humbug!"

"What? What's humbug in her loving you?"

Krishnan was relishing the leg piece of the roasted bird. He looked up at me and said, "Why not humbug, my friend? Lust! It's only lust that predominates this bloody world. You say love. Do you know what love is? Love between man and woman leads towards a single ultimate aim and that is to sleep with each other. I had my own concept of love - I never gave importance to physical needs.

"Do you know what real love is? It is not lust; it has neither physical attraction nor any expectations. There is no feeling of winning or losing. Only love. Pure sacred love."

I laughed at him.

"Don't give me those Utopian concepts about love, Krishnan. No love exists that matches your definition."

"Yes, I know how difficult it is to love someone the way I described it to you. But does it mean that we should accept whatever comes our way? Vani wanted me to be her mate for life. Why? What did she find in me during those short interludes? Could she fathom the depths of my soul? No. She liked my company because I suited her ideals; I could satisfy her feminine ego. She thought I would be crazy for her. Stupid girl.

"No, that was not love, Venu. She thought I would worship her beauty. I will hum around her like a bee. I will make attempts to touch her, to kiss her, and she, with all her queenly glamour, will keep on protesting my attempts. I will praise her heavenly beauty and woo her. I will tell her how I dream of her and how so much I love her. But I never gave her what she expected of me - I never even attempted to kiss her. I never took her to my room under some pretext to screw her.

Sanjay Sonawani

"No, I did not do all that, I simply could not. She left me only because I didn't do all those things to her. And then no more was I her dream lover. What kind of love she had for me after all? Lust, Venu, only lust, for I smelled it. All lovers keep on loving each other with a secret dream to sleep with each other. To make this secret dream true, they shower all the loving words and false emotions on each other, with the hope that one day they will fuck each other. They keep on using sweet words, try to become poets, singers or even dashing Romeos. They make a show of tears. They say it's real love. They feel it's real love. Do you think I could love her to satisfy her passions? If at all it was love, she could have accepted me as I was. But it never happened that way, Venu."

His bold statement shook me. Was my love for Janaki just lust? I tried to remember all the events till our marriage, and I found none resembling what Krishnan had just painted before me.

"You couldn't understand what love is," I protested.

"Yes, I do."

"But you have not loved anyone."

"I did!" He said softly, gazing into the leaping flames.

"Who was she?"

"Dorothy Hillman."

"And what was she?"

"Our lecturer. She lectured us on human relations. What a lady she was. Her mere entry into the classroom would impress me. I fell in love with her."

"Then? Did you ever propose her."

"No, why should I? And if I had, it would have been a

great joke."

"Why?"

"She was sixty years old."

I looked at him agape.

"It was platonic love. And then age, sex...nothing matters. Response, rejection... doesn't matter. Love is as eternal as the sun and the moon. It is unchangeable... unperturbed... unmovable."

He had a wild philosophy that was difficult to digest. But his voice held a primitive passion and I listened to him with equal understanding.

We had finished feasting on the wild fowl. The fire burned low. The twinkling stars above, through gaps of the branches, made me feel a part of an unbelievable world unfolding its myths before me. I felt dazed.

Krishnan had spread his body on the soft grass. I do not know what he thought. Why on earth had he pushed me into the world of psychopaths? Yes, he was responsible. Yet, I loved him very much.

I too lay down on the grassy earth from where I looked up through the branches at the twinkling stars, the constellations, decorating the vast sky. Everything was as mute as death itself. The forest murmured and I listened to its spell of deep silence. No sound of rejection. No begging for satisfaction. There was only silence, only forgiveness, and only giving and only peace.

It too was a world within. And the world outside, unknown to us, but breathing with us; yet so strange. It too had the same eternal existence as humans. Not like humans, it had a far greater history. Many enchanting and frightening dramas had taken place on the stage of that vast eternity. There simply did not exist the impudence of boasting history on one side and the spoiled present and future on the other.

For a while, I forgot my pains. I forgot the dangers. Like a child, I drowned myself in nature.

As if flying through the clouds, the next moment, I felt I was being driven towards stinking filth. The darkness surrounding me was suffocating. Its sticky, warm touch nauseating. Then, suddenly, a piercing ray of light shook me from my vain efforts to fight out darkness. The light did not bring any relaxation. I grew anxious and frightened. The awakening within me had the stench of a curse. I was still alive and it was not at all a comfortable realization.

I opened my eyes. Through the dense leaves overhead I could see a bright sunny sky. The wind was blowing gently. The birds chirped welcome songs. The stream down the slope flowed with never ending enthusiasm. The reality, that I was alive, slapped me from all directions.

Krishnan was still in deep sleep. His face looked like that of an innocent child asleep in the arms of his loving mother.

I sat up and then walked slowly towards the stream. The crystal clear water running to meet the sea reflected various shadows. I dipped my hand in the cool water. Its touch was soothing, like a balm on my wounds. As if in a trance, I watched the water flow, its mesmerizing sound filling my thirsty soul. Nearby, frogs were jumping underneath shrubs that bordered the stream. Birds swooped down and when their beaks touched the water, flapped their wings into flight.

Serenity like that of the blessings of the Almighty enveloped my being. Still, I was unable to understand what next I was going to do. I slowly cupped my hands and splashed some water on my face. The touch of the water was refreshing. It cleared my mind of the fog that had gathered there.

"Venu...Venu." Krishnan's voice snatched me back to the world to which I belonged. This nature, its soft caress did not belong to me. It was merely an incident that happened to me accidentally, a dream.

I hurried back.

"Are you alright?"

Krishnan nodded. But as he moved he shivered and his face contorted in deep pain. His shoulder was swollen and he could hardly move his left hand.

"The bandage must be changed," I said, worried.

"Later," he replied through clenched teeth as I helped him get up.

"Let us move now, Venu."

"No, let us wait, instead. You're not okay."

He gave a weak smile.

"Waiting will do us no good, my friend. Let us start now."

I nodded sadly.

Our journey had begun.

There was not much left to discuss now. Busy in our own bizarre thoughts, we kept on walking side by side.

The forest thinned. We could now see large stretches of farms; we were just about to enter into the so-called civilized world. The very thought annoyed me. And an unknown fear started to grip me. I felt uneasy but I said nothing. Krishnan was walking slowly. I knew he had fever. He badly needed a doctor, but how could I take him to one? Life was not at all blissful.

Then we saw a hamlet.

"A village must be somewhere nearby."

"Yes, we must reach a phone first," Krishnan said. "We must call your residence."

"Let's try," I said weakly, without much hope.

We descended the slope. A pathway led us towards the hamlet. Beside a mango tree, I saw a young girl tending a flock of sheep.

I beckoned her.

She came forward with a curious look on her face.

"Which village is located nearby?"

"Dotti Palayam," she replied.

"How does one get there?"

"Keep on this same pathway. Right there," she said, pointing north, "You'll find a road. Take a right turn and keep going straight and you'll reach Dotti Palayam."

"How far is it?"

"Two, three miles."

I nodded. We were tired. But yet a two-three mile walk was not too far. I thanked the young girl and followed her direction.

Walking on the dusty, uneven road under the hot sun was not an experience that one enjoyed. After a while, we halted and ate the salted fish and bread we were carrying with us. At a distance, we could see farmers and workers busy in the fields.

Nobody took cognizance of our presence. That satisfied me.

"This area is not much infiltrated by the LTTE," said Krishnan, "Mahabalipuram is not for away from here. But, at Dhanush Palayam, a handful of supporters do exist."

"Krishnan," I said, abruptly. "If they tape the phone, they will come to know of our whereabouts. How can we possibly get her out?"

"I am thinking that only," said Krishnan, "However, at least, we can gauge the situation. We need to know that she is safe."

Once again, I got lost in the labyrinth of my worries.

❖ ❖ ❖

Ten

Janaki was two years younger to me. She came from a
well-off family, her father was a retired deputy collector. They
owned a large farm, too. Frankly speaking, ours was not a love
marriage. Yet, you cannot categorize it as an arranged marriage
either.

I was working with Tarapore Fishing Corporation, when
Ganapathi, one of my colleagues, invited me on his engagement.
Honestly speaking, I dislike attending social or religious
ceremonies. But Ganapathi's insistence forced me to attend.
He had very few friends, and his wish, that his closest ones
should witness the most important event in his life, couldn't be

neglected.

The ceremony was organized at his fiancée's house, situated near the Integral Coach Factory. When I arrived at her home, the sacred sound of conch shells, coconuts and garlands of flowers indicated an auspicious occasion was at hand.

The hall was covered by a carpet, on which close relations sat cheerfully.

I sat beside Ganapathi.

Then the girl entered the hall, surrounded by her friends.

Watching them approach my eyes caught the glance of a doe-eyed young woman with a glowing complexion and hair that streamed down to her calves. She looked so innocent and charming that I simply surrendered my soul to her at that very instant. When she smiled, her eyes lit up like the sun. I was mesmerized. For a fraction of a moment, our eyes met and as if a million thunderbolts struck my heart. I did not pay any attention to the ceremonial proceedings after that.

At regular intervals she would look at me, as if to intimidate my bold gaze. But the moment the ceremony ended, she walked back into the house without even a backward glance at me.

I returned home restless. I did not know who she was, what her name was, but her image resonated in every atom of my body.

The days went by.

My father, in the meanwhile, undertook the Herculean task of finding a suitable girl for me. But in the depths of my heart, I nourished the image of the girl I had seen at Ganapathi's engagement ceremony as my soul companion. I desperately wanted her. I dreamt of her. But, as I did not know who she was, it appeared to me as if I had indulged myself in an insane game. I rejected the proposals that came for me. I even tore up some of the photographs of the girls given to me by my father with a hope that I might select one of them as my wife.

One evening as I reached home, my father pounced on me. He threatened that if I was not yet prepared to get married, he would simply throw me out on the streets and the doors of his house would be shut for me forever. There was an obstinate force in his voice that made me think seriously. After all, how long could I wait for the girl of my dreams?

I reluctantly nodded and assured him I had no plans of remaining a bachelor for life. That seemed to satisfy him. He gave a warm, victorious smile. The next day, he handed me a bunch of photographs of some girls and some letters detailing them. Reluctantly, I took them to my bedroom and lying down on my bed, started to shuffle through the photographs with disinterest.

Suddenly, I froze.

It was she. Looking out of the photograph at me with those doe-eyes, smiling mischievously.

I sat up erect and looked at the accompanying details

Janaki Padmanabhan, B.A. Honors. No Mars!

I was elated.

I rushed back to my father's room. He was sitting in a chair, engrossed in reading J. Krishnamurthi's teachings.

He shot a glance at me.

"What's it Venu? What happened?

Sanjay Sonawani

I said nothing and stood like a wooden block, gazing down on the floor.

"Have you selected any of the girls?"

I nodded.

"Which one?"

I silently handed him the photograph as if it was my own heart.

He glared at the photograph for a long time. He then removed his specs and looked up at me.

There was a smile on his face.

"Good choice, son," he said. "It's a good family...sound financial background..."

I returned to my room. A fear gripped my heart - what if she rejects me? What if the largely circulated photograph of hers is selected by many of the prospective grooms and if they happen to be better off than me, why on earth would such a lovely girl choose me over them?

I prayed desperately to God that night to let her select me. 'Let her be mine and I will shower all the love on her. I will make her happy and content.'

How miserable waiting can be I experienced it that night. I was worried whether my father had informed her parents or not. Time was running out. What if she got engaged before my acceptance reached her family?

The morning was sunny. The sun shined brightly. Birds soared high in the sky, as if reaching out to steal a kiss. Yet, in a corner of my heart, a despicable animal sat. The fear that lurked in the corner was overshadowing my happy dreams about her.

But my dreams came true. Her family sent an invitation for a "seeing ceremony". I went there with my heart in my hand, confident and at the same time afraid. But all went well. I was even granted a meeting with her on Marina beach to open our hearts and understand each other.

The sun was setting in the western horizon. An intoxicating smell of the sea filled the air. Its sound the roar of emotions in my heart that wanted to take shape in words. I was like a crazy stag that was bounding towards some unknown far away destination. I wanted the moment to freeze. I wanted that she hear the outbreak of my emotions; I was simply crazy for her!

She sat looking at me seriously, poised and confident, without showing any shade of her inborn mischievous nature. I slowly took her hands in mine and asked in a trembling voice -

"Will you be happy with me?"

Her eyes gazed at me unwavering in her silence, as if her answer lay in them.

I understood what she meant and gathering her in a warm embrace placed my lips over her forehead. She said nothing. Her entire being seemed filled with acceptance of me.

"I will never abandon you. All the time you will be in my heart," I murmured.

She said nothing. But her silence told me that she too shared my ideas about our being together for eternity.

I just kept on looking in the depths of her eyes with a mystic passion.

That was beginning of a heavenly bliss.

◆ ◆ ◆

Sanjay Sonawani

The dusty pathway leading to the village twisted and turned as it wound its way through lush greenery. Unknowingly, our pace increased as the village came into sight. Evening was approaching and the dusty road leading to it was gradually becoming busier as villagers began returning from their fields.

"Where is the post office?" I asked an old man.

He casually directed us towards an alley, at the end of which was situated the post office.

Fortunately, it was open.

Behind the counter, a middle-aged man occupied a chair with an antiquated phone in front of him.

"We want to make a call."

"Where?"

"Madras."

"It might take some time."

"It is urgent."

"Let me try. These bloody fools at the telephone department take a lot of time, you know?"

He snatched the hand set and asked us to write down a number. When his call was answered, he repeated the number asking it to be connected immediately and then slammed the receiver back on the cradle.

"Never seen you before. Where are you from?" He asked us with a curious look seeing our ragged outfits and Krishnan's bandaged shoulder.

I avoided his gaze and said, "From Mahabalipuram."

Was he suspicious? I could not tell for sure. And even if he was, the hell with him. After all, he was just a postmaster. What harm he could do to us?

Sanjay Sonawani

We waited for almost half an hour before we were connected to my residence.

My heart was pounding with the intense emotion that had gripped my body. I could not sustain the pressure - "Krishnan...please."

Krishnan understood the gravity of the moment. He took the receiver from my hands.

I kept on looking at his face as though the end of the world was in front of us.

What could have happened?

Had those bastards held her in custody to avenge my stupidity?

"Hello..." Krishnan's voice was barely audible. He pressed my hand gently commiserating my anxiety.

"Can I speak to Janaki?" He asked.

So Janaki had not answered the call. I could not imagine who else could have picked up the receiver; she was always alone at home while I was away.

"Me? I am her distant relative...I am planning to come to Madras...when will she be back? Okay...is Venu there? Never mind, I will call later. By the way, who am I speaking to?...Who...? Okay... Alright."

Krishnan slowly put the receiver back on its cradle and looked helplessly at me.

I wanted to cry. I wanted to curse, but stood silent, all my distant hopes having been shattered.

He snatched his wallet from his hip pocket and taking out a hundred rupee note threw it at the postmaster. "Keep the change," he said and walked out of the door.

Blindly, I followed him.

"Something is wrong, Venu;" he murmured

"Your brother-in-law was at your house. Please...don't interrupt me, I know for sure, he couldn't be your brother-in-law, even if you had any. He told me, Janaki was at her parental home and did not know where Venu was. He was asking my name. I could give any, but he would know I was lying...something is wrong, extremely wrong, Venu."

I was speechless. My heart was frozen, legs paralyzed, I was unable to think, to react. I stood still. Rage surged within me for the bastard Krishnan who had brought this nightmare upon me. But my limbs felt weak; I could not even say a word. I was terrified and on the verge of fainting.

He forced me to walk on, even more careful now so as not to attract the attention of the villagers.

"They are using her as bait. But don't panic, Venu, they will not cause any harm to her until we are caught. They are waiting and as long as they are waiting, Janaki is safe. The moment they feel holding her is of no use, they will simply do away with her. Let's hope for the best.... We are their enemies, not she, try to understand..."

His assurances did not help me in any way. I was scared to death. Wild images of the worst kind had begun to haunt me.

"Let us first get out of this village, Venu. They will try and trace all calls. They will easily locate us. I know their ways. By this time they would have sent out a large team to locate us."

This scared me even more.

Sympathy poured out of his eyes for me. Was there any

guilt in it? I wanted to know. But my mind was numb; unable to grasp anything.

"Hell! We must get out of here."

His voice shook me out of my stupor. I looked at him helplessly.

"They must have tapped the phone. It will take a few moments for them to know from where the call was placed. The search will put more hurdles in our way. They need to know that we are dead and till then they won't rest, Venu."

I was terrified.

Krishnan held my hand tightly and dragged me along with all the frightening thoughts that were erupting within me. I felt like a piece of paper surrendered to a storm. I had no aim, no direction. Yet my soul cried out in vain protest. My mind was crazed. I wanted to set the entire earth ablaze, kill each one who came into my sight. I wanted them, those bastards, to burn alive and laugh at them while they died. I was blinded by anguish.

The image of my father appeared before me. That lousy bastard laughed at me. Yes, he was the man who threw me in the abyss of sorrows and death. If he hadn't worked for the demons, I wouldn't have landed in this mess. Yes, he was responsible for the morass I was in.... and yet he laughed...I wanted to shoot him. Batter his beaming face beyond recognition. Trample him and dance over his miserable body.

Krishnan dragged me out of the village. The dusty road ahead through the green fields appeared like a white strip on the body of a leper. The sun was setting behind the woods. The soul within me too was setting. All was dead for me.

Sanjay Sonawani

The sun disappeared after a while and the world seemed a sinking ship. Soon, darkness established its deathly grip over the world.

O God! What crime have I committed for which you punish me so? Where is my Janaki? Where is she, you bastard? Tell me!

The night was a painful journey of bitter memories. We walked fast keeping pace with the speed of our thoughts.

"She must have been taken away from your house," said Krishnan, after a long silence.

I had nothing to reply.

"My friend, rest assured, you will meet her again, I give you my word. Wherever she is, wherever those bastards have hidden her, we will find her. I will take you to her. Even if death crosses my path, I will fight it."

I looked at him through tearful eyes, not trusting a word of what he said.

"They are bastards, I know. They know how to avenge their enemies. But I too am in their league with their own explored philosophies. We will checkmate them. We will bring them to their knees."

There was an echo of solid assurance in his tone. Yet it did not inspire any hope. Didn't he know that we were only two and they were numerous? How on earth were we to mitigate their force?

All of a sudden, the blinding headlights of a jeep lit up the dark road.

Krishnan grabbed my hand and pulled me behind a bush.

Sanjay Sonawani

I was surprised to see that he had the revolver in his hand. But as soon as the vehicle screeched to a halt and a couple of men jumped down hurriedly with guns in their hands, my surprise had turned to fear.

They opened fire wildly.

One of them shouted - "We know your are nearby. Surrender, or face death."

Again a round was fired into the darkness.

I was unarmed. Krishnan lay beside me with the revolver in his hand, ready to attack.

How these bastards got to us so fast?

I was wondering through the myriad of fears.

They must have located our direction as soon as they knew from where we had called.

They began firing blindly.

A few bullets stuck the tree next to the bush we were sheltering behind.

I saw Krishnan crawling towards the right.

I was afraid not having him beside me. But I could not speak. I was scared as hell.

Krishnan was then invisible to me. I was alone and these demons were shouting and shooting aimlessly. Trying hard to hold my breath, I tried to hide myself into the earth.

Suddenly, I heard counter shots.

In an instant, three of the men, who were visible in the light of the jeep, fell on the road. The others ran helter-skelter in search of safety.

But a couple of explosions made it sure that those who tried to run for safer abodes never found one.

The eternal silence of the night enveloped us once again.

"Come on, Venu," Krishnan said in a low voice as he moved into the light of the jeep's headlamps. "Let us escape from here at once."

"Can you drive this jeep?" He asked

"Yes," I said and got behind the steering wheel. As soon as Krishnan seated himself beside me, I sped the vehicle towards our unknown destination.

"Let us avoid villages. They have their supporters spread everywhere, we can't use this jeep for long; they'll be looking out for us," said Krishnan as if in a trance. He was trying to regain his composure, but I realized how drained he was.

"Then... where will we go?" I asked.

"Dhanush Palayam."

I looked at him in astonishment.

He was asking me to drive into the militants' lair!

Eleven

Krishnan motioned me to stop the jeep. Automatically, I applied the brakes, shifted gear to neutral and cut the engine. My mind too had ceased to function.

We were near Dhanush Palayam, forty kilometres from Madras. We sat still for a few minutes in total darkness. The starry sky above loomed as if an eternal curse. Occasional trucks roared by, their headlights lighting us as they passed.

In the distance, we could see the street lamps of the township making a feeble attempt to illuminate the streets. Dogs barked, accelerating the series of barking in the vicinity. Rows of trucks stood by the roadside where they had halted for the night.

I touched Krishnan's arm. The touch startled him out of his reverie. He sat erect and said, "We must move now."

"Alright," I said and was about to start the jeep when he stopped me.

"No, let us abandon this here. We don't want to be noticed."

"As you say, *Tambi*..."

We got out of the vehicle and began walking towards Dhanush Palayam.

Darkness was melting with the gradual advance of dawn and the crescent moon gradually faded in the coming daylight. Our tired legs gradually increased pace.

Krishnan reloaded his revolver without a pause and thrust it back into his hip pocket. After the series of earth-shattering events, my fears and anxieties had now sunk deep within me from where they could bother me no more.

I was curious.

"What are we up to?" I asked in a flat tone.

"The most unexpected," he muttered mysteriously.

I grew even more curious.

"You must tell me," I insisted.

"They do not know as yet that we have survived their attack. It will be morning before they come to know that we have once again escaped. They'll then be thinking that we are running away, scared to death. They'll be looking for us but won't know where. It will infuriate them and cause confusion. But before they know we are still alive, I want to sabotage their secret centre in this town. I know its location for I was the man who installed the advanced communications system here."

His sinister motive shocked me. I stood still.

"No Krishnan... we can't do this. They will simply kill Janaki if they know what we've done."

"We have already done many a thing to make them angry enough to kill Janaki a thousand times over," he said in a cold voice. "Even if we don't attack, they have reasons to kill Janaki. Believe me, I am doing all this to protect her... at least till we reach her."

The reasoning did not sound convincing enough to me. I was confused.

"Venu, try to understand me. I have been with the Tigers for years. I know how they react to attempts to disregard them. I know, we too are in danger... Janaki is in danger. We have no friends to help us. They are hurt. We have caused major damage to their reputation. Think, Venu... think."

"Leave me alone," I said flatly, "I have saved your life. Now you can go anywhere you wish. I will go back. Let them do whatever they want with me. At least, they will release Janaki. My seed is growing in her womb. Even if I die, I will grow within her and will see the world again with the fresh innocence of a newborn. Let me go alone."

As I started in the opposite direction in a frenzy of emotions, he held me back.

"You are a fool, Venu," he shouted at me. "You'll be dead before you can even start to plead with them. Janaki too will be dead. None of you, including your child will ever see this world again if you act on some foolish impulse. I implore you, do not go. Let's be united, only then there is a chance that we can save her life."

I looked helplessly around. The erupting volcano of emotions within me held back by his words, the man responsible for my plight. I did not know how to react and what to do.

"Okay." I had resigned myself to the fate, "But if anything happens to her, mark my words, you bastard, I will kill you."

"Fine. Kill me, if I fail," he assured me. "Now, let's move on before the town awakens."

Krishnan led the way, with me following him in silence.

We crossed the highway, where the illumination was weak and from there ducked into a dark alleyway.

Krishnan bent down and whispered, "We are just behind that godown. Let us go and see how well it is guarded."

I looked in the direction he pointed. A huge structure stood in the dark like a sentinel. I sensed no existence of any living soul around it.

But Krishnan crouched and slowly crossed the alley and pressed his back against the wall of the godown. I followed his motions.

"Now, you walk along the wall to the front. If you see any watchman, hit him hard enough to allow him to rest for a while with no botheration to us."

I moved forward. My heart was thumping against my ribs. For a moment I felt I would loose consciousness. But some unknown force kept pushing me ahead.

Through the narrow pathway, I crossed the long wall and stood still at the corner. I closed my eyes and prayed. Then I bent slightly to see the front portion, which was badly illuminated with a small bulb.

A young watchman sat dozing there.

I looked back. Krishnan was not to be seen. Dawn was approaching at an alarming pace. The sound of speeding trucks on the highway grew even more frequent.

I looked around in the hope to finding something, which I could use as a weapon. I grabbed a stone lying nearby and held it tight in my sweaty palms.

I glanced at the watchman who dozed oblivious to the approaching danger.

I braced myself and then gathering all my strength leapt forward and hit the stone on his skull real hard.

The guard gave a loud moan and fell on the ground with a wild shudder. A rifle that lay on his lap too fell to the ground with a clatter. I collected the firearm and looked all around trying to make sure that no one had heard anything. Blood racing in my veins made me almost crazy.

Then remembering Krishnan's instructions, I bent down and fumbled for the keys.

I found the bunch.

"Open the door..."

An order was shot at me.

I rushed to the huge door and tried the keys. The lock opened. I furiously slid the bolt and opened the door.

"Push the watchman in or someone will see him."

The alarming order made me even more active.

I rushed back to the unconscious watchman and dragged his lean body in. I tried to control my labored breathing.

Sanjay Sonawani

"Good job," muttered Krishnan under breath.

It was a typical godown, full of gunny bags and a peculiar smell, nauseating and yet familiar.

"Get in."

As if well acquainted with the arrangement, Krishnan led me in.

He stopped near a locked door.

"This leads to the basement," he murmured. "Down there, must be at least three-four guys busy with the usual communications."

He knocked the door in successive, deliberate, intervals, as if relaying a coded message.

"Be alert," he whispered, as we heard footsteps approaching the door.

I leapt back and crouched in anticipation of danger.

Krishnan stood still in front of the door.

"Who?" A weary voice sounded through the closed door.

"Prabhakaran is the sun of tomorrow," announced Krishnan.

"Okay." I heard the voice say from inside, followed by the sound of the bolt being moved.

Krishnan held his revolver ready.

As soon as the door opened, he fired. The shriek of a wounded man resounded for a brief moment followed by a commotion down in the basement.

Krishnan again moved back.

I heard a frenzy of activities and rapidly approaching footsteps. I held the rifle tight and tried to take aim. But how ignorant was I in handling firearms. I simply did not know how to use a rifle.

I could hear intermittent firing. Krishnan lay flat on the ground taking pot shots into the basement. Then there was silence, as if I was the only living creature left on earth.

I got up. Krishnan too stood up and started to descend the staircase to the basement. I followed him.

The basement was not more than 15 by 20 feet. In one corner, was a foldaway bed, few bottles of unfinished liquor and in another corner, on a table, was the most sophisticated transmission system I had ever seen. On the walls hung weapons, amidst a large portrait of Prabhakaran.

The scene was shocking. It was amazing how deeply the enemies had penetrated the system.

Krishnan hurried forward and placing his revolver on the table sat down before the system. He donned the headphones and began pressing various buttons. I stood still, unable to fully comprehend what we had done and what sinister outcome could befall us. Then Krishnan began speaking into the microphone in some strange language. In an impulse, I placed the rifle on the floor and selected a revolver from those that hung on the wall. I did not know what Krishnan spoke. I did not know what awaited us out there in the daylight. But I now had a weapon that I could manage.

As soon as Krishnan finished with his strange communications, he shut down the system, took off the headphones and stood erect. He gathered the revolver in his right hand and fired point blank at the transmitter. Sparks crackled from the system and after a while silence established its rule once again. The transmission system was as dead as the men Krishnan had fired at.

I stood still, expectant and yet not knowing where all these incidents were going to lead us.

"This is the only powerful transmission system the Tigers have in this region. I had established the system for accurate and immediate communications. The Government of India can never locate these systems for we applied our brains while setting them up. All the instructions regarding the assassination of Rajiv Gandhi were received here and then passed on to the executioners. We have destroyed it. Now, at least for a few hours, they will have no means available to know what is going on."

"I've just informed them, in our code language that we are dead. To forward this information to the LTTE high command it will take them a few hours and the confirmation of the message will take even more time than that. Now let us move," he said and shoved his revolver in his hip pocket.

We traced our footsteps back into the open under the early morning sky.

It was almost quarter to five in the morning. People had begun to awake. We locked the door and tossed the bunch of keys in the gutter and approached the highway, as if nothing had happened.

"We must reach Madras at once," Krishnan said in an urgent voice.

I looked at him in bewilderment.

"Janaki is in the custody of Varadrajan. I have received

certain instructions that verify this," said Krishnan.

"I've informed them that we were killed and burnt to ashes. They told me to give a counter message to Varadrajan to do away with Janaki. You see, they don't know as to who received the message. The people sitting in Sri Lanka don't know all the names of their activists down here. But Varadrajan is a sort of a leader and he knows everything. We cannot fool him. We simply cannot communicate with him; he would at once sense some irregularity and get suspicious. That would be dangerous."

I tried to gauge his reasoning, but failed for never in my wildest dreams, could I imagine how these demons reacted.

"We must reach Madras. At once!"

"But..."

"What now?" Krishnan asked, irritated.

"The owner of the godown will know what has happened to the communications system. And there are many dead bodies down there in the basement. We cannot suppress this, you know? The police will be on high alert after this. And they will just kill my Janaki."

"Don't be stupid," he yelled at me. "They won't know. In such incidents, who shall contact whom is carried out typically following the rulebook. They simply cannot bypass the regulations. We have got a few hours, and before that we need to reach Madras. Is that understood?"

His voice silenced my doubts. After all, I had surrendered myself to destiny's cruel hands.

"It will take time for them to understand what we've done. They may even fail to attach any significance to the event, for they know we are just two and could not possibly have caused this havoc. They cannot take it too seriously, as they are confident of their power. This weakness we must capitalize on. We are on the right path. So far we've misguided them. And most important thing is that we know where to attack."

Reluctantly, I nodded in affirmation. I had to depend on his wisdom, for he was one of them until recently when they tried to kill him, and knew best how they functioned.

"How much do you know of Varadrajan?" He asked me in a hushed voice.

"I know nothing, frankly." The whole episode of our first meeting in middle of the night flashed before my eyes. "I know not who he is or what he does when he is not taking part in illegal covert activities. I simply met him because my contractor, Thyagarajan, told me to meet him. Now I blame myself why I did not neglect his message. Varadrajan had minutely explained me the consequences if I refused to accept their offer. My father was a militant and I did not know that being a son of a militant could be so dangerous. I'm not a strong man, Krishnan. I could not afford to act stupidly."

***

With the morning's first yawn we were on the highway. I looked all around. There were many trucks parked alongside the road. The eastern sky was lighting up. We could spot sleepy men, with water filled bottles or tumblers in hand, crossing the highway and slip behind bushes. The calmness of the morning was hurting, as we hadn't slept since the night before. My body was cursing me for stretching it beyond its limits of endurance.

"We need a vehicle to take us to Madras," Krishnan muttered. "We have to hijack a truck."

Sanjay Sonawani

I knew that was the only way we could get transportation.

Fear knotted my stomach making me uneasy. We were committing one crime after another. And there seemed no end to it until I had my Janaki in my arms and we both were far away from this crazy world.

I fixed my eyes on a truck parked just ahead of us.

I looked at Krishnan.

"Will do," he said.

I held the revolver tightly in my right hand and tiptoed to the front. I held the door handle with my left hand and through the window glanced inside. Krishnan kept watch on the road. The driver was curled up in deep sleep.

"Open the door and kick him awake," said Krishnan. He sounded cold and heartless.

I pulled open the door in one smooth swift action and fiercely shook the driver who muttered a few abuses and tried to shift his position.

"Kick him, Venu," Krishnan said urgently

I hit him with my left fist.

The driver, a frail looking man, sat up irritated. He shot a fierce glance at me, opened his mouth to shoot a mouthful of obscenities, but the sight of the revolver in my hand silenced him. Astonishment, then fear, made his eyes bulge out. Meanwhile, I had positioned myself beside him and pressed the revolver in his ribs. I motioned Krishnan to get in. Painfully Krishnan managed to climb into the cabin. As his left hand could not assist him close the door, he looked helplessly at me. I leaned over and pulled the door shut.

I turned to the gaping driver, speechless and horrified.

Sanjay Sonawani

Pity touched my soft heart, but an urgency of life and death forced me to become vicious.

"Start your truck and drive straight," I ordered him.

"But..."

I pressed the gun against his neck. "Say one word and you are dead."

"Who... are you?" He trembled.

"Start the truck," I hissed through clenched teeth; I'd turned vicious. In Madras, my wife was in the hands of murderous people. She was in danger and no other life could ever matter to me before her. I could set on fire this whole bloody world if something untoward was to happen to her. I could even press the trigger and kill this bastard right now if he refused to obey me.

He obeyed. He knew he had no choice. He was frightened. And no one wishes to encounter death when millions of dreams beckon them far away. And everyone wants to reach there, and so did he. He turned the ignition on. The engine roared and he pushed the gear with a trembling hand and pressed the accelerator.

I looked at the street coming alive to the soft early warm rays of the rising sun.

I thought, 'Soon they will know we have destroyed their communication centre. They will be outraged and like bloodhounds they will follow us. They will shoot us at sight and leave our bodies to be dumped in some cold morgue... what would happen to Janaki...and the baby.'

I shuddered at the thought. Merciless destiny had hit me hard. It had ruined my life. I cursed my father. I cursed the moment I was born. I was an outcast, an outlaw, a criminal. I was followed by untold dangers. I did not know how long my breaths would last. But, for now, I had to run. I had to try everything possible to save my love, whom I had promised to be with always, in good times and bad. I loved her. I could never abandon her.

The thought strengthened my resolve. If I was destined to die, why not embrace death fighting?

The truck was speeding towards Madras. The driver had his eyes fixed on the road ahead. He never turned to look at us nor posed us any question. He was in his late thirties sporting a ten-day stubble and a greasy vest and a worn out *lungi*.

" C...can I light a *beedi*, *Saab*?" He asked after a while.

"Go ahead," I assured him.

For the first time, I realized the power of a weapon - you can get done whatever you want.

By the time the sun started to cast its strong heat, we were on the outskirts of Madras city. The traffic was heavy with people hurrying about with unfathomable determination. The wind blew fast and cool through the window. Sleeplessness was now overpowering me. I desperately wanted to rest. But I knew there wouldn't be any sleep.

Madras was my town. It was where I was born, where I grew up, made friends and adversaries; fell in love and got love in return. This was the city where I took my first lessons of life, where I learnt to become a polite social being and I learnt to love my society, my caste, my religion and my nation. Where I learnt to respect those great souls who had sacrificed their lives for the well-being of this nation and for mankind, and those who preached solidarity and non-violence.

This was the city where, like all other young men, I too devoted myself for the prosperity of my family. Where I worked hard and tried to earn more and more, through legitimate means. This was the city where I had dreamt of living a happy life into a graceful old age and a painless death.

But was really there such a society as I had thought of? Weren't there people like Thyagarajan and Varadrajan around, hidden behind the mask, ready to destroy the system they lived in? Weren't there bastards who made lives of innocent people like me miserable? Haven't they uprooted our well-nurtured beliefs? Had they not also learnt all the things that I did, from the same society? Then why on earth did they behave like cruel monsters?

Today, I was entering Madras city with a vengeance. Today, the sight of my beloved city did not soothe me. It was as if an alien town, never before seen, and yet known. My heart sobbed as I looked at the familiar streets we passed by. Unconsciously, I looked at Krishnan. He too looked completely exhausted.

"Where to?"

"To G.P.K.," he muttered.

I repeated his order loudly to the driver who accepted our destination with a nod; he had not yet recovered from the initial shock. He knew the roads of Madras and drove us towards our destination. G.P.K. was near Kamraj Memorial.

Krishnan was alert once again. He held the seat tight and

kept looking at the buildings we were passing by.

"Are you alright, Krishnan?"

He gave a slow nod.

I noticed pain in his tired face.

"You don't move. Just tell me where I have to go and I will do whatever has to be done. You are not in a position to strain yourself anymore."

"No. I am alright," he said in a weak voice. "We will finish the work together, don't worry."

Krishnan had high fever. Though the bullet had passed through his back, I was afraid that the wound would get infected. He also needed rest. His strength had drained out. He was just hanging on...trying hard to be awake...and alert. I felt great pity for him. But I really did not know what we were up to and for guidance, at least, I needed him badly.

Within twenty minutes, we were near Kamraj Memorial.

I told the driver to stop.

He obediently found his way through the vehicular traffic and brought the truck to a halt in a corner.

Getting off the truck I threw at him a hundred rupees note and said, "Thanks, and sorry for the inconvenience."

He said nothing, only nodded his head violently.

Krishnan too got down.

It was almost eight thirty in the morning. An occasional cool breeze brought relief from the humid atmosphere. It was going to be a hot day.

"Let's discuss our strategy," he said, leading me to the beautiful memorial.

"I know who Varadrajan is. I've met him a few times for

his assistance. He is an influential man down here, having close contacts in the Ministry. He had helped me in locating a safe place to install the communications system. Now, he is the man who rules over the militants here. A bastard, no doubt, but a trusted man in the higher echelons of the LTTE. He arranges to hide and smuggle out militants. A hardcore LTTE man living behind the facade of a gentle and faithful citizen. The attack on us must be his idea. We must get to him. His office is just in the next lane."

"But it must be closed right now."

"I know," Krishnan said in a hoarse whisper, biting back the pain that gripped him as he tried to straighten his wounded hand. "He must know where Janaki is. In fact, she must have been abducted on his direction."

"But how can we reach him? If he is as dangerous as you have described, he must be well protected."

Krishnan gave a scornful laugh.

"Of course, he is well protected, but in a different sense. He cannot deploy an army to guard his life. He has to show that he is just an ordinary citizen, not an outlaw, who needs ramparts all around him. He cannot afford to act that foolishly. Therefore, he is not as safe as you think he is."

"What do you mean?" I asked warily. A shadow of worry was overpowering me. I could not imagine attacking Varadrajan's residence in broad daylight. It would most certainly mean our deaths or arrest. It could not be a safe approach to solve the problem.

"Simple," he said, in a low voice. "He is protected by his facade. Not by armed men surrounding him round the clock. He has secured his life through the contacts he has established in the ruling class. But, still, we cannot risk entry into his house and fall into some trap. In the next alley, right there, is his office. I know because I've visited it once before. We need to be careful. He is the only man who can lead us to Janaki. No, he is the person who will have her delivered to us safely. Hence, we need to lure that bastard out of his lair and into our hands. We can then use him as a shield to get Janaki back, understood?"

I nodded silently. His plan was difficult to digest. I knew Madras as a monstrous city, not a place where one could do anything and get away safely. The police was everywhere and so was Varadrajan's little army of hardcore militants. We two could not possibly make a perfect attack that could save Janaki and us as well. I tried to think of some other option, but failed. I had no choice now, but to rely on the wit of a wounded, semi-iconscious man.

"I am thinking how we can entice a rabbit in our snare and use it as our shield.... Varadrajan is that rabbit. We must get him out of the safety of his home and out in the open where no one will suspect what we are up to."

I nodded again with quite understanding how we were going to force him out of his castle.

"Are you ready?" He asked.

I nodded. I had no choice but to follow his instincts.

"Varadrajan is far from being harmless. He is a shrewd and cunning beast. The moment he knows that we are on the run he will have increased vigilance. We, therefore, must accelerate the chain of unexpected happenings, only then we can achieve our aim. Is that clear?"

I nodded again, for the want of any better idea.

"Tell me, what we are going to do?"

"Right now, Varadrajan will be at his home, unaware of the fact that we have fought back his vicious people and they are dead and that the communication centre is no more functional and that we are alive and here in Madras. It'll be quite later when he comes to know what exactly happened. We have to use this time lead we have over him and act fast. We have no scope for speculation."

"As of now, they are well assured that we both are dead and pose no further threat to them. And we also have time, as he is not the person to decide as what to do with the hostage they hold. They will wait till they receive instructions from Sri Lanka and we know what the orders are going to be, okay?"

I nodded my acceptance to his logical thinking.

"Fine. Now tell me, how are we going to lure that bastard out of his house?" I asked.

"Look, it's almost nine a.m. now. He, even in his wildest dreams, cannot imagine that we are alive and here, in Madras. They have another communications system in Coimbatore and they will have to use it when they come to know that the other centre is dead. We have time until then. So let's capitalize on it."

He finished his sentence emphatically.

"Okay. But what are we going to do?" I asked, impatient to get on with the execution of our plans.

"Janaki is in their custody and Varadrajan is the leader of

the people holding her."

"Come on, Krishnan. All that I know," I said in an irritated tone. "Tell me, how are we going to get hold of that dirty rat, Varadrajan?"

For a few moments, Krishnan kept on looking at me without batting an eyelid. A firm decision was embodied on his face.

"There is a petrol pump near by. Go and buy five litres of petrol, a funnel and a rubber pipe. If pump attendant gets curious and asks, tell him that your scooter has stalled on the way. Hurry up now. I'll wait for you in the end of the alley. Do it fast. Come on, move...now." He shot an order at me.

I was confused, but still I moved quickly.

Yes. Just a few blocks ahead I read the sign 'Hindustan Petroleum'. Before that, at a provision store, I bought a can, a funnel, and a length of tube and ran towards the pump. It was almost quarter to nine. Time was running out.

It took almost five minutes to get the can filled. Handing over a hundred-rupee note to the cashier, I impatiently waited for him to return the change and as soon as I had it, ran to the alley Krishnan had indicated earlier.

He was there waiting for me.

As I joined him again, he began to move towards the other end, making sure I followed him.

The alley opened on Ennore Street, which by now had got a little busy with all the rushing cars, autos, two-wheelers and pedestrians. It had become hot and sweat was rolling down from our aching bodies. Our hearts were beating violently against the rib cage.

We turned right and walked casually. No one seemed interested in us. Just a few curious glances. I wondered what if someone knows who we were?

I did not know what Varadrajan did for a living, besides being a director of a local bank and heading the local LTTE outfit. Here somewhere was his office. It was too early to find his office open or his presence there; most commercial outfits open not before quarter to ten. Even in my wildest thoughts, I could not imagine what we were up to. But I was now too scared to ask.

I carried the can of petrol carefully. With the haversack on my back, I felt as if I was Atlas lifting the earth on my shoulder; too much burden for me...unbearable.

We approached a tall building. Krishnan abruptly slipped in through the small gate which stood open. I followed him, his Man Friday. Marble steps led us to a wide porch and then to a staircase on the left. The lift was switched off. There was no sign of any activity in the vicinity as yet.

"Third floor...Varadrajan Syndicate," he whispered.

We climbed the stairs. This was not going to be easy. The overpowering silence in the vacant structure cracked under the sound of our footsteps on the marble flooring.

On the third floor, the huge corridor seemed like an anaconda, ready to swallow us alive. I wished I could lie down and embrace the deep eternal sleep of death and forget that we were ever alive.

"Hurry up, Venu," Krishnan hissed.

His sharp tone shook me. We were in front of a closed door on which a brass plate announced it to be the office of Varadrajan Syndicate.

"Push the rubber tube through the gap... slowly...ensure the other end reaches inside."

I followed Krishnan's instructions mindlessly.

The tube was flexible enough to push through the narrow gap at the bottom of the door.

I had begun to comprehend what his plan was - we were to set fire to that bastard's office.

Krishnan gave a satisfied nod and instructed, "Now, fix that funnel at this end and pour in the petrol...hurry up...any moment now the cleaners will start coming in."

I poured the petrol carefully. Then when the fuel almost touched the bottom of the can; I pulled out the tube, poured the rest of it on the door. Within a few moments I was through with the task. My body was taut with excitement.

Krishnan retreated a few steps and produced a lighter from his pocket. A sharp flick on the knob and a flame appeared. In the soft yellow glow, he looked like some vicious animal. He then took a deep breath and threw the lighter at the door. The petrol caught fire instantly. The flames sneaked inside the office where an even larger pool of petrol was waiting to get into action.

Krishnan gave a satisfied nod.

"Now, let us get out fast and find a telephone."

I said nothing. We had just torched a building. It would take no time for the fire to spread everywhere, first in the adjoining offices and then the whole building. We had become arsonists, too.

I could hear the hissing sound of the fire as it blazed. It sounded like a wounded serpent, coiling and uncoiling in rage, ready to strike.

We reached the ground floor. I glanced at my wristwatch... 9.15 a.m.

Now to find a telephone.

"Call that bloody swine - you'll find his number in the directory. Tell him you are calling from the fire brigade and that his office is on fire. He will rush here immediately. He won't realize that this could be a trap."

I looked at Krishnan in astonishment. He was wounded but he was thinking logically. He was accelerating the confusion within the militants' camp. They could never imagine that two men on the run would walk into their well-protected castle.

I nodded in assurance. We were now back on the street. For the people there, the fire was sheer ecstasy, as they gathered around shouting and pointing at the third floor of the building. I turned around to look. As yet the windowpanes had not shattered, but I could see thick smoke trying to escape through every opening it could find.

"Quick, Venu," Krishnan called in a weak voice.

Though I felt completely drained and was on the verge of collapse, I followed his instructions and rushed to find a telephone. Where the hell could I find one?

Twelve

After a few blocks, I found a shop where a yellow board read: 'Local calls - Rs.2 each'. The shopkeeper was an old, uninterested sort of man, who just waved his hand towards the instrument placed at another end of the counter when I asked to make a call, and continued with his morning newspaper.

"I need a telephone directory," I asked in an urgent voice.

The shopkeeper lifted his head from the newspaper and with a grimace, pulled out a thick, tattered directory from the lower shelf and shoved it at me and then sat back again to read the item that caught his fancy.

I wildly rifled through the pages trying to find the name S. Varadrajan. There were numerous Varadrajans listed there, but as I knew the exact address, it took me only a moment to locate the right number.

'Will he believe in the call?

Will he rush here with no protection?

What if he verifies the information with the fire brigade?' I was gasping as my mind thrashed about violently with bizarre thoughts.

I frantically dialled the fire brigade first.

The call, after endless rings, was received by a heavy male voice.

"Fire Brigade."

"There is fire at Shehnaz building, on Ennore Street." I tried to sound urgent and genuine. The shopkeeper put down the newspaper and looked up interested.

The fire brigade personnel shot a few questions at me, some of which I answered and then banged the receiver on the cradle and wiped the sweat from my forehead.

I remembered Varadrajan's number. I was gasping for breath and my body was bathed in sweat. Every cell of my body was taut. I remembered the meeting with Varadrajan. Would he know it was me who called? Would he be able to recognize my voice? But time did not permit me the luxury of waiting to answer self-raised questions. I would be an idiot if I failed in my mission. I had to convince that bastard that his office was ablaze and that his immediate presence at the site was necessary. I could not afford to raise any suspicion in that shrewd son of a bitch.

I took a deep breath and dialled his number.

My heart was pounding in my chest missing an occasional beat. Sweat dripped from my palms. The throat had dried υρ...

Sanjay Sonawani

The call was received.

I heard the maid's pleasant voice.

"Get me Mr. Varadrajan," I snarled.

"Who is on the line, please?"

"Police." I tried to keep my voice flat.

The shopkeeper became suspicious.

I looked away from him.

"Just a moment..." The maid said politely.

Again the wait... I furiously tried to find the appropriate words to announce such information...

"Yes?" Varadrajan's husky, assertive voice hit my eardrums. This was the bastard who had forced me into this maze of uncertainty. He was the one who had ripped my life to shreds. He was the pig that had gorged on my soul.

"Control Room, Sir," I tried to sound normal and disassociated. "Just now we were informed by the fire brigade that your office has caught fire."

There was a long pause. It increased my anxiety.

"When did it happen?" He sounded shocked, which relieved me.

"A few minutes ago, I suppose," I told him. I could imagine how flabbergasted he would be.

"Fire brigade is on its way."

"Who is calling...your name?"

"Pillay... Shankar Pillay, Sir."

"Thanks for the information, officer."

I hung up satisfied. But would he show up, I wondered? The shopkeeper had become suspicious by now, for he had heard me giving a fake identity. But at that very moment an explosion deafened the atmosphere, people on the street ran to shelter, few vehicles collided with each other and a frenzy changed the color of the peaceful morning. The old man's suspicion turned suddenly to fear. He jumped up and with just a glance at me rushed towards the street pavement. I had done what I could. Exhausted, but satisfied, I ran to where Krishnan was waiting for me.

Krishnan stood at the corner where an excited mob had gathered at a safe distance from the burning building, jamming up vehicular traffic on the streets. Shouts, advise, suggestions and orders were being thrown about amongst them while they watched in wonderment as the fire engulfed the building, each trying to soak up all the sights and sounds keeping an alert ear for all the rumors they could spice up and narrate authoritatively later on to their colleagues, family and friends.

I looked at the building. It was an inferno. Flames were spreading like an epidemic. Fiery explosions shattered the windowpanes and the heat competed with the sun overhead.

I was doubtful whether Varadrajan would come personally. We had created enough drama with the hope of luring him out in the open. Only if he fell into our hands, would I see Janaki again.

Janaki, my love, where are you? Where have these bastards hidden you? Are you safe?

The next moment two fire fighting water tenders arrived at the spot with their sirens wailing, followed by a police van.

In the presence of the frenzied mob and the police, we had blatantly set ourselves to kidnap Varadrajan!

We waited in desperate anticipation. The mob was now

like a unified monster with its thousands of heads shouting and screaming. Yet, I was deaf to it.

The uniformed men in yellow helmets set about their job. Hoses were unwound from the fire engines and collapsible stairs were erected as near as possible to hose down the inferno. Water was pumped at high pressure in and on the building. The hissing sound became even more frightening - a tumult between fire and water, each trying to assert itself. The traffic police had an uphill task diverting the flow of vehicles.

Suddenly, Krishnan held my hand. I followed his glance.

It was Varadrajan, arriving in his car, looking shocked, obviously.

"Bend your head down. If he see us before we reach him, we will never get him."

My eyes searched for him. He sat rigid at the wheel trying to steer his vehicle through the screaming crowd. Parking anywhere nearby would be impossible. He was trying not to look at the raging fire.

Varadrajan's sight drove me crazy. The pounding in my chest ceased and blood became as cold as Arctic ice. All anxieties and pressures of life were blown away in an instant. I reached for my revolver and rushed forward. No one took any note of me - all eyes were glued to the towering flames.

Varadrajan had moved ahead a bit and was looking at the distressed state of the building. He was shouting loudly at the crowd to clear the road for him to pass through.

Just like Arjun in the Mahabharat, I saw only him and no one else. He was the bastard who had pushed me into the black hole of misery. How could I forgive him for what he had done to my life? And my love was in his clutches. Her life too was in danger.

I pushed aside the crowd violently and rushed towards him with the revolver in my hand. I did not give a damn to the observers. Krishnan followed me.

Varadrajan had found a gap between the sidewalk and the milling crowd to park his car. He was about to open the door and step down.

Krishnan moved forward and in one smooth motion kicked the door shut and signalled me to get into the car from the other side. I followed his signal and before Varadrajan could shout for help, I pressed the revolver to his neck.

"A word and you are dead, you bastard," I hissed.

Krishnan too quickly opened the front door and got in.

I felt Varadrajan stiffen. He gave Krishnan a helpless look.

"Start the car and follow my instructions," Krishnan shot his order in a cold voice.

"W...Who are you?"

"No questions, or you die."

"But..."

It was the end of my patience. I pulled his hair viciously - "You bastard, drive the car."

Without another word, Varadrajan turned the ignition on and, trying not to commit any fatal mistake, slowly waded the car through the anxious crowd and turned into an alley.

"Who are you?" He asked, meekly.

Krishnan did not answer.

Suddenly, Varadrajan collected himself as he realized what must have gone wrong. His body stiffened and he shivered in cold fury. In a flash, his look turned to that of a vicious savage and then unwillingly surrendered to the grim reality that faced him. He tried to clear his throat, but failed.

"What you are going to do with me?" He asked with recollected bravado. "It all is your mistake. You proved untrustworthy, treacherous. Why you are after me now? It's of no use. Even if you kill me, you cannot avoid the inevitable, my friend. You shouldn't have come here and done all this nonsense. It is not going to help you in any way."

Krishnan said nothing. He kept on looking intently at the ashen face of the old man who was wicked enough to play bloody games with innocents.

The situation was maddening. I did not know what are we going to do to extract information from such a hard core person.

"You burnt my office. You set the whole building ablaze. You have gone insane," he said, in an aggrieved tone. "If you wanted any explanation, you should have contacted me."

I wanted to laugh at him. He was ingenious. He was acting as if he was a grandpa consoling naughty kids.

"I will burn you alive, if need be," Krishnan retorted.

How much Krishnan had changed in the short course of time. His moves were cunning. His actions quick, suitable of a militant. He knew of no soft approach to his enemies. 'Give no chance to your enemies to think,' he had said in the jungle, 'and no time to act on it!' I never saw him so excited since we had met on the trawler. He was wounded and, because of the pain, had not slept even for a minute. Nevertheless, he did not complain. His mind was as strong as that of a militant. He thought and acted meticulously - he had surprised our enemies.

"Take us towards the Integral Coach Factory," Krishnan ordered.

Varadrajan took a left turn at the next crossing.

"Now answer my questions, one by one," said Krishnan in an emotionless voice.

My heart leapt. I knew what Krishnan was going to ask.

"I know nothing, Krishnan," Varadrajan protested. "I am a very small fish in the pond - you know that, Krishnan. You have got the wrong person. I am just an old man, devoted to the cause. You know that I simply follow the orders. Why ask me questions? Please, let me go."

I looked at Krishnan. I wanted to tell him that this bastard was wasting our time. He knew everything - even where Janaki was confined. Krishnan seemed to hear my thought.

"Tell me, where is Janaki?"

"Who Janaki?" Mimicked Varadrajan in surprise.

At this I lost my patience and leaping at him, I grabbed his hair and jerked him around violently. "You bastard, you don't know who Janaki is?"

The car swerved invoking violent reactions from the passersby. I let him go.

"Just drive on, and don't stop," said Krishnan, impassively.

Varadrajan said nothing. With his left hand he ran his fingers through his disheveled hair.

"You must tell me, Varadrajan? Or the death I have planned for you will be so horrible that even the Gods in the heaven will shudder seeing it.

"Tell me, in the first place, why have you taken Janaki hostage? She is in no way related to our world of crime. You want to avenge me for a crime I have not committed - okay. If you want me dead, you can pursue your endless efforts to do that. Why Janaki?" Krishnan said in a calm, controlled voice that could send shivers in the heart of devil himself.

An unbearable silence followed. My vision blurred and my throat dried up. I was on the verge of committing murder. But, as yet I had to be patient, for I knew this was the only chance I had. Losing it would wreak disaster. I could meet my beloved again, only if we handled the situation rightly.

Would he tell us?

In his long drawn silence, Varadrajan was considering the gravity of the threats. He knew that the two of us, already under the shadow of death, could easily do away with him...and who is not afraid of death, after all?

"It was Thyagarajan's idea," at last, he mumbled. "I told him repeatedly to let her be and let us keep a watch from outside your home. It would have been more profitable, as I now come to think of it. We could have easily got both of you. But he was insistent, the fool. He reasoned that you will not return home if you found out that Janaki is safe. He wanted a bait and that could only be your wife. And how could we let you go when you have caused such great damage to the system; I had to admit that there was a point in his reasoning. So Thyagarajan employed his men and got hold of Janaki, moved her to a safe place, then planted his men in the house and tapped the phone to ensure that you returned to Madras

"He was sure that you would call. And you did. Then it was not difficult to find out from where it was made. We were damn sure, at least until now, that you both would not escape from our previous attempt to punish the two of you. But it seems you somehow outsmarted our people and now are after me."

"Where is Janaki?" Asked Krishnan.

"That I don't..."

Krishnan hit Varadrajan on the side of his head with a clenched fist.

Varadrajan cried out in pain and lost control over the car. Krishnan grabbed the wheel and kept the car going steady.

"Answer my questions. Dodge them once again and that will be your end. Have I made myself understood?"

Varadrajan nodded his head.

"Now, where is Janaki?"

"In George Town."

"Where exactly in George Town?"

"If I tell you that, Krishnan, it will be treachery and I am not a traitor...as you are."

"I've never been a traitor."

"Then why did Sivrasan have to consume cyanide? We lost a gem of a man because of you."

"Why do you think that I cheated on you?"

"That's something you should know better."

"What do you know, you son of a bitch?"

"We knew that you turned on us when you met Dorai Swami."

"I met him, but how can that mean that I turned on you?"

Varadrajan gave a scornful laugh.

Sanjay Sonawani

"Everybody knew that he was an undercover agent of RAW!"

Krishnan looked at him in shock.

"What? No, it can't be true." Krishnan was aghast.

"Yes. It's the truth. Dorai Swami, we knew, was an agent of RAW. But we never let him feel we were suspicious of him. We supplied him with misinformation. We always kept him on the wrong track. That was the reason why RAW always thought that we will execute *him* somewhere in the north. Not in an obvious place like Sriperambudur! We successfully off tracked the RAW and also the CBI via him. We manipulated the security lapses and meticulously executed our operation. But you failed us, Krishnan."

"But..."

Krishnan was obviously shocked to hear these outrageous details. "But I did not speak to Dorai Swami of anything concerning the assassination. And how do I know if you are speaking the truth? Why should I trust you? You people made me a scapegoat, isn't it? And by the way, where is Dorai Swami now? How did you know he was a RAW mole?"

"We knew of him from the day he joined us. We need such defectors who can supply information to their superiors, the misinformation we want to pass on so that they mobilize their efforts in the wrong direction. We occasionally make them happy by allowing them to capture a few of our militants who are of no use to us. It was so damn easy for us to pull wool over their eyes and carry out our major operations unobstructed. We have always succeeded in that. Right, Krishnan?"

Krishnan was speechless.

Sanjay Sonawani

"And do you know an interesting bit of news, Krishnan?" Varadrajan asked, benevolently, as if he was in control of the situation. "Till the day Sivrasan was captured dead, he was an invisible man even for us. No one except the top brass and you knew where he had taken refuge. Now we know that you were the man in charge to take care of his transportation and asylum. When we ourselves were in the dark about his whereabouts, the possibility that RAW, who all the time acts on inside information, could find him and Shuba was extremely remote. The obvious reasoning is you became a turncoat. You informed Dorai Swami about what was going on. That alerted RAW and naturally poor Sivrasan had to end his life in order to evade arrest and subsequent torture and save the organization the repercussions. We lost so many things with the death of him. Many people have been arrested since his death. There is fear everywhere and it's you who has caused it. We found out that you met Dorai Swami and came back to Madras and only a day after that, Sivrasan's hideout was surrounded by the police."

"Whatever you people feel I am not the man who blew the whistle on Sivrasan, okay? I don't know what makes you think I defected to Dorai Swami, a person whom I hardly know."

"Then why did you meet him?"

"It's a long story," said Krishnan in a deflated tone. "His brother was captured in Sri Lanka during the army attack. He himself contacted me and begged me if we could do something to pressurize the Sri Lankan army to release his brother. He knew I was a responsible man in the organization. He expected me to..."

Varadrajan let out a hearty laugh. "You fool, tell this crap to amateurs."

"I am telling you the truth."

Varadrajan did not try to control his filthy laughter. As soon as the waves of laughter receded, he said, "Dorai Swami never had any brother. He was the only son to his parents."

The shocking revelation stabbed Krishnan in the chest like a sharp knife.

I watched him turn ashen and his lips twitched in anguish.

"But why would Dorai Swami lie to me?" He asked in a pained voice.

"That," said Varadrajan, triumphantly, "Only you know. Dorai Swami could not contact you unless he knew exactly who you were. For him, we always kept your identity intact. We could not afford to let him know who you were."

"But he did contact me," Krishnan protested.

The conversation was not at all proceeding on the right track. It worried me. Krishnan was getting upset. The sides were reversed, as though Krishnan was now the captive. It bothered me. Any moment now, his emotions could explode and he would bump off Varadrajan. It was immaterial now as to why they thought he was a traitor. The question was how were we to rescue my wife, Janaki, from their clutches?

Tears rolled uncontrollably down my cheeks. "We don't have time, Krishnan. Don't try to prove your innocence to him, for heaven's sake, it's a waste of time. They won't ever trust you. And even if they did, we have caused them enough damage by now as not to allow us to go unharmed. Please, ask him, where Janaki is," I begged.

Sanjay Sonawani

But Krishnan was deaf to my pleadings. He stared at Varadrajan as if in a trance, his became face white as a sheet of paper. I had never seen him like this before. Even under the shadow of death, he had always maintained his poise. What had happened to him now?

"Krishnan!"

"Someone has framed me, Venu. Someone has played a dirty trick on me...I swear," he replied, after a while, looking me directly in my eyes, his own ablaze in anguish.

"Ah!" Exclaimed Varadrajan mockingly, enjoying his temporary superiority, and forgetting for the moment that he was in our custody.

Krishnan squeezed his eyes shut in a silent bid to control the erupting volcano in his heart, then, with a deep breath, said, "Let's go to George Town. We want Janaki. And you, you'll bring her to us."

Varadrajan said nothing and for a long while drove silently towards George Town.

"This is absurd," he said, finally. "I have no authority over Thyagarajan, Krishnan.... You know it. They'll let you kill me but won't release her under any circumstance. You are putting your as well as my life in danger. She is safe until you both are roaming free and alive. The day they come to know that you cannot be captured or killed only then they might release her. It would be better if you got out of this city and found a safe haven. Place your trust in destiny and hope that death doesn't approach you."

"I know your ways of functioning, so shut up. You know where she is, and you will take us to her. Then, we'll decide

Sanjay Sonawani

what to do with you."

"The place where she is kept is well protected, Krishnan. And I can see from your faces that you both have not slept for a long time and are starving. Under the circumstances, you cannot fight, and neither can you use me as a shield to get in there, because I too cannot get in there without prior instruction and approval from the high command. You all would simply be blown to bits along with her. Those are the instructions to everybody...try to understand."

"I know," said Krishnan thoughtfully, adding, "Tell me the address."

"Fourth street. B-54, if at all you want to put yourself in danger. As for myself, I am an old man who has seen enough of life - I have lived for the cause."

"How many men?" Krishnan asked, paying no heed to his plight.

"At least twenty."

"Why? You believed that we were dead, then why such tight security?"

"We always believe in taking precautions. Come on, Krishnan, you know that!"

"Yeah! It was just yesterday that I joined your filthy organization," retorted Krishnan with a sneer.

Varadrajan preferred to remain silent rather than invoke Krishnan's ire with some stupid comment.

"Where's Thyagarajan now?"

"How should I know?"

"You'll call him."

"No, why should I?"

"You will obey me, you old fool. You say that you are not afraid of death, but I can see in your eyes how afraid you are. Trust me, I will execute all my threats to extreme accuracy if you don't phone him. Got it?"

"I'll do it. But it won't yield what you want."

"That's my problem."

"Alright, I'll phone," Varadrajan mumbled.

I did not know why Krishnan was considering contacting Thyagarajan instead of forcing this big fish in our attempt to rescue Janaki. But then, I didn't in the least know how the LTTE functioned. For me, Thyagarajan was some petty contractor dealing in fish trade. And Varadrajan, a LTTE supremo.

But Krishnan was no fool. He knew their ways inside out. He seemed confident about what he was doing. Thyagarajan might be an important man, at least in this case, I summed up. Would he release Janaki, if Varadrajan phoned him up? The question pounded my heart, accelerating many more counter-questions.

"You will stop the car when I instruct you to and then you'll get down. No bravado or else you are a dead man. I'll be right behind you covering you with a gun. So just follow my orders as accurately as you follow Prabhakaran's. You people are fools. You have tried to sacrifice my life and now you are after innocent people. I won't let you do anything to her. No matter what happens to me. Still I have not contacted RAW. If I do and strike a deal with them, you all will land up behind the bars awaiting your death sentence. I have much valuable information that will certainly be of great interest to them. But I still have enough faith in the cause that I have taken up as my life's mission to put my life in danger instead of calling on the enemies, the RAW. However, rest assured, I could do it anytime."

Varadrajan reflected on Krishnan's sincere statement. "What do I tell Thyagarajan?"

I shot a glance at Krishnan in anticipation.

"You shall inform him that both, Krishnan and Venugopal, have been executed and therefore there is no need to keep Janaki in custody any longer. Got me?"

"He won't believe me. He will smell foul play. It's useless, Krishnan."

"He will believe you, trust me. I have already informed headquarters of our deaths - I hope you know that it's I who installed the communications system at Dhanush Palayam. I used the same system to pass on the information to them. So even if Thyagarajan needs confirmation, he'll have it."

Varadrajan looked at Krishnan in disbelief...

"You couldn't possibly have done that. We would have known if some unauthorized person had entered the centre."

"Your three goons over there are dead. The transmission system is destroyed after passing on the information I wanted to convey. There is no way how Thyagarajan can confirm the news until he comes to know what happened at Dhanush Palayam. And the fact is that they accepted the message of our deaths only because they were expecting such news. For now, we are dead for your bloody organization, so there is no reason why Janaki should remain in your custody. Ask him to release her at once and he will be more than happy to do so."

"And what if he does not release her?"

"Then until she is safely handed back to us, you will remain in our custody... Varadrajan, don't force my hand. Okay?"

Varadrajan nodded in the affirmative - he had no choice.

"You are insane," he muttered.

Krishnan gave an impassive smile.

Just then I saw a yellow board indicating 'Telephone booth' and pointed it out to Krishnan.

"Stop the car beside the booth," Krishnan ordered coldly. "And remember, I am behind you with the revolver. You just call Thyagarajan and say exactly what I have told you to and no tricks. Okay?"

Varadrajan nodded as he slowed the car to a halt next to the telephone booth beside the footpath. The booth was empty.

The air was hot and damp. Sweat beads appeared on my brow which no amount of wiping helped. Uneasiness filled my empty mind. Varadrajan slowly bent over the door, opened it in slow motion and stepped out in the blinding daylight. Krishnan too moved out of my blurred vision. My mind screamed to be alert, but numbness grasped me in its cruel clutches. I tried to focus my vision on the stealth movements of the two men moving towards the PCO. What was happening to me? Was it a sign of my surrender? Was sleep overpowering me? Or was it a nightmare that would soon be over and I would awake in the warm embrace of my beloved? I did not know. I shifted position and again wiped the gathering sweat from my face. I tried to concentrate on the booth, now occupied by both the men. Time was speeding up, making blurred imprints on my mind.

All of a sudden, I saw Krishnan sag and fall. I was shocked. I thought, Oh! God, we have lost, we have been outsmarted by those fucking bastards. Janaki, would I ever see her again.

In a flash, the thought of me separated from Janaki shook me wide-awake. I looked at Varadrajan's figure running away from Krishnan into the crowd.

Krishnan now stood erect, but his wound was open and bleeding, bereft of its dressing and his face contorted in unbearable pain.

But, no, we could not afford to lose that bastard, Varadrajan.

I pushed open the car door and, revolver in hand, ran after Varadrajan who was now trying to cross the road. Age was by my side and charged by the outrage, I ran fast after him.

Varadrajan looked back.

I saw the look of surprise on his face on seeing me with the revolver in my hand.

I pulled the trigger. The explosion brought the passing vehicles to an abrupt halt and some collided with each other as some drivers slammed their brakes. Fear overpowered the morning tranquility and peace. The mob ran helter-skelter. I saw Varadrajan stagger and fall, a trickle of blood staring to flow through his back where my bullet had struck him. He withered in the throes of pain. He was not dead.

Don't die you bastard…I need you, alive.

Then, police whistles sounded in the distance.

I looked helplessly at Krishnan walking towards the car.

"Hurry," he called weakly.

The police were approaching and the people around too had started screaming in hysteria. I wanted to take Varadrajan with us, alive…but in that very instant I knew we had lost the opportunity. My helplessness angered me.

This time I aimed at his head; if we could not take him with us alive, there was no reason why he should be allowed to further pollute the earth with his filthy presence, I squeezed the trigger. He gave a violent jerk and lay still. He was now just a body lying dead in a pool of blood on the road. I turned towards the car, weak...tired...angry...defeated.

"Drive the car," yelled Krishnan.

I threw the revolver on the back seat and jumped behind the wheel and sped like an arrow released from the bow.

I was drenched in sweat.

"Slow down, Venu," Krishnan said.

"Sorry..."

I could well imagine the reaction of the police. There had been a shoot-out in broad daylight. We had to abandon this car fast and find some shelter. The circumstances were certainly not in our favor.

I looked at Krishnan. The sight shocked me. His forehead had a deep cut, which was bleeding profusely.

"Does it hurt a lot, Krishnan?"

"Forget about me and concentrate on the road...we are being followed. Take a left into that alley ahead."

"Police?"

"No, it's a red Maruti car. They must be our dear friends whom we've been fucking so royally."

I stiffened. In the rear view mirror I could see the red car that Krishnan had noticed following us. It was maintaining a safe distance from us.

I looked at Krishnan desperately.

'This is going to be a deadly end of our desperate endeavor,' I thought. Krishnan was wounded and I was a novice in dealing with such a crisis. The LTTE or the police would certainly seize us. Either meant certain death. I was scared. How had the LTTE got to us so soon?

"He informed them," Krishnan answered my unasked question. "He did not speak as I had instructed him to. He hit me on my head with the phone, I stumbled and before I could recover, he finished with what he wanted to say and started running. These people are hard core militants, Venu, they don't bow before threats even that of death...

"I took a chance, Venu, but failed."

It was destiny playing cat and mouse game with us. Now that my tears had dried, only a feeling of detached vengeance and an acceptance of the naked reality was imprinted on my mind; how much can a person weep over his or her misfortunes?

We had approached Saint Thomas Square.

"Turn left and increase speed," instructed Krishnan.

Not caring a damn for the traffic, I spun the steering to the left. The tyres squeald and suddenly the statue of Saint Thomas was in front of us standing tall. The road was empty, except a few speeding vehicles. The red Maruti, too, followed us at a threatening speed. In a flash, I realized that the last battle would take place here.

"I can see a gun barrel stretching out of their window...they are about to shoot, Venu, take care."

What should I do? How do I save us?

The Maruti was now trying to come parallel to us. It was in full speed. Suddenly, I slammed the brakes and, with the screech of tyres, we came to a halt. The Maruti zipped past and before its occupants could realize what had happened, I spun the car around and sped in the opposite direction. My heart was crashing against the ribs violently and blood pounded in my head.

"They too have turned, but we have gained some distance. The only fear is that they are equipped with sophisticated weapons," continued Krishnan, like some cricket commentator.

I knew we were not safe, we could not be. We were simply trying to prolong our impending death, nothing else.

Again the statue of the benevolent Saint Thomas was in sight and a crowded road ahead. I was doubtful if they would attempt to fire at us in the crowded street, but soon I remembered the many shoot-outs that took place on such busy streets. Why would they spare us? We were their enemies. And then, an undefined feeling for vengeance filled my mind.

All of a sudden, I heard a crash. Certainly, there should be no cause for it, but I had heard the explosion. Then various colors flashed before my eyes. Gradually, the colors turned grey. My senses froze, but some hidden power forced me to pray-

'Oh God! Help me. Let me not loose consciousness.'

But God did not seem to hear my prayer. And I gradually slid into the cold embrace of unconsciousness.

The feeling assured me.

I was at peace.

Thirteen

There was quiet all around. A terrible whiteness enveloped me and it felt as cold as a morgue. It touched me with its icy fingers, caressing me.

'No, I don't want to die. I want to live for my beloved Janaki, to avenge those bastards who had pushed me into the crevasse of misery and agonies.'

I shut my eyes to escape the terrible scene. A redness began staining the canvas of my mind and fear clutched my heart with monstrous force.

What did that redness indicate? Was it a sign of my death?

I desperately wanted to run away from that ghastly scene. I wanted to be enveloped in a cocoon of calm and peaceful darkness, feel safe and protected. But the darkness did not favor me - it ditched me like an unfaithful friend. The whiteness and redness suffocated me. I wanted to escape, but, sharp as ice needles, it went on piercing me causing unbearable pain, and I could not scream.

The tormenting memories of the past suddenly came alive. The past and the present got caught in an unending fight, a battle that would only result in pain. I was suffering in the realms of death and life without end. I preferred death to these agonizing moments. Where was that blissful death? And if I was dead, then why this pain?

God! Why have you created life?

Janaki...where have they imprisoned you? I could not give you happiness. Fate should be ashamed for that moment when it graced my life with your existence. Why did it get us together?

I am a bastard... My father was a rogue... Wasn't his involvement with the terrorists responsible for the curse I am under? I have become a prey to his treacherous past.

I am afloat on the raging waves in the sea of pain.

But...these moments...this pain...

I cannot be dead.

I cannot see darkness...nor light...

Only the sticky redness...

God, in what state of existence am I...

Gradually, the heavy curtain of unconsciousness slid away. The stormy thoughts gently slipped into the vacuum of my mind.

I slowly opened my heavy eyelids. The curtain of mist was getting dispersed and I could make out some movement. I

Sanjay Sonawani

moved my eyes to see where I was. It was a room, whitewashed, not large, but enough to accommodate weird surgical equipment and the movement of the visitors. There was no picture on the walls. I did not understand where I was. A doctor stood by my side watching me intently. I turned my eyes to an old nurse shuffling the pages of a chart at the foot of the bed on which I lay.

Suddenly, Krishnan's image flashed on the tired horizons of my mind.

Where was he?

Had he survived the accident?

"He is improving," I heard the doctor confiding in the nurse. Then he bent over me and asked –

"Can you hear me?"

I tried to speak, but only my lips moved...there was no sound. My mouth was parched like a desert.

"Don't try to speak. Just give me a nod."

I nodded positively.

"Thank God," the doctor beamed.

I had many questions to ask, but I could not speak. I tried to move my left hand...thankfully, I could. But my right arm was as stiff as a board. With my left hand I touched my face. I was shocked. Whose face was that?

"Your face is swollen. However, the wounds are healing well," the doctor informed me.

What does he mean? How long have I been here on this bed?

Reasoning let me down, and again I got lost in the maze of irrelevant thoughts.

When I woke up next, my mind was calm. I opened my eyes and saw a dim bulb illuminating the room. I was alone. For a moment, my heart froze with fear. Where was I? I tried to listen, but there was a deadly quietness. I could only hear the whirring of the ceiling fan. I shut my eyes and tried to remember the moments of the accident, but my memory betrayed me. As if there never had been an accident, just a dream, a horrible dream which has left its mark on the canvas of my mind. I could not recall anything.

I must, in all probability, be in the hands of the LTTE. Then why on earth are they trying to save my life? Wouldn't they prefer to see me dead?

Where was I?

Where was Krishnan?

I turned my face towards the left wall. The small movement raked up a volcano of pain in my body. I closed my eyes and waited for it to subside.

Gradually, I opened my eyes once again. The white wall seemed to stand like a barrier between my awakening and the world I belonged to.

I looked at the switch that was hanging by my bed with an imprint of a bell over it.

Call bell...

For a moment a flood of wild expectations rushed to my mind. Should I press it? Who would answer?

Then reality dawned upon me. I had crossed a boundary and had entered an unknown world. It was immaterial knowing what awaited me next.

Sanjay Sonawani

I pressed the button.

The silent wait was agonizing.

Moments passed by.

I then heard the door creak open.

A young nurse entered the room. Her face was sleepy, but as she looked at me it became alert.

"Should I call the doctor? Are you feeling all right?"

"No," I uttered, the first word, after a long night of speechless existence.

"Do you want anything?"

I shook my head.

"Who brought me here?" I asked anxiously.

"Why think of that? You are safe here, and that should be enough."

"Where is my friend...?"

"He is alright...back in his senses. In fact, he is worried about you."

"Where am I?"

"Sorry, no more questions. You must rest now," said the young nurse making the sign of the Cross. She then checked my pulse and scribbled something on the chart.

"Is there much pain?"

"No... Not much. Sister, how long have I been here?"

The nurse looked at me patiently.

"Today is the eleventh day," she said softly.

"Eleven days!" I exclaimed in shock. "Oh God... my Janaki..."

"Don't get excited. It's a miracle that you are still alive. Thank God for that."

But I was anxious.

"At least, tell me where am I?"

"Sorry," she muttered, as though unhappy restricting information from me. "You have not yet recovered. It may take days or weeks before we can allow you to move around. But that you are alive is in itself a miracle, believe me."

She handed me few pills to swallow. For a few minutes, a perfect stillness took charge of me. I looked at her intently. She was dark complexioned, just like us Tamils, and possessed a well carved body of flourishing feminine self. She was of medium height with a slim waist that swelled to a luscious fullness at the hips. Through her tight uniform her breasts blossomed enticingly. Gradually, as I looked on, a gentle mist surrounded her beautiful frame making her look like an angel. Slowly the mist entered my eyes and enveloped me in its softness. The only thought that came to me then as I crossed the threshold of sleep was what if she had given me poison instead of medicine?

I was on the road to rapid recovery. At regular intervals, doctors and nurses would come, check me, and then retreat to their world of safety. I was now able to eat. It would pain me a little, but soon I got used to it. The deadly pain, like a terrible nightmare, was now far away from me. The stiffened body slowly accepted a little movement without giving me much pain. It was as if life was taking over once again.

As yet no one would speak to me much. Just casual talk about my pains, diet, etcetera. By now I was able to stand on my own feet without any support. But I could not walk beyond the doors as they were closed from outside. I tried to think who these people could be who had imprisoned me in this white cell. Even if they were the police, they wouldn't have brought us to such a hospital where secrecy would be so strictly maintained. I thought hard but no plausible answer came to me. I could not believe that it was a hospital of any kind. I could hear muffled sounds that indicated the presence of other people outside my room. I would broach the many questions that came to my mind with the nurse, but she would avoid the answers with a warm smile, as if she had taken a vow not to satisfy my curiosity.

I was weak, tired and frustrated. My wounds were nearly healed. A few teeth were absent from their usual place and my right arm was in a cast. I would walk around the closed room like an animal cursing one and all in a vain attempt to overcome my frustrations.

Soon, I found it difficult to breathe even for a single moment in the company of my agonizing thoughts, which would erupt at regular intervals. I would sometimes feel that I was in the hands of the militants who would torment me mortally. They would throw me once again in the ocean of calumny from which I had tried to escape, I feared.

And Krishnan, how was he? What about Janaki? Where was she? Was she still alive? I would dream of her suffering, of her bleeding corpse. I would open my eyes and find myself drenched in cold sweat. I would say to myself, 'Look Venu, you are alive and well even after that deadly accident. It was certainly a miracle. God really does exist, otherwise, how was it be possible that you killed the bloodhounds that were after you and are still alive? You have done nothing wrong in the past. You have always been helpful and kind to others. You have never sinned in your life. That's the reason you are still alive. God is with you. He will not let you suffer anymore. You will go back to your home where Janaki will be waiting for you. God has saved you and he will save Janaki, too! The consolation would then wither away at the cold touch of reality. I knew well, I was alive only because I had to suffer even more. I knew, as long as I was alive, the vengeful LTTE members would not rest. Till they find me, they will continue their chase. Some day or the other, my death is certain at their hands. How and where, is the only question. I had read many stories about the LTTE and their operations. These people, who were fanatic; enough ready to swallow cyanide if they feared arrest and could volunteer themselves as human bombs, could not be expected to be merciful to the man who had caused heavy damage to their organization. I sensed, they must be around, ready to swoop on me. The thought would frighten me... It would chill me.

I was alive. But being alive was not a blessing. It was just a coincidence. I was simply prolonging death from knocking on my door.

For now, I was left with only one choice - fight or die. Defeated souls think of suicide. I never thought of ending my own life. I was not a coward. Deep inside me there existed a warrior...

I had been left with nothing but a mind with scorched hopes. I had been robbed of my earlier straight, simple, happy life. Why had they forced me to take their bloody path? I never had any compassion for them and their cause. I had nothing to do with politics and the bloody games it involved. Yet, they had entangled me in a chain of inevitable incidents.

Sanjay Sonawani

Now to save myself, I would wage war against them. I would take revenge, such horrible revenge that even the angels above would tremble in fear.

This dialogue with the friend hidden inside me would make me feel strong. I would pace about in the room. This end to that end... one... two... three...determined steps, head down, mind alert. Don't think, just go on walking, till you are tired. Then go back to the bed and lie down. Stare at the white ceiling but try not to think. If at all you want to think, think of the diet, think of the food that they might serve you this evening. Try to talk to the doctor...You know very well that he won't speak about anything relevant to your detention, but you can talk to him about the weather outside; ask him whether it was a sunny day or a cloudy one! Ask him about his wife and kids, if he has any; he can talk at least that much. No harm in discussing family affairs; you can tell him how your wife is pregnant and you are expecting a son, and if at all Janaki delivers a daughter, she would be as beautiful as her mother. Your can speak to him about your flourishing business. How you are able to predict the weather by the color of the sea. You can speak as much as you want...

Then there is the nurse. You can speak to her too. You can ask her if she is married. If not, is there someone for whom her heart races? Does she live with her parents and how deeply she loves them? Is she happy with the present job, where she is restricted to be frank with her patients? Does she have to look after many patients like me? Is she tired? Does she attend church and pray to God regularly?

But how weak was the consolation. It would not soothe me. It would scream...it would deafen me... I would go on walking... one... two... three... infinity...sweat pouring from all sides. My wounds would cry for relief. And I would return back to bed exhausted. I would shut my eyes tight and try and forget that I was alive...

◆ ◆ ◆

Occasionally, I would get angry at Krishnan. I would clench my fists and abuse him loudly. Had that scum who boarded my trawler not been Krishnan but someone else, I would have kicked his butt off my trawler into the mouth of death and returned safely to Madras to collect my reward. My life would have been safe; my Janaki would have been in my arms. But for treacherous destiny. And who is capable of turning down its verdict?

I also knew, anger apart, I could never be so cruel as to throw Krishnan, or any other person for that matter, into the jaws of death. It was my weakness. I detested those who forced the humble people to bend before them only because they possessed the power. Who gave them the right to destroy the lives of others? After all, what eternal values were they fighting for? They were selfish. They desired power, and for the sake of their insane dreams, they had forced people to serve them. They were hungry wolves. Not mine alone, they had destroyed the lives of many others. Rivers of blood had irrigated the land. Why? For the race whose purity has vanished long ago? Today, which race can stake claim of its purity? But they stoked the deep sense of racial egoism inherent in the people. Masses are always blind. They accepted the philosophy, and such philosophies never value life, and the goals remain far away from the grasp of those who lost their lives for the cause.

We have always been afraid. Afraid of violence, power,

government, social values... This fear is well exploited by the scoundrels with a fair understanding of the human psyche. They capitalize on your fear and turn your life into a living hell. We never have enough courage to denounce them. How easily they play with other's lives! Where is humanity, after all?

They were masters of mass psychology. They profited from that knowledge. They encouraged violence. Ironically, they claimed that only violence could bring about peace! They made violence their profession. History is witness to this. Many rascals have come to power by preaching similar philosophies. Is this the same land where Mahavir, Buddha and Gandhi walked?

No. The creed of the enemies of society is spreading like an epidemic. They must be crushed before they cause further harm to the establishment. Let the rivers of blood flow - not that of the commoners, but of these bastards. Let them be shot dead in public. Let vultures feed on them.

How strange is human life. Since the day we are born, we start to form opinions, whether good or bad, about the world we live in. Teachers teach you that only truth, strong character and non-violence are the fundamental principles you need to grow with. They impress upon you that honesty is the only ornament human character should be proud to display. They impress upon you ideals. They tell you to become ideal personalities.

But, as you tread ahead on the path of life, one by one the ideals start to fall by the wayside, just like the brothers of *Yudhisthir* on their way to heaven. The ideals you learn in your childhood go on shattering before your eyes as time progresses. You feel they were never the ideals and go on wondering how foolish you were to have believed in them. But again, in an unending effort, you form other ideals and keep walking on. Then, one day, you find even the new ideals to be as filthy as the ones before. You then try to console yourself with the thought that, after all, the world is like this only. Later, as a grown up man with shattered faiths, you try to form your own image in the world you are living in. You construct a facade around you, as yet pretending to be a man of deep values. You try hard to impress upon others how successful you have been in the proximity of ethics and morals. But you know in the depths of your heart that it is not the truth. You know very well how bitter and violent the world is and how you too are a part of it. Life teaches you to shut your eyes to naked facts. You live in illusions. It deprives you of your real duties towards life and you do all the things that are otherwise denounced publicly...

You then come up with a new philosophy. You keep on telling yourself, if the society is bloody well not bothered of its own devastation, then why on earth you only should think and be bothered by it? And, yet, you are such a hypocrite that you teach your own blood, how morals and ethics matter! You get angry when your son lies to you. You thrash him. You never try to think how shrewd and tricky you have become in your endeavor to become a pillar of society. Few people, for example, the extremists, walk out of the society. They, with their acute knowledge of the human psyche, threaten society and force it to acknowledge their existence. Okay, they are insane. They are perverts, but, truly speaking, very similar in nature with these gentle beings. An impotent perversion and another a violent perversion, aren't both equally dangerous for the human race?

Sanjay Sonawani

But we are ourselves responsible for it. We let the sins flourish and we let their propagators flourish. We tend to look up to false powers. The true strengths we always neglect. True power lies not in weapons, not in governance. It is in morals. But with morals alone you cannot fight evil.

Fourteen

Days passed.

Sitting on the bed, I got engrossed in meditation. The mind in its tranquility has an edge of strength.

The door opened and the doctor entered.

"Come. Someone is waiting for you."

I could not believe my ears. Had I heard him right?

"Who?" I asked, heart in hand.

"You see for yourself; you are all right now," he said in a soft voice.

I spoke to him with deep gratitude, "I don't know in whose hands I am, but, doctor, I shall be ever grateful for all that you have done for me."

The doctor gave a warm smile and patted my back.

I stepped out of the room and for a few moments stood like a statue, soaking in the sight. My gaze ran across the neatly manicured lawn and shrubs, enclosed within the huge wall surrounding the three buildings, which stood in a semicircle. I was amazed by the view of the outside world. I slowly realized that this was a strange place, located amidst wood; there was not a single sign to identify as to where the hospital was located. A fear began to grip me.

"Come on," said the doctor, impatiently. His voice startled me. I looked at him as if seeing him for the first time.

"Okay, doctor," I said in a hollow whisper and followed him through a huge corridor. I could sense that almost every room was occupied behind their closed doors. But I could not see any other human being around. It perplexed me.

For a while we kept on walking. The slapping sound of our *chappals* on the stone floor consoled me. Then we turned left, then to the right, into a dark corridor.

A dim bulb spread its weak illumination. A muscular guard stood alert at the door at the end of the corridor. The guard saluted the doctor.

"Let him in," the doctor instructed the guard.

"Good-bye, young man...and good luck," the doctor said to me and went back.

My condition, for a moment, was that of a man awaiting verdict in a murder case. I did not know where exactly I stood.

The guard opened the door for me.

It was a huge hall with no windows. In the centre was a

round table with a few chairs around it. The light green walls had no photos or pictures adorning them. A lamp in the corner was the only decorative item I could see there. The low hum of an airconditioner could be heard over the sound of my pounding heart.

A chair was occupied. A tall man sat on it with his back towards me.

My God! It's Krishnan.

He too sensed my presence and turned to look over his shoulder. He eagerly rushed and embraced me. Tears of joy came to his eyes. I could feel the outburst of his feelings.

A sob choked my voice. I trembled with the force of emotions that took over my body.

We stood embracing each other for a long time, consoling each other. We did not know whether we were happy for the reunion or sad by the outcome of our endeavors.

A huge wave of emotions had drowned us.

Then it receded slowly, making clear the bare facts of life.

We watched each other intensely.

Krishnan's wounds had healed, but he looked weak.

"How are you?" He asked with deep concern.

"Alive, I guess" I said, "But you look so weak."

"It's the grace of God that we are alive," said Krishnan.

There was then a wall of silence between us for some time.

I broke the silence.

"Where are we, Krishnan?"

"I don't know for sure," he shrugged. "Just a little guess.

In a few moments we will come to know where are we and in whose hands."

I nodded.

"They have brought us here to break the suspense," he said, in his peculiar mischievous tone.

We both occupied the chairs. We had many things to discuss...many questions to ask, but words failed us. The waves of bizarre, abrupt, eager, sentences rose and broke against rocks of destiny, leaving a sense of defeat in our hearts. And that curiosity...deadly curiosity made thinking even harder.

After a long wait, the door of the hall opened. A tall, impressive looking man in his late thirties walked in holding a black attaché case in his left hand. He strode confidently towards the table and took a chair opposite us. He gently put the attaché on the table and tried to gauge us with a look. He did not waste time in preliminaries.

"Well, where you are, in whose hands, and who am I, are some of the questions that must be bothering you the most, I assume." His voice was deep and mesmerizing. "But before I answer these questions, I would like to brief you about the situation you are in. I know who you are. I have deduced the circumstances you must have been caught under. But let me tell you, the circumstances now are not at all in your favor. You are a prey surrounded by hunters. You may try to run away, but let me tell you frankly, death has already cast its shadow on both of you.

"You are militants in the eyes of the government. You both have been associated with the most vicious gang on earth. One of you is directly associated with the assassination of a former prime minister of this country. You both are the most wanted criminals today. SIT is digging deep. No pardon to the crime you have committed, knowingly or unknowingly, will be forthcoming. The government, if you fall into their hands, will charge-sheet you. The trial, a very brief trial, indeed, will take place and then both of you will be executed. I hope you know the consequences of the crime. Do you?"

We did not answer.

"Suppose, even if you escape the trial, you will be out on the streets, to be hunted down by the LTTE. You have caused heavy damage to their organization. They won't rest until they find you and ensure your death. Krishnan, you know well how strong a network they have established in Tamil Nadu. No one has so far been able to destroy this network. The Chinese, the Mosad are their guides, trainers and suppliers of ideas, as well as armaments. SIT is not at all in a position to encounter this reality. Krishnan, you know this very well...don't you?"

Krishnan did not reply, but I could see his muscles twisting.

"Not only that. The people are well trained and equipped. They also have public sentiment in their favor. You won't be able to break that huge rock of sentiments that stands in your way to survival. No. You can't. Hence, your position is of a man who may jump either side, but is still in danger. We all, including you, know that. Yet, I must admire your courage and bravery, which forced you to rebel against a formidable force. And look at the miracle, till this moment, you both are still alive. Would you not like to thank us for saving you?"

His polite face was full of self-assurance. Then Krishnan went in for a soft attack.

Sanjay Sonawani

"We would have thanked you, if we knew who you were. But please don't spend time detailing the possible dangers we may be facing. We know we are in danger. We know very well that we could lose our lives at any moment. So stop raising the boogey of fear. We are used to it. Okay?"

The man stopped drumming his fingers on the table. He tried to control his disappointment and said,

"Well…it's not important as to who I am."

"Yes. It's important."

"Aren't you happy that we saved your life?"

"Why should we?" Retorted Krishnan. "Death and life is nobody's sovereign. No one saves, no one kills. It's destiny. If at all I am grateful, I am grateful to God. Not to you. Is it understood?"

The man's confidence seemed a little shook up by Krishnan's approach. He seemed confused at Krishnan's bluntness. I was afraid. After all, we were in the hands of unknown people. They might just kill us for all that it mattered to them.

But I let Krishnan speak, for I was ignorant of the rules of the game being played.

The man sitting opposite shrugged and shut his eyes for a moment to think.

"Let me finish," he said, sounding irritated. "First listen to me and then you can raise your questions. I've just told you what condition you are already in. Now, it is up to us to decide which side we should hand you over to."

"So you are not government officials," retorted Krishnan like a whip.

"Do you think this kind of discussion would be possible with the government's dumb officials?"

"You are right, but that does not mean you are smart."

"That's your look out," said the man in front of us. "Now will you let me finish? Your bravery and bluntness is admirable, I must admit. Very few have that courage. That's the exact reason why we are interested in you."

"Proceed," said Krishnan in a calm voice.

I became attentive.

"Whether you admit it or not, the fact remains that we saved your life. It was not at all an easy task. We had chased you for a long time; we knew something strange was happening. I have never seen or heard of anyone in the LTTE turning rebel in the past. You are the only case and we were waiting for it to happen since a long time, Krishnan.

"Now you have two choices, walk out from here, be on your own, and face all the possible dangers from both the parties. Alternatively, join hands with us. We can help you immensely, to what levels you can't even imagine. We know you are important and we know how to help you in your revenge. We were in search of people like you for years. Finally, we have got you...Think of it, now that you know where you stand."

I looked at Krishnan buried in deep thoughts. A silence enveloped us like the shadow of death.

The man sitting in front once again broke the silence.

"Krishnan, I know your past. I've a file on you."

He opened his briefcase, snatched out a file and browsed through it, as if the whole life of mysterious Krishnan was jotted down.

Sanjay Sonawani

"You were arrested at the airport by police authorities when you landed at Chennai airport from London. You turned against the Indian government because you felt ditched by your own motherland. But you do not know the mystery shrouding your arrest. Murli, your friend at London, needed recruits like you - brilliant and enthusiastic. He was the one who tipped the Indian Embassy saying that you were returning to India to execute dangerous plans. Of course, he supported his information with proof, to incriminate you. You were arrested, just the way they had planned, and subsequently, jailed. Your fundamental right to be produced before proper court of justice was denied to you due to the home secretary at that time, who also pressurized police authorities to keep you in detention.

"Then, all of a sudden, you were rescued by them. Your arrest and your deliverance did cement the possibility of your turning into an LTTE supporter and made you an enemy of the State. Due to the subsequent rescue, you did become a supporter of the LTTE, which they badly needed.

It was not your fault. Not at all!"

Krishnan's face flinched. He looked like a man defeated. His shoulders sagged and head dropped.

"Why did they do this to me?" He muttered in a helpless voice.

The man sitting in front gave a shrug.

"They needed...always needed smart guys at higher levels. The commoners, the illiterates, can be easily motivated on emotional issues, not the educated class, who possess enough brains not to challenge the system."

Krishnan nodded, as if he understood what that man had

said.

I, too, was shocked at the revelation. How cunningly had Krishnan been baited by the militants.

Now the man sitting in front turned at me.

"You are a very ordinary man. By a stroke of destiny you had to do the things which you never would have done under ordinary circumstances. I do not have much information on you. However, we need you too! Those bastards have destroyed your life. I feel pity for you."

His voice had a touch of deep feelings. Or at least, I felt so.

Unknowingly, words from my mouth reeled out.

"My wife...Janaki...those bastards kidnapped her...will you help us rescue her? I will obey every order you give...can you do that?" I cried. Tears rolled down my cheeks and dripped onto the table. I was looking at him as if he was the judge who was to decide my fate.

His face turned stony and he did not speak for sometime. He then flipped open his briefcase and produced a day-old issue of a newspaper and gently pushed it in front of me.

I grabbed the paper and held it with both hands. A marked news item screamed at me in bold headlines-

"Fisherman's wife burnt alive"

My universe exploded in a flash. Storms raged within me. My sight blurred. I held my head in both my hands and screamed. Slowly my own scream became strange to me rushing far away behind dark clouds. As if the clouds were waiting for some cruel opportunity to begin drizzling bad omen. I drenched in it and forgot even to scream. For a while, I was as if dead!

The stream of conscious returned to me slowly. Someone was patting me on the back. Pushing aside the heavy curtain of mist, I tried to see where I was. All my strength was drained out. The Almighty had deceived me. He had killed me and yet so mercilessly had kept me alive! The bastard that He was.

I was defeated. I knew not how to react; my mind had taken leave of my senses. I tried hard to push away the thick mist swirling about me. I desperately wanted to know if I was dead.

Krishnan stood beside me and kept on patting me on my back and head. I detested his touch. I vehemently shoved him away, I abused him. I hit him. He did not protest. I looked at him. He was weeping.

I too sobbed and with the flood of tears, all humanity was draining out of me.

The storm receded. It had to recede. I had no control over it. I pressed my back to the chair and clenched my fists as I tried to win control over my emotions.

I wiped my tears with the back of my hand.

Krishnan produced a glass of water.

"Have some."

After some time I calmed down a little.

"I am sorry," said the man sitting in front. I just nodded. Krishnan too resumed his seat.

"After you killed Varadrajan, Thyagarajan did it to your wife. The police tried their best to arrest him, but before they could get him, he fled to Tanjawar and from there to God knows where. No one seems to know where he could be. He may be back again in Madras or anywhere. We don't know whether the police will ever succeed in arresting him. He is well protected. As far as we know, he sailed to Sri Lanka, near Elephanta Pass. The sailor who is supposed to have taken him there is now in SIT's custody and we know very little about his interrogation and the outcome of it."

I was not interested in the details. Nothing mattered to me now that Janaki was no more.

"I already have clarified to you your position. It was we who brought you here and saved your lives rather than let you fall into the hands of the LTTE or the police. Now you both are in good physical state. They are searching for you everywhere like rabid dogs. But if you join hands with us and undertake a mission, which, I dare say, you yourselves are planning, things could be quite different for you.

"...So, should I say you are with me?"

"With the CIA?" Krishnan's voice cracked like a whip.

The man sitting in front of us was unperturbed.

"Why do you think so?" he asked.

"You are not from the government. You are not from the LTTE. And as far as I can deduce, the CIA was behind the assassination of Rajiv Gandhi. I know it for certain. Now why do you want us to join hands with you? All the way you have been backing the LTTE, not only financially but also with arms. You don't need us. Just go to hell, you shit head."

I was amazed at Krishnan. How could it matter now to us whether these well-organized people were the CIA or anyone else? Our lives were in extreme danger.

A broad smile appeared on the face of the man.

Sanjay Sonawani

"You have no choice," said he, bemused. "Have you? You are in an extraordinary situation, which means you have no choice but to do what we ask of you. Now, whether you wish to stay with us or not, it hardly matters. Really...It is useless to know who we are and why we saved your life. What matters is whether you are going to jump at the opportunity I am presenting to you. All I can tell you is that if you grab it, may be you will be safe. If not, die a satisfied death in the quest of avenging your enemies."

Memories of Janaki flashed in my mind.

I looked at Krishnan in intense anticipation. His face was wooden. And it frightened me.

"Speak up, Krishnan. What should we do?" I asked for I did not know what trap would we be walking into now.

Krishnan looked at me, his face reflecting the great pain he too was feeling. He nodded silently and looked again at that mysterious man.

"What you want us to do?" He asked hoarsely.

The man nodded in approval and shuffled the papers in his hands, as if to remind himself what he was up to.

"You know very well, Krishnan, why the LTTE was formed and with what objectives. You know how the organization was helped and how it was despised by the masses. You know its friends and enemies. You know how the LTTE has disturbed the otherwise peaceful atmosphere in the subcontinent. First, your own country supported it, but could not stand firm in its stance as the Indian political climate is so uncertain. Then China supported it and then the other superpowers followed suit. Because there are some people who do not wish your country to become another superpower. India, despite all its weaknesses, has remained all the time a united country against the vicious wishes of the entire world. But the fact also remains that this country is now weakening by the day. The LTTE posed to be the best opportunity to shake India's very strong democratic foundations for those who desire that this country be divided into many small, weak nations. Therefore, everyone assisted this organization in its objective of fomenting trouble.

"Prabhakaran, an ambitious man, was an excellent scapegoat who could be used and sacrificed whenever they thought it necessary. But he proved much wiser and cunning than their general assessment. He killed all his opponents and his would-be successors. Padmanabhan was the last of the rebels who got killed by the carefully laid plans of Prabhakaran. He systematically assumed supremacy within the organization. He used Tamil Nadu at his will. He assassinated Rajiv Gandhi, because he proved to be a major impediment in achieving his ultimate goal-"

"Stop!" Roared Krishnan.

That man looked at him in surprise.

"What's on your mind?"

"Rajiv Gandhi's killing was not Prabhakaran's plan, though he despised him like hell. Rajiv Gandhi was the one who had sent the Indian Army to destroy us. But we fought like lions and defeated the mighty army. Prabhakaran was satisfied by the outcome. He never wished that Rajiv Gandhi should die."

"Then tell me, why was Rajiv Gandhi so brutally assassinated?" The man seated before us smiled.

Krishnan's voice was now as cold as ice. "Because the

USA wanted Rajiv Gandhi to die."

"And why would the USA want such a thing...?"

Krishnan shrugged.

"You know it. Rajiv Gandhi had to die. Prior to him Indira Gandhi had to die, as did her other son, Sanjay. The family, with all its weaknesses and strengths, was loved by all the Indians. With them lay vision, wisdom and the wit to lead this country to superpower status."

"You have quite an imagination!"

"Do I?" Krishnan gave a weary laugh. "No, I don't. We discussed this in the jungles. Wherever the US finds that it can poke its dirty nose in local political affairs it takes sides, supplying money, arms and information. But I have never been surprised at this, for I knew, as does the rest of the world, how the US wants to enforce its position in the world as a global cop. For that there must be trouble all over the world. And when they find there is no trouble, they create it!

"But forget all this. Tell me, what you want us to do?"

Silence enveloped the hall for a while. I was ignorant of all these subversive happenings. I never could have thought that the USA would ever plan the assassination of Rajiv Gandhi at the hands of the LTTE? What I knew was an entirely different story, that which the newspapers published.

"I don't agree with your view because the CIA has nothing to do with Rajiv Gandhi's assassination. India, for decades has been USA's friend."

Krishnan said nothing.

"Really, people always seem to have funny ideas about the CIA. I wonder why? Any assassination anywhere and the

CIA is to blame. The CIA has never come out openly and denied the charges against it, and that's what creates all the noise. All right, we are not here to discuss the CIA's role in Rajiv Gandhi's assassination. But very soon I will prove that the CIA had nothing to do with it."

Krishnan glanced at me, as if to see whether I was getting all what was being said.

I gave a nod.

"Actually, Prabhakaran has gone beyond his limits. Rajiv Gandhi's killing has caused ripples of doubt about the role of the CIA, which has helped him with all the possible means for certain reasons, but not to assassinate any leader of this country, as you think is the case. The blemish is false. Prabhakaran has exceeded the limits. He may still go ahead and destroy the original purpose of our collaborations. We don't want this to happen again."

Krishnan gave a sardonic laugh, which perturbed the mystery man sitting in front.

"You may not agree, Krishnan," he muttered. "Really, we need not convince you. But here we are in a peculiar situation, you must admit. As you rightly said, most of the intelligence agencies secretly believe that the CIA is responsible for Rajiv Gandhi's assassination. The government has set up a commission to inquire into this matter and the possibility is that they may stumble upon wrong proofs and will then blame us by inferring wrong meaning. We want to prove our intentions that we have nothing to do with the assassination. We also wish to eliminate Prabhakaran, who has turned against the original purpose of the collaboration."

"And how do you propose to prove it?" Krishnan's voice

was still sarcastic.

"We want you to eliminate Prabhakaran."

"Bullshit," muttered Krishnan.

I was stunned at the suggestion given by that unnamed man.

"You need not be surprised."

"Why?" Asked Krishnan, "I am flabbergasted. Your suggestion is outrageous. Have you been in a mental asylum lately? You, a most powerful gang of vicious, scheming and dirty brains are suggesting us to assassinate a man who is highly protected. Ah! I can't even laugh at you."

"Krishnan, do you know the reality?"

"What reality?"

"The CIA cannot touch Prabhakaran."

"Why?"

"We lack the means. We cannot reach him. No white American can even come near him - killing him is a distant dream. There are other possibilities, such as using local men, his opponents, or to bribe his close men. But the efforts to locate such people have failed us. If someone can kill him, it's you, Krishnan. You were one of them. You know their routes, secret forts and methodology. You know how the organization functions. Your presence in Jaffna will not cause any suspicion; you can roam around freely. And you know the area as one knows the back of his hand.

"And you have a motive to kill Prabhakaran. He is the one who destroyed your career. It is he who put your life in danger and that too for no fault of yours. He killed the wife of your dearest friend, burnt her alive. Try to listen to her screams when her body was put to flames."

My fists clenched. I wanted to yell and say, I want to kill that bastard. He has killed my soul. But as I opened my mouth to speak, Krishnan gave me a hard look and signalled me to stop. I looked at him in seething anger, but said nothing.

"It's true, he has caused danger to our lives. I may kill him one day with my bare hands. But why do you expect us to kill him for you? We are not kids to obey the orders of some juvenile thug."

The man gave a slimy grin.

"Do you have a choice?"

"Yes. We do."

"And what might that be?"

"We can refuse to agree to your suggestion."

"In that case, I will mourn over your untimely death."

"You are threatening us?"

"Why shouldn't I? We saved your lives. We have brought you back from the land of the dead. You should be thankful to us, Krishnan."

"Ah! Death is sometimes better."

"Then should I consider you are not with us?"

Krishnan leaned back in the chair and closed his eyes as he contemplated the fallout of not complying with what the man had suggested.

"What's your choice, pal?" The man asked, directly addressing me for the first time.

I frowned. A mist had covered my eyes and I could barely hear my own voice -

"I have nothing to do with your vicious games. I don't know why on earth you people pollute the society. You play dirty games and then expect people to be happy and content. I can't understand this at all. I am not that wise and neither do I possess your sharp wits. I used to be a happy man and dreamed that one day I will own many trawlers and father many children and die after having led a contented life. Even after my death, people would remember me .

"But everything has changed. Was it a destiny that wrote for me these hellish verses? To undergo these pains? To lose all I had and become a runway criminal hunted by all? No. It does not matter to me now, whether your schemes are dirty or wise. It no more matters to me now whether I am dead or alive. I have nothing now to weep over.

"And why should I bother about this strange world, where people go on living, feeding on their own flesh? Everything is so dirty, so filthy. It's like a curse. Everything that I see is spiteful. It's nauseating.

"I don't know whether a lamp of peace was ever kindled within you or not. You look at us as machines to use against your enemies. You may have reasons to eliminate Prabhakaran. But I have only one ambition left and that is to avenge my destruction. And that I will.... I accept your proposal."

Now that the outburst of my feelings had ebbed, I sat back tired and exhausted.

Krishnan was looking at me awestruck. He probably never expected me, a simple man, to take such a fatal stand. He stood up and, turning his back at us, walked around the room with his hands in his pockets. Then after a moment that seemed like ages, he turned. His eyes now were blazing in rage. But his words were steady and as calm as the sea in winters.

"I know for sure this is another dirty game of the

scoundrels. But I agree. I have every reason to kill Prabhakaran and I will. I will avenge Janaki and riddle him with bullets. Now, should we discuss the details?"

"Good!" Nodded that mystery man and shuffled the heap of papers placed before him.

As if a heavenly bliss had enveloped me in that peaceful moment, I closed my eyes and in my mind killed Prabhakaran a thousand times with my bare hands.

Fifteen

Krishnan's eyes glittered as he looked at me in anticipation.

"Are you really ready, Venu?"

"Yes," I said in a firm vice. All confusion was cleared, like fog in sunlight. I had no aim left in life but to kill that bastard hiding himself in secret bunkers in Jaffna.

"Don't you feel it strange?"

"Strange? I think so…" I gasped.

He gave a faint smile.

"It happens in life…. Once or often." He slowly stretched his hands and closed his eyes, as if he was lost in the mist of memories, obviously unpleasant ones. I kept on waiting for him to speak, as I too desperately needed a philosophy to substantiate the change in me, which so far I had failed to inspire.

"Venu," he mused, "Don't you hate me?"

I looked at him sharply. I was crestfallen. I never had prepared myself to answer this question though, I knew, I hated him. And yet, I never could understand, why on the earth, I was not deserting him.

But this was a question I had to answer sooner or later.

I thought...what should my answer be?

"Krishnan..." A hoarse voice trickled out of my throat, "True... I hate you."

"Why?" He asked softly.

"You ask me, why!" I shouted as a volcano of emotions suddenly erupted within me. "You, who has destroyed my life, dare ask me why I hate you."

Krishnan sat upright glaring at me in a strange way.

"Yes. You must hate me. Good that you admit it. It consoles me. I don't expect you to love me after all these disastrous happenings." He tried to control the quiver in his voice as he spoke. "But what has happened cannot be altered in any way. Life is cruel. It goes on punishing innocent souls. Who can argue with destiny? I tried and have failed. Yet, life is a mysterious game. Yes. It is so, my friend. Life is full of mysteries. And it intrigues me.

"Let us not fight over the past. The past is irreparable. It would be unwise of you to repent over the past deeds. Isn't that what is stated in the sacred *Bhagvad Geeta*? Yes. It was unfortunate that the LTTE chose you to escort me to Sri Lanka. It turned into a nightmare for you. The course of future events was inevitable under the given circumstances. It was I who was responsible for Sivrasan's escape from Sriperambudur to Bangalore. I was the only man who knew the whereabouts of Sivrasan. And yet, he was exposed. Someone has been dangerously treacherous and the crime has been stamped upon me. Well, it serves the bastards right. But yet, I'm immensely curious to know, who did it and why? What gain would Sivrasan's mentors get by his capture?"

For a few minutes Krishnan was lost in deep, ponderous silence.

"Why are you interested now? Aren't you too now a runaway militant?" I said in a cold rage. "What angers me is the brutal murder of my Janaki. And I hate you because, if it weren't you in that trawler of mine but someone else, I would have kicked the bastard off to face the bullets. It was you and that's why I could not do that. I saved your life in exchange of my dear wife's."

"Have you ever thought what I would have done if you weren't the sailor? If it was not you but some other fisherman?"

I glanced at him quizzically.

"I would have shot him dead and would have turned towards India again, without remorse, of course!"

A chill ran through my spine at his cold-blooded statement. His face was as hard as granite.

"But it was you and for you I decided against my will to climb down and face an inevitable death! Nothing was planned, my friend, that it would be you who would sail me out. It was a coincidence, a fatal coincidence, that brought misfortune upon you."

I had to believe his every word. Because he was honest...

Sanjay Sonawani

sincere.

"And we're going to avenge –"

"No emotions, my friend. At least, not now. We have entered a maze of mystery. Let me finish my reasoning. I need to think deeply now, as we are only allies in the entire world and only we have to fight out their ugly schemes. There are so many things that are startling, so many things that are obscure and there are many more things unknown in the heinous dark. Even if we are meant to die, we must know what brought about such disaster to our lives. We must know who it was that leaked the whereabouts of Sivrasan and why. We must know why one after another from the Gandhi family is destined to die 'accidentally'. We must know why the CIA, that has constantly supported the LTTE with all the possible means so far, is so interested in killing Prabhakaran. Another curious thought occurs to me: Why on earth the CIA thinks that we can kill Prabhakaran, when it can eliminate any person with ease and that to without stirring any doubt."

The questions raised by Krishnan turned my mind into a world of confusion. I could not understand the importance of knowing all these things. Why such things go on happening and what ulterior motives are there behind them? Does it change our lives? Does it soothe our pains and sufferings? Or are they the real culprits who take our day-to-day life away and our dreams? What kind of a world is this in which we live? Why Sivrasan, a brilliant brain, ends his life with a pill of cyanide? Why on earth do fanatics get followers to end their lives in the abyss of holocausts? Why all the time there is trouble and violence in the lovely planet we live on? Why can we not live peacefully and enjoy the fruits of life? What is that, which leads us to the quest for blood and power?"

The questions whirling in my mind had no answer; they simply dashed against a cliff and shattered into oblivion.

Krishnan was watching me intently.

"The world is different," he muttered.

"Yes, it is different. I never could think or even imagine of it even in my wildest dreams."

Leaning back in the chair, he closed his eyes and said, "Look. I don't know whether we will ever get answers to our questions. But I am curious to know. After all, of what use is life if it is not curious? This is a second life we have got. We could have been killed in that fatal accident. But we are alive and well. Few unknown people have saved us, not for the kindest of purpose, but to use us to achieve their ulterior motives. I am not even sure the man we contracted this morning belongs to the CIA. We don't even know his name. Why he did not give even a false name? I wonder. It boggles my mind even to think that the CIA could built this huge outfit, amidst woods without stirring any curiosity in the government. It is unheard of. Unimaginable. But yet, we are in the custody of unknown hands. They have resurrected us. They have decided to provide us with every means to kill Prabhakaran. Why that kind of faith in us? And yet remain anonymous to us? Although our lives are in their hands, I am curious to know.

"And most importantly, what happened after the shoot-out in the streets of Madras where we killed Varadrajan. How is it that there has been no search for our missing bodies? With the police and public as witness how could these people manage to whisk us away from the accident site? Not that this was some obscure incident not to invite the attention of the Rapid Action Force deployed in Madras. And yet, in broad daylight after that accident we were removed unconscious to another vehicle and transported to this place, unnoticed. How?"

Krishnan had a point. How could it be possible? There must be a lot of confusion in the police, public and the media. They cannot have remained silent when they have a corpse on the streets and a fatal accident where the injured or dead bodies are untraceable. There must have been chaos. A massive manhunt for the assassins who killed a reputed banker on the streets in broad daylight and then survived an accident and were transported by unknown people to some unknown destination.

"But the man we met today seems unperturbed over the possible repercussions. Or, have they even been able to manage all these things? I have a doubt that many people in the government are on the pay rolls of the LTTE, though no one can prove it officially. Is it the same case with the people we are with today?" He sighed. "And the main question is, are they really the CIA? I am not sure because, again, we haven't any proof."

There was an agonizing silence in the room. I was caught in a whirlwind of emotions. I was trying to go along with Krishnan, but complications and intrigue was so intense, I could reach nowhere.

"This man," said Krishnan in deep voice, "Unknown to us, seemed well in control. He was certain that we would agree. We have agreed because we have no choice. These all are borrowed breaths we are breathing. But why he was so sure we could assist them in the assassination of Prabhakaran? Prabhakaran is practically unreachable, even by those belong to the inner circle. The LTTE is hunting us. How did this mysterious man assume that we could possibly reach Prabhakaran, crossing all these fatal hurdles, and kill him and return alive to live happily ever after? Isn't it irrational thinking?

"But yet this man confides in us the reason why the CIA is wanting to eliminate Prabhakaran. Then why can they not undertake this operation on their own, when they have all the means available at their disposal? Why did they risk saving our lives under such extraordinary circumstances? Have you got any plausible answer to all this? ...It intrigues me." He leaned forward emphasizing his urgency to know the answers to the questions he had raised.

I looked at him in great anticipation.

"Yes. There are questions and still more questions and I desperately need answers to them," he exclaimed in frustration.

"But, Krishnan, isn't it enough that we are alive and have got a chance to avenge our misfortune? Why should we bother whether they are the CIA or anybody else? Why should we think why they have saved our lives? Shouldn't we instead be grateful to our unknown saviors? Why should we think how their scheming minds work? We need no answer to the questions you have raised. I know you are curious and are in quest to find the answers. But what purpose will it serve that we jump into another maze when we are not out of one as yet? For me, my friend, it is enough that we are alive and are to be supported with the means in our endeavors. Right now, life is meaningless as we know not why the past was as it were and so blind we are about the future. Let's try again with the only hope that we can avenge the brutal minds that have caused irreparable damage to our lives. In my opinion, let us not think of what we know nothing about. Let us plan how we can best use the means provided to us to succeed in our mission."

Krishnan sighed. "My friend, true that now there is no point raising foolish questions. But I am curious. Life and death no longer matter to me, as I have experienced death. Now I wish to know why is everything happening to us that is not supposed to happen. Without knowing how and why, will death be a bliss? My friend, how easy it is to live without knowing anything. But is it a true life then? It may so happen that we never get the answers and die. But why can't we give it a try?"

Krishnan had a point. There was definitely no harm in trying to decipher destiny's code, as long as we were alive.

"Then, what do you think we should do?"

"Time is in our favor. At least till these people send us to Sri Lanka. From then on, in my opinion, we will be on our own and may hardly find the time to deliberate over the questions stirring in our minds today. I have to make plans to outsmart them. I need to think."

I knew he needed to think deeply, as I knew nothing. All I knew was that I had a dream and had to reach it somehow, to get all those bastards who had caused so much misery in my life.

I let Krishnan be in his maze of thoughts and leaned back and dreamed how beautiful life was with my wife.

◆   ◆   ◆

The next few days were busy for us. The day would begin

with lectures by that unknown man, armed with maps and notebooks. We would then be brought into the open to exercise, to regain our lost strength. A thick coconut plantation surrounded the building and we could see not much activity as the rainy season had begun. There was a rich smell of fresh earth, which made us feel life rushing through our veins.

Krishnan knew most of Sri Lanka. He knew where the LTTE secret posts were stationed. This information would please the mystery man. There would often be arguments about the moves that we were expected to make when in Jaffna. He suggested we practice handling the weapons that we would be carrying with us when we landed. The evenings would be spent in target practice under the shadow of gunmen covering us, ready to kill us if we played smart.

The unknown man kept a close watch on our progress. He continuously kept harping on the importance of not giving up. "Remember, courage, and only courage is going to assist you when you are on your own."

We were in agreement. Courage was our only support, how could we ever lose it?

After a few days, the mystery man announced, "I think we are ready now. Tomorrow, you shall begin your journey."

"You haven't yet updated us with the latest developments that are taking place in India and Sri Lanka," said Krishnan in an aggrieved tone.

The man laughed.

"As I told you there is no special development that you should know of. SIT is still in search of other suspects and I think that at least 18 people have been arrested so far. A few others have preferred to die before the police could get its hands on them. There is complete silence in the LTTE camp. That's all I can tell you."

Krishnan listened to him in rapt attention knowing well that he had been provided all the information he had asked for. But he let it go at that.

The day dawned with mixed feelings. We had nothing of our own to pack. We were ready to face another unknown universe. We knew not what destiny had in store for us. However, I was determined to avenge the people who had destroyed our lives. I prayed to Lord *Ranganatha* in deep devotion. I took a vow that if I returned safely, I would serve Him for the rest of my life.

We were driven in a jeep, accompanied by three gunmen who scarcely spoke. The road was muddy and with the drizzle, had turned to slush. I didn't see any living creature on the way except for some birds perched on the branches seeking shelter from the rain and some animals. No thoughts came to mind and slowly, a calm enveloped me.

I know not how long we drove. Somewhere on the way the men accompanying us blindfolded us.

This made me uneasy as an unknown fear gripped my heart. Without the sense of sight, I tried to listen to the outside sounds and determine the direction we were proceeding in. I knew the coast of Tamil Nadu well. We must be somewhere near the coast, I thought. The premises we were locked in must then be just a few miles from the coast. What area would this be? Forests are scarce in Tamil Nadu except on the border of Karnataka. Such thoughts kept me busy so that the uncomfortable travel and the blindfold did not bother me much anymore.

Suddenly, lightning split the sky with a thunderous clap followed by a heavy downpour. The man beside me cursed under his breath and shouted some instructions to the driver. It was hot and sultry in the closed jeep and yet the sound of falling rain was pleasant to the ears. I longed to feel the touch of rain on my body. But the windows remained closed, confining the airconditioner's humid hum to us alone.

The rain played its mysterious tunes invoking pleasant memories within me. I remembered Janaki. I remembered the passionate moments we had shared together. I remembered my days in college filled with subtle fighting and passionate arguments with Krishnan. I remembered how pleasant it used to be when at sea during the rains - it used to bring out the poet in me, feelings that I could never express otherwise. Do you know Janaki liked to accompany me on sails when it rained? I knew it could be dangerous to sail too far from the shores under such conditions, but such opportunities were rare and too pleasurable to miss.

Now, all this appeared to me but a dream lost forever.

Why does one not dissolve in the moods of nature and become a part of it? Why does one need power and wealth? Why was this beautiful earth under the yoke of ugly men who cheated everyone they came across? My heart was rending in a deep agony that I could not understand. I cursed myself, I cursed Krishnan, I cursed Varadrajan, Thyagarajan, my father, and the system I was a part of.

I wondered what time it was. Was it afternoon or evening? By now I had lost all sense of time and direction. How far had we travelled? How much longer would we continue like this? There was no point in pestering our companions, who spoke nothing to us. I knew their guns were pointed at us in case we tried to play smart and cause trouble. I tried to speak to Krishnan but he did not respond to my questions. Finally, the man sitting besides me shouted at me to shut up.

Sixteen

Though blindfolded, I sensed it was nearing nighttime. We were near the sea. I could hear the rushing waves pounding the shore in rage. The familiar odour of the sea assailed my nostrils. It comforted me somewhat.

A thought flashed in my mind and blood began rushing through my veins. Here was a great opportunity. We had regained our strength. We could easily dodge these men in this darkness and rain. We had done it before. We could run away and find our own means to seek revenge. We need not be at the mercy of these people whose motives were yet unknown. It was a chance, certainly a great chance.

But with the approaching sound of the sea, the initial rage

was slowly ebbing away. Uncertainty started to undermine my initial resolve. There seemed no sense in vengeance now. I did not even know whether we would achieve success in our mission against Prabhakaran. I was not even sure whether we could ever reach him. We were a two-man army trying to take on the might of the well-organized LTTE. Their forts were well secured. They had all the possible means to protect themselves, whereas we had none. They were ruthless and would only be happy to punish us with death.

It would not be easy to avenge- vengeance meant violence. Would violence bring back the life I had lost? Would killing Prabhakaran revive my Janaki from the dead?

No. We must not rush and jump from the pot into the fire; we already had enough misery in our lives. It would be better that we found some way out of this situation, found a safe haven and let those bastards rot in their self-created hell.

I must turn Krishnan away from his disastrous motives...

I touched him in eagerness, trying to convey my thoughts to him through my touch. The jeep was descending the curves leading to the shoreline. The roar of the savage sea was getting nearer.

Krishnan responded to my touch with an angry shrug.

A surge of anger erupted within me.

The jeep had now come to a halt on the wet sands. There was a rush of instructions being passed to and fro. Tension was mounting by the minute.

My blindfold was snatched off abruptly. Darkness engulfed me, punctured by flashes of light. It took some time for me to regain my sight. Rain was crashing down,it was an encouragement to my secret plans to dodge our escorts and escape. The gunmen were confused as to what they should do under the circumstances even as they continued to cover us with their guns.

"Krishnan, let's get out…please…" I whispered.

"No, don't be a fool. Just hold on."

I thought Krishnan had lost his senses and power of reasoning.

"Alright, I am going," I said in frustration.

"Stop, you fool," he roared in my ears. I hated him for this, never before had he behaved like this. I did nothing, though I knew I just had to kick the door open, kick the gunman, standing under heavy rain, real hard and make a dive for cover under the darkness. I knew that the possibility of being hit by a bullet in the dark surroundings was slim and I could walk away safely till I reached a safe distance.

An opportunity was there in front of us and I wanted to make a go for it. And yet, I could not. I still don't know what poison Krishnan had filled in his voice that kept me from trying.

"Come down. Step out." The order was barked at me. I reluctantly stepped out of the jeep. Within seconds I was drenched. Flashes of lightning were illuminating the vicinity and it was followed by the sound of thunder. I could see a launch dancing viciously on the savage waves some distance away from the shore.

"Krishnan!"

"Keep on walking…follow them…it's just a hundred steps

ahead."

I staggered on, following the guides who tried to light our way with their torches. How easy it would be to run away! I cursed Krishnan. I hurled hundreds of abuses at him while I maintained my pace carefully behind the guide.

The shoreline was like an untamed beast. The crashing waves were threatening us with their deafening sound as they crashed headlong onto the shore, only to go back hissing in frustration and then return once again with renewed might. As we stepped in the water, the waves fell on us with deadly force, so much so that we had to fight to keep our balance. The wind was furious at the hurdles that nature and mankind had put in its way and seemed determined to smash them down.

The man following us yelled - "Let's give the signal. I know they have seen us."

Another man yelled something else.

Then our guide approached us and shouted, "You have to wade through these waters. Keep heart, it's shallow. They will put down the ladder for you to step aboard."

"We won't. I can't swim. The water is wild. If we lose our lives, you too shall lose yours. Your boss won't like this," Krishnan yelled back.

It took some time for the man to understand what Krishnan said. He was furious but he knew he had to get done with the job assigned to him somehow. He did not know what to do. Probably, he had not expected such a savage attack from nature. He rushed to confer with his fellowmen and then flashed his torch in successive flickers at the launch and came back to us.

"There will be a rope from the boat to us. We shall hold one end of rope from this side. All you have to do is grip it tightly and advance. Trust me, the water is shallow, so there is no need to panic. They have been waiting for us in this wilderness for a long time."

Krishnan said nothing.

I went on observing the frantic activities on the shore.

The occasional lightning revealed hurried movement on the launch. Then two men ran across to get hold of the thin rope thrown by a sailor from the boat. Meanwhile, another man kept guard. Somehow, one end of the rope was now in the grip of one of our escorts. He then rushed to us and asked us to get going through the raging water.

"We still have a chance, Krishnan. This journey is not going to lead us anywhere."

"Keep on walking," roared Krishnan through the lashing winds.

Gripping the rope tightly that would lead me to the launch I entered the fierce waters, trying hard to keep my balance, and started to wade through the brief moments of life and death.

Krishnan followed me. He was determined to take this journey. He was determined to undertake something I could hardly fathom. But yes, he was determined and had forced me to be with him. Was it true that he was curious about the magic of life? Didn't he know that only death could satisfy his final wishes, the point where all quests end up in disappointment?

He walked firm and erect, his stride careful and alert. I yelled for his assistance as we reached the end of the rope. He looked at me and gave a weak smile and climbed the rope ladder.

Aboard the boat, I embraced him tightly. Tears started to roll down my cheeks.

There was a frantic activity on the deck. The lights were suddenly switched off and darkness swallowed us, only to add to the confusion. We could listen to footsteps, yells, and orders being shouted and then we were shoved ahead rudely. I understood we were to be locked up and that the launch would be moving soon. I would never have dared to sail under such weather conditions. Will we be able to make it to the destination or drown halfway?

It was a small room below the deck, cluttered with implements, bundles of ropes, nets, etc. that one can find on almost every fishing boat. The room was damp and heaving up and down with the force of the waves.

"You two will remain here throughout the journey. Food will be served right here. Only one man at a time will be allowed to come out in the morning. Meanwhile, make yourself comfortable. Food will be served as soon as we move." Our escort informed us in a tired voice.

We nodded a silent acceptance as he left hurriedly securing the doors behind him. The mention of food infuriated our hunger. Since morning we hadn't eaten a morsel.

After a while, there was a heavy jerk as the boat moved forward. Somehow we managed to maintain our balance, cursing at the abrupt start. I looked around the room hoping to find folded beds and a can of drinking water and then sat down on the

Sanjay Sonawani

wooden floor and stretched my weary legs.

"What do you think might have happened to my trawler?" I asked Krishnan trying to divert my mind from the terror of nature I had witnessed a few minutes ago.

Krishnan looked at me in surprise, "What trawler?" Then he remembered the trawler we had left deserted on the shore…in a cove. "Ah! Your trawler! Yes, now I remember. It appears as if it happened ages ago. It should be safe…no one seems to go there and even if someone happens to stumble there by accident, what would he think? Sailors must be around somewhere that's what he would think... We have buried a huge sum of money over there. I hope we can go back and collect it some day. What would you like to do with the money, Venu?"

Was he mocking at me?

"That money…hell…I won't touch it again."

"Life is far mysterious, Venu. People do unusual things…against their will…against their values under unusual circumstances."

"What would you do?" I asked in annoyance.

Krishnan's eyes twinkled. He smiled and said, "I don't know. But life can be restarted. It is a large amount. What if someone comes across it accidentally? Say, he is just digging to bury some corpse and lands on that bag? He would be hysterical, no?" He laughed. "He might even die of a heart attack."

I tried to express my amusement at the absurdity of such a situation but laughter evaded me. My mind simply wanted to erase all that.

"Do you think these people really are from the CIA?" I asked, perturbed.

"I don't know for sure," Krishnan replied. "But why bother now? Let us somehow find Prabhakaran. Let us plan meticulously. The monsoon is in our favor. By now it will have considerably slowed the LTTE's movements in the jungles of Jaffna. They should also have assumed us dead by now, which too is to our benefit. I know the region, their command stations. But I still have no plans, *Tambi*. I badly need to think."

I didn't pester him any further. I too was tired and hungry and, for now, bereft of questions.

Food was served after a while. The throb of the engine was consistent as the sound of the rain in the backdrop. We ate like hungry wolves and when finished, shoved the plates aside and sprawled out to sleep.

It was a great sleep. No dreams, no nightmares and no haunting memories.

In the morning - or was it morning? It was hard to tell as no outside light penetrated down - there was a heavy rap on the door and a call for us to come out.

It was a pleasant morning. Nature's rage of the previous night was no longer in evidence. It had calmed down to a slight drizzle that felt sensuous as it fell on our bare heads and faces. The sky was still dark and I could see the glow of the morning sun behind a veil of clouds on the eastern horizon. The wind blew like a mischievous child; playful. I strolled on the deck under the drizzle to relieve my body from the strain. Then I leaned over the rail and looked at the dancing waves. The sight of the ocean always mesmerized me.

Sanjay Sonawani

The journey onwards was without any event. Towards the end of the day, I smelled the approaching coast.

"It's time, Krishnan."

I was worried. From now on, we would be on our own. No outside help would be forthcoming in our suicidal assignment.

I saw the dense forest through the thick curtain of maddening rain. Krishnan was calm, as usual. He had hardly spoken to me during the journey. I knew he needed to think and so I let him do his job.

"Give us our luggage," Krishnan said to the man who appeared to be the leader of the group.

"Not now," the man replied. "Let the launch get near the shore. You two then go ahead and wait there. Your luggage shall follow."

"We want to check what all they have provided us - we may need a few more things."

"I can't help you, *Tambi*. Orders." He laughed. "But take care...succeed in your mission whatever the hell it is!"

Krishnan said nothing. He stared at the shore and the advance of the launch through the wild waves.

It was about an hour before we anchored.

"Now, bye friends," said the leader, slapping us on our backs. We moved forward into the open and got drenched within seconds. I climbed down the ladder. The water was chest deep. The waves made my movement even faster. They kept me pushing ahead with a determined force. I rode a wave and made ot the shore. There I sat on a rock gasping for air and waited for Krishnan.

He followed soon after and sat beside me on the rock. Then I saw a man wading through the waters carrying two haversacks. He reached us, threw the baggage before us and hurried back to the boat.

Now we weren't in a rush to get hold of the stuff provided to us in the haversacks. Whatever was loaded in them would have to be suffice.

Evening had cast its mysterious shadows under the cloudy sky. Krishnan got up to pick the luggage. It appeared heavy. I too got up to assist him. The haversacks were bulging with loaded inventory. Krishnan unzipped one and slipped his hand inside.

"The rain is against us, *Tambi*. We can't afford to get all this wet. I think there are guns, cartridges, clothes and some food…maps too. We must find some place where we can halt for the night. I don't know where exactly we have landed and how far is the nearest village. Night is approaching, so, for now, we will follow a general direction and try to find some shelter and organize ourselves properly. The guns are dissembled and it will take some time to reassemble them. Let's start now."

Through shrubs, puddles and thick woods we advanced our march from unknown to unknown. The rain made it a difficult, tiresome and painful walk. We could hardly see a few yards ahead of us. The storm had left its outrageous mark all around. A few trees lay uprooted in our path. A couple of them struck by lightning stood like dark skeletons of monstrosity stripped off all foliage, a reminder of the awesome power of nature. We could not make out any habitation nearby, which may be the

Sanjay Sonawani

reason why they had deported us here. They could not afford to approach populated shores.

The darkness now was enveloping us. We stopped, cursing the situation we were in. Krishnan put down his haversack and from it brought forth a torch. He switched it on. It was powerful. "Now it won't be that difficult," he said, hopefully.

I nodded. There must be another torch in my sack, I thought, but we preferred to use only one between the two of us and save the other till this one's battery ran out.

Our walk continued.

We were slowly ascending a hilly slope. Seeing the uprooted coconut trees stripped of their fronds by the strong winds and the rainwater rushing down towards the sea was an altogether different experience.

"Should we continue uphill or change direction?" I asked Krishnan.

"Uphill is better. We may see lights somewhere from the top."

My breathing grew heavy as we walked through the mud and shrubs. But the need to find shelter forced me to trudge on.

The ascend was not as sharp as I had perceived. Yet, it took a long time before we reached the top. From there only woods could be seen all around. Then, Krishnan stopped and flashed the torch beam around on the ground. I do not know what he saw. But he took another direction and asked me to follow.

Suddenly, lightning flashed and I saw a vague structure eastward in the direction we were proceeding.

"It seems to be an abandoned Buddhist shrine," he said.

"How did you find it?"

"Oh! Just luck, that's all. I saw a faint pathway and thought that here in the wilderness it must only lead to some old religious site. Now, hurry up…"

Half an hour later, we were inside the shrine, which seemed on the verge of collapse. The stones were loose and looked as if they would fall at the slightest touch. We entered the main hall. Krishnan threw light in all directions. Bats fluttered their wings, shrilled and then settled as soon as the torchlight went off them. A huge statue of Lord Buddha, though disfigured by the passage of time and negligence, was a peaceful and welcome sight. Unconsciously, I prayed to him, bowed and sought his blessings.

"We shall be safe here. At least for the night. The floor is dirty but let's not worry about that. We need rest. First, let us light a fire. Will you go and fetch some wood, Venu? There's plenty of it stacked near to the main door."

I put my haversack down and taking the torch from it walked towards the main door.

It was frightful in the dark. The ghosts from the past, I thought, might alight and haunt me for trespassing their territory. Krishnan was left far behind to help me. *This is a temple…no ghosts can ever enter a temple…*I tried to reassure myself. I approached the main door cautiously. Outside, I could see scattered statues, some broken and some intact, lose stones that bore strange carvings and crumbling walls that surrounded the main structure. There was a projection near the door under which was a stack of weathered wood. Worms and insects had hollowed most of it and I was afraid to touch it. What if a snake showed up? I was afraid of snakes. But I knew I had no choice. Holding the torch firmly in my left hand, I picking up a stick in my right, pushed at the stack of wood. It tumbled down. No snake appeared. Satisfied, I selected some comparatively dry wood, as much as I could carry in my arms, and hurried back to Krishnan.

Krishnan was sitting close to the statue on a stone platform with his torchlight on.

Without a word I organized a small bonfire. Krishnan, in the meanwhile, had emptied his haversack and was examining the contents that he had laid out neatly in front of him. There lay a Sten gun and a revolver, besides a set of clothes, a pair of binoculars, some maps, a heap of cartridges and packs of food. Of all the things, the sight of the guns was most assuring; we had something to fight with.

After a while, I added a little more wood to the fire and turned to look around the shrine.

"Must be a thousand years old," said Krishnan. "There are plenty of such as this one in this country, so many that you will fail to count. Buddhism is widely popular here. And the Buddhists go on building new shrines every year while the older ones tend to get neglected and gradually fall to ruin, may be because of difficulty in approaching them or the distance they are from the populace. We used to come across many of them in the jungles when on the run or on some mission. Except for the shepherds, no one turns up at such places nowadays."

Sanjay Sonawani

I was watching the huge edifice with tired curiosity. There were blurred paintings on the walls, the victims of mildew and the elements of nature. The floor was of cobbled stone, which reminded me of the huge temple of Lord *Ranganatha* at Trichi. I was awestruck when I had first been there.

"Buddhism is a religion that preaches non-violence and yet the Sinhalese have been oppressing the Tamils for centuries. The violence they have perpetrated can never be forgotten and it is the very reason why the Tamils had to unify and fight back the injustice. The Sinhalese never wished for peace among their fellow citizens; they have kept on inciting the issue instead. You know, in a way, the Tamils are a humble people. They prefer peace. It is difficult to infuriate a Tamil in ordinary course of life. He will prefer reasoning. He will suffer negligence. He will worship Gods and his heroes with equal zeal. He loves art. He loves knowledge and hard work. The Tamils crossed Indian boundaries centuries ago and established themselves in many Asia Pacific countries. No one has ever heard of a Tamil causing any harm to the local order where he has settled. He cherishes his destiny and explores new avenues for the future of his family. The Tamils are most religious...more than the north Indians. They like to preserve culture and religion. No modern thinking can humble his ancient traits. He will adapt very fast to the changing technologies and yet at heart he will remain an orthodox Hindu.

"Then, why is he so outrageous over here? Why he is supporting militancy and becoming a militant himself? The Sinhalese have caused irreparable harm to his very existence in the most impertinent manner in the recent past. The chaos and civil war is a sort of fruit of their evil politics. They went on oppressing the Tamils. They feared - what if tomorrow the Tamils come to rule over them! They thought, after freedom they were the only people destined to rule the country. They denied equal rights to the Tamils - the right to employment in government establishments, the right to preserve their culture...

"Venu, we too are Tamils. I am not fanatical about anything. I am not a racist. I know we Tamils sometimes get carried away by our emotions. We too have some ugly traits that we are not ready to reckon with. We tend to support our leaders with no reasoning whatsoever, when we know that they are looting us and causing great damage to our faiths. We are too sentimental. Our sentiments can hardly be justified many a time and yet our people go on suffering and praising their idols.

"Venu, but this does not mean that one should suffer just because he happens to belong to some particular race. Caste is an evil in our country and also around the world, but it hardly calls for violent reaction. The Sinhalese have asked for it and they are getting it."

Krishnan was speaking as if in a trance. What he was trying to tell me? Why was he now advocating the Tamils' fight? Why was he praising the enemy? I looked at him in confusion not understanding much of what he said.

"Krishnan, the Tamils moved to Sri Lanka centuries ago. All right, they had to suffer for they were in minority and following the new circumstances that independence threw up, they became competitors to the aspirations of the natives. But couldn't they fight back using the means adopted by Mahatma Gandhi? Today, we are forgetting our past. We are forgetting our traits," I said in vehemence.

Krishnan gave a weak smile and asked, "Then why should we not fight injustice they did to us with non-violence? Why not throw away these weapons and start a hunger strike? Don't live in a fool's paradise, Venu. The means to fight depends on the culture of the enemy. We are here to fight the worst culture, one that demands blood for blood. I am not justifying Prabhakaran, my dear friend. I just am telling you why we Tamils had to undergo this vicious civil war.

"But motives keeps on changing when the initial euphoria is over. The same thing has happened with the LTTE. Their initial goal, they now realize, is too far away to achieve. They also know that after such violent reaction to the injustice, there can not be an eternal peace with the natives. The wounds would never heal even if the demands of the LTTE are accepted and executed to its fullest satisfaction. Enmity will be everlasting now.

"Prabhakaran knows this very well for he never lives in fool's paradise. Now he is just pulling ahead with some different goals to satiate his hunger through his organization. He is a treacherous man, treacherous to the Tamils and to the rest of the world. First, he had help from India, then China and then Mosad, and now from the American intelligence agency, the CIA. USA needs trouble everywhere, you know it. Its existence will come to an end if there is no trouble across the globe. They need to cause the trouble if it doesn't exist. They are immensely resourceful and rich. They need madmen like Prabhakaran to help them in their ugly mission. They know he is god for the Tamils in Sri Lanka and for many in Tamil Nadu. They also know that the Indian government helped him initially. But later, when they found they were mistaken about this man, they backed out. Prabhakaran always had been furious about it and he used to call it a treachery. He never forgave Rajiv Gandhi for sending the Indian army against him in Jaffna despite his pleadings.

"But he never wished to taint the LTTE with Rajiv Gandhi's blood. He knew it would be a disastrous setback to his plans and to his position, as his supporters in India would then back out. Also, the possibility that the Indian government might undertake some severe mission to punish him for his impudence. It would be crazy to assassinate Mr. Gandhi when he was not even a premier and opinion polls showed he was about to lose majority in the coming elections. Even then the execution was planned and executed. It baffles me. It baffled me even then when I was asked to accomplish certain duties after his execution. It shocks me why Sivrasan's hideout was revealed. There are many unanswered questions I am curious to find answers to.

"Venu, the CIA, I suspect, has played a major role in this assassination. They had all the possible motives. They plan for the next hundred years. They silently go on sowing poison that yields a fortune for them. They wish their supremacy lasts forever. I am sure by now the Indian investigation officers must have reached a conclusion about the motive behind this assassination. There must be many people knowing this in the Central Government well in advance. But they didn't try to stop Rajiv Gandhi from coming to Sriperambudur or make enough arrangements to protect him from any possible attack.

"You know how easy it is to bribe Indian citizens and so the leaders. We too have done it before. We too have our lobby of supporters in New Delhi. They are MPs, astrologers, gurus, mahants and journalists. We pay them handsomely. They support our actions and oppose every move that the Centre decides against us.

"You know, Rajiv Gandhi was forced to call back the Indian Peace Keeping Force only because we had mounted tremendous pressure over the Indian polity through our supporters in the media, through so-called think tanks and MPs. And all this support is bought. These crazy bastards never work on sentiments.... You understand why all that which is possible for us is easier for the CIA. The Indian investigation team must realize this some day. They will or they might already have, but what can they do? What can they prove? Their hands are tied. In my opinion, they will declare Prabhakaran the main culprit and file cases against those they might arrest and those who are dead already.

"This is all that is going to happen. No real culprit will they ever prosecute."

After a haunting silence I said - "Krishnan, all these events have baffled me. I am not as knowledgeable as you are. May be the CIA is behind this conspiracy. May be the real culprits will never be known to us; they never will be brought to justice; they will laugh at our stupidity and weakness. May be those who were simply pawns in the conspiracy will be hanged. People will then soon forget that their leader had been assassinated. People are cold blooded here in our country. No hue and cry will ensue. By now, I am sure the people are not even paying heed to the news appearing in the media.

Sanjay Sonawani

"Now I begin to understand that all that appears on the surface is hardly the truth. The event makers remain behind closed doors and laugh at the effect they cause. But, my friend, the world cannot be governed forever by such malicious people. The world needs a breath of fresh air. The filth must be scraped off. We are here not only to avenge our disaster, but also the villains who have become pawns in the hands of merciless people. At least let us try hard to punish the pawns and send a message out to those who use them.

"You know how pleased I was when I learnt that Janaki was pregnant. I dreamed for a child who would grow up to become a great person. A person who would be kind and be an asset to society. I used to speak out my dreams to my Janaki at night. I wished I would earn enough to support his carefree life and high education.

"And see, Krishnan, the evil that has befallen me. My wife and unborn child were committed to flames. What did I do wrong to this world? Didn't I pray faithfully to the Lord every morning? Did I ever commit a sin? Did I ever harm anyone? Then why? Why on earth?" I sobbed. I wept incessantly, ever since I had set sail for Sri Lanka at Varadrajan's behest.

Krishnan held me in a tight embrace.

"We shall avenge them, Venu, we shall. I am sorry, I could not save her; I could not even see how she looked. She must have been an angel. She now must be in the sacred court of the Lord you prayed to with such great devotion."

◆◆◆

Seventeen

The morning was warm and cheerful. The rain had taken a recess and the clouds were but a scattering of woolly clumps in the azure sky. Sunlight after many days. The vicinity was clearly visible. It was a flat tableland crowded with shrubs and trees. The water had flowed away and before my eyes lay a carpet of green grass. The birds chirped cheerfully and flew high, over the trees and in the sky. Nature seemed to be in a festive mood. Nobody was in sight and it pleased me that the area was deserted. But we had to start…

Krishnan too was ready. A bath was out of question. We already had been washed so thoroughly by the rains that for many days we could do without a bath. We had our guns assembled and loaded and our haversacks strapped to our backs. Krishnan was studying the map.

"We may be here, or near Kankesanturai, some forty-fifty kilometres away," he said, pointing at the map. "We are in the red zone. Here the LTTE is powerful and has a patrolling system in place. But let us not worry too much about them. This area is covered with thick forests, so we can possibly escape their notice."

"Which direction are we going to proceed and, moreover, what we are supposed to do?"

"Just follow me," he said, mysteriously.

"Alright," I said irritated at his curtness. I turned and bowed to pray to Lord Buddha.

Krishnan stood silent. I looked at him in astonishment.

"You never pray to God, Krishnan, do you?"

"No."

"Why?"

"When He does not exist, then why pray?"

"Why are you so cynical?"

"God is the creation of mankind," started Krishnan's sermon. "It is a creation of fear. Primitive man was afraid of darkness so he made fire a god. He was afraid of death and so he created another god. He created religion because all the time he was afraid of the elements of Nature and wanted its blessings. Religion was succor. He then created an umpteen number of gods and myths to establish them in order to feel safe and secure. He needed all the consolation because he was afraid. Why after all should God exist to assist the mankind that is filth that breathes and pollutes the earth?

"If at all God exists why would He be different for different sects and religions? It is so foolish. No God exist and there is no reason why He should exist. You know that people who do not wish to stand in queues pay money to get a *darshan* of their deity at temples. These fools think that God will bless them with prosperity and so try to bribe Him!

"You have every right to do what you feel is right. Do not ever ask me such a question. For me, God never exists and never shall. There is no place for God in my universe.

"And see we are not alone here," he said in a sharp voice that forced me to shut up and scan the area in fear.

I could see nothing unusual. The sunlight was warm and insects and birds were chirping happily. A gentle breeze was rustling the foliage. Everything was peaceful, serene and in perfect order.

"What's it?" I asked, hesitantly.

"There are people around here. I wish they were on their usual patrol. I would kill those bastards if they were looking for us. Now, just a moment. There is no reason for them to patrol in this area; there is no Sri Lankan government post nearby."

I kept silent. I was tense.

He crouched and made his way stealthily forward, making good use of the bushes and the clumps of tall grass. I followed suit. Near the ruins we stopped. He looked in all directions and then pointed me to look in a particular direction.

He was right. I could make out secretive movements of a man in military fatigues through the shrubs.

"They must have been searching for us throughout the night," said Krishnan, bitterly. "Our arrival is no more a secret."

Sanjay Sonawani

"But how?" I asked, on the verge of panic.

"That's what we need to find out."

The uniformed man had now stepped behind the shrubs to allow his colleague to move ahead. The other man was looking at the shrine when he produced a handset and started speaking into it. Krishnan watched the unsolicited scene through his binoculars.

"They are not the army. They are our friends, the LTTE. Be ready for a fight, Venu."

I tightened my grip over my gun. My mind was spinning. How had they found us!

"Let's see how many are they. Not many, I hope. They must have known the general location where we would land. The rains last night must have delayed their actions but now it seems they are ready."

I cursed God now. Tears were gathering in my eyes. I knew I had to rely on Krishnan's wits. He was right, I saw another man get up from the shrubs and join his colleague.

"They suspect we might be around here but are not sure. They may turn in our direction. This is the right opportunity to take them unawares."

"Krishnan!" I exclaimed in disbelief.

"Yes, just fire at them. They are well within range. Don't flinch, just fire...you are great at it..."

Suddenly, gunfire erupted. I didn't know whether it was Krishnan or I who started to fire first. It echoed from all directions. The man who had appeared first, stumbled and then with a wild jerk fell down. The other one tried to run across, faltered and caught a few slugs. He died instantly. Frightened birds took wings and swept high in the air with loud shrills that faded away in moments. Silence was reestablished.

"I hope they were just two of them. It is a practice we adopted. Others may be elsewhere in areas assigned to them. Normally, they move in teams of two and keep in touch with other pairs over the wireless at regular intervals. So, if communication is broken, they know that the others are in danger and get moving in that direction calling out to all others in the area to zero in on the enemy."

"Krishnan, what if we had left the shrine from behind without taking them?"

"It would have been a temporary respite. They know for certain that we are around here, in this area. It is not at all a coincidence that they have undertaken a manhunt in this deserted area. You know, the LTTE, though powerful, does not have that many soldiers to cover the entire countryside in the remote chance of capturing the enemy. They only have one enemy in this region and that is the Sri Lankan army. What they were doing just now was hunting us.

"These men most certainly are on a manhunt and are searching us. All right, at least we have eliminated two of them.... There may be more of them hidden in the shrubs waiting their turn. Here we are much safer with the ramparts of the ruins to take refuge behind and even to defend ourselves. Let us wait for a while and see whether other intruders come."

"As you say."

We lay there silently for about an hour. Nothing happened.

Sanjay Sonawani

The trees stood silent and tall. The birds chirped as before and the sun spread its warmth without bias. There was no movement in the shrubs or in the grass.

Krishnan was alert. Suddenly his grip started to tighten over the gun.

"They are coming. They know there is danger awaiting them around here but are not sure where. They are coming in, that's for sure. Be ready. Let's take them by surprise."

The fight had begun. They already knew we had landed in their territory and wanted us dead.

But how did they know that we were alive and had come back was the moot question.

I noticed a sudden movement in the southwest. The bushes shook violently as a man burst forth, gun in hand, and ran in the direction opposite to where we were. He came upon the two corpses lying in the shrubbery where we had left them and he jumped back into the cover of the shrubs. Another man followed him ready to cover his mate in case of attack.

There was no movement for a long while. Then, slowly they crawled forward in our direction.

"Now!" Shouted Krishnan and opened fire. His aim proved fatal for the man covering his teammate. He shuddered and fell as a hail of bullets from Krishnan's gun struck him. The other man started to fire blindly in our direction. Then realizing that he was wasting ammunition, he pulled out his handset and started yelling something into it.

"We must get this bastard before he can make another contact," Krishnan hissed.

I fired in the man's direction. The shrubs jerked wildly but none hit the man who continued calling for support over his handset.

"Stop, Venu."

"But he will call...."

"Let him."

"He now knows where we are hiding."

"We shall remedy that."

We rushed to the other side, where there was a ruined staircase leading to the top of the wall. We somehow managed to climb up. From the top, we had a better view of the region. We saw the frightened man speaking agitatedly into the wireless. From atop the wall we could better aim and both of us fired at him at once. How easily he had got himself killed!

The shrine of Lord Buddha had proved safe and useful!

Krishnan knew there would be more activity soon. He proved right as a stealthy movement in the shrubs about 500 metres away caught my eye. It was another two-man team moving ahead with extreme caution, their guns aimed in the general direction ahead. They were now looking directly in our direction, though they seemed unsure of our hideout. Slowly both separated trying to cover each other in case of attack. Krishnan kept his gun trained on them, waiting for them to come within killing range.

"I shall take the man at the left, you aim for the one on the right," Krishnan whispered.

I nodded in agreement.

The sun was now behind the clouds, casting a weak

shadow over the area. I took position and concentrated on my target crawling ahead. I squeezed the trigger and kept it pressed till I saw him stagger and fall like a rag doll. Krishnan too had killed the other militant by then.

There was silence after the shattering noise.

Soon the birds settled in the trees and bushes. The wind blew swift.

"Let's wait for some more time."

We waited another hour. Nothing happened. Then Krishnan made another move. He forced me to walk down the ruined stairs with him to the dead men. There he picked up the transmitter belonging to one of them. I could hear some static and then a voice…

"What happened? Why did you break contact?"

"There was a fight. We lost three men, but now both are silenced. Any order that I shall follow?"

"State your location, the support team will be there in two hours time."

"Hello, I can't hear you, repeat orders."

The man out there repeated the order. But Krishnan still pretended to be unable to hear him and then switched off the communication set.

"Let's move now," said Krishnan, as he searched the dead man for any bit of information that might prove useful to us.

"Nothing has changed since I left them."

"Couldn't we have slipped away from the other side instead of waging this encounter?" I asked, worried. "They would have searched the area and not finding us here would have left.

Now we have alerted them. They will be searching for us with even more men now."

"Venu, they would have found this shrine and evidence of our overnight stay here. They still would have done the same, trust me. We now know their nearest support station is about two hours away. Let's move."

He was abrupt, busy in his own thoughts.

"We have to do better," he said, half to me, half to himself. "The jungles are treacherous here. We must take some other route. Let us get to the coast. We need to takeover at least one of their support stations, which ever might be nearest, to give shape to my plans. I need to use their communications system."

He started towards the northeast. I followed him like an obedient servant.

We did not hurry this time, though our walk was brisk. All around us I could see the destruction caused by the heavy rains. Rivulets of water were still rushing forth with full vigor. Several small animals and reptiles lay dead in the mud. The smell of death prevailed everywhere. I knew there would be rains again in the evening, the atmosphere was getting to be hot and humid under the sun. The ground was slippery and muddy. We made our way cautiously through the shrubs and trees and made our way to the sea.

The seacoast was quiet except for the sound of the waves crashing against rocks.

"We have to penetrate deep in there," said Krishnan, pointing towards the dense woods. "By now, they'll be aware we are still alive and must be planning some strategic move. We have to outsmart them to prolong our deaths. This is war now that we have declared."

"How could they possibly have come to know that we had landed, that too at this particular spot? There must be some information leak. Or, is that mystery man playing some game with us?"

"I don't know, *Tambi*." Krishnan was irritated. "Whatsoever, it doesn't matter now. The fact is that they know for sure that we are here. I don't know whether they were expecting us for some time. Nothing comes to mind how it could have happened. But, all right. We are here to fight, and fight we will."

He then gave a wry smile.

I was intrigued. I thought hard trying to find an answer. But I too was in total darkness.

It was almost quarter to four when we took a curve that led us southeastwards. Keeping the sea to our left we walked on carrying our misery with us. The sky was overcast with dark clouds. The wind had stopped and I knew any moment the rains would come. My whole body was aching after this long walk and the excitement of the morning.

"We must stop," I whined.

"Keep walking," snapped Krishnan without a break in his pace. I swore and followed him. We were now in dense woods. An uneasy calm was prevalent here. The rustle of leaves was deafening to our alert ears. Our pace had slowed down but Krishnan seemed in no hurry. He stood for a moment or two and then said,

"I feel we are somewhere near Command Station Four. It used to be headed by Virupaksha sometime ago. I do not know whether he is still heading this camp. He is a master in guerilla warfare and a most trusted man of his superiors. He has caused severe harm to the Sri Lankan army as well as to the Indian army, in the recent past. He knows me well but will now be only too happy to shoot me dead. I am a traitor for them."

He then laughed.

I could hardly understand Krishnan at times.

"From here on we shall proceed cautiously. No noise, no talk. Just follow me."

I nodded.

"I know this region well. I have been here many times. Let's see how we can use my knowledge to our advantage."

I didn't know what was on his mind, an ignorant fool that I am. With no other choice, I just followed him.

We moved forward with care as deafening thunder followed by a deluge tried to caution us against the impending dangers. I cursed and swore, but in my heart I knew the rain was to our advantage. Our movements would go unnoticed. Our hunters wouldn't dare enter the woods knowing we could be anywhere. They knew we were suicidal. We had nothing to lose. We were breathing borrowed moments from destiny. There was no more remorse for the kind of mess we had placed ourselves in. We had killed six of their men this morning and would kill as many as we could before they got us.

But weren't they suicidal too? They were willing to lay down as many lives as may be required to eliminate us. They knew the jungles and all the secret paths therein better than we did. The thought chilled me.

Sometime later we approached a small open space littered with huge rocks. Water was rushing through the uneven gaps in the rocks. We climbed up a large slippery rock and sat down. We were soaked to our skins.

"I think, Venu, it would be unwise to keep going on till the rain eases. We can't see how close we are from Command Station Four. Plus, we need to recharge our energy." Saying this, he sprawled out on the rock and started humming to himself unmindful of the savage rain beating down on us. I removed my shoes and tried to revive my numbed limbs with a brisk massage.

The rain was incessant and the sky thundered as bolts of lightning crackled and fell on the ground. Since the beginning of the universe it must be happening like this every season. And yet nature was flourishing with promises of new life to come. We were amongst eternities. No remorse for calamity of nature could be sensed anywhere. Only bowed surrendering could been seen all around. The water rushing towards the ocean was only too happy to lose its separate existence, when we, mankind, were so specific to paint our deeds on the canvass of time. In the world of mankind there was chaos, stupidity and selfishness. What Krishnan had said was right - mankind always tried to buy out religion and gods. It wants to establish its supremacy over nature's rule. This nature was breathing just like the human soul, but it didn't have any deity. Mankind wanted to kill and get killed. What curse had we been blessed with?

I was deaf to the tunes of the rains for some time.

What a meaningless life was I leading, now that the villains had destroyed my family and me. I had been leading a peaceful life, the life of a gentleman. I wished everybody happiness. Never had I cursed anyone or had caused them harm in any way. And see, what was happening to me.

Darkness enveloped us. The crashing rains continued to soak us. I felt hungry. I yelled out at Krishnan. He opened his eyes and sat up.

"Let's eat."

"Alright. I am hungry too."

"Hey, Krishnan, remember the feast we had in the forests on the Indian coast? That wild fowl? I can still smell and taste it. Can't we find one here?"

"May be, but not in this rain," he laughed.

"Alright, let's open some of the packet stuff."

Before we could open a can, torchlight fell on us. Instinctively, I dived to one side and rolled down the rock grabbing my revolver at the same instance and releasing its safety catch, ready to open fire at the intruder. Krishnan too had repeated the same action.

I looked at the source of the beam. It was impossible to see the person behind it.

"Please, don't shoot," the voice pleaded.

It was, to my surprise, a female voice. I kept my revolver pointed at the intruder, trying to make out who she might be and what the hell she was doing here in this weather.

"Switch off the torch and come forward," yelled Krishnan. When the torchlight went off and there was no activity that would stir violent reaction in us, Krishnan switched on his torch and threw light at the woman who stood there in military outfit.

Sanjay Sonawani

"Krishnan, it's me, Himani... Himani Cherion. Have you forgotten me?"

Eighteen

Krishnan was silent during those agonizing moments.

He slowly got up still pointing his revolver in her direction. "Come forward...and don't try any games. Keep your hands up, behind your head...come slowly...come on. Sit here...Where are the others?"

"I am alone...shoot me if you want to."

"No. Why should I shoot you? Tell me, what's up? Why are you here? How did you know we would be here? How did you find us?"

"One question at a time, Krishnan. Don't be so impatient."

"Alright." Krishnan was irritated at her.

"Why have you walked into this trap?"

"I don't see this as a trap."

"Don't be a fool. This is a trap, and you know very well. I know how you outsmarted six men this morning. They were searching for you. They were expecting you to walk in here. They know everything. Don't you realize this, Krishnan?"

"There is nothing I don't know of. Tell me, why are you here and how did you find us?"

Himani took some time to answer him.

"I have been following you since the moment you landed."

"Impossible!" Shouted Krishnan, vehemently.

"But true, Krishnan. We knew you were being deported here. The location was known. They wanted you both eliminated. But the rains caused some confusion and that's why you are still alive.

"Krishnan, you have walked into a death trap."

"That should be our concern. Tell me, why have you come here?"

Himani gave Krishnan a look that I very well understood. The same look I had seen many times in Janaki's eyes.

"I was following you through the rains and thorny shrubs. I was out there when you found shelter in the shrine. I witnessed how you fought this morning... Forget it, it is so immaterial. I wanted to meet you, to warn you, but then I had a message from the Command Station so I had to rush somewhere else. But I came back, retracing my footsteps.

"Why did you return, Krishnan?"

"If you already knew that we were coming here, then you must also be knowing why we have come back and who brought us here, and for what!"

Sanjay Sonawani

Himani was silent for sometime. I was witnessing a nightmare that could well be true. The militants were not far away, not in the dreams, or at a shooting range, they were right here, alive, and in possession of emotions too!

"I knew you never were a traitor, Krishnan, but it seems that the Sivrasan incident has destroyed you. I know you had nothing to do with it. I always knew it, Krishnan. Since the day the news reached here, there were frantic activities. Rash decisions were taken about your life. I protested, Krishnan, honestly, I did. I pleaded for you. But they decided to eliminate you. How much I cried that night only I know, Krishnan."

"Himani, are you honest to your feelings?" Krishnan's voice had softened. He wanted to touch her, caress her, and soothe her. But he checked himself.

"If you still have any doubt left, you can kill me, Krishnan. After all these treacherous events, I have lost all interest in living any more," she said with a sob that turned into a muffled cry.

I wanted to curse Krishnan for his impassive attacks.

"They were in a hurry to execute you. I don't know why. They could have questioned you if they had any doubt left. They could have punished you if you were found guilty. But they were insistent to kill you. I don't know why, what happened in higher circles!

"Sivrasan, I feel, someone wanted him dead. Someone was sure he wouldn't surrender himself alive if threatened with arrest. They were right. But why then did they frame you with a false charge? You were the only man knowing his hideout. You had organized it. Framing you was so easy for them, Krishnan!

"But with Sivrasan a mystery has died. They so hurriedly

passed orders of your elimination that it really shocked me. I don't know who leaked the information. But I know for sure, my heart says so, it wasn't you."

There was an uneasy silence for some time.

"I am here to find out who cheated on me. I know not who saved us from that fatal accident and backed us to come here to avenge my destruction. I don't know what politics you all are playing. I know we hardly can succeed in the mission we are on. Politics, I know, keeps on changing its colors every moment - chameleons are far simpler! We are victim of their ugly politics.

"But the main question remains, who benefited from Sivrasan's death? Who was so anxious to leak out the news to SIT? They say I spilled my guts before Dorai Swami who they think was a mole in our outfit, fostered to pull wool over the Indian forces' eyes. But I didn't do it. I know for sure there wasn't anybody who knew where Sivrasan was being taken, except for Prabhakaran and me. I surely didn't leak the information, for there was no obvious reason for me to do so. I was on my way back after installing him where I thought he would be safe, in Bangalore, along with Shuba. I was not allowed to be in touch with any other person and I followed the instructions strictly. I reported only to Prabhakaran. And yet the hideout was made known to the Indian Police. There certainly was a leak and I am sure it was by someone who had access to covert developments.

"I know Prabhakaran, or someone from his coterie, is responsible for what happened at Bangalore. I have been victimized with some ulterior motive. I wish I could see him to know why this ugly game was played against me."

"You are expecting the impossible, Krishnan. I pray to you, go back. There is nothing you want to know. There is nothing you ever will know. I am here. Sometime later I may learn something and soothe myself that they had wronged you. But if at all you remain here for some more hours, you shall be dead. Please try to understand."

Krishnan was in no mood to pay heed to her prayers.

"Tell me, who were those saviors of ours from that fatal accident? Why did they inform you of our arrival when they too could have killed us so easily? Who alerted you of our deportation? Tell me."

Himani gave a helpless shrug. "I don't know. I knew only that you were being deported here. I know not what kind of conspiracy is this that forces you to walk into their den. I do not know who saved you. The news in the beginning was that you both were killed. There was a sudden calm about you out here. True, you caused confusion and violence out there in Madras and during your passage to India. But then it all was forgotten for they assumed you were dead. I mourned your death. And then, suddenly, there was this rumor that you were alive. They said that you had been protected by someone whose identity they were unaware.

"Your saviors sold you out. I am sure they must have struck a good deal. Do you know, Krishnan, that we are receiving a delivery of armaments from abroad? Of the latest technology. We may even be able build an atom bomb with it.

"...That's all I know. I don't know who saved you and why. But they must be powerful men?"

"Yes, they are the most powerful gang on this earth. They must have sold us for some timely gains. But does it matter to us now, Himani? Our own men first got me arrested in order to infuriate me. They forced me into jail for months to brainwash me. They destroyed the career I longed for. They forced me to become a militant to benefit their cause. They wanted to eliminate me just to cover up their heinous acts when they had enough of me. They used me as a pawn. So meticulously that I failed to understand what was about to befall me. So stupid I have been. Now, I am here to avenge their treachery, Himani."

"Go back, Krishnan. Respect my feelings. You know I too have been prey to their motives. I told you several times of my deep agonies, of how they raped me disguised as Lankan soldiers…twenty times a day to infuriate my soul, and then stage-managed an encounter to release me. It made me think that the LTTE was a humanitarian organization and not at all like what the media portrayed of them. But now I know they too were the LTTE who raped my existence. They wanted my special skills in logistics at their disposal. I was a happy young girl at that time looking forward to a career as a professor.

"Let me tell you, the LTTE has now nothing to do with the pride of the Tamils. It is using the Tamil pride as a weapon in its selfish mission. They used you. They used me…after such humiliation. But now there is no way out. I have to be amongst them following orders. I have no place to go. But you are a man. You can fight your way out. You can lead another life. There is no place for you out here, only vultures are awaiting you. Forget all the politics, it's an evil. Forget the past and lead a new life…"

I looked at Krishnan with a renewed passion. What she

said was right. We were unwanted men out here. They knew we were here - No secret anymore of our arrival! That meant the men who saved us and wanted us to kill Prabhakaran had changed their mind sometime during our journey through the outrageous weather. Or there was another political upheaval that forced them to change their course of action.

"I shall not go back," said Krishnan in a firm voice, "Unless I avenge myself. Even if I run away, death is written, now or later. I wish to die a man's death. They have killed innocent people without showing any mercy. They killed a man, who was beaming and waving at those who garlanded him in affection and then a human bomb blew him to pieces.

"I have many questions to ask. Please answer them, if you can."

"I know so little, Krishnan! You go back, please. You can still save yourself."

"How did you know that we were alive and coming here?"

"People were talking. They were being alerted for some time. First the news was that you both were killed in an accident after shooting Varadrajan dead; I wept when I heard the news. I felt as if my life was shattered. And then, there was talk of your walking back to life. Who saved you Krishnan?"

"You tell me, you know that."

"No, I don't know. Who send you back here?"

"I don't know," Krishnan replied, honestly. "The fact is they didn't tell us anything. I said they were the CIA and they didn't deny it! But they must be LTTE's enemies or why should they take such pains to save us and organize our passage here? But then, who told you people that we were alive and reaching here and when? The question troubles me. I need answers to many questions."

"And who do you think can or will answer you? They will first riddle you with bullets. No answer can you ever obtain here. You should go back." Her voice was full of passion and prayer.

"From the beginning, someone has been cheating me. There is some deceiver out there hiding behind a façade. First, the leak of Sivrasan's hideout. Now, this leak. Who is playing ugly games with me? And why are you here? Why do you wish to save me? Why are you pleading my return?"

"You are a hypocrite, Krishnan. You know I have my reasons to risk my life for you. I always had tremendous affection for you. You know it, you bastard. You knew it all along and still never admitted it."

Krishnan kept silent. I could not see his face in the dark night.

"When I learnt that you were here, since then I have been secretly watching and following you, neglecting my superiors' orders. You don't know what a risk I have taken coming here to meet you. You truly are a cruel person."

Her voice was choked with emotions.

Krishnan moved slowly forward and caressed her face and then took her in an embrace. He said nothing. My heart lit up with the light of a million suns. I was drenched in a shower of feelings.

Krishnan released her and watched her intensely.

Both were still like the statues at the shrine where we had sheltered for the night.

Then Krishnan moved back.

"Go back, Himani. Never you shall entangle yourself in mortal affairs. Do not risk your life anymore. I am here to avenge the disaster that has befallen my friend for no mistake of his. I am here to know the truth and I shall have it. I know I will have to slay many people or it may so happen that I will die before I know anything. Yet, there is satisfaction in trying. Please go back."

Himani stood silent for some time, as though her mind was not ready to accept leaving her heart behind.

"As you wish, Krishnan. I pray that you be safe. Do not go deep in this area. They have laid booby traps that may cause you great trouble. Watch every step carefully as you walk. Another thing, Sri Lankan armed troops are camping not far from here and there is talk that there soon might be a brief encounter with them. Our men are worried for they don't have adequate supplies; there was some problem with our friends. So in case we don't receive the new shipment in time, we will be in trouble."

Krishnan nodded in understanding.

"Don't tell us anything more. It is dangerous for you. Now you better go. If destiny permits, we shall meet again under better skies."

Himani bowed to touch Krishnan's feet.

Krishnan touched her head in a silent blessing.

Himani then turned around and disappeared into the dark shadows of uncertainty.

Krishnan broke the silence.

"See, *Tambi*, this is love. Here no companionship is

expected. No burden of responsibilities is ever thrust upon the other person. True love is like this.

"I know her for a long time, ever since I have been with the LTTE. She is a commanding officer with them and has accompanied me on a couple of missions. I knew she had been deceived, humiliated. She was forced to join the organization. She adapted to all the hard practices of life here in her fury. And still she was full of liveliness. Her eyes would speak of her heartfelt sentiments. I knew she was deeply in love with me but I never wanted to love anyone - I have no love left within me.

"Do you know, I never tried to contact my parents afterwards? I don't even know whether they are alive or dead. I have become dispassionate about all worldly relations since then. I knew no true relationship could ever exist in my life to console me. But this woman, playing with arms and killing others so mercilessly, has a heart that could love.

"And yet I cannot trust her. I know, it may be a ploy. She may have come here under certain circumstances. May be to misguide us for reasons we don't know. And still, I feel I should trust her. I should have behaved sensibly when she was in front of me. Now she has gone and I don't know whether I shall ever see her again."

◆　◆　◆

"Let's discuss our next course of action. We now know that there are traps laid in the jungles and that the LTTE is lacking in supplies. She said their friends are causing some trouble and who else could it be but the USA? They are their latest allies. That mysterious man's deliberation to convince us to undertake this mission matches with these latest developments. The CIA

Sanjay Sonawani

is not having the same romance with the LTTE as before. And yet a shipment of arms is arriving soon to these coasts. Mind-boggling incidents have taken place and, alas, how little do we know!" Krishnan was pouring words out just like the dark sky above, without a reflection of remorse for the moments he just had been through showing on his countenance.

"However, the question remains, why the news of our walking back to life and into this region has been leaked? Who did this and why? Why the CIA has changed its mind, *Tambi*. And it has put us in a vulnerable position in these jungles.

"Is it their moles in the CIA who still desire that American friendship be continued with the LTTE when their other fractions have something different in mind? This is possible. The Indian operations of the CIA is much stronger. They have several establishments and they continue to operate several missions. They buy thinkers, politicians, scientists, journalists... They are like missionaries working all the time on forming and deforming public opinions to their benefit. They wish to topple governments and provide support to all the possible insurgencies in this continent.

"In India, it is easy to establish terrorist training centres and remain overboard. Many spy networks are active there but neither the RAW nor the Intelligence Bureau, or the CBI has ever come to know of their existence.

"But it's alright. Ours is a poor country where money is God. With money anybody can be bought. However, the main question is, how do we proceed. We need to enter..."

A sacred thread of moments had just been woven into a fabric of emotions here and as if oblivious of it, Krishnan was speaking as usual. Couldn't he wait for sometime? How cruel could he be, even to himself?

I cut him short. "Krishnan, what Himani said is right. You are cruel and a hypocrite. You don't respect the essence of life. I know we can't sit tight and let them capture us, but still, Krishnan?"

Krishnan looked at me in surprise.

"Hell! Don't be stupid, Venu. I am not here to weep over my misfortune. Can't you see that there is no time left for remorse? We are amidst deadly surroundings. We are here to avenge ourselves and to know, not to weep over our past. Yes, she loved me. So what? Aren't there many affectionate people who weep alone in misery for their bygone love? I am not the first and nor the last person on this earth who has been loved with all the care and affection and has still not responded to the heart's wrenching outcry. I never had any feeling for her. But I do respect her feelings, that's all. I am not here to reunite past emotional ties.

"See, Venu, sometimes one reaches a point in life when there is no goal left to advance to. No achievement is desired. Defamation matters no more, nor does fame. Only you have to quench your thirst. Here, no emotions or logic can help us. We have to be on the alert all the time. So don't be a stupid fool to get engrossed in meaningless feelings. You had many feelings and all you have seen and experienced is shattering before your eyes. No feelings, my friend, there's no place for them now! Just listen to me for we have no time."

I forced myself with great effort to extricate myself out of the dense marsh of emotions that had bogged me.

Sanjay Sonawani

"You continue your rubbish," I said in a heavy voice.

"They are everywhere. They know we are somewhere in the vicinity. Moving about with them on our lookout is dangerous. We are left with scarce choices. Somehow we have to do better. They must be thinking the same as what we might think. We have to surprise them, somehow. We have to mislead them.

"We cannot wage a face-to-face battle with them, it would be suicidal. They are experts in guerilla warfare. It's their forte. We must be careful and avoid encounters. Our goal is not at all to eliminate those common militants, but Prabhakaran. So let's focus our efforts on reaching him somehow.

"I know Prabhakaran is normally in Puranthan, but reaching there is as good as impossible. We have to take some other course of action. We have to bring him out in the open where we wish him to be.

"I know there are ministers in the Lankan government who secretly support the LTTE for their own political reasons. I know a few of them for sure are involved in LTTE activities. To reap benefits out of the insurgency they need men like Prabhakaran. It's a tragedy but let's use them to our advantage.

"So, Purantham is out of the question. Those bastards who thought we can ever kill Prabhakaran must be crazy. Prabhakaran is highly protected. He is terribly secretive. His movements are unknown even to his closest men. He keeps on changing his place of stay. He is the most wicked man I have ever met. But, we need him. We need to face him and after we have our answers, kill him. We have to play a trick to lure him in the open. And for that we need to do a little exercise. The rains are in our favor. Their shortage of arms and supplies is also in our favor. The LTTE can't survive for long without an adequate and constant supply of arms.

"Fortunately, I know something that may play a vital role in our operations. We have to take a chance. It may be our last chance. But if my judgement is right, we will succeed."

I was at a loss for words. I could hardly understand what he said. I didn't know the rules of the game we were playing. And the game was dangerous. What he had said was true; after all, we were here to avenge ourselves. And avenging a powerful and merciless organization like the LTTE was not as easy as I had thought in a fit of outraged emotions. True, the enemy was far more powerful and well organized. So unless one knew their secrets, it would be impossible to penetrate into their home turf.

I felt helpless and weak. Then Janaki's image appeared before my eyes. She was screaming, her body contorted in terrible pain and she was calling me.

"No, Krishnan. No matter what happens to me, I shall avenge myself. At least let us kill as many as we can. Let's go ahead and wage a war on these bastards."

"We must move now. Let us change direction a little. It may take at least five to six hours to reach our destination," said Krishnan, adding excitedly, "I need a communications system urgently."

"Are you sure you really need a communications system, Krishnan? You have done it before. This time they will definitely suspect foul play."

"I am not at all going to call them. I need someone else

this time and know very well who that person is. I only hope that I am right, that's all. If I fail...sorry friend."

"You need not to be," I said in a soft voice.

"Alright then. Let us try to abort this trap of theirs first and then let's go back the way we came."

"As you say," I muttered.

The rain was incessant. We had nothing left that was dry.

"Let's move," said Krishnan in hurried tone.

I didn't know what was on his mind, but I had to follow his judgement. I got up, slung the haversack on my back and held the gun in one hand and the torch in the other. I was ready.

Krishnan too was ready.

Our retreat had begun.

Nineteen

It was a dreadful journey, as we retraced our footsteps for more than three hours under the cursing skies and an unfriendly jungles. Then changing direction, we headed northward or whatever direction it was. We were now walking through small farms and could see the illumination of the villages near them and hear the barking of dogs. This was the first sign of being around civilization. I had heard that the villagers in this region were LTTE supporters and most of the youth had joined the organization.

"Now I know the general location. There is an army camp somewhere nearby. Before morning we have to enter it."

I was shocked to hear him.

"Are you crazy, Krishnan? How can one enter the military area unnoticed? They will shoot us at sight."

"We have to take the risk. There won't be many of them, trust me. It's only a small command station. We are still at the outskirts of the LTTE zone. The army here has many bunkers and quarters on the disputed borders. They patrol during the night. However, in the rainy season no hectic activities are carried out here as then both parties suffer badly; we may have a chance."

"But Himani told a different story, that she suspected an encounter to take place in this region. They shall be alert and ready to shoot at intruders. It doesn't makes sense to risk our lives."

"Himani may be wrong," said Krishnan in a tone of finality. "I do not think they are preparing for any battle at this time. If that were the case, Himani wouldn't have dared to follow us. I know womankind - they are treacherous when under pressure. May be she has the wrong information and if I am not being skeptical, she might have said it because she wanted us to go back."

His voice was stern and emotionless. It stunned me.

"But why do you wish to enter a military area? They are not our enemies," I protested.

"I agree. But I do need to use their communications system, just for a couple of minutes. I have one urgent message to transmit. Our success depends on how precisely I do that. Keep moving on."

I asked him many questions, but he didn't answer any one of them.

Sanjay Sonawani

Frustrated, I walked on.

We passed a hill that spread eastwards only to curve westward in an awkward twist. Krishnan had increased his pace as if he knew that we were nearing our destination. Then we were in thick forests again. The rain had stopped and a cold wind kept lashing our drenched bodies.

It was then that I heard a harsh command that froze my heart.

"Stop. Throw down your weapons and raise your hands."

Before I could guess what calamity was about to befall us, I saw Krishnan leap sideways and throw his body flat on the grass. I too, in a frenzied reaction rolled down till my body crashed against a tree trunk sending shooting pains through my body. Somehow I managed to take position behind the tree and watched, alert for any further signs of trouble.

There was no movement but a rustle of leaves and stealth footsteps from behind the bushes. Then I heard a slight noise not far from me in the bushes. I aimed my gun in that direction but before I could pull trigger, Krishnan fired a shot from his revolver, shattering the calm of the night. A painful moan and instantaneous counter-gunfire at us followed the sound of the gunshot. There must be many of them, I thought while trying to wipe my eyes with the back of my hand.

I pointed my gun at the place from where the gunfire had come from and pulled the trigger.

A thunderous roar echoed in the hills and I heard a thrashing sound in the bushes and then a thud.

Soon, the earlier peace had settled back in the vicinity.

Sanjay Sonawani

We waited in silence. Fear had tightened its grip on me. The sound of gunfire would carry a long distance in the night and we were somewhere near an army outpost.

"Let's move," muttered Krishnan. "We have to change our course a bit now."

I got up, adjusted my clothes and the haversack, and followed him without a word.

"Don't get frightened. Such encounters are not new out here. When they find corpses tomorrow they will blame the LTTE for it and may kill some militants in retaliation. Actually, the Sri Lankan army is tired of this prolonged civil war. But as long as the LTTE is active, they have to hold fort."

I said nothing.

"I am sure they are not many of them out here, but even then we have to be careful. Human rights activists are attacking the army and, hence, they are afraid of taking brutal action. The same thing is happening in Kashmir. They simply can't shoot the militants at sight. These human rights activists are fools. They just don't seem to understand the seriousness of the militants.... These militants just can't claim they are humans!"

There was bitterness in the voice of the ex-militant turned avenger. Wasn't it an irony?

"What's up Krishnan? With whom do you want to communicate?"

"I wish to mislead them. I want to use a little information I have and use my guessing ability to our benefit."

"Whom are you to contact?"

"Kondathaman."

Sanjay Sonawani

"Who is he?"

"He is one of the ministers in the Sri Lanka Parliament. Let me update you with some background.

"In May '1990, I was in Jaffna. At that time a plan was hatched to assassinate the leader of opposition in the Sri Lankan Parliament. Actually, to my understanding, that is, the instructions were issued from abroad. I was the man who used to receive and decode the instructions. I was chief of communications, remember? And these instructions were relayed from Colombo.

"I suspected all the time that there existed secret supporters of the LTTE within the Sri Lankan ministry. There was cause for my suspicion as many a time they had used the LTTE to eliminate their political rivals. Prabhakaran happily helped them and, in turn, gathered support and money and information that could strengthen his position. Had the LTTE desired ultimate victory over the Sri Lankan army it wouldn't have been that difficult, for the LTTE was better equipped with armaments as well as with ruthless supporters. But Prabhakaran never attempted the final war. He just went on tightening his grip over the organization and reaped as much benefit as he could by befriending foreign contacts and the government authorities. That was also the reason why the Sri Lankan government did not wage an all-out war against the LTTE as well. There were two possibilities. One, the LTTE would win over and establish its formal rule in the framework of democratic norms; two, Sri Lanka would win and the ethnic war would come to an end and there would be peace on the island nation.

"I debated these possibilities with myself and deduced that there must be a secret truce between the two parties.

Politicians could then go on denouncing the LTTE publicly and infuriate public sentiment to their benefit - to get themselves elected to power. The insurgency helped them to remain in power without doing anything for the public. For they could blame the LTTE for everything - for the slackened economy, for the rising inflation, for the worsening international relations. Everything.

"They needed the LTTE. They needed a shrewd man like Prabhakaran. Do you know, Venu, when Rajiv Gandhi diplomatically forced the Indian Peace Keeping Force upon Sri Lanka, no one was happy in this government. Not even the Sri Lankan army. I know for the fact that there was a lot of exchange of information, which led to the ultimate defeat of the Indian army on this island. The Sri Lankan army wouldn't cooperate with the Indian army, but would even mislead them at times. And when Mr. Gandhi realized this, he had no choice but to withdraw his army, and so he did.

"The LTTE is not as powerful as it is made out to be. It is entirely dependent on the disillusioned youth to fill the ranks and foreign countries for the supply of armaments. And now, as Himani was telling us, there are disputes with their new allies. Their supply of arms is endangered. Which means - No arms, no LTTE.

"There was Padmanabhan, the leader of another militant fraction - Tamil Revolutionaries was the name of his organization. When I received the earlier message from our friend in the Sri Lankan government, I deduced that he must be a powerful man. The opposition leader was raising a hue and cry over many issues and had put the government in an embarrassing situation. They had no choice left but to eliminate him. And they did; a human bomb took his life. Then the issue of Padmanabhan was bothering Prabhakaran. Padmanabhan had a different ideology. He too had many supporters who had brought him in the position to bargain with the Lankan government independently. He was a pain in the neck. A secret meeting was summoned and was attended by only four people. Then for the first time I saw this man. Kondathaman. He was a minister then; though the revelation supported my deductions, it came as a shock.

"Everybody had their own private interests in Padmanabhan's elimination. The Lankan Government wished they had a single enemy and Prabhakaran desired his sole supremacy. He wished to rise above all as the messiah of the Tamil liberation movement. So a plan was hatched to kill the opponent who could one day challenge Prabhakaran's supremacy. And Padmanabhan was brutally eliminated.

"Moreover, did Kondathaman represent his power hungry party? No, he represented the CIA, the new allies. He promised them a regular supply of arms and also limited warfare strategies. There was a blemish on him few years ago when a Member of Parliament had attacked Kondathaman for being a CIA agent, manifesting anti-national activities. The media had covered this sensational accusation with wild headlines. The charges, of course, were denied and then there were just allegations and counter allegations for some time and soon everyone had forgotten it.

"Kondathaman has a lot to do with the LTTE. He is the LTTE's strong support outside. A mediator between the LTTE, CIA and the Sri Lankan government. This is the reason why the USA pokes its dirty nose in Kashmir but has never expressed its concern over the insurgency on this small island nation. They were already in it. They needed to be there, not to check the Sri Lankan government, but to undermine Indian unity. Their motives were ulterior. I was afraid to speak out my concerns even to myself. They had nothing to do with the well being of the Tamils. They capitalized on the Tamil pride for their benefit."

"And still you were with them?" I said in a bitter voice.

Krishnan was silent for a moment as we crossed a spring.

"I had no choice, *Tambi*. Where could I go? I had no other destination to go to. I had destroyed my life already by then."

There was no remorse in his voice, just a matter-of-fact explanation. It pained me. But I was eager to listen to his deductions.

"Now, it appears that though the CIA was somehow involved in the matters concerning Rajiv Gandhi's assassination, it has backed out temporarily for some reason. But why would the CIA back out? In such a case, there must be a threat, a threat to expose the CIA connection and it had to stop supplies to the LTTE. Now, surprisingly, the misunderstanding between two parties seems to have been resolved as they have let the LTTE know that we are alive and approaching the coast.

"One thing is sure, *Tambi*, both the parties, in a way, are scared of me. See how they sold out Sivrasan and then tried to eliminate me. They know my living is dangerous to them. They must get rid of me before I let the cat out of the bag and derail their well-laid plans. But I knew what was on their minds at the time they involved me in that highly secret operation.

"Again a question remains. Why there was dispute and

why there has been a hush-hush deal between them? There must have been a quiet understanding and attempts are being made to seal further leaks that may pose a threat to their existence. There must have been some development that forced the CIA to change its mind and sell us out. Truly, we are of no significance, in a way. They knew that once we were in Sri Lanka only luck could save us. Even then, to be doubly sure, they leaked the information, and cheated us. They notified them during our passage here that we were being deported, for some kind of timely advantage.

"I am curious to know what transpired between them.

"I am curious to see Prabhakaran.

"I am curious to know why the CIA backed out and tried to use us as a weapon against their friends. There must be some reason. It just can't happen without any cause."

He stopped. Everything seemed so dubious and untrustworthy. How so many incidents kept on happening without anybody knowing what really caused the change of seasons!

"Tell me, Krishnan, did they really believe that we could kill Prabhakaran? Prabhakaran is not that easy a target, even for his most powerful enemies. Then why did the CIA think that we could eliminate him?"

Krishnan stopped, patted my shoulders affectionately and said, "They knew they had nothing to lose. They saved us in order to use us against the LTTE if things got worse. They knew I was a key person in Rajiv Gandhi's assassination. I was the man who escorted Sivrasan to Bangalore and the only one to know of his hideout. Till then, no CIA connection was in the picture. The secret communications and supply of arms could never be proved in any court of law. Only physical evidence matters when one confronts the law. And I am the physical evidence. The LTTE wanted to kill me, blaming me for Sivrasan's exposure, not only to punish me but also to erase evidence. Mind you, I am only deducing all this. I have been deliberating with myself from the day I regained consciousness after our accident.

"Why did they leak information about Sivrasan's hideout, I wonder? There must be a reason. They put blame on me and tried to kill me because they wanted to eliminate the proof and safeguard their sinister secrets. And, why the CIA took so many pains to save us? I feel it was to secure a proof. And why the CIA decided that we could be used as a weapon to eliminate or attempt to eliminate Prabhakaran? Because during that period of our convalescence our need as a proof might have become insignificant... So much water has flowed during that unfortunate passage of time. But they had brought us back to life and then found that they had no use of us. They had resolved the misunderstanding among themselves. They knew they couldn't let us walk out and roam freely in the open. It would cause another scandal. We might remember our secret saviors' hideout and might attract unsolicited attention to it. They wanted us away when they found we were of no other use. They wanted to infuriate our feelings and use it as a weapon against the LTTE. They wished to capitalize on our disaster.

"They wanted us away from Indian soil, in this treacherous land where we could hardly succeed. The CIA is extremely powerful, my friend. Killing Prabhakaran would be just a routine job for them. And still they tried to convince us that we really could eliminate Prabhakaran! They thought that at least we would cause them some damage; some fruits still could be reaped in exchange for saving our lives. I don't think they ever believed we could even reach Prabhakaran. But that we would be killed in the bargain, they were confident.

"They tried to use us somehow even when we were useless to them in the light of the new events that had taken place. What these incidents were, we do not know. But certainly weird."

A sharp-edged silence prevailed for a long time. I was bothered. Would I ever get to avenge my destruction? Would I ever avenge Janaki's death? And if at all we were to fail, why we were treading this dangerous path? Couldn't we sneak away from this dangerous coast, as Himani had suggested?

"*Tambi,* we surely can kill that bastard. We only need a little luck and the right opportunity. I am here to prove we can destroy their sinister moves as they have destroyed us. I wish to make them repent for whatever they did to us. They have underestimated us, Venu. I won't let them play any more games with us. And so we need to get hold of a communications system."

We walked in silence. My heart too was now on fire. Krishnan was doing the right thing. He had not forgotten the death of my Janaki. He hadn't forgotten all those treacherous games they had been playing with us. He was enraged. His calm countenance didn't mean that he was about to surrender to their machinations. He was not as selfish as I had thought him to be.

I was willing to die to avenge Janaki's brutal murder. I had no zeal to breathe and survive on stale and defeated moments of life. I had no desire left to achieve anything else other than the destruction of my enemy, even at the cost of my own life.

We had crossed a roaring spring surrounded by tall grass, when I saw a streak of light through the trees.

"Krishnan," I hissed.

Krishnan dropped to his knees - he too had seen the light - and crawled stealthily through the bushes. I followed suit.

As we came forward, we saw a couple of structures surrounded by coils of barbed wire. Occasionally, a search-light mounted on a watch-tower would sweep the area illuminating the structures and the few armed sentries standing guard.

"Venu, you stay here. I shall enter. I guess there wouldn't be many soldiers inside. I have to find the communications room."

"It's dangerous, Krishnan. There will be more armed soldiers hidden from us in the darkness and also inside the buildings. The communications room won't be empty either."

"Venu, it's almost quarter to three in the morning. If at all there are more soldiers, they must all be asleep, barring these tired sentries outside. It won't be that risky. And, also, do we have any other option?"

"Then let me also join you." I insisted.

"No," he said, firmly. "Supposing they catch me, you go back and save yourself."

"But…"

"No buts. I must start now before it's too late. Trust me,

I shall be back. I know how the Sri Lankan army acts. This is a very small outfit as compared to others. And they are not expecting anything unusual - during the monsoons they don't expect an attack on their regiment."

I was desperate to convince him to take me along but his firm voice stopped further argument.

I nodded silently and wished him luck.

I lay flat on the grass behind the shrubs and through the branches watched him crawl stealthily towards the barbed wire fencing.

Reaching it, he bent a couple of strands of the wire.

Suddenly, he froze.

Footsteps of the patrolling sentries could be heard.

Two sentries passed him by without a break in their stride. Krishnan then continued with his efforts. It took him almost ten minutes to make a gap large enough to crawl through.

Thereafter, I could see nothing. He had blended himself into the dark surroundings of the army premises.

Waiting in the shrubs was a severe punishment. I was sweating with anxiety. My heart was beating rapidly, as if it was about to explode. I prayed desperately to God for Krishnan's safe return, peering anxiously into the darkness, fearful of every movement. Every minute seemed like a year to me. I glanced at the sky, still crowded with dark clouds. The gurgling sound of the spring that we had crossed was sharp and bothersome. I glanced at my watch. Half an hour had passed since Krishnan had left me.

Sanjay Sonawani

I tried to avert my mind from Krishnan.

What will I do if he doesn't return?

I knew nothing about the geography of this region. I had no knowledge what I should do under such circumstances. I could fight, but how? On my own, how could I reach Prabhakaran's secret hideout? How could I outsmart these militants by myself? I knew nothing of their ways. No. Alone I would die.

An uncertainty loomed over me. Truly, revenge is not easy when you are fighting against a group of crooked people unless you know their traits and have inside information. They can play a cat and mouse game with you and kill you once they are tired of it. You simply meet an unfortunate death. And, now without Janaki, there would be no one to mourn my death.

Another hour slowly ticked by.

I then heard a rustling sound in the darkness. I froze. I was terrified. It was as though death had finally caught up with me. I shut my eyes tight in fear.

Gradually, I opened my eyes and shot a glance at the dark figure that appeared before me.

I stared in disbelief.

It was Krishnan.

He was back.

I rushed towards him, without thinking of the danger I was calling upon myself should I be seen or heard by the military men, and helped him through the thorny bushes.

Silently, we crossed the spring trying to put a safe distance between the military camp and us.

"I had to kill two soldiers. They were guarding the transmission room, " he said finally

"But were you able to use the system?"

"Yes, I have sent the message. I don't know whether they will believe in it or not but I have tried my best. If I have successfully convinced them, they shall come tomorrow evening to a place on the banks of Fanoma River."

Now was a time of excitement after deadly uncertainty. Krishnan had done it.

"Whom did you send the message to? What did you say?"

"Oh! It's all so weird. As I told you, I had given some thought to the recent happenings, and deduced that Kondathaman has something to do with the LTTE, as well as the CIA. I tried to use this to our advantage. I informed Kondathaman that a meeting with Prabhakaran has urgently been summoned to thrash out some matter of grave importance. The rendezvous is now marked. Or so I hope."

I was not in the least bit convinced that a minister would rush to the rendezvous site without a thorough verification of the message.

"It is impossible, Krishnan, that they can be fooled like this. They know better. They know any stupidity on their part can bring disaster upon them."

Krishnan laughed.

"There is one thing, Venu, you should not forget. That is, each party to the recent chaos is in a quandary. It is the first time that the LTTE has ever handled such a gruesome assassination that has caused ripples across the globe. Killing an opponent militant head like Padmanabhan or some local ministers is a different ball game altogether, you know. Rajiv Gandhi had many friends as he had foes and still he had international standing. The LTTE, in the past, has resorted to a lot of violence, but within its own territory. What significance does Sri Lanka have on the vast international political canvas of the superpowers? This land is being used to cause unrest in this part of the world, so that India busies herself in resolving the crisis and has no time to peep out of her windows.

"My heart says, they laid plans to eliminate Rajiv Gandhi not only to avenge his action of sending the Indian army to mitigate the LTTE's stronghold. He had to be killed for some other reasons, too, at someone else's behest whom they couldn't turn down.

"That someone got it done at the hands of the LTTE. But then failed to understand Prabhakaran. He just couldn't perform such a gruesome act just for the sake of Tamil pride and unnecessarily put himself in extreme danger. If at all this was the case, that the LTTE on its own eliminated Rajiv Gandhi, then he would be calling for another vicious attack from the Indian army in retaliation. A fight which he could never expect to win. Under the circumstances, the Sri Lanka Government could hardly deny its support to the Indian army. He must have ensured this doesn't happen and such assurance he only could have got from a superpower that has adequate control over Indian policymakers. You must remember, in the ordinary course of things, no one can challenge India's supremacy and play around with the lives of its leaders, unless one deliberately plans for it.

"He, Prabhakaran, is the shrewdest man one can ever

meet. He just couldn't do it for the sake of supplies of arms or money, but for more important promises that we don't know of. He did it, used his suicide bomb and the best brains to execute the operation, and waited till he knew he had control over the situation. Sivrasan's incident is not at all a coincidence. There must be something more to it. I sure didn't leak any information. Then the only man left who could have done it is Prabhakaran himself. But then why should he do it when Sivrasan was lodged safely and not at all in any position to cause any harm?

"As I am telling you, my friend, there must be some greater dimension to that incident which I am failing to decipher. Why did the CIA get annoyed with Prabhakaran and yet, why they had to form another hush-hush pact with him? They are not true friends in the conventional sense of the term for they have come together to achieve their own ulterior motives. Prabhakaran is hardly a man you can trust. He is treacherous and has hellish ambitions. He must have somehow threatened his new allies that he can cause harm to them if they just keep on safeguarding their own interests and leave him in the open to face the music. And why should Prabhakaran feel unsafe when the execution was orderly and perfect? What could possibly have happened to strain the relations when they were supposed to be closer than ever under the circumstances? Did the CIA turn on him when its motive was fulfilled?

"We know nothing. And now we are the proverbial sacrificial goats at their reunion. I'm perplexed by the complexity of what we are facing here. The assassination has raked up something that they couldn't have foreseen and that's why there is confusion and distrust among them.

"But I am not sure whether they are sure of anybody. They seem to be cautious, ready to take advantage of the situation that time provides them with. Think, why on the earth those men, whether CIA or anybody, should be watching the streets of Madras in a scarce hope that we may alight there of all the places left on earth? How did they know we were in the heart of the matter? Let me tell you, our escape from that fatal accident was no coincidence. The CIA, or whosoever it was, was on the lookout for us. When that bastard Varadrajan tricked us, none except the police was there to take cognizance of the situation. And still they could step in, that too, in time and take our unconscious bodies to their secret hideout and revive us. Is it a mere coincidence? No, my friend. It can't be. They saved us and led us to this path that we, under different circumstances, would have avoided. What does this mean? Tell me!

"They wished to outsmart each other if the circumstances turned against them and tried to hide an ace up their sleeves in order to surprise the other. There are people on this earth who didn't like the recent disaster, Russia, for example. They might be eager to expose the CIA connection. And even China, for that matter. They all despise USA, you know, though they claim there's a political marriage between them. Who is the LTTE then? Its so-called smartness is the doings of its allies. Even if the Indian Intelligence arrives at the conclusion that the LTTE was just used as a pawn, what can it do? The system has been so greatly undermined by the surreptitious infiltrators that society is no longer ready to fight.

"Do you really think that the Indian investigators, even if they come to know what might have gone wrong, can blame the

CIA? No, my friend, India would never do it, as it is a dependent country. But suppose someone else takes the lead to expose the USA?

"Then not only the LTTE but the integrity of the CIA too is in danger. All connections must be hidden, as if there never were any relations between the two. Their machinery has to work hard to eliminate all the possibilities of unsolicited exposure. And when everyone's existence is at stake, they have to reconcile the relations so that they can fight out the common danger. They need to deliberate and extract maximum benefits from each other so that they can carry on the same activities uninterrupted in the future. They are vultures of some primitive kind, ready to attack and ready to defend equally viciously should the situation turn against them. And here now in front of them is a unique situation that needs clarifications! Isn't this possible?

"We don't know the current political scenario that is taking shape in India or across the world. Hence, we are left only with wild guesses, which might be absolutely wrong. But in the last couple of weeks, SIT must have reached at some conclusion through its endless investigations. India still has a caretaker government. The acting prime minister knows he can't execute his powers unless the election process is complete and the democratically elected government is sworn in. The timing is so perfect that the assassins have scope to seal all the probabilities of exposure before the new government is formed. May be the new government will again be in minority; that's what has always been desired by the Western think tanks and shrewd politicians. For them India must remain a slave to the superpower.

"But all this is unimportant, for all these are my deductions based on my previous experiences with my now alienated friends and I cannot be sure that I am right. But, for the time being, I only hope that my message to Kondathaman causes some uneasiness. He knows in what mess he has put himself and also his allies. He too needs meetings and assurances that in case of any adversity, Prabhakaran does not expose the other partners."

The deliberations that Krishnan continued endlessly made no sense to me, as we truly knew nothing. And what was the use of it when we weren't even sure of seeing another dawn. What lay ahead was important and how could I assure myself that Krishnan's little game would succeed?

"But he can counter-check whether the message came from the right sources. He may smell something fishy. He may not be as important a person as you say. He might contact his superiors. And what if they sense this is but a decoy planted by us?" I asked, anxiously.

"My friend," Krishnan said mildly after a while, "I have sent a counter-message to the LTTE headquarters; I was afraid that they might have changed their codes and communication methods after what we have done to them in India. But it seems that as yet they don't have any replacement for me. They lack technicians out here in the jungles, my friend. I, a man, having expertise in social sciences, could grasp the training under white men that got me promoted to In-charge of Communications. They have many experts in unarmed combat and in guerilla warfare but they still lack in technocrats. The original system remained intact, just as I had left it.

"I sent a counter-message to the LTTE headquarters on

some other specific frequency and relayed a message saying that there had been a leak about the CIA connection to two rival political parties and that they are in discussion with the Indian premier, and it may call upon them unsolicited attention from the rest of the world. Hence, Kondathaman desires a meeting to discuss this issue on top priority."

"But wouldn't they cross-check?"

Krishnan laughed.

"My dear friend, they could if at all they had a chance. But I have now changed all the frequencies. They can't call each other for confirmation, at least for some time. That's why I took that much time in the army communications room. The modern systems are perfect - if you don't know the technology you can't play around with it. But I have mastered electronics, as I had nothing else to do while being an active member in their outfit. I know new emerging technologies that an intelligent man can use as bugs, and I have bugged their system. Kondathaman should come out there and so too Prabhakaran.

"Do you know how their meetings are held? You will wonder at their extraordinary management abilities which even the great corporate houses lack. Everybody is well protected. Kondathaman doesn't come alone. He has his own men to protect him, for he doesn't trust anyone and so does Prabhakaran. Prabhakaran is highly selective about the locations where he meets other people or delegations. He ensures his safety first.

"The place I told you is the safest place for him, located on the banks of Fanoma River. Firstly, dense forests blanket the place. Secondly, all the villagers around the place are hard-core LTTE supporters. They also have the best modern surveillance equipment to check all activites in the vicinity. Even if he doubts the message, he would come there, as it is the safest place for him.

"And Kondathaman. He too will come because he knows Prabhakaran can't harm him. He is an important man for him, a link between the two parties. No gain can Prabhakaran extract out of his death. So why should Prabhakaran or Kondathaman suspect foul play?

"They are in a dilemma and need a lot of interaction. We are giving them a chance to interact. They are isolated and it is very easy to make those who are lonely and uncertain of everything uneasy.

"So, my friend, the chances are good that both will be present at the meeting place, where we can reach safely since I know the area very well and I also know how to outsmart their surveillance system."

Krishnan seemed damn confident of what he said and it gave me confidence. I patted his shoulder for his brilliant logic. He said nothing loosing himself in the depths of his thoughts as he continued to walk on through the shrubs and bushes.

***

I noticed we were heading for the coast, that too from an entirely opposite direction. We hadn't had any sleep and we were tired but the prospect of the coming day forced me to tread ahead.

"Where are we going?"

"We are heading for the harbor. It's a small one, near Kankesanturai. We need to hijack a boat now or steal one. Fanoma River is about one hundred kilometres away. We should at least be able to reach Elephanta pass, somehow. I don't know whether we can sail through the waters of Fanoma as it is usually flooded during this time of the year."

"What if they don't come?"

"Then we shall have to find another way out. Venu, nothing is in our favor. We are groping in the dark. We have to take chances. The way ahead is dangerous. They are searching for us. Let's see how we can overcome the problems destiny has posed before us."

I said nothing, still doubtful.

Suddenly, we froze. We could hear the barking of a dog and then hushed whispers in the woods.

The voices neared us.

We hid ourselves in the darkest shadows, behind a clump of trees.

They were three men and were coming towards the same tree we were hiding behind. Any movement would be dangerous now.

"Where the hell are the two hiding." One of them exclaimed in frustration. "And this rain. How to find those bastards? They may be anywhere; this is such a large area."

"They must have been killed by some other group by now. They were only two and we are so many looking for them," suggested another.

"Or they might have fled back."

"Not possible. Not now. There are launches watching the coast. And haven't you heard about the ship that has just arrived from India. Something deadly serious is on. But nobody is willing to say anything. Tell me, why are those two fuckers so important to us?"

"I know a little- one of them has cheated us."

"To hell with them and to hell with these rains! Let me light a *beedi*," replied the other, and he walked directly towards the tree we were hiding behind.

Krishnan pressed my hand. I understood the signal. By now I could touch that militant by just extending my hand. I held my breath in anticipation. Blood was rushing through my veins.

He was fumbling in his pockets for a matchbox when I leapt at him, hitting him hard on his head with the stock of my gun. The man moaned and collapsed under the sudden attack. It all happened in a fraction of a second. His startled colleagues jumped and went for their guns.

Krishnan opened fire. They were at very close range. There was no chance he could miss them. The two fell on the ground where their bodies shuddered and thrashed about for a moment as they died.

Now I was on my feet attending the militant who was trying to get up groggily and defend himself.

I pressed my foot on his stomach so hard that he gasped and then pushed the barrel of my gun in his chest.

Krishnan, reassuring me that none of them whom he had fired at was alive, came to me and took charge of the situation.

"Don't make any sudden move. Just get up and put your hands behind your head. And don't try to play silly games," Krishnan ordered the militant I had knocked out.

The man just babbled and cursed.

Sanjay Sonawani

Krishnan searched him, taking away his weapons and whatever else he could find in his pockets.

"Now, tell me about the ship that has arrived from India?"

He didn't reply. He just spat on the ground and touched his injured forehead.

"Who is it that has arrived? Why the ship?"

"I don't know."

"You must tell us or you shall die a miserable death."

"Who cares? You both are bastards. You have been a curse to the cause. You deserve to die."

"Do you know what death is?" asked Krishnan in a mocking tone. "You people have killed hundreds and thousands of innocent people. You say you people are courageous. You can swallow cyanide and end your life if you are captured. Take it now, if. you have the guts. Aren't you as yet disillusioned? They are using you, as they did me. But then you are mindless people. Tell me what ship has arrived and why?"

The man was in no mood to answer Krishnan. He spat again and remained silent.

Krishnan moved back a few steps, aimed his gun at the militant's leg and fired.

The roar of the gun that echoed in the dark, rainy night was matched by a long agonizing scream from the man as he hobbled for a moment and then fell on the ground. There he lay curled clutching his leg cursing and moaning.

Krishnan waited.

"If you don't tell me I shall go on torturing you."

"You bastard, you traitor, why don't you just kill me?"

"I shall. But first I shall hurt you so much that you'll regret having been born. Tell me where the ship is docked?"

"I don't know anything. I have just heard about it. It must be in the harbor."

"What's its identity?"

"You can never reach it. You both shall be dead before you reach it."

"That's our problem, you swine. Tell us what kind of ship it is?"

"I don't know. I haven't seen it. I just heard about its arrival. They say it is a liner of some kind...small, not big as other ships, and has arrived here for some kind of immediate crisis they wish to resolve."

"When did it arrive?"

"In the night. I don't know for sure. Now kill me please."

Krishnan stood there in moments of grave uncertainty.

"Throw light on him. I want to see his face," Krishnan ordered me suddenly.

I followed his instructions.

The man was in his late twenties, dark and mean looking.

Krishnan fired.

The bullet hit the man's forehead and he was dead in an instant, as he had pleaded for.

"What's up, Krishnan?"

"I don't know," said Krishnan honestly. He seemed a worried man.

"Everything that's happening is so weird, that my brain has stopped functioning. Why should someone risk a voyage to this place from India, that too taking a liner? Who could it be?

Sanjay Sonawani

Why is he here? With what?"

I didn't know either. "What difference does it make to us, Krishnan?"

"We should know for our planned meeting very much depends on the current circumstances. We have been shooting arrows in the dark for a long time. We need some enlightenment now so that our desired impact is achieved. We should not walk blindly into the landmines. Something is happening of grave importance, can't you sense it? They are on the run. They are no more in a mood for games. They certainly are damn serious. Something drastic has happened, otherwise, there is no reason for someone to come here risking their whole game plan, and the person who has landed here couldn't be any ordinary person.

"The question is, what could possibly have happened? We must know, Venu. Our success depends on the knowledge as we have on the current situation. They are not fools to risk their lives sailing through open waters with danger lurking all around them unless something has shaken them badly.

"Someone else is frightened, too. There must be threats, and Prabhakaran, being the so-called ultimate leader, has to resolve the problem. He has to revive contacts. And, ironically, all are dependent on him. What if he does otherwise? His uncanny wits must be a threat to his allies. He is the man in the open, taking all the risks and so putting all his fellow being's lives at risk. He must secure his way ahead. The world hardly knows what all took place behind closed doors, but the fact remains that it was Prabhakaran who signed Rajiv Gandhi's death sentence. Now, he must ensure his safety. He will use his trump cards if his mission is jeopardized by his allies or if his own life that is in danger. It seems he too is in a dilemma.

"I don't know anything and yet, I feel as though I know a lot, maybe because I have been with them and I know their traits. I know how and when they plan their attacks. I know the inner circle that is involved in taking major decisions. Nothing is done single handedly. Prabhakaran risks the LTTE to meet the wishes of the other powers. From them he gains what he needs to strengthen his supremacy. He is a power hungry man and if he loses their support he is no more. His game is tricky.

"But this time, Venu, they have disturbed a hornets nest. They are in big trouble. They have to resolve the strained relations and do whatsoever that may be required of them to ease them out of this crisis. My gut feeling is that they need each other to avert any sort of scandal. For I know the uneasiness that had plagued the high command when it confirmed Rajiv Gandhi's death warrant. None were sure whether they were doing the right thing. And yet, they had to do it because the pressures were mounting so terribly that they couldn't think otherwise.

"And I am sure they still are uneasy. SIT will go the whole hog to find out what all happened and who all were involved. They may take a long time to fix the blame on the culprits, but they won't sit idle. They have to bring evidence of conspiracy before the law, before the government. The masses won't keep silent over such a brutal assassination of their leader, beloved or not. May be some bought-out thinkers and columnists, in order to pollute public opinion, will start indirectly blaming Rajiv Gandhi for calling upon his own death by sending the army to Sri Lanka. It is typical of what happens in India"

Krishnan paused to breathe in new thoughts that the dark

jungles inspired him with. I was perplexed, as I was ignorant about much of what he said. I never had seen Krishnan so passionate, so frustrated and still enthusiastic, reeling out thought after thought as if it was the last chance for him to speak his mind. I thought he was also trying to justify the course of action he had chosen to undertake. I knew he was angry and felt deceived and was trying to apply salve to his tortured mind.

Though his convictions later might prove wrong, they were justified, for he was the one who had suffered extreme humiliation. It also was true that a leader of a sovereign country was brutally assassinated - how could one term it as a mere violent reaction from a militant group? There must be many unknown dimensions to the assassination.

There was nothing else to do but think and discuss and keep our minds alert as we walked on through the dark jungles.

"Why you are so depressed, Krishnan? The think tanks may even call for severe action against the LTTE. Why shall they wish otherwise? Wasn't it an attack on Indian pride and sentiments? Why wouldn't they pressurize the government to avenge the assassination and send the right message to all others like them across the world? Isn't such thinking logical and expected of each and every Indian?" I asked as we crossed a flooded stream.

Krishnan exploded in an outburst of pent-up feelings.

"Do you know, almost all the think-tanks in India are so-called members of the Brahmin community? A Brahmin never seeks vengeance, for it is not in his cowardly blood. He prays to the power humbly and is content with his own security. That is the reason India could never succeed as other nations have in the past. The bloodstained history of India's enslavement, in a way, was their doing. It was the Brahmins who enslaved themselves first to the invaders and taught them devious ways to rule the Indian's soul. It was the Brahmins who were the masters of deception and misled the Indian psyche! For thousands of years they let people rot in the dark morass of illiteracy for their own selfish motives. Those self-proclaimed custodians of knowledge and religion polluted the mindset of the true warriors so that they should become idle bastards and dance to their tunes. They made sure that the community by and large remained unaware of the outside world. The Brahmins used their cunning on the local seats of power to satiate their own selfish interests and undermined the system by using religion as a tool. And when they found that bravery had been raped to the point of uselessness and they could no longer gain from it, they enslaved themselves to the invaders to keep their supremacy intact.

"They poisoned the mindsets and preached that it was *Kaliyuga*, where destiny is written based on the wits of a bygone past. They produced proofs from the *Puranas* and from the *Bhagvad Geeta*. Tell me, who was there to know whether it was true?

"But they themselves never made any sacrifice for the cause. They reaped all the benefits they could from the illiterates masses as well as from those who needed their wise counsel to rule this land. They taught and guided the invaders how to rule the Indians. They used religion as a weapon then and now they use their wisdom gleaned over the centuries to defeat all those tasting the fruits of freedom and the light of knowledge. There were a few visionaries among them but they were soon outcast by their own community that also raised some of them to the status of demigods when they found that their vision was to their benefit. They never wanted any visionary from other castes to rise above them. What if Mahatma Gandhi was a Brahmin? Would they have assassinated him? No. They wouldn't have killed him for his nod to Partition! He was killed for they felt no other caste in India had the right to command the masses, and it were they, the Brahmins, who had the birthright to do so. When they found that freedom was inevitable and that the doors of knowledge were about to open to all, whether an untouchable or a common man, they united to play a game of deceit on the gullible, ignorant masses saying that they wished to win back the lost glory of the Hindus. But let me tell you, the Brahmins were never Hindus. They wanted to reestablish their supremacy by confusing the rest of the community and seeking their support, for in a democracy numbers matter. They needed numbers and so they lit the pyre of hatred. They masterminded schemes that would confuse and divide the populace in order to gain back the power they had lost in the wake of the new awakening in the illiterate masses.

"Venu, I too am a Brahmin, and yet I hate being one. For the Brahmins are more treacherous than any other caste in India. History is evidence and since they have the means to read and write they go on distorting the facts. They keep on forcing inferences from history that suit their purpose to blanket their own heinous sins. They can easily be bought. They love USA far more than anyone else in this country. They hated Mahatma Gandhi and killed him. They hated Nehru for his non-aligned policies. They hated India's friendship with the USSR. They were cowards but the best in Gobbles policy. They penetrated the Indian psyche so deeply that those who never read history could easily debate how Gandhi was wrong! They wish India to be a powerful country, but only when they occupy the seat of power. They feel, nobody else has any right to lead the nation to its supremacy. I know, for in my community, even when we used to meet men belonging to other castes, they would congratulate them for their development and progress but in their own privacy would laugh saying what those lowly castes were ever going to achieve! And then I would listen to the elders expressing worries, what if these illiterates grab important positions tomorrow! What a hell it would be to work under a low caste officer! What a future their kids were going to have in this unholy country! They would abuse Mahatma Gandhi and the Congress. They used to be furious on the issues of Partition. But would they ever wage a war against Pakistan even if they were in power?

"So they had to find other means. Religion all the time was their domain and they wanted to use it to its full extent. Hence, they had to rake up religious issues to incite the masses. They knew how after their thousands of years of efforts the Indian community still was religious minded and a Brahmin was a living god for them! They said national sentiment, but when have they themselves ever displayed national sentiments in the past? What kind of nation were they thinking of? Constructing temples everywhere and looting the faith of the common man was their contribution towards the making of this nation in the past. But when the invaders came and looted their domains, they were the first to surrender. They decorated the royal courts of the aggressors and praised them and forced others too to follow in their footsteps. They said it was *Kaliyuga* and outside rule was inevitable. Those who raised a voice against the oppressors and won were denied their religious rights.

"They played such heinous games, Venu, that I, despite being a Brahmin, hate my caste with every breath. We deliberately denied the right of education to each and all for centuries. We had utter hatred for equality. We deliberately sidetracked those who could fight.

"And yes, Rajiv Gandhi's assassination is to the benefit of all those who are dreaming of grabbing power. But as long as the Gandhi family is alive and safe they can't dream of being in power, for the Indian community knows their future lies with the sacred principles of true equality. The moles in the Indian system are those who think they have the birth-right to change the course of the current Indian system. They know they must deflate the prominent personalities who believe in equality and communal harmony. Don't you see why the Ram Mandir issue is so hot? Who has anything to do with Lord Ram in today's circumstances? Why rake up dead issues? Who is the true and honest follower of Lord Ram these days? He was a warrior. He was not at all a cowardly Brahmin! And still the issue is kept hot, not in order to rebuild the temple but to stoke disharmony and confuse the mindset of the people.

"And innocent and ignorant masses follow them. They are unfortunate for they never had a Brahmin idol that could be worshipped all over the country. They had to choose Krishna, Ram or Shiva. The day is not far that you will find another breed of fanatics in India. They are the think tanks and they are the very people who attempt to plant seeds of chaos in the minds of the people. They always had a passion for the USA and all things American and most of them are now migrating. They fear that they might not have a stronghold in this land anymore. And those who are still here try hard to infuriate the illiterate masses in order to garner support for their own selfish motives. They are still doing it and shall not stop till they corrupt the blood and spirit of this country.

"Rajiv Gandhi's death is not incidental. It is not at all an accident or the fanaticism of the LTTE at work. It is the handiwork of some ignorant people who never knew what they were up to. And still there is hectic activity out here in the jungles of Jaffna when everything has been done with. The CIA, or whosoever those were, who saved our lives, for their own benefit sent us here as we proved useless to them to cause lateral damage to the LTTE. But yet they informed the LTTE that we were in their territory. It's all so ridiculous.

"Hell! I know they have panicked.

"There are so many questions that remain unanswered. I am curious, Venu, let us find answers to the baffling questions before we die. So, my friend, do not weep over bygones. It was all inevitable. Time is lord and master of all substance. Those who were destined to die have died. My soul has died. Your wife too died. There have been many like her and me from the past to the present. People die blaming their misfortune and the people who cause it are demonic. We must fight them till our last breath.

"Remember, we are not at all here to blame the time we live in, we are here to avenge in the light of knowledge. Let's be united and alert. Let's find out what went on behind the thick curtains. I am curious. I need to know before I die."

Krishnan's impassioned speech was so intense, so honest that I didn't say a single word. Not being a Brahmin myself, I knew how we had to suffer at their hands. The taunts I had to suffer silently when I had exemption from fees in schools and in college, due to being poor and belonging to a minority caste. Even the annual drama competition, mostly performed by the Brahmins, would blame the system for reservations. We were so naïve that we could never fight back the injustice they meted out to us since centuries because we were fishermen. We never wrote chapters of history about our heroic deeds or the agonies that we suffered over the centuries while fighting the so-called custodians of religion. No one was interested in what we suffered and never wrote a single line, forget about a saga, of our determination to cross the deadly hurdles that were put before us by them. We lived and all that mattered to us was life's eternal song in all those hardships and the negligence of the leading society. They killed our psyche, reiterating that our being outcastes was the retribution of the sins we had committed in our previous births. We trusted them. We praised them and called them to religious ceremonies to conduct sacred rites and were happy to donate fat amounts in the hope that all our sins would be washed away and that in our next birth we too would be sacred as them. Yes, they did it to each caste and reaped all the benefits, not allowing any of us to enter the fields they commanded.

They denied us the right to live a humane existence by cunningly propagating the practice of non-violence. Yet, when a man from some other caste than their own raised his voice and followed non-violence even then he was to be blamed and executed!

"Krishnan, I never befriended you thinking you were Brahmin, or anybody else. I liked you. I sensed in you an awakening, though I always felt conscious of being an inferior caste when I visited your house. I loved you always, immaterial to which caste you belonged. Your reasoning may be right or wrong and yet there are so many historical facts that point to the brutal distortion of facts. But, my friend, it again is yet another kind of fanaticism that is storming our culture. It has been prevalent from ancient times. Each race thinks it is superior to others. They have their own ideals and philosophies.

"Tell me, Krishnan, why does this racism exist when the world has entered the scientific era where only knowledge and wisdom matters? Why, isn't this yet another kind of fanaticism being exhibited by the superpowers to gain control over political streams in this sub-continent? They are ruthless in their functions and aims.

"We are living in a world of instability. No values, substance, morals or truth exists anywhere. Terror and fear exists everywhere, may be in tiny fragments or in traces, but still they exist in everyone's heart. The torments of the past agonies no more matter now, as we are the victims of our present system. The fight going on here is racial but then who possess the wisdom to think and act accordingly to kindle the light of humanity? I find us in a moral as well personal dilemma to avenge ourselves.

"Anyway, forget it. Let's find out who is there on the ship that has come from India and why. If they have panicked for something unusual they must be frantic to resolve the issue at once. They will easily fall to our strategy."

I was excited and blood was rushing through my veins so wildly that it seemed as thought my heart would burst at any moment.

After another hour's walk through the drizzle and a sloppy land covered by woods, I smelled the wild sea and surf. I could hear the waves crashing against the shore, resonating in the wilderness. As we advanced we saw the dim lights of Kankesanturai and of the harbor through the curtain of rain. I could see many boats anchored in the open sea. None dared to sail in such calamitous weather. How could we find that unknown liner?

"We have to make a careful search. Let's first get hold of some launch or trawler. There are many...look at that side. We have to sneak into one and get to the sea."

The fishermen's hamlet was spread across the seashore. We circled it and approached a pier where many trawlers and launches were chained.

"The ship in question may be a little away. They can't risk anchoring directly in the harbor. Let's have a look."

There was a calmness of the early morning. The hamlet would soon be awake. We had to hurry and sneak out fast. I saw Krishnan inspecting a couple of trawlers, tied with chains to wooden stumps. Suddenly, with the butt of his gun he broke a lock releasing the chains hooked to it and jumped onto a trawler. "Hurry. Take charge of the helm. I don't know how to run this machine."

Sanjay Sonawani

I rushed to the engine room and started the engine. Then I rushed to the control cabin and steered us in the direction of the open sea. Despite the wind, I was sweating in fear of being caught for stealing the trawler. But I smiled as Krishnan came beside me.

"How simple everything becomes when you are determined," I said with a laugh. "Now, we are murderers, intruders and thieves, as well. It's fun!"

"Take a straight direction. Visibility is so poor that I am sure they wouldn't risk anchoring in the harbor. They must be at a safe distance awaiting someone to join them or to ferry them to their destination. If it weren't for the rains they would have long vanished. But let's see."

The east glowed orange in the light of the rising sun, reflecting myriad hues on the clouds above. Seagulls swerved high above catching sacred moments of the morning light. The sea seemed uneasy, just like me. As the sun came up, visibility improved and now we could see a farther distance. I looked back. The shore was far away. On our left, I could see some ships anchored. Most of them were containers and a few of them, liners. But nothing seemed unusual about them. Could our friends be hiding in one of them?

"Look at the northwest side, can you see a ship there? It is far...close to the shore...at the curve where no one in his right senses would dare to anchor," said Krishnan.

"But still they have risked anchoring there, Krishnan. The Coast Guard can easily spot them and cause trouble."

"I know…I know," said Krishnan urgently. "This is unusual, what they have done. There is something definitely on. Or there must be some orders from Colombo…Kondathaman can do wonders at times, I tell you."

I turned the trawler towards the ship slowly so as not to draw attention to us, as there was a chance we were under surveillance.

"We have to act smart," said Krishnan, with an urgency in his voice. "When I signal you, you fix the helm in the northern direction maintaining the current speed. We shall then jump into the water and swim towards the ship. The waves will make our movements easy."

I nodded. We couldn't dare to approach the liner with this trawler. It would call for unwarranted attention and before we could embark on the ship, we would be fed to hungry fish.

What if this liner wasn't the one we expected it to be?

But there was no time for doubts. Now that the ship, medium-sized liner, was in front of us.

"We are about half a league away from it," I said.

Krishnan nodded.

"Let us carry only our revolvers and enough spare cartridges. Let us say goodbye to our things and this trawler and say thanks to its owner. Now set it going north…. Oh! No. You can't…let's see… northwest will do."

I followed his instructions blindly as no better thought came to my mind.

"We shall jump from the other side. First, I'll move from here, then after some time, you leave the cabin."

Krishnan slipped out. I frantically fixed the helm and

adjusted the speed and came out onto the deck. Krishnan was ready and was pushing his revolver securely into the waistband of his trousers. He handed me my gun and cartridges. The waves were high. Trawler was moving swiftly in the set direction.

"Dive," he yelled and jumped into the water.

I followed.

A huge wave bore down on me as I dived. I surfaced fighting for breath; being a sailor, I knew the techniques of swimming in the open sea; you ride the waves and you need not waste energy as the salty sea-water keeps you afloat; this way, you can swim for miles without exhausting yourself.

I followed my instincts and rode a wave.

It was an exalting experience. The sea-water embraced me in its soothing arms and my aching body forgot all pain. I looked forward to the impending danger that I was soon to encounter.

I looked around for Krishnan. He too was moving forward with the force of the sea.

We were nearing the liner wave by wave.

Twenty

It took us about an hour to reach the ship.

As I drew closer, I was cautious of my approach, not wanting to be spotted by someone from the deck. When I was about a 100 metres away, I started to swim just below the surface, occasionally raising my head above the water to take a breath and survey the surroundings.

Slowly, we neared the black metal that formed the stern of the ship. The ship had weathered many seasons and layers of chipped paint told me the story of its age. I looked in all directions trying to fathom the gravity of the situation. All I could hear was the rushing sound of the waves, the wind and the drizzling rain. I tried to find some means of getting on to the deck. I found none. Then a thought flashed in my mind. The ship was anchored. I could use the anchor chain to climb the ship.

Krishnan came closer to me. His face was pale in the dim morning light. I sensed how tired he was. What energy was forcing him ahead I didn't know. I felt pity for him. He was not made for such kind of hard work. Last night had been one long walk without sleep or rest. I was used to hardships of life. Being a fisherman, I had many a time passed sleepless nights and that too fighting the elements of nature.

Krishnan seemed exhausted.

"Krishnan, let us swim towards the anchor. You hold the chain and keep afloat in the waters. I shall climb up and find some way to get you aboard."

"No, Venu. You don't know what to find there. You don't know what danger you could be walking into. Let me do my job and you just follow me."

"Krishnan, this ship may be an ordinary liner. We don't know as yet whether this is the one where we might find someone important. This all is instinctive action we have embarked upon. Those soldiers might have been lying. You are tired. You can't bear any more physical strain."

"Do not worry about me. Come on, let us swim to the anchor chain."

I said nothing. There was nothing I could argue about. We had no time. We approached cautiously where I had seen the huge anchor chain dip into the sea.

"Krishnan, give me just half an hour's time. Let me climb up and find out whether we are on the right ship. I shall signal you then you can climb up. It is not easy to grip this iron chain and climb. It's wet and slippery. I know some tricks that you don't. Let's not waste our energy in futile efforts. Okay?"

He nodded wearily. He was too tired even to argue.

I touched the cold iron chain. It was wet and slippery just as I had perceived it to be. It was heavy and rigid. The ascend to the ship from this side was sharp and allowed no space for a foothold. I still went ahead. I knew it was important. I clutched the chain in a firm grip with both my hands and taking a deep breath started to climb up like a monkey till I had to stop to fight for breath. I waited for a couple of seconds to regain my strength and then started again.

It was exhausting. My fingers were numb and paralyzed and my arms, heavy wooden logs. I was fighting for breath. My thumping heart felt it was about to give way. I tried hard to control my breath and forget the pain in my fingers, arms and legs. Finally, I made it.

I peered cautiously over the edge of the ship. To my relief the deck was deserted. The rain hadn't stopped as yet. Were the Gods in heaven helping us or were the rains entirely against us? I wondered.

I somehow managed to get a hold on the large protruding metal ring, through which the anchor chain ran and shoved my body in. It was about a five feet drop to the deck. I first held the ring tightly, slipped my legs to the other side and jumped. Then I looked down at the sea to see Krishnan. He was right there where I had left him, looking up at me anxiously.

I again surveyed the deck. It was still deserted. I could see numerous drums and coils of ropes and containers scattered about.

I controlled my anxiety. My heartbeats started to get to normal. The only disturbing thing was my cold, numb hands. I tried to put life back into them with a vigorous massage. I tried to get hold of the revolver that I had hidden in my T-shirt. It was a painful effort.

I started crawling through the mess they had spread on the deck to a protruded portion that led downstairs. The poles and other usual things that you notice on any ship I neglected and crawled ahead using them as cover.

It was a long distance, but I sensed nobody's presence around me. On my left, I could see a row of lifeboats. I knew all the important cabins and control rooms would be downstairs, so I entered the oblong structure from where the steps would lead me down.

As I was about to take my first step, I heard footsteps on the dark staircase. I bounded back behind a table that was affixed to the floor in the corner. There I waited with bated breath.

Someone was climbing up the steps. I was curious to know who it was. But when I saw a gun barrel held high followed by the heads of two men, I ducked down instantly to hide myself. I knew Krishnan was right in his assessment. Ordinary liner crew doesn't carry guns.

The two men casually climbed up without sensing anything amiss and went to the aft of the deck. I could see their careless walk and hear the curses they hurled at the inclement weather.

I released my breath and started to climb down the stairs stealthily, the revolver held firmly in my hand, ready to shoot at the first sign of danger.

There was no one in the long dark corridor in front of me.

I knew I must find something that could help us to go ahead in our mission. I wanted a clue. Some sound that would suggest the presence of someone behind the closed doors that lined either side of the corridor. But there only prevailed a threatening calm of the cold wet night gone by.

There was something weird about this ship. It was already morning but there was hardly any activity to be seen. It was as if the ship was deserted!

I moved on expecting to come across something useful. Then I came to a branching of the corridor. I wondered for a moment as to which direction I should take. I could go straight ahead to find the Captain's cabin or I could take the left turn where I would possibly find the dining hall, as is the typical layout of such ships.

I went straight ahead moving as stealthily as possible. There was no sound. No voices. Not even a snore to be heard.

Then, from behind a cabin door, I heard a commanding voice threatening someone.

I carefully peered through the glass peephole.

The scene inside was so shocking that it made me gasp. I could see five or six gunmen pointing their LMGs at a man sitting in a chair in front of them.

Blood rushed through my veins. I could hardly believe the scene before my eyes.

It was Thyagarajan, occupying chair. No, the bastard was

not sitting. He was bound tightly to the chair with ropes and had guns pointed directly at him.

Why? Why did they want to kill him? Wasn't he their trusted man? Or had Thyagarajan defrauded his mentors?

No. They hadn't any right to kill that bastard. Only I had that right; he was the one who had shoved me into the maze of treachery and had taken the life of my wife and my unborn child.

Rage was overtaking me. No matter if death graced me, I wouldn't allow them to cheat me of my right.

I gripped the door handle and jerking it open, fired blindly.

My rage served me well. For, in an instant, four of them lay sprawld on the floor gasping for life, the sudden attack had taken them by surprise.

The other two tried to fire at me in shocked reaction. The bullets tore apart the weak cabin door, shattering the silence of the morning, without coming anywhere close to me.

I carefully aimed my gun at the man trying to point at me and fired, and then at all those who lay shuddering on the floor from my first burst of bullets putting an end to their misery.

Without any sound they lay still.

I then aimed at the leader who stood frozen on the spot. He was unarmed. He looked frightened and said something that I couldn't discern. Without a second thought, I fired recklessly at him in his belly. He gave a shrill cry and collapsed on the floor.

I felt a burning sensation in my arm and saw it was bleeding profusely. I had caught a bullet. I looked at Thyagarajan through the pain that exploded in my body. He too was looking at me as if he had seen a ghost.

Sanjay Sonawani

"Save me, Venu. Please, save me!" I heard the bastard plead.

"I'm not here to save your miserable skin, you son of a bitch. I am here to take it... with my bare hands. You don't deserve a man's death. You are just a worm that eats its own flesh and soul. I wish you rot in the hell forever."

I was enraged. I screamed all the possible abuses that came to mind.

"I'm here to kill you, you bastard. You snatched away my life from me. You are the cause of all those calamities that have befallen me. I won't let you get away."

"Venu, you are my friend. I have helped you all the time. I am the one who has been purchasing your catch for a long time. Don't forget this…" He pleaded while his eyes bulged with the terror of death that stood before him. He looked pitiable. But how could he expect to be forgiven.

"Thyagarajan, you are a bastard. Worse than the scum of the earth. Don't you ever think I'll let you go on breathing on this earth."

"What wrong have I done to you, Venu? I always have been your well wisher. I…"

"Shut up." I trembled in rage. "What good you have done to me? You destroyed my life. You burnt my wife alive. You forced me to run away from a happy life, you bastard."

"No, Venu. How could I kill her? She was just like a sister to me. I pleaded for her safety, but these people turned treacherous. They now wanted to kill me too…but you have saved me. Now please release me…let's get away from here. There is death lurking all around…please, Venu, trust me."

Sanjay Sonawani

Hatred for this man was eating me alive. I held the revolver tightly in my sweaty hands and aimed at his head.

Before I could pull the trigger, I heard Krishnan - "Stop, Venu."

Why had he interrupted my verdict on this bastard? Why was he so pained by my wanting to kill this bastard? I slowly turned to look at him.

I was shocked to see Krishnan. He was bleeding. His whole body was drenched in blood. His steps were uncertain as he staggered towards me.

"Krishnan, what happened? Why you did not wait for me?" I wailed, not trusting my eyes with what I was seeing.

"How could I leave you alone, Venu? Aren't we brothers? Wait…give me something to sit."

I looked frantically around. A wooden chair was there in the corner. I rushed and brought it for Krishnan and helped him sit down. He moaned as pain wreaked his body. He had caught numerous bullets in his body and blood was flowing out of the wounds in spurts.

The fear of losing him gripped me. I couldn't think of anything.

"Why did you do this, Krishnan? Why didn't you wait for me till I had had my revenge? This man is none other than the devil who devoured my soul!" I wailed in anguish hugging him, trying to will away his wounds.

"You need a doctor. We must get away from here."

"No." He said in a firm voice, shoving my hand from his shoulder. "I'm alright. Don't worry. I can see and I can hear… They were two…suddenly, they shot at me…somehow I opened for them the gates of hell. But now life seems to be ebbing away from me. It seems like bliss!"

He then looked intently at Thyagarajan, as if realizing for the first time what had happened.

"Tell me, Venu, who is this bastard?" He asked in a drained voice.

"Thyagarajan."

Krishnan nodded. He was still holding his gun in his left hand.

"So you are Thyagarajan!" said Krishnan in a low, vicious voice. "It seems to me that you were about to die before we got to you. Just like the way you people had voted to eliminate me. I didn't do anything that could warrant a death sentence, did I? But, tell me, what earned you your death sentence?"

Thyagarajan blinked his eyes in fear, not grasping fully where all this was leading.

"They thought I too was treacherous. But believe me, I didn't do anything untoward. Release me. I shall help you both get back safely. I still have many contacts reserved for such emergencies."

"What did you do, Thyagarajan?" Asked Krishnan, as if he hadn't heard him.

"I told you, I didn't do anything. They were accusing me of treachery. They thought I was the one who brought in the Chinese on the scene by selling them the information they needed. They said I had leaked information to the Chinese due to which their plans had come under the danger of getting derailed. They said, due to me they were forced to change all plans and policies and form pacts which they didn't want."

Sanjay Sonawani

"So you didn't play Chinese checkers, huh?" Krishnan said with a sneer.

"I swear I have never ever involved myself in such tricky business. Though all along I have known that China always wanted to reestablish relations with us. Several times in the past there had been instances of them bribing our key people. These people were watching the developments in this part of world very closely for obvious reasons. I knew that they wanted some control over the LTTE. But trust me, my life is at your mercy, I shall never lie…I never had anything to do with them.

"And see, still they were blaming me for leaking information that brought the Chinese into the present scene allowing them to take advantage of the new conditions. It is ridiculous to blame me, a true devotee of the cause and interests of the Tamil people for so many years. I dream of a Tamil Eelam. I joined the LTTE to be of some use to the cause. I risked my bloody life for them. I smuggled weapons and drugs and men and what not? Though I was deeply afraid within myself while doing what I was asked to, I used to keep on thinking, what if I am caught? What if I am killed in an encounter? What about my family then? And still I consoled myself with the hope that even if I did die for the cause, the day the dream we saw together comes true, they will treat us as martyrs and would rewrite history in golden ink with our names in it.

"Yes, Krishnan, I set aside my feelings and risked everything I had for the cause and the organization. I worshipped my leader like Lord Shiva and Lord Ranganatha. Prabhakaran was a deity to me! And even then they questioned my loyalty. How could they? Those bastards, they can never do anything good for the Tamils or for humanity."

I wanted to laugh at him; shoot the miserable swine dead. What humanity was he talking of?

I looked at Krishnan.

His lips quivered. He leaned forward and looking straight into Thyagarajan's eyes, asked, "Tell me, how come you are on this ship? Tell me, why were you asked to come here and why by sea and not an aircraft? You, I know, are not on the Indian government's list of suspects. If at all these people wanted you to be here, you could reach here by easier and faster means. Or if at all they have forced you to come, why on this ship? Who owns it? What is it carrying?"

I found no sense in Krishnan's questions. It made no difference at all to me why Thyagarajan took this means of transport. But I waited, cursing Krishnan for wasting precious time. He desperately needed medical aid. Every minute wasted was reducing his chances of survival.

"Krishnan," said Thyagarajan, "Eight days ago, I received a message from my superior officers stating that I must be onboard a certain liner to supervise a covert operation regarding an arms shipment. This is the liner, Krishnan, and, to my knowledge, it is carrying large quantities of RDX and some machinery for printing counterfeit currency notes. They said my presence was necessary onboard this ship as the leader of this mission had fallen ill and they couldn't trust his team members with the cargo.

"They told me that this liner was scheduled to leave from Calcutta port and the exchange of goods was to take place mid-sea. Most of the crew they said were Bangladeshis, whom they couldn't trust. I believed in what they said. I knew that, following Rajiv Gandhi's assassination, the Indian Navy and Coast Guard were on extremely high alert. But then our fellows here desperately needed ammunition and money, so I agreed to take the risk. I knew shipping such kind of explosives, that too in such dangerous circumstances, needed an expert on this part of the Indian Ocean, which I am. I also know the people well with whom I was to transact the operations.

"I accepted the assignment because I thought it was an honor being bestowed upon me by the high command. He trusted me with such a deadly mission. Three days ago, I joined this ship. I found nothing unusual in the behavior of these men, who now lie dead in front of us. I roamed freely everywhere. I even had a look at the crates of machinery and RDX. I found everything in order. I had no reason to suspect anything till the last night when we reached this shore. Though, since no mid-sea transaction had taken place, my mind was nagged by the doubt that something was amiss.

"Krishnan, Venu, I swear on my mother, I am telling the truth. It was as if they wanted to kill two birds with one stone: Punish me for a crime that I didn't commit, and also get a dangerous task accomplished.

"But please, let's now move from here. I promise to appraise you with all the facts that I know. Further delay may lead to our death. Please…"

"Don't worry about our death, you bastard, worry about yourself. Now tell me, I am sure you know, why was I framed?" Krishnan took a deep breath as he asked.

Sanjay Sonawani

Personal vendettas had to be settled. More than the gunshot wounds, he had been mortally wounded by the stigma of being branded a traitor. He was anxious to know why he had been framed. He didn't seem to want to know why I had been dragged into this quagmire and had unnecessarily lost the life of my beloved who was at that time carrying a new life within her belly. Nobody seemed bothered about my tragedy. They had many issues to deliberate under the shadow of death. They were talking about the truth and their false accusations.

What wrong had I ever done to anyone? I didn't ever commit any crime that could even attract the attention of the harbor police. Then why this punishment? But nobody paid any attention to me. And I knew nothing was ever going to change. I knew that only destiny was responsible for my destruction. I had always trusted in the Almighty, which made me discern that this was all temporary and unimportant and that my agonies would be taken care of by Him. God now seemed to be my only support.

"I'm not worried about my death and yet, I so earnestly wish to live!" Thyagarajan sighed, as he continued, "I'm worried about what is happening all around. I am worried why they wanted to connect me with the information leaks to the Chinese. I doubt if there is any…"

"There you are wrong. There are hectic activities taking place on this island that indicate that they are not just worried but have panicked. And that's why before they could find out who the real culprit was, they needed a scapegoat. You were picked because you were the ideal victim. You knew the waters of the coast and the people, the ideal person to accuse, to sacrifice and ratify the situation, whatsoever it is!

"There are moles everywhere. But tell me, why *I* was framed?" Krishnan moaned as he gasped for breath.

I leaned over him, trying to soothe him with a gentle caress. "Krishnan, please don't raise any questions now. It is all irrelevant! Useless. Now it doesn't make sense anymore. We should have paid heed to Himani's advice and gone back... Relax."

"I want to know…"

"Don't be a fool, Krishnan! You never will come to know what the truth is and what the lies are. Truth keeps on playing games with us. Only yesterday, we were fiercely discussing the US connection and now, today, this new Chinese connection is mocking us in our face. What have these outside countries to do with the internal matters of our country? You shall never come to know who was responsible for your or my disaster. May be the men behind it all will remain safe forever and we will kill those who are merely a front! And still we never would know who or what induced Rajiv Gandhi's death.

"I beg you, Krishnan, come back to your senses. You are a genius. I know this man Thyagarajan. He is a bastard. He is a ruthless son of a bitch and people like him are a menace to the society. So fuck him off. Let him die here. Let's get you to a doctor."

I pleaded to a crazy man who seemed determined not to listen to me.

"Forget your Chinese connection, damn it. Just tell me, why was I framed?" Krishnan screamed at Thyagarajan.

Thyagarajan licked his lips. "Let me brief you on some obscure happenings that you might be unaware of.

"When after previous attempts in north India *that* plan was executed to our complete satisfaction, we failed in our attempts to ship the most obvious suspect, Sivrasan, to a safe place. Then we received orders not to establish any contact with him. Our hands were tied and had to sit tight awaiting whatever decision they might take. The pressures was mounting. Varadrajan too was worried. We wanted Sivrasan away, for the heat was intense. The government had issued a red alert. The Indian Coast Guard had sealed the shores. No unauthorized ship or even a boat could sail out to the open seas. Everybody was scared.

"Sivrasan too must have been uneasy and so must have been Shuba. Suddenly, a ray of hope emerged. We were informed that you, Krishnan, would be coming and would take this pair to some safe haven. We were relieved. We never wanted to know where they were being taken. We knew how SIT was combing all the places and employing all kind of tactics to unearth the real culprits.

"That's why, Krishnan, you came into the picture. You landed on the coast of Kerala and from there travelled to Madras and then taking hold of the situation, transported Sivrasan and Shuba to Karnataka, though we didn't know the destination then. Meanwhile, the couple got married as if they too might have suspected that they would soon be dead!

"I do not know what transpired between you and that couple but when you were back in Madras, we were ordered to make arrangements to ship you back to Sri Lanka. Varadrajan was handling this task and I had to bring Venugopal into the picture as I knew he would accept this assignment due to his father's past and also because he had a spotless record and owned a trawler.

"And then, when you were already half way to the Lankan coast, I received orders that shocked me. I was ordered to inform Sivrasan's hideout to the authorities, just the way they had briefed me."

I shot a glance at Krishnan in shock. But his face was expressionless, as if nothing surprising was being disclosed to him.

"I was perturbed by these orders and the briefing on how I was to leak the news. I demanded confirmation over and over again. They said the orders were from Prabhakaran and couldn't be altered. I knew I had to follow their instructions or I would be calling upon my own death. Everybody knew, in case of attempted arrest, neither Sivrasan nor Shuba would surrender alive. And so it happened. When the police surrounded their residence on my tp off, both embraced death.

"Now they needed a person on whom the stamp of treachery could be placed. They readily had you, Krishnan, walking in the trap so innocently unaware of what had transpired."

Thyagarajan paused trying to rearrange his heavy frame enmeshed by ropes. I was gasping, suffocated by these shocking truths that I would never ever have come to know during the course of my ordinary life. Krishnan was sitting calm and expressionless.

"Meanwhile, you both had escaped the trap set for you.

I desperately wanted to know why they wished Sivrasan dead. Obviously, there was bound to be some reason. So I started my little exercise, digging around a bit, keeping myself in the background.

"Then I landed on a grave truth. It came to me as a shock. No more was I dealing with Tamil pride. Suddenly, my being a soldier to the cause and all my doings were nothing. I was merely a pawn in the ugly game being played by those hypocrites."

He stopped and looked at Krishnan. He was desperate and yet seemed fairly composed.

"What did you find?"

"Make a guess, Krishnan."

"Guess? Why should I? I could easily kill you if you don't answer."

"Krishnan, I know you desperately need to know what went wrong and why. I have told you enough to let you understand how you were victimized. But, my friend, truly speaking, I am now sure that they too know what I know and that's why they called me here. That's why they wanted to kill me. The Chinese connection is just a red herring. The fact is, they just want to bury the truth.

"Now I wish you to make a guess…"

Krishnan closed his eyes in pain. I patted his shoulder to soothe him. After a moment he looked at Thyagarajan.

"My guess? You want to know? I suspect foul play. I am trying to understand why Sivrasan was anxious to marry Shuba. He, I feel, didn't marry her for the sake of love or romance under the shadow of death. He knew he would be safe and would soon be transported to another safe place and then abroad somewhere. He had ensured his safety before he involved himself in the mission that would open all floodgates of danger. He needed his safety assured and no leaks of his whereabouts under any circumstances. He had been promised everything he demanded. Then why was he so anxious? What he was afraid of? Why he needed Shuba in his complete control as a wife!

"I feel, he was up something else. He wasn't willing to trust any of his superiors. He had different plans and needed Shuba's total cooperation to execute them. He wanted to ensure his safety in his own way. He couldn't do it all alone. He was a one-eyed man, very easy to spot. He needed to take Shuba into his confidence. And what better way to ensure this than marry her?

"But I do not know what was on his mind, what safety net he planned to cast about him. Why he didn't trust the security plans laid out by his superiors, I do not know. Tell me, was he in touch with some other party that could use him to their benefit, may be by assuring him complete safety for life? Tell me."

Thyagarajan nodded.

"Yes, he had decided to decamp. He doubted whether he would be safe in the hands of our people. He knew the enormity of the wrong he had committed. He had decided to say good bye to this country with the help of others. To my utter disbelief, this help he had arranged was from a media tycoon. He had agreed to disclose the complete story and in exchange was promised a new identity and a new start to life in the country of his choice. He chose a place no one could ever think of - He had chosen Sri Lanka to migrate to!

"He was a brilliant chap. But one never knows what

tragedy can befall a person, even the most brilliant ones. He must have planned everything meticulously to the last detail with the highest possible secrecy. But unfortunately, nothing remained secret. His plans came to the knowledge of our superiors, or at least they suspected Sivrasan of something fishy.

"Anyway, whatsoever might have happened but the fact remains that he had to die. He had to swallow cyanide after shooting Shuba dead.

"...This is what I came to know from my sources. I don't know whether the information disclosed to me is entirely true and not tainted. Though now I am sure that the same sources leaked my discreet inquiries to them. But they don't know what all I know about Sivrasan's secret arrangements and wanted to silence me and seal all possibilities of a leak. They had me by my balls...till you came along.

"Now, Krishnan, you have all what you wanted to know. Better option is that instead of killing me use me for your safe passage...release me from these ties."

"Yes, I'm about to do that," said Krishnan in a weak voice. Blood was still oozing from his wounds. His face was pale and it took a great effort for him to speak.

"No one can dodge the responsibility of his deeds," continued Krishnan. "We all are fools. We lead our life to hell with all our stupidities. Life is not the property of an individual. All of us are being sailed through the river of death in a dinghy of life. Our dinghy is now about to shatter and drown us in the river of death. Shouldn't we rather jump into the river, Thyagarajan?"

What was Krishnan talking about? Was he delirious as he

struggled to hold himself together on the edge; between life and death?

"I must say, you too are a bastard, Thyagarajan. The amusing stories you tell don't entertain me for Varadrajan too had his version as to why I was framed and I see that the versions don't match. Nothing makes sense. Not then; not now. The truth is still far away and, sadly, you cannot quench my thirst for the truth. I am tired of you people. Ridiculous things have been happening when cohesion was expected. But it is meaningless now to debate over all these stupidities. I never shall know what the truth is!

"How could you burn Janaki alive? Wasn't there even a drop of humanity in your miserable heart when you ordered her death? You were the only man in command after Varadrajan's death. You could have let her go. But you still wished to be honest to your treacherous commanders. Now the time has come for you to go to hell for whatever you did to an innocent woman," said Krishnan, and in one slow motion raised his revolver and fired point blank at the wildly protesting man.

The bullet hit Thyagarajan's throat. Blood spurted from the wound drenching his grotesque body. He grunted in disbelief and then with a shudder his head dropped to his chest. He was dead.

I bent over Krishnan and tried to communicate my gratitude to him through my touch. I saw his eyes trying hard to focus on my face, whitening as they started to roll back in a final journey into the valley of death.

"Hold yourself, Krishnan. Everything is over now. We

must get out. You need a doctor. You need to rest," I cried out to him in desperation as I tried to lift him from the chair and lay him on the floor of the cabin. Earlier too, I had nursed him, but now his body was becoming cold so rapidly that fear of the obvious filled my mind.

And then there was a light shudder in his body.

He was not listening to my outcries.

I ripped his T-shirt off and removed his shoes. I knew I must hurry. I tried to assure him while checking his wounds. The bullets had penetrated his upper torso ripping apart his organs.

"Krishnan," I shouted trying to keep him from slipping into the darkness.

There was a slight movement of his eyeballs. I knew all efforts were in vain. The blood under his slick body was darkening as it started to congeal. He was looking straight at me with lifeless eyes. Death had carried him away to some unknown realm. He had ditched me after making all those promises of never leaving me alone.

I collapsed on the floor, my throat painfully choked with emotions.

Twenty One

I don't know for how long I lay in a deathly stupor. Then I heard movement around me. I opened my eyes. I saw one of the men wounded in the stomach crawling towards me. When he saw I was conscious, he tried to raise his gun at me. But before he could fire, I had my gun pointed at him.

"Get up," I said, rising to take the gun from his hand

He moaned and fired. The bullet from his gun hit the edge of the wooden partition spraying splinters all around.

"Drop the gun and get up, or I'll kill you."

The man seemed unsure of his strength.

"I can't," he grunted. "I'm hurt."

I looked helplessly at Krishnan. He lay still. I knew I was

on my own now. No more did I have his expert guidance and consolation. All alone, how was I to conclude our avenging mission? So little did I know of this area and the enemy. Thyagarajan was dead. My personal vendetta was concluded. But was it so? After all, he was just a pawn in the hands of those hidden players who had orchestrated this dastardly symphony of death. He had but obeyed the orders of his superiors. I needed his superior's blood to quench my thirst.

How was I supposed to achieve it? I had, till this moment, ardently followed Krishnan in his wisdom. He was now no more. I was alone and tired. I grieved his death.

I looked at the man still gazing at me, like a dying serpent at a mongoose.

"Tell me, is there still someone on this ship?"

He took a long time to understand what I asked.

"How could there be?"

"Then you must pull yourself together. We are going to sail."

"Impossible, I can't do it. Can't you see I am dying."

"I will carry you to the control room and dress your wounds with the medication you have onboard. But you must cooperate with me or else you definitely are going to die."

He deliberated his death in all its certainty should I leave him unattended. He must have thought of some way to cheat on me, even if he was a dying man, but to execute his plans he needed to prolong his death for a while. He knew he needed immediate medication in order to survive. He had no choice but to assist me till he had recovered his strength to outsmart me. But now I didn't care. I needed him.

Sanjay Sonawani

"I can't walk," he said.

"Better to take some pains than ask for death. I shall assist you but do not try any foolish games, or else." I repeated my threat.

"Where do you want to sail to?"

"To the mouth of river Fanoma."

"You must be crazy! The river is in flood and the weather is at its worst."

"It doesn't matter. You just do what I say."

"If you want to die with me, I don't have any problem, but I need medication first. I am bleeding to death."

"Don't worry."

I said and got up.

It was a laborious task helping him to his feet and then forcing him walk towards the control room. He cursed me as a wave of pain rushed through him, but to me it hardly mattered. I needed somebody to assist me. I had never captained a ship of this size.

He guided me to the ship's infirmary where an abundant supply of first aid was available at hand. Why then hadn't I tried it on Krishnan? Why was he so desperate to know the truth? What good had the truth brought him? What satisfaction did it give him as he lay dying?

I nursed the man's wounds and gave him a handful of painkillers to swallow assuring him that he would be all right. He seemed comfortable and fairly in control of his senses. He was still cursing me, reiterating that I was a person about to die. I told him that I didn't care. He laughed.

He was a dark man in his late thirties. I asked him his name to which his cheeky reply was that he was a nameless person. He requested me that if he would sail me and drop me wherever I wanted to go, in case of my capture, I should not disclose who had sailed me to that area. I wanted to laugh at him but controlled myself. Even on the threshold of death, he wanted to be assured of his safety. One harbors hope when he sees light at the end of the tunnel, and starts planning and scheming. He starts thinking how he can get to safety. But it didn't matter to me for the time being. I somehow wanted to get to river Fanoma and find the location where the expected guests were to have their secret rendezvous. I was hopeful of Krishnan's trick succeeding. I didn't even want to give any thought to the possibility of their having uncovered the ploy and lying in wait for me. With my wife and friend dead and my life in a shambles, I already considered myself dead. I had nothing to lose or to fear.

When the 'nameless' man seemed sufficiently recovered, I forced him to the control room. The rain had stopped by now and the vision was fairly clear. I wanted to get away from the shore. He said he was in no position to steer the ship but would guide me from the chair where he had seated himself. I didn't mind. He instructed me how to lift anchor using the buttons and levers that adorned the panel in front of me. He then told me how to start the engines and speed up the ship. I frantically followed his instructions and got the ship going.

"You too are frightened, aren't you?" He asked in a

despicable voice. I wanted to spit on him, kick him in his wounds, but somehow controlled my fury. I needed him.

"Why should I be frightened?"

"You know this is a fight no one can ever win. Better if you take my advice - let's turn the ship to the Indian coast. You will be safe there.

"...If I take you wherever you want to go then I shall be all alone and in this condition of mine, you know very well, I couldn't maneuver this ship. I am badly wounded and have no strength left in me. The place where you wish to get off is covered with landmines. You'll never even know when you step on one and are blown to bits. They cover every inch of the land. Those men are cunning in their ways. They have guarded their forts well. Listen to me, you cannot win this war; you are alone. It will be like attempting suicide."

I said nothing. Nothing could discourage me; I knew my destination. I knew I had to reach there somehow and find them. I looked at the man in cold fury. He smiled, which hurt him. I laughed meanly.

"You are live and safe, so why not shut up and sit quiet. Gather your strength, it'll help you to try and play some dirty tricks later."

I took charge of the helm, fixing my sights on the gray sea ahead of us.

The beeping sound from the transmitter startled me. Someone was trying to contact the ship.

Who could it be?

I pointed my gun at my companion and asked viciously,

"Who's it?"

"I don't know. May be they are calling from the base to know what's happened to Thyagarajan."

I nodded. It was probable. I decided to ignore the call. It beeped for a long time and then fell silent. After a while, it started again.

"Answer it or they will suspect something is wrong," said the man.

"Then you speak to them and don't try anything smart or you are finished."

"I tell you, you are driving yourself to death. There is nothing there that you can do anything about. Listen to me, let's get away from here."

I looked at him thoughtfully. The beeping sound was irritating me. It was driving me insane. I turned and pointing my gun at the transmitter let off three rounds at it. The damn thing was blown to smithereens. The sound stopped. I sat on the chair for a few seconds and then turned my attention back to the sea.

"What's your name?" I asked him.

"Why do you need to know my name? It is immaterial. You have almost killed me and you know I cannot sail this ship alone in this condition. I need a crew to assist me. The weather too is bad. I wish you would turn the helm elsewhere... Don't be suicidal, these people are everywhere."

"How deeply are you involved in this?"

"Oh! I just transport goods for anybody who can pay the price. This is not the first time I have come to this part of the sea. But I seldom come to know what we ship. Except for a few people, nobody knows what is being ferried. Secrets, you know!"

I wanted to laugh at this cheeky bastard.

"You were questioning Thyagarajan. Why? Unless you were the leader and connected with the LTTE?"

He sat expressionless for some time and then said -

"I heard what he told you, you know? I was semi-conscious when he was telling you the long story. An excellent fabrication! I was not asking him anything about the Chinese or whatsoever connections he had. What do I have to do with his being treacherous to his people? I'm a shipper shuttling stuff for anybody who can pay for my services. It has nothing to do with the LTTE or anybody else for that matter. I was only questioning him about the covert communications that he established from this very transmitter last night when he had a chance to sneak in unobserved.

"We are in the business where we have to be cautious, you know. We simply cannot let anyone use our transmission system without authorization. Thyagarajan was not authorized. He was representing the other party. The men you have killed were all ours. Before we deported him, I wanted to know with whom he had talked and why? Couldn't he have sought my permission before using the transmitter? That's the reason we delayed our departure, telling them that the weather was bad and we couldn't take the risk.

"What he told you about our questioning was a very well fabricated yarn. In no way are we related to the LTTE except for the transportation that we provided them in exchange of a little money. What the hell do we have to do with his secret knowledge of Sivrasan's motives or of Rajiv Gandhi assassination? We people mind our own business."

Was he telling the truth? I doubted it. But if you gave it a thought, his reasoning seemed logical. Then why had Thyagarajan told us a different story? But it hardly mattered anymore. He had satisfied Krishnan's soul before he died.

I sat motionless for a while looking at the wounded man through the maze of my destruction. Insanity was taking over. I leaned back and said in calm voice, "May be you are being truthful. These people are the scum of the earth and I hate them. I too am just an ordinary man who got involved in this mess for no fault of mine. Do you know, I have lost my wife to them...she was pregnant and they burnt her alive.

"I never have had any sympathy for their treacherous and merciless paths. I too minded my own business. I fished in the vast the sea and tried to accomplish my dreams through hard work. My dream was to earn enough to buy more trawlers, to employ many sailors and be successful. And then one day, hand over my business to my son so that he need not have to struggle with the harshness of life, as I had to.

"But what cruel games destiny plays with us! Didn't the same happen with you also? Yes. You were sailing this ship with some objective, so sure and confident of your safe, unobstructed return. But now, all your men are dead and you are wounded. You too are afraid of death...so was I! Death is one thing that no one in his right mind desires to court in a hurry. We want to overlook its very existence. But see how close it always is to life! In fact, it walks alongside you from the time you are born.

"Isn't the life that we live an illusion? The truth is but all untrue and the love of mankind is love no more. Hatred. It's all hatred and I despise it. And yet, I too am a fool who thinks that somewhere exists truth!

"Look. You know you are about to die. The pain of the gunshot wound in your stomach is troubling you. Then, you bastard, why try to breathe stolen moments? Why not die just like the innocent child in my wife, Janaki's womb? Why are you trying to convince me with your slimy ideas? Why should I give you painkillers, eh? Why should I nurse you and prolong your agony? You deserve to die. Just try to get up…Oh, no…you will collapse and that will cause you even more pain. Just sit there and don't move. I will not cause you any more pain. Death will welcome you."

With this I got up gripping my gun with both hands. The man sitting in the chair looked at me in astonishment. "You must be crazy…" he started to say as I shot him.

His eyes bulged. He looked at me in horror and disbelief, then let out a cry and fell silent.

I was sitting on the chair, dazed, for I don't know how long. Then I realized that the ship was heaving heavily. I looked ahead and found I was in dangerously shallow waters. I got up and spun the wheel in the other direction gunning the throttle at the same time.

I somehow managed to stabilize the ship and get it on course again.

◆◆◆

Twenty Two

I glanced at the map. Fanoma river was a few leagues away now. I peered at the coast through the veil of rainy weather. I remembered my friend who lay lifeless in the cabin. My heart ached as I lamented his death. Cursing myself for having landed ourselves in this mess, I fixed the helm and then ran towards the cabin.

The cabin was the same but my mind's reference frame had changed. The room appeared as if the scene of a bloody massacre. A thick curtain of meaningless pains blocked my vision. The room smelled of death. Everywhere there was blood - drying, coagulating, darkening - and in it lay numerous bodies; I failed to count how many. And amongst them lay my soul.

How could he be dead? He must be sleeping. I approached him. He was like an innocent child in deep sleep.

"Wake up, Krishnan, we are near our objective. Don't worry, everything is under control," I said through the tears that were flowing down my cheeks. I looked at him hoping for some response.

He said nothing. His face was bloodied, his jaw slag.

How could he ditch me? How could he not respond to my calls? How could he die like some ordinary mortal? He was supreme...

But he was dead. And now no insects or enemy should torture his body if at all they captured us. He must be in safe hands. For us sailors, the sea is eternal and so forgiving that all those who can reach its bottom attain supreme life after death. The sea deity must take over his caring.

I took Krishnan in my arms. His limp body making me cry even more. Then lifting him gently, trying not to cause any more pain to him, I went to the deck.

The sky was overwhelmed with grief. It shed tears on us with the soft, caressing touch of a mother trying to sooth her child's anguish.

I looked at Krishnan. His face looked so pale, so relaxed. And so lifeless!

I kissed him and whispered my eternal love for him in his ears as I lifted him high above the rails. Then, with a prayer to the deity of the seas, released him from my arms. He hit the surface of the water, where gentle waves were waiting to embrace him in their arms as they took him on his final journey. For a moment, I could see his serene face. He seemed finally at peace with himself.

◆　　◆　　◆

On reaching Pedro harbor, I turned the helm south. It was almost afternoon. I knew the meeting was fixed for sometime in the evening, but not where the secret fort was located. I had to reach the place before it was too late. I tried to speed up the ship.

The sun was hanging low over the western horizon, behind dark clouds, by the time I approached the mouth of river Fanoma. Water churned furiously where the river met the sea in a show of strength. It appeared as if it would be impossible to penetrate this wall of water that roared like an enraged beast. Against it was my will and the power of this ship.

Concentrating on steering the ship accurately through the sandbanks, I increased throttle. Soon the ship was breaking through the wall of water, as it first slowed down, seeming to surrender to its might, and then charged through to emerge at the other side to greet the mouth of the river.

Dense plantations covered either bank of the river whose reddish waters were rushing towards the sea like avenging beasts. The force of the water was so intense that even after putting all the engines at full throttle, the ship was moving slowly. I had to fight back my frustration against this force and safely reach…

Where was I to reach? How far had I to move up the mouth of this vicious river? Krishnan hadn't told the exact location where the meeting was taking place. All he had said was 'a little in…' What had he meant by that? Now with the sun going down, a mist was rising, gradually reducing visibility by the hour. I couldn't afford to get mired in the sandbanks.

Then I heard a familiar hum above the noise of the rushing water and the rains. I tried hard to look around through the drizzle and the mist. Everything seemed as usual. I then looked up at the sky. In the distance, I saw a helicopter, its rotors cutting through the air and lights twinkling, further up the river. It was descending somewhere in the jungles. What was a helicopter doing in this area and, more so, in such inclement weather? There definitely must be a helipad nearby where it would land.

I watched the helicopter lowering itself in the woods so intently that my eyes hurt.

I inferred I must be somewhere near the site of the secret rendezvous, and the arrival of this helicopter meant that the meeting was taking place exactly as Krishnan had planned.

I fought the rushing waters. It was reckless but I had to find some place where I could anchor the ship safely - It might later serve as a possible means of my retreat.

I wasn't afraid. Insanity had me in its clutches. I had not much time left. I had to enter the premises where these bastards were gathering. I had to reach the place before they realized that they had been fooled. I had to kill them and get back, if possible.

I cast anchor where I thought the ship could sustain the vicious force of the water. It wasn't the best of places but I hadn't any choice. I let the rope ladder down the side and climbing down it, braved the rapid currents to reach the other side of the river where the chopper had landed. From there, I started hurriedly towards my destination.

Dusk had fallen and darkness was rapidly covering the entire area. Fate, it seemed, was against me. The rain was incessant and heavy giving birth to numerous streams that rushed with terrible force towards the river. The jungle floor was slippery and thorny creepers made my advance difficult and painful. I wanted to run as fast as possible, before it was too late, but the thick jungle slowed me down. I was using the carbine I held in my right hand to push aside branches and creepers that blocked my way. I cursed God for creating so many hurdles in my life.

There was a small open space where I stood in silence with bursting heart and lungs and watched the scene before me. There were lights on that made the surroundings visible. There were three barracks standing in an L shape. The building in the middle was the largest of the three and a few jeeps were parked in front of it. There was a watchtower at the periphery manned by a couple of armed guards, alert and watchful. On the ground, about a hundred metres or so away from me stood the helicopter. There were no guards around it. They must be so sure of the security of this place! But then, how could anybody, for that matter, imagine that a man would be able to cross the raging Fanoma river and walk through the dangerous jungle littered with landmines and attack them! The thought provided me some relief in the face of mounting tension.

I decided on an immediate strategy to move ahead and enter the main building. I was now sure that Prabhakaran and Kondathaman were inside that building. I started circling the opening, keeping myself hidden in the woods. I crossed the watchtower with a thumping heart and moved forward so that I could reach the spot nearest from where I could easily reach that building.

I stood under the dark shadows of a tree watching the main building carefully. I could spot a guard standing by the door under an overhang smoking a *beedi,* its glow reflecting the barrel of the gun he held in his hand. I looked around. There was no exceptional activity taking place to be of any cause for concern. But the casualness about the atmosphere troubled me. Then a doubt cropped up in my mind. Had I reached the right place? But the helicopter had landed here and I could not imagine any entity using a helicopter to reach this place, unless he was involved in some subvert activity. The area was under LTTE control and no one could reach here unless he was a welcome guest of theirs.

I had no time to deliberate. I looked around again and then started in a straight march towards the main building, as if I too was an integral part of the scene. My heart was beating like drum. Any moment my courage would have given way but then I thought of Krishnan and Janaki and bravely stepped ahead.

I walked on, nervous in the fear of being challenged by someone or sudden gunfire getting me before I could achieve my objective. But nothing happened. In the darkness and the heavy rains, visibility was poor and I went unnoticed.

I reached the main building where the guard stood smoking his *beedi* oblivious to my intrusion. I waited beside a pillar where rainwater was rushing down from the roof with a loud noise. I crept slowly behind the negligent guard and raising my gun high, I hit him hard with its stock on his head. He collapsed with a faint moan, which in the noise of the falling rain went unnoticed by anybody.

I stepped through the door into a long, dimly lit corridor. I walked in, tightening my grip over the gun in readiness. To my left was a hall, empty and dark and ahead another closed door, behind which I could hear faint voices. So that's my target, I thought!

I waited for a few moments to gather all the courage I possessed and kicked the door open, yelling, "You bastards..."

I gasped at the view that was exposed to my sight. I was dumbfounded.

Around an oval shaped table sat three men and a woman. I felt I had seen her somewhere before. They didn't look at all surprised by my presence. They continued to sit without making any move. Then a tall and commanding looking man raised his hand and ordered me to put down my gun. I had no desire to obey his command. This bastard must be Prabhakaran, I thought, and opened fire at him amidst a shower of abuses.

The other two men dived from their seats and tried to hide themselves under the table yelling something that I couldn't make out in my frenzy. I bent down and fired at them too and when I realized I was wasting bullets on corpses I stopped. I was breathing hard.

I then turned my attention to the woman sitting at the table.

It was Himani Cherion.

What was she doing here? Why was she present in this

meeting of top ranking LTTE officials?

She didn't flinch. She seemed unmoved by my sudden attack and the killing of her supreme leader at my hands.

"Where's Krishnan?" She asked in a voice that sounded like the breathing of a dying man.

I didn't answer. I kept on looking at her.

"You take care of yourself. It's time for me to leave... I must go." I said softly as the intital euphoria started to subside. I had earned the ultimate satisfaction.

"Yes, you must go...as fast as you can. And keep safe." she said, as if in a trance.

Yet, it was so difficult to move away from her. I owed her the truth about Krishnan. But how could I tell her?

"How did you reach here?"

"There is a ship anchored in the river. It's yours. I hijacked it."

She nodded in deep understanding.

"Now you must rush. There's no time left for you," she almost yelled at me. I looked at her in disbelief for a few brief moments. Her face was contorted in an unusual urgency that I failed to comprehend.

I obeyed her command and walked out of the room.

The guard still lay spread-eagled across the door, unconscious, just as I had left him.

The rain was intense. It thundered and exploded from all sides. I was exhausted. I had had my revenge. An impossible mission I had accomplished. I wished Krishnan were with me to celebrate our victory. But he was now in the realms of the Gods.

Sanjay Sonawani

Never again would he speak to me and mock my faith.

I started towards the jungle at a slow pace through the pouring rain. The water and the liana were making my advance difficult. In the darkness, I didn't know whether I had taken the right path to the ship.

Then bright beams of lights suddenly blinded me. Terrified, I threw my body to the ground and tried to shoot at the source of the light. I fired a number of rounds before I realized that I had hit nothing and that a large group of armed men was advancing towards me. I fired at them till I ran out of ammunition. Then with a curse threw my empty gun aside and started running in the opposite direction. I staggered as I felt several hard punches on my back followed by bouts of intense pain before I finally collapsed into a world of darkness.

◆　　◆　　◆

When I awoke, I looked around for several minutes without moving. I felt that I had been roused from sleep by some terrible nightmare. I then thought of Janaki preparing morning tea for me and of where I would sail today with my crew.

I lay enjoying a warm, pleasant morning. I tried to change position and pain exploded within me in a flash yelling at me that it was not at all a fine morning! I let out a scream and felt myself slip once again into the infinite darkness where hounds waited hungrily to tear at my flesh!

I don't know for how long I remained suspended in the dark void. When I awoke, I felt I was at sea. The bed where I lay was heaving up and down with vicious force. All around me was darkness. I did not move in fear of the pain I remembered having felt the last time I had tried to. In whose custody was I, I could only guess. I tried to recollect the events that had transpired before I had surrendered to the pain that wracked my body.

I remembered the scene at the barrack where I had killed three men, including my chief enemy, Prabhakaran. The remembrance made me happy and my pains faded for a few moments. After all, I had been victorious.

May be they have captured me and now are shipping me somewhere where they could torture me at leisure. But it hardly mattered now. I had avenged myself. I had wiped filth off from mankind's' slate.

But if at all I had killed him, who were the men who had fired at me? If they were ready with all those hidden searchlights why had they not used them when I had entered the premises? Where were those guards when I had walked in? Why had they waited till I could kill that bastard?

I had no answer for the multitude of questions that hammered in my stupid mind.

A new awakening came with the brightness of day. The light was mellow and warm, reminding me of life. My body felt dull and heavy and was heavily bandaged. I could sense the presence of someone near me. But any movement I attempted wracked my body in a flood of pain.

Bracing myself, I looked around.

She was standing with her back towards me pouring some liquid into a glass.

Her frame silhouetted against the morning light was like a

picture postcard.

"Himani…"

I tried to call out to her.

She turned towards me.

She looked like an angel as she stepped forward, her face full of concern. She looked so frail and weak and at the same time like some deity.

What was she doing here? Why was she there in that secret meeting? Why was she nursing me when I had caused havoc in her organization? Why had she asked me to run away? And then, was she the one who had captured me?

"How do you feel now?" She asked softly. "I was worried. I wouldn't wish for my fight to go in vain. But now everything is all right. We are on our way to somewhere safe.... It was a hard task. I had to fight those damn guards and drag your unconscious body through the darkness and the thick jungle in heavy rain to the river where you had anchored your boat...

"I have aged doing so," she grinned, showing her glittering teeth. But somewhere in her smile was the shadow of gloom.

I looked at her in deep gratitude.

"Krishnan is dead, isn't he?" She asked in a matter-of-fact manner. I tried to avert her inquiring gaze. I wished the earth would split and swallow me.

"So he is dead." She continued in a monotone that was filled with more agonies than one could ever express through tears. "I thought so when I saw you walk in alone. Krishnan never would have allowed you to do so. He was a mastermind. He would have immediately sensed that his ploy had failed and that a counter-trap had been laid for him. He was a genius who could read their dubious minds."

"But I was able to kill those bastards. That Prabhakaran…and Kondathaman." I was excited at my victory.

She nodded deeply in sympathy and continued in same monotone, "Better if you could succeed in your mission, but it is not the case. Don't ever think Prabhakaran is a fool. He is the master of all masterminds. They anticipated all the moves you could possibly try and wrer ready to trap under all circumstances. In fact, he used you by anticipating that you would come to the resort where you had organised the meeting. He was ready with all the bait necessary to lure you. He let you come in unobstructed only because he could get rid of all those he wished to have killed at your hands. I too was supposed to die in this encounter and was asked to be present there in the afternoon. I knew I was walking into a trap and still was so unaware of what was happening.

"You think you have killed Prabhakaran, Kondathaman and someone else whom you cannot place. Have you ever seen Prabhakaran in real life? No. You have only seen his photos. At times like these, you never know whether the man is the same as the one you suppose he is. And Kondathaman? You have never seen him either. The men you killed were brought there by another fake call that informed them that they were going to meet other LTTE delegates to discuss the crisis that has cropped up following the deaths of Sivrasan and Thyagarajan. I too was told the same thing. I do not know why they thought I was treacherous; I have always been so careful; now I know that they knew it. They wanted me dead. If you hadn't been able to reach there, in that case, the guards would have killed all of us and blamed you for it.

"I think you are perplexed at the complexity of the situation. For me, such complexities are a routine. There is nothing straight about anything out here. Everybody is a friend of everybody and everybody is an enemy in that disguise. Everything they speak is the truth and yet there exist no truth. The LTTE never meant the pride of the Tamils. It always was just another group of power-hungry gangsters in the control of the foreign powers.

"The truth no one will ever know. But the fact remains that the leader of one country was assassinated mercilessly, that your wife was burnt alive, that there is now going to be political chaos in the Indian subcontinent. The greed of the power hungry will continue unabated and cause hurt to the innocents who dream in them is a messiah! Sadly, this is the world we live in - full of chaos and uncertainty. Deceit and untruth prevails over the values preached by one and all.

"Truth is truth and yet it never is. We live in a world of illusions. Most people wish to believe what they read and try to praise or refute it. But they never desire to come out of their illusions. That is the very reason that these power hunters never let you have peace of mind. They understand the psyche of the masses and keep on polluting our minds with distracting actions. They have even fooled Prabhakaran, even though he thinks he is a smart man. Only circumstances can survive him in the times to come.

"I name names because I was closely involved, just like Krishnan, in planning the execution. We both were a part of it.

We thought we were avenging the Indian attack on our mission for freedom. I was enraged at the merciless attacks on us from the oppressors. And so was Krishnan. But when the tide is changed, you think otherwise. Now I too think it was a mistake to get carried away with the racial outburst and that I was involved in the wrong mission. But what is the use of it now when all is over and life had taken its toll?

"Who cares about one Venugopal who lost his wife while fighting his misfortunes? Who is Venugopal, after all? Who then are Krishnan, and Himani, and even Rajiv Gandhi, in the passage of cruel time? The true rulers are always shrouded in dark clouds of secrecy. They prefer to keep a low profile for then they can enjoy the results of their doings without endangering themselves.

"The world we live in is such. All your personal ambitions and faiths too are ruled by some vague entity whom you never know. You just keep on following the new norms of life thinking this is a new world where new actions are necessary to be enacted to survive and achieve success over others. And what a mess all this is!

"The world! What a wicked society we live in! They raped me because they thought my joining them with vengeance in my mind was necessary. They wanted me as an enraged woman so as to use my talents for their benefit. In doing so, they also destroyed all my dreams and aspirations about the world and life. They needed me and they had me. They used me and then wished to kill me.

"But now, it is alright, I guess. I cannot re-enter the past and rectify all that went wrong with me. The only soothing thought for now is that at least we are alive and can experience the magic of a new dawn. May be one day we will reach unknown and untouched shores where the virgin beauty of sanity smiles on us and takes us in its forgiving embrace.

"You are an innocent man, Venu. You are alive because God wanted it so. Never thank me. The Almighty never deserts his true followers."

"Then why did Krishnan have to die?"

"Don't ask. He always was a missionary of truth. He risked his life to seek and to know. Unrest within him was so obvious that I sensed it whenever I met him. I loved him with my heart and soul. But now nothing can be changed.

"The only fact that remains is that all those who think they are going to rule and possess enormous power to enslave the earth are only temporary existences and shall be defeated by the likes of people like Krishnan and you. The truth is that the oppressors of mind and soul are bound to fail sooner or later. So why worry about the temporary punishment that the innocents have to undergo? If the innocents are meant to be victims, then why worry about them - even about yourself when you are made a victim?"

Himani's voice had reached a crescendo and it bothered me. I had nothing to say. I had had enough of life. Life had drifted away from me and I could hardly believe that I loved it.

"It's alright," I said, weakly. "Bygone is bygone. I tried my best and it appears that I failed. My revenge proved fruitless. They proved smarter than we did. But who is there to account our history? No one. Then why worry? It's great that you are alive and so am I. I do not know what tomorrow is going to bring us.

"Life is always so beautiful, so bewitching that it ensnares us in its eternal clutches. Let us forget the ugly games those bastards play with human lives. Let us think how we shall live for a better tomorrow, for everybody..."

And then I was floating on clouds of dreams.

The End

Sanjay Sonawani

THE JUNGLE

By Sanjay Sonawani

He laboured under the burden of his own indecisive-
ness and moral blunder, misconstruing it to be his mag-
nanimity. But the ghost of his past pursued him even in
his exile on a solitary island.

Yashovarman was an ordinary soldier who, by sheer hard
work and perseverance, became the commander of the
Kausal Army. He fell in love with princes Mahadevi
and to fulfill her condition, reestablished a dead empire. But circumstances forced him to renounce his
throne and order the execution of his own son and
daughter-in-law.

In the backdrop of serene nature unfolds scene rocking
the very basis of human perception and all philosophi-
cal and moral hypothesis raising fundamental questions.

An ancient perspective of a contemporary question!

THREE NO TRUMPS
By Raj Supe

Three enigmatic characters are playing a game of faith when Brian D'Souza, a Victim of unrequitted love, bumps into them. What follows is a monstrous trial of his heart and soul. He slowly awakens to the bold and bizarre art of 'No Trumping.' And gains a faith which is more spiritual than moral.

A breakthrough in the narrative tense, this novel reads like a dramatic dialogue. Four biographical testimonies drive its story line like a moving reminiscence: It has metaphors at play, speaking the secularity of Indian Spirit and an immense appeal for seekers around the world.

LAST OF THE WANDERERS

BY SANJAY SONAWANI

The modern man is still a wanderer, wandering in his mind, as it were, in the quest of psychological settlement.

Last of the Wanderers, in the guise of the astounding tale of the Kushan is, in reality, a journey through the realm of human society, its strife, its agonies and affliction- physical and psychological, of a society in the pursuit of imaginary goals.

It is a poignant depiction of the tormenting transformation of a wandering society to a civilized one.